THE PARIS
DIVERSION

ALSO BY CHRIS PAVONE

The Expats

The Accident

The Travelers

CROWN
NEW YORK

THE PARIS
DIVERSION

A NOVEL

CHRIS PAVONE

Copyright © 2019 by Christopher Pavone

All rights reserved.
Published in the United States by Crown, an imprint of the Crown Publishing Group, a division of Penguin Random House LLC, New York.
crownpublishing.com

CROWN and the Crown colophon are registered trademarks of Penguin Random House LLC.

Library of Congress Cataloging-in-Publication Data is available upon request.

ISBN 978-1-5247-6150-9
International edition ISBN 978-1-9848-2493-6
Ebook ISBN 978-1-5247-6152-3

Printed in the United States of America

Book design by Elina D. Nudelman
Interior photography credits: (title page) Getty, Sam Salek/EyeEm; (Part I: Louvre) Getty/Purestock; (Part II: Champs Élysées) Getty/portishead1; (Part III: Palais Royal) Istock: isaxar; (Part IV: Notre Dame) Istock: IakovKalinin; (Part V: Tour Eiffel) Rogdy Espinoza Photography.
Jacket design: Tal Goretsky
Jacket photographs: (running figure) Chris Tobin/DigitalVision/Getty Images; (Eiffel Tower) borchee/E+/Getty Images; (bridge) ESCUDERO Patrick/hemis.fr/Getty Images.

10 9 8 7 6 5 4 3 2 1

First Edition

THE PARIS DIVERSION

What the eyes see and the ears hear, the mind believes.
—HARRY HOUDINI

PART I

LOUVRE

1

A siren wails, far away.

Kate Moore is lingering in front of school, her daily dose of sidewalk-swimming in a sea of expat moms, gossip and chitchat and a dizzying ping-pong of cheek kisses, usually planted on both sides of the face but sometimes three pecks, or for some lunatics four separate kisses.

It's an international school. All the parents are transplants from dozens of different countries, with different ideas about what constitutes the proper sequence. It's an etiquette minefield, is what it is. And etiquette has never been Kate's forte.

She cocks her head, trying to discern if the siren is approaching or receding, an instinctual habit—a professional obligation—of assessing potential levels of danger. Here in Paris, at this hour, sirens are unusual. This city is less noisy than other global capitals, London or New York, Mumbai or Hong Kong. And much less than where Kate lived before here: Luxembourg, perhaps the least noisy capital in the world; and Washington, which doesn't even make the cut of the twenty most populous US cities.

But Kate has traveled plenty. For her job, dispatching her to far-flung destinations in Latin America and Europe. And for the past few years for adventure, driving around the Continent in their aging station wagon, with their EU driver's licenses and bilingual kids.

Other metropoli have all seemed like more aggressive aural assaults than Paris, with more insistent car horns honked more frequently, more idling trucks and unmuffled motorcycles, jackhammers and pile drivers and bass-heavy music blaring from souped-up sound systems, fire trucks and ambulances and police cars in hot pursuit, the unmistakable urban sounds of urgency, emergency.

It's in the mornings when Paris feels especially hushed, and in particular this slice of the *septième,* sleepy cafés on the quiet corners of narrow streets, well-dressed women depositing well-groomed kids at the towering green door of the school's fortress-like façade, forbidding stone walls from which no sounds can escape, nor for that matter children.

The siren grows louder, nearer.

A curbside fence prevents the kids from running into the street, getting hit by cars. Every school's sidewalk is lined with these fences, festooned with locked-up bicycles and kick-scooters decorated with decals of football clubs, pop singers, flower petals.

The kids are absolutely safe in there.

After the *Charlie Hebdo* massacre, sirens began to take on a new significance, triggering more vital concerns. Then the November attacks ratcheted up the tension further, and then again the Champs-Élysées shooting, these events produced a permanent propensity to generalized panic.

Sirens no longer suggest a multicar pile-up on the *périphérique* or a gangland shoot-out in St-Denis—somebody else's problem, somewhere else. These days, sirens could mean a nightclub shooting, hostages in a grocery store, a madman in a museum. Sirens could mean that Kate should storm into school, drag out her children, initiate one of her emergency protocols, go-bags from the linen closet, the always-gassed-up car in the garage, speeding out of the city toward the secret farmhouse in the Ardennes, or the airbase in the Ruhr, or somewhere else, anywhere else.

These days, sirens could mean anything.

It's what everyone is talking about, the shopkeepers, restaurateurs, hoteliers. Tourism is down. Locals are wary. Customers scarce. Soldiers and police patrol the streets in threes and fours, heavily armed, flak-jacket clad. Not only near the ministries and embassies, the busy commercial boulevards and the famous monuments, but everywhere, soldiers are loitering even here, on sedate residential streets.

The military has become a permanent presence, the new normal. Sharpshooters have taken positions in the latticework of the Eiffel Tower, the flying buttresses of Notre-Dame, the neoclassical roof of the Arc de Triomphe. Everyone is getting used to it.

This is how a police state happens, isn't it? An emergency that never subsides. Everything is getting worse all the time, so the far-right steps in and promises to solve it all—the taxes, the unemployment, the poverty and immigration and terrifying violence out in *les banlieues*, Balkan gunrunners and Albanian drug dealers and Corsican mobsters.

The police suit up, and never stand down.

People are talking about getting out of town, buying a crumbling pile of château in the country, starting a biodynamic vineyard or an eco-friendly bed-and-breakfast. Or to hell with it, leaving France entirely, moving to Zurich, to Helsinki or Lisbon or Edinburgh, places that are immune, or seem to be.

Kate hears a second siren, coming from another direction.

The other moms seem to be oblivious to the noise, nattering about nothing. Kate tunes them out, scans the bulletin board next to her, push-pinned with notices for kids' activities, community meetings, nannies, holidays, the week's lunch menu—symbols for organic, for local, for vegetarian—next to the list of every kid's allergies, right out there on the sidewalk for anyone to see.

The goodbyes begin. With all this cheek kissing, it takes forever to say hello and goodbye. Like adding a whole new category of daily chore, now every morning you have to iron a shirt, mop the kitchen floor.

"What time would suit tonight?" asks Hashtag Mom. "And what shall we bring?" Hashtag Mom never lived anywhere except New Jersey until she was thirty-one, when she moved with her global-banker husband to London, then Singapore, then Paris. Somewhere along the way, she apparently started pretending to be British.

"Bring nothing," Kate says, "except your good company. Everyone's coming at seven."

"Lovely." Hashtag Mom leans in for her final air-kiss. For Hashtag Mom, everything, always, is hashtag lovely.

As much time as Kate needs to spend kissing all these women, she's increasingly unwelcome to kiss her own children, not in public, especially not the mortified older one. But Kate is confident that her younger boy is just going along with that pose because that's what younger siblings do;

she knows that Ben still wants his mother's kisses. So she sneaks them onto his head when Jake isn't looking, an open secret right there in a crowd.

The sirens are closing in.

Now other people finally begin to react, to tilt their heads, dart their eyes, searching for whatever proximate threat might be attracting the police.

Cautionary tales, the things you hear: the aroma that turns out to be a ruptured gas main, the staph infection that over the weekend becomes an amputated leg. Lessons in vigilance, the things you could've done, should've done, if only you'd been worried enough, if you hadn't been so lazy, so selfish, if you'd had the courage to follow your fear from the very first flush. But it's only in hindsight that you see it clearly: this was one of those moments.

Everyone turns in unison, to where the narrow street ends at a broad boulevard, glimpses through the gap of a convoy zooming past, motor-cycles followed by squad cars followed by armored trucks then more mo-torcycles sweeping up the rear, all those dark-blue vehicles with lights flashing, a thundering herd galloping in the direction of the river, the museums, the presidential palace, it's all just over there, spitting distance.

Shooting distance.

It's terror that's amassing in Kate, a sense that something is very wrong.

Maybe it's finally here: payback for all her mistakes. Her parenting mistakes and filial ones, her professional mistakes, matrimonial, her wrongdoings in every segment of life. She wakes up every single morning prepared for it to happen, for her life to be assailed.

Maybe it's today.

2

The biggest concern is safety. A distant second is discretion. But if you are concerned with neither unintentional detonation nor with being noticed, your options multiply immensely.

There are so many different ways to build a bomb.

Mahmoud has occasionally wondered if he has hallucinated this whole thing, the past two years, everything. It all *seems* so real, but is that not what people think when they are hallucinating?

The bomb that Mahmoud is wearing under his windbreaker is the type that can be easily identified by any layperson, at first glance: bricks of Semtex and a battery-powered detonator connected by wires to a flip-phone, all of it duct-taped to a canvas vest, everything easily visible. Everyone knows what this is. That is the point.

This bomb can be delivered by foot, then detonated remotely, even if the delivery system is no longer functioning.

The world has become prepared for this sort of thing, in the sorts of places where it makes sense. Places like here.

Mahmoud is the delivery system.

This type of bomb is as close as possible to fail-safe. The only drawback: one person must be willing to die. But what is one death? Hundreds of millions of people die every year. We all, obviously, die. Nearly all of us before we think it is our time, many by surprise. So it is a luxury to know when, exactly.

Mahmoud will also carry a second device, not as easily recognizable. The police will have their suspicions: Why would a man wearing a suicide vest also carry a briefcase? What could be the point of the luggage? They will be prepared for various possibilities, they will have detectors, sensors, a mobile laboratory. They will guess just from Mahmoud's body language, from his location, what the most likely scenario is. They will use their equipment to make measurements. Then they will be sure.

⚜

He sits in the rear of the panel van, GOUPIL ET FRÈRES ÉLECTRICIENS on the dingy side.

After months of planning, the final arrangements were pulled together hastily. Mahmoud does not understand all the factors, or perhaps any; there is much more to this than anyone is telling him. For all he knows, he has been lied to repeatedly, more or less constantly, about everything.

Nearly everything. Some things he knows to be true. He has seen proof.

The problem with the van—although not, in the end, Mahmoud's problem—is that because the event will happen in a heavily monitored neighborhood, the police will have access to copious surveillance footage. It will take only minutes to procure the video of Mahmoud stepping out of this vehicle, then trace the van's movements backward through the various state-owned surveillance cameras that are affixed to the walls, streetlights, and traffic lights, as well as the private cameras at jewelers and banks and hotels and ministries, new cameras are mounted every day, ever cheaper and easier to install, to network, to identify a specific timeframe, compress the file, e-mail it to investigators.

There is no way to evade surveillance.

This necessitated complex logistics just to get Mahmoud into the vehicle. A system whose sole purpose was to deliver one man to one spot on one occasion.

Him, here, now.

⚜

This tradesman's van is hand-stenciled with a nonexistent address, a fictional phone number; there is no Goupil in Paris who is an electrician with his brothers. There are no tools in the rear, no supplies, no other passengers. The steel floor is hard, the shock absorbers ineffective. Mahmoud feels every bump and pothole in his tailbone, his spine, even in the back of his head as it clunks and thumps against the side, which he does not much try to prevent, even relishes to some extent.

Recently the concepts of pain and death have been consuming his thoughts, especially late at night, when he reaches to the other side of the bed. His hand always comes away empty.

There are no windows back here. It is weak light that comes through the front windshield, on the far side of the high-backed seats. Mahmoud's angle does not allow a view of any but the tallest or closest structures, difficult to identify in the whir of whizzing by, set against a small slice of sky.

Mahmoud cannot tell which direction the van is headed in, cannot keep track of the turns. Even the passing of time has become difficult to gauge. He does not know the exact destination, but he does know it will be in central Paris. All the same to him. He has lived here only a few years, but that has been long enough to learn to hate the whole beautiful place.

⚜

The van swings around a turn, too fast, and Mahmoud slides on his seat.

He tries to adjust his tight rubberized underwear. A very uncomfortable garment, but he understands the necessity. In fact he asked for it.

Mahmoud catches a glimpse of something through the windshield, a tall wide column, nothing on either side of it, just the bright blue sky pierced by this verdigris bronze. He recognizes this structure, it is . . . he knows this . . . ?

There are so many monuments here, statues, obelisks, fountains, the French are keen on memorializing events, celebrating themselves. What is this one called . . . ?

Mahmoud visited many of these sights back when they first moved here, dutifully trekking to one tourist attraction after another. He noticed the looks he received, he observed the security guards, many of them just like him, North Africans, Middle Easterns, dark-skinned men issued uniforms and badges and walkie-talkies, told to keep an eye on anyone who looked like themselves. Jobs to pay the rent, to feed their families, to purchase the things you need, maybe sometimes a few you simply want.

The driver shifts into PARK, hops out, then seconds later jumps back in.

Mahmoud wondered if these security guards lost sleep, wracked with guilt about how they earn their livings, about the types of men they had become, men who themselves were subjected to the same injustices and sleights and distrustful looks, all reliable constants, like the gray skies. It was only their absence that surprised—a sunny day, how glorious.

Today is a sunny day.

Ah! He remembers the name of this place, that square with the column in the middle, perimeter lined with the most expensive of jewelers, the fanciest of hotels: the place Vendôme.

It is a relief that he has not completely lost his memory. But then, what does it matter?

It was not Mahmoud who had wanted to move to France. That had been Neela's desire, her dream. He had been swayed by her passion, her conviction. For the children, she said. For me.

And then look what happened. What they did to her.

3

Hunter Forsyth doesn't register the sound of the siren.

Later, when he's second-guessing his decisions, he'll understand that he did hear this first-wave siren but failed to acknowledge it, standing on the balcony off the formal dining room, which during the year that he has owned this apartment has never, not once, been used for formal dining. He's ignoring the spectacular view of the Eiffel Tower in favor of the ordinary little screen in his palm, index finger swiping, and swiping, reading this message, dismissing that one, deleting, deleting, responding with single-syllable answers, *yes, no,* trying to project not only his general level of importance but also his extra-impatience with matters that are below his purview, decisions people should make without consulting him, problems they should solve on their own.

Today, of all days, nibbled to death by minnows. It's important to retaliate. Controlled rudeness can be an effective tool.

Hunter hears a car ignition turn over, and sees the police cruiser pull out of its customary space. The car's lights start to flash as it accelerates, then the sedan tears around the corner.

This penthouse is a spectacular apartment—high ceilings and tall windows, herringbone floors and marble fireplaces, the romantic ideal of a Parisian home. On the other hand, it's just off the Champs-Élysées, with the attendant riffraff crowd, and who the hell wants that? Not Hunter. But when he was looking to buy, he discovered that at any given moment there are only a handful of quality apartments available for people like himself—American businessmen with no titles of nobility or royalty, no above-the-title film credits.

Compromises were necessary. This place is just a few minutes from the downtown office, which is the European headquarters of Hunter's multinational conglomerate. There's another Paris office with far more employees, way out in La Défense, which he visits much less frequently. He doesn't like it out there.

With all his long-haul travel, Hunter tries to minimize his commutes. For the on-and-off month per year that he spends here, he'd much rather be somewhere else, maybe out in Passy amid all the Art Nouveau and ossified old ladies, or the Left Bank, not so artsy-fartsy anymore, perhaps now even welcoming to people like him, the kinds of people who can arrange for the local police to serve as private security.

So why did the cop car just leave?

⚜

"Colette?"

Hunter's efficient, officious assistant hurries from the kitchen, heels clickity-clacking. Colette wears monstrously tall heels that make her legs—her entire figure—look spectacular. The shoes seem impossible to walk in, but she does it with aplomb, as everything. Colette is the most competent human Hunter has ever met. That's one of the reasons—one of many—that he is utterly, helplessly in love with her.

"*Oui Monsieur?*" Phone in hand, ready to answer his every question, cater to his every whim, solve his every problem, those big hazel eyes gazing at him expectantly. It wasn't until last year when he realized just how beautiful Colette is, and since then he hasn't stopped kicking himself for how long it took.

"Do you know why our police just left?"

"I will find out" is what she says, what she always says, and what she always does.

In all other aspects of his life, Hunter is supremely confident. But with Colette he feels like a scrawny sophomore with a crush on the prom queen: flustered, hopeless. The more he becomes convinced of her perfection, the more he envisages all that could go wrong. Beginning with his wife finding out, prematurely. Or Colette's husband.

She hits a button on her phone, which connects her to the woman out in La Défense whose job it is to find answers for other people.

Hunter steps back out to the balcony, just in time to see a new car pull up, a strobing blue light on the roof. Both front doors open, and a couple of uniformed policemen climb out of the unmarked car, looking around.

"Colette?"

"Oui Monsieur?"

Of all the mistakes he'll make today, this one is perhaps the stupidest, for the most irresponsible reason: he doesn't want Colette to go to the bother of calling the office, then dialing the police station, then connecting to the operator, then a supervisor, then whoever arranges for Hunter's not-exactly-legal security detail. . . . He wants to save her these half-dozen conversations. Why? Because he can't stop thinking of her as his true love, instead of one of his five assistants. He's putting Colette's interests ahead of his own, the inverse of their professional relationship.

"Forget it," he says. "A new police car just arrived."

"Parfait."

She types into her device—fingers flying, greasing the various wheels of her boss's life—while walking back to her perch at the kitchen counter.

Then he hears her gasp.

The small television on the counter shows police cars amassed in front of a train station, MENACE À LA GARE in big red letters across the screen.

"A bomb," Colette explains. "At the Gare de Lyon."

His mind jumps to how this will impact him, his today, his tomorrow, when he'll be flying to Hong Kong. A bomb in a train station on the other side of Paris is not his problem. Not with the police stationed out front, and his bodyguard in the hall, in a neighborhood teeming with military, police, the presidential palace, the US Embassy. He's safe.

Tomorrow's flight will be brutal. What Hunter needs—it's so obvious—is his own plane. Not some chic little Gulfstream for short hops to vacation spots, but a big jet that could get him from anywhere on the planet to anywhere else.

After today, he'll be able to buy one of those planes. After today, he'll be able to buy anything. Have anything. Maybe even Colette.

4

Kate watches another pair of police cars zoom through the intersection, breaking the peace of the rue du Cherche-Midi still in the process of waking up for business, doors unlocking, signs being turned over to OUVERT.

It's easy to become uneasy these days, there's a general foreboding in the air, plus an extra dread that's special to Kate: the specter of her career imploding. She keeps hoping that she'll be able to relegate it to the background, stop seeing it in the stark foreground at four A.M.

Flashes flood her consciousness, all her worst visions parading through. The life going out of Santibanez's eyes, slumped against the tree trunk in the dark park in Oaxaca. The surprise of a woman's pleading face in New York, her blood blooming into the carpet. The hateful, determined look on Julia's face, drenched in the pounding rain atop the medieval wall of Luxembourg, the muzzle of her gun just inches from Kate's forehead.

That seems so long ago, when they were still new to Europe.

Until she moved to Luxembourg, Kate didn't have any experience with this variety of high-street retail, the same clerks working the same schedule for years, for lifetimes, closing up for lunch hours, for a whole month during *les fermetures annuelles*; half the people are gone in August, the other half in July. Back in DC, Kate did her shopping in supermarkets and big-box stores, a hazy blur on Saturday mornings, driving from this parking lot to that in the rain, waiting with other sensible cars in left-turn lanes, the household chores a halfhearted afterthought to distracted parenting and autopilot marriage and faltering career, one that had once been rewarding, exciting, and invigorating but recently had become frustrating, terrifying, and ultimately untenable.

One night, Dexter came home from another dispiriting DC day and asked, "What would you think of living in Luxembourg?"

Just like that: a whole different life. Expats.

There's even a name for those traditionalists who take their holidays in August, and another for the upstarts who prefer July. *Aoûitiens* versus *juilletistes*.

Around the corner from home is a squeaky-clean, brightly lit new supermarket, but Kate prefers to shop the traditional way, beginning at the farmer's market on a boulevard's shady meridian, the fish guy and the fresh-fruit guy, the onion stall, the potatoes, the olives, the rotisserie meats, the butcher's yellow chickens and quartered rabbits. Kate is buying a fistful of flowers when everyone pauses to watch a tight caravan of *gendarmerie* people-movers tear past, big blue vans with red-and-white-zebra-striped accents, blue sirens, ten *flics* ready to leap out of each, with riot gear and assault rifles over their shoulders plus automatic pistols in their holsters, a lot of armor, a lot of firepower.

Her phone chimes with an alert, an explanation for all this activity: a bomb threat reported at the Gare de Lyon.

Another day, another threat.

She continues her rounds of the commercial street, everything anyone needs, pharmacist and housewares, *fromagerie* and *boucherie,* a veritable explosion of health-food stores, *bio* this and *nature* that and fresh-pressed juices that all incorporate ginger or echinacea. With the bike-shares and smoking ban and electric-car chargers, the place is becoming California, there's even a rash of burger joints, the type of fad that Kate thinks of as an American phenomenon, outsize passions for pit barbecue, for craft beer, for stuffing ducks into turkeys into cauldrons of deep-frying oil.

The longer she lives away from America—has it really been five years?—the less she identifies with her increasingly foreign homeland. The less she can imagine working her entire career for the American government. It was different when she had supreme confidence in the system, in its mechanisms for sorting leaders, for choosing the people entrusted with the privilege—the responsibility—of making decisions. But recent events suggest an institutional failure of epic proportions.

Yet still she remains over here, following orders from back there. And still she doesn't know who, ultimately, is giving her the orders. That makes her increasingly uncomfortable.

What Kate does know is that her position is growing more precarious by the day, as her past failures are not offset by new successes. As Hayden continues to be disappeared. Peter too. As every day it becomes more possible that her career is over, it's just that no one has yet bothered to inform her.

She takes her place on line among the women in the *boulangerie,* catches sight of her reflection in the store's window. She's a well-put-together woman on the early end of middle-aged, a working mom who hasn't yet succumbed to the inevitable short haircut that French women all seem to adopt somewhere in their forties. That haircut isn't something she's willing to admit about herself, not yet.

Kate wants to look to other people the way she sees herself. She wonders if anyone, ever, has attained that goal.

Maybe tomorrow she'll find something new to do for a living. Maybe tomorrow she'll need to.

⚜

Kate's work begins first thing every morning by checking on a handful of persons of interest scattered across Europe, their homes under surveillance, their devices hacked, wifi networks penetrated. She scans these updates before even getting out of bed.

Then she breakfasts her kids, clothes them, escorts them to school. Kate's end-of-day professional hours are unpredictable: meetings with assets, with sources who want to be bought a drink, with snitches in need of cash. These obligations tend to arise beginning late afternoon; nobody stumbles across valuable intel when they're asleep.

So her mornings are for householding, for making the rounds of her *bonnes addresses,* for meeting her husband at the café, an important component of her marriage-rehabilitation program. After Dexter's betrayals, and her own behavior, Kate realized that she couldn't continue to be a passive participant in her marriage. She couldn't assume that everything would work out, as if marriage were a perfectly engineered rocket hurtling through the infinite expanse of outer space, with no friction, no resistance, no reason to slow down or veer off-course, to crash and burn.

There's ample friction. Also plenty of foreign bodies that exert their own gravitational forces, magnetic attractions, repulsions.

Somebody needs to be active about keeping this marriage moving forward, on-course. Kate has lived with Dexter long enough to know that he isn't going to be the pilot. So she instituted these semi-regular morning dates, eased into their schedules subtly, one proffered invitation after another, until it became a habit.

Kate is the pilot.

✤

She glances at her watch, a guilt-induced anniversary present from Dexter. Are all men so transparent? Or just her own feckless husband?

The workday ahead of her will probably be uneventful—futile, even. But her dinner party tonight won't. There's a point to these relationships, working at them. It has been Kate's turn to host for a while, a responsibility dodged too long. The guests will be school couples: the inevitable Hashtag Mom and her Hashtag Husband; the charming Dutch couple who look like siblings; the quiet Norwegian banker whose garrulous wife once drunkenly shared that he has a colossal penis—she held up her hands, staggeringly wide—and this subject now comes up every few months, during that portion of a girls' night when someone invariably admits to some level of dalliance, an innocent crush on the math teacher, a not-so-innocent tryst with a bartender, backroom blowjobs and a brief pregnancy scare—though never Kate's indiscretion, that never comes up, not to anyone, not ever—and sooner or later someone will ask, straight-faced, "So has anyone seen Olaf's cock lately?" and they'll all crack up, double over, trying desperately not to laugh wine-bar pinot noir through their nostrils.

It's not a bad life.

5

Dexter Moore hears sirens, somewhere in the distance.

He glances at his wristwatch: just past the dot of nine o'clock. He looks over his shoulder: once again, no one is waiting. Throngs used to queue up for these half-dozen tennis courts, everyone wearing whites, sipping coffee, leafing through newspapers, chattering away.

Not today.

Dexter has played badly this morning, distracted, his mind wandering unproductively around unpleasant subjects, building up his anxiety, degrading his play, a vicious cycle.

He suspects that the reason these courts have become unpopular is their proximity to the Sénat. Nobody wants to be playing tennis here if a bomb goes off at the legislature, possibly lethal and—worse—deeply shameful, to be killed that way, your Lacoste'd body found under an umpire chair, a sweatband around your wrist. *Insupportable.*

"*Bon match,*" he says to Luc, in what he knows is a poor accent. Dexter has lived in French-speaking countries for a half-decade now, and he really did try his best—private lessons, vocabulary memorization, verb-conjugation exercises—but with limited success. Which is another way of saying: failure.

"You sure you don't want to come tonight?"

Luc looks up from unwrapping his knee brace. "It will be four married couples?"

"That's right."

Perhaps nothing seems like a bigger waste of a night to a guy like Luc, a divorcé constantly on the make, always hyper-aware of every woman within striking distance, who isn't wearing a ring, who's most attractive, who's most likely to sleep with him. Luc never stops collecting phone numbers and drinks dates and notches on his belt, morning-after regrets and disappointments and exes. He sees his kids only on Sundays, after kicking out Saturday night's date, burying the condom wrappers deep in the bin where the children won't see them when they're tossing away the wrappers of the chocolate bribes, ticking off every divorced-dad cliché in one fell swoop.

"*Merci*," he says with an indulgent smile, "*mais non merci.*"

Dexter doesn't expect Luc to accept. But it's the invitation extended to the lonely person that's the nice thing, not the occasion itself. Dexter doesn't even want to go to his own dinner party, he doesn't especially like those people from school. And certainly not tonight, with so much on the line today. He'll be lucky to make it through the afternoon without throwing up.

"You are ready for today, Dexter?"

"Yes, I think so." He looks up from his tennis bag, navy canvas, racquet handle sticking out. "I hope so. Thanks again for the tip."

The Frenchman laughs. "Do not thank me yet, *mon frère*. I promise nothing!" Luc too is a self-employed investor. They met online via a message board, then in person at a freelancers-in-finance meet-up where everyone was too young at a bar in Oberkampf, a whole neighborhood where everyone is too young. "Can I ask, what size position you have taken?"

"Enough to be worth it." Dexter smiles, a look that he hopes is light-hearted, untroubled. "Not enough to break me."

If only this were true.

There are plenty of people in the world who spend most of their waking hours—maybe their sleeping ones too—thinking about money, about margins, about currencies and credit and equity and debt, market share and cost ratios, different ways of considering relative valuation. Dexter never imagined he'd become one of them.

His path hasn't been straightforward. There was the ultimately disappointing Silicon Valley sojourn, then the more satisfying DC years, the complicated detour in Luxembourg. He wonders if Paris will be the longest stage. With their kids in their cosmopolitan school, Dexter in his home office day-trading, his wife doing . . . what, exactly . . . ?

Doing whatever the hell Kate does.

Dexter has been forced to accept that she's entitled to her secrets. He's had plenty of his own.

⚜

His day: first tennis, now coffee with his wife, then his computer for London's opening, a couple of hours of trading before lunch, then New York's bell followed by a tense afternoon, late pickup of the kids from school, and somewhere in there he must scour the city for Ben's birthday present—something Dexter should've bought weeks ago, but didn't—and finally the dinner party.

A normal day, just a bit busier. And hopefully a bit more profitable.

Scratch that: a shitload more profitable.

Dexter has too much riding on today's outcome, he understands this in the rational part of his brain, knows that this investment is not a level-headed solution to his myriad and mounting financial problems, and the not-unrelated personal ones. He's reluctant to even acknowledge the extent of the problems to himself, unwilling to write off his bad choices, situations that continue to deteriorate on an almost daily basis—

He fights back the sense of doom, the tsunami, the hurricane, the uncontrollable force that threatens everything—

It's *not* uncontrollable, he tells himself. It's *not* doom.

Everything is going to be fine.

Fine.

He looks around at the manicured trees and shrubs, the neat tan-pebbled paths, the thoughtful orderliness of it all. When they first moved to Paris, this park was the kids' favorite place in the world, queuing up for the zip line, scaling the tension-rope climbing pyramid, stopping at the café for juice, for candy, for ice cream. Dexter used to purchase playground tickets by the ten-pack, earning a tiny volume discount. French culture does not embrace discounts, and any markdown sales are generally illegal, except during specifically delineated periods—*les soldes*—when a blanket of ads proclaims the sorts of modest percentages that wouldn't even convince American shoppers to slow down on their way to Walmart.

Then at some point the kids simply stopped asking, "Can we go to the park? Please? *Please*?" Just like that. Finished not only with this particular playground but with all of them, with slides and swings and seesaws and sand pits, that whole stage of life was concluded; done and done, no sentimentality.

Dexter quickens his pace through the tall wrought-iron gates, and turns to watch a police car zoom by at an unusual speed, a terrifying speed, from which he turns just in time to crash sideways into a woman—where the hell did she come from?—her groceries spilling, apples tumbling, potatoes, even her cheese is round, everything in her shopping bag seems to be rolling in different directions across the sidewalk, and Dexter is apologizing profusely, jettisoning his tennis bag, lunging for errant produce.

"*Je suis desolé*," he says, depositing the grapefruit into her bag, one of those big sturdy recycled-material things. Nobody uses plastic anymore.

"*C'est pas grave.*"

"*Ça va?*" he asks. "*Sûr, ça va?*"

Most mornings Dexter doesn't interact with anyone except his family, sequestered alone in the apartment with his computer. But today there has been Luc and the old man who spoke to him while waiting for the traffic light and now this woman, who stands up, her hands full of round fruit.

"*Oui Monsieur.*" She smiles at him. "*Merci bien.*"

It's a nice smile. She's an attractive woman, in fact she's beautiful, and Dexter has a vague inkling that he's seen her before, though he can't place where, and realizes that he's trying too hard to figure it out.

6

T he van pulls to another stop. This one, Mahmoud suspects, is the final. This one is his.

Mahmoud was never told the ultimate destination, and he did not object to being kept in the dark. But in the minutes since he identified the place Vendôme, he has been trying to guess where he will end up.

He has no idea what other elements are involved, what other people, in what other parts of the city, of Europe, the world. He could be one piece of an immense puzzle; he could be a solo operator. In the end, it makes no difference, not to him.

The driver is dressed like any other Frenchman, the type of outfit that can step out of a van and merge into the pedestrian flow, anonymous, unnoticed. Mahmoud does not even know his name.

The man turns around. *"Nous sommes arrivés."*

Mahmoud had been told that it would be a familiar shape, something well known to everyone, and even more well known to him than to most others. Like a riddle. He worried that he would not understand this riddle, that these people had overestimated the breadth of his knowledge, his powers of deductive reasoning, his overall intelligence.

"Là-bas"—the driver points at the pedestrian passageway through the sturdy building. "Do you know it?"

Mahmoud nods, of course he knows it, everyone knows it. Now that he is here, it is completely obvious, and he cannot believe he did not figure it out beforehand. Maybe he really is, after all, an idiot, just like his father used to yell at him.

"Bonne chance."

That is what this guy is telling him? Good luck?

When he met the driver for the first time this morning, Mahmoud was surprised that he was not from the Middle East, nor Africa, nor Asia. In fact he seemed like an American; spoke French like one too. And he was not the only American involved. For a mission that really did not seem like an American thing.

Mahmoud does not know how to respond to the man's good-luck wishes. Thanks? He simply turns away.

"Hey!"

Mahmoud looks back. The driver is now facing the other way, reaching toward the passenger seat, then back, extending something through the window—

Ah, of course! How could he have forgotten?

This heavy reinforced-steel briefcase is supposedly the only thing that will give Mahmoud any chance of surviving the next few minutes.

He reaches up, takes hold of the smooth handle of the shiny case. His palm is sweaty, wet—he is growing more nervous with each second—and the metal handle slips through his slick fingers, and both men gasp as the thing falls, clatters to the sidewalk—

One second—

Two—

Three—

Nothing happens.

They both exhale.

⚜

It is just a few steps from the van to the gold-tipped gates at the entrance to the pedestrian *passage,* where it is cool, dark, moist, echoing with the sounds of footfalls, which are suddenly drowned as a city bus enters one of the roadway bores, filling the space with roars.

On the far side he steps out into the bright light of the expansive vista, the little arch, the carousel, the trees and flowers, all under a tremendous sky, the Eiffel Tower on the distant horizon. The sky is often visible in Paris, there are many open spaces, the buildings are not tall. It is unfortunate that all this sky is so often gray.

People had once tried to explain to him about the weather in Northern Europe, but he could not understand it, not until he lived here.

Large marble spheres line the sidewalk, as well as square concrete blocks, protection against attack by car, by truck. But there are no closed fences, no police, no security guards, nothing to impede a pedestrian's progress on this walkway.

Mahmoud pauses at the lightweight movable fence. This is his last chance to turn around, to wade back into the scrum of vendors from sub-Saharan Africa selling Eiffel Tower keychains and water bottles and selfie-sticks, of pedicabs and tour guides, of every species of hustler preying on tourists who are lost in guidebooks and phones, double-checking the opening hour, wondering why there is such a long queue.

Mahmoud knows: the queue is for security, which everywhere is increasingly tight these days, with everything that has happened in Paris, in France, in the rest of the world.

It is a dangerous time to be alive.

In truth it is always a dangerous time to be alive. But now it is dangerous for Western Europeans and Americans, not merely for the overwhelming majority of the world's people who live and die all over the earth in places that are pretty much always dangerous, places where sizable populations are exterminated in genocides, in famines and epidemics, in floods and earthquakes and hurricanes, in civil wars and counterrevolutions and political purges and sectarian strife and tribal feuds and deeply ingrained religious conflicts that have been going on for decades, for centuries, for millennia.

Yes, these metal detectors make people feel safer. But it is just a feeling, not a fact. In reality, none of these people are safe. There is no such thing as safety for anyone, anywhere. Not anymore.

1

Her arms are growing tired, with the big bunch of flowers, and the bag filled with a heavy dome of bread and a box of assorted *gâteaux apéritifs* for the obligatory cocktail hour, and fresh fruits and ripe cheeses and a bottle of Armagnac. She dutifully marinated her chicken in red wine, braised it last night, ready to reheat.

Kate cooks, it's now something she does, she even owns an apron, which was a birthday present supposedly selected by the kids, though it was probably a not-so-subtle gesture by Dexter; Kate pretended to be overjoyed. She has even started teaching the boys to manage for themselves, nothing complicated, no fingertips shaved off by a mandoline, forearms scalded by burbling oil. Just marinara sauce, grilled cheese sandwiches, those sorts of things.

She spots Dexter across the boulevard, already installed with an espresso and *Le Monde,* still wearing his tennis clothes. As he crosses his legs, he kicks over the racquet propped against a chair, then bends to retrieve it and bangs his head.

Jesus.

She can't help but smile. If she didn't know better, she'd think it was an act.

They've been in a simmering feud for the past few weeks—no, it's months now, but it was that recent trip to Champagne that really put her over this edge. It was Dexter's idea to go see the cathedral in Reims, go on a winery tour. Evincing an appalling lack of awareness of how his children want to spend a Saturday. This ill-conceived trip came fast on the heels of a recurrence of Ben's health crisis, reminding Kate of Dexter's role in failing to mitigate it, to manage it. Also her own disappointment with herself for not being home to prevent it. Her reason for not being home.

But day by day, Kate's anger has been ebbing away. She is once again willing to be amused by her husband. Though not yet willing to let him know it.

The traffic light changes. Kate steps off the sidewalk, not especially paying attention—

A flash of danger, coming fast on her left, it's a truck swerving in her direction, turning onto the rue de Rennes, clearing out of the path of a pack of police cars speeding past, lights flashing but sirens silent, there must be a dozen of them. Kate leaps back, just barely not getting hit by the truck, which careens into the crosswalk, braking but not quickly enough, not before a few people scream as the tires screech and—

Kate drops her shopping bag, her flowers, and sprints over, ready to help, her mind running through first-responder checklists, don't move any neck or back injuries, examine pupils, apply pressure to lacerations, tourniquets—

It's a dog.

It's a brown-and-white springer spaniel, still tethered to its leash, whose other end is held by a natty old woman whose mouth is wide open in horror.

The driver jumps out of the delivery truck, leaving his door open, and looks around like he's coming upon the scene as a curious bystander, not his problem.

The old woman starts to yell at him.

People are converging from every direction. A young woman kneels to the dog, puts down her motorcycle helmet, wearing tight jeans and tall boots and a distressed leather jacket, cigarette dangling from the corner of her mouth. She examines the dog, who with no warning clambers to his feet and shakes himself off, a full-body electrocution shake, as if he has just emerged from the cool lake, ooh that felt good.

The old woman bends over to stroke her pet gingerly, checking for injuries, the legs, paws, skull. Staring into the dog's eyes, as if for signs of a concussion, asking the spaniel to count backward from ten, what's today's date, who's the president.

A few people have begun to berate the driver, and Kate can hear a hysterical woman phoning the police. But the dog is now wagging his tail, thrilled with all this attention from strangers, normally the morning walks are so uneventful, we just go get the newspaper and then return to the apartment, plop down at the door and wait for something fun to happen, maybe today is cleaning-lady day.

Kate feels sorry for this truck driver, who's trying to explain that the police were swarming in his rearview, it was his civic duty to get out of the way, the dog impossible to see down there . . .

The guy's points are valid; some people are nodding in agreement, others are still livid. A middle-aged man with a terrifically hooked Gallic nose has anointed himself moderator, he's wearing magenta jeans and a puffy vest over his tweed jacket, the outfit of a man who sees his rightful place as the center of anything.

Kate is finished here. She's not going to get involved in any police reports about an uninjured dog.

"What's all that about?" Dexter exchanges a peck with his wife.

"Spaniel got hit by that truck. Dog fine. People up in arms. How was tennis?"

He grunts, then turns back to the paper, studying up for another day at the computer, in this new career of his, which is not really so new. Kate thinks anything in the past decade is new—new to be a parent, new to live in Europe, new that Dexter is a day-trader. The Internet is new. Cell phones.

"Hey," she says, "what's with this?" She points at his new cap, made by the preferred brand of French outdoors enthusiasts, the requisite head-to-toe outfit to *faire de la rando* in the Pyrenees or the Dolomites. This brand doesn't really belong in the wardrobe of the man who's Kate's husband; Dexter doesn't hike, he's not French, he's not trendy. "What happened to your tennis cap?"

In Luxembourg he'd belonged to a club built on the grounds of a noble family's old estate, a place where the whole village used to come every year for a hunt, back when that things like that went on. The land eventually evolved into a suburban development surrounding a tennis club whose logo is a kneeling rifleman, which makes a small amount of sense if you know the club's history, but otherwise suggests that the club is a hunting one.

"That's a good question," Dexter says. "I can't find it."

Kate's phone vibrates. She doesn't like being a person who jumps to attention at every electronic interruption, but with all the police zooming around, today is different. Many days, she tells herself something similar.

It's a text-message from someone who's identified in her contacts app as Pierre, at the butcher shop, telling her something she already knows: *Undetonated bomb at Gare de Lyon.*

The guy's name isn't really Pierre. He's not a butcher.

8

The driver is trying to look like any other guy killing time in a tradesman's vehicle, window down, arm on the door, waiting. His orders are to give it one full minute, in case the other man needs to return, for some unarticulated reason.

He glances at the phone resting on the passenger seat, next to that bag that he sometimes has to carry around. Forty seconds more.

This is a risky minute, perhaps the riskiest. He can hear sirens, a whole chorus of them, rushing somewhere. But he knows that it can't be here that they're coming, not yet.

Deep breath.

Remember the money. That's what he's been telling himself, over and over, ever since he signed on to this op. Except there was no signature, obviously. No contract. No record of any sort.

It'll be just another few hours. Then he'll be rich. Or at least no longer broke.

His phone beeps: the minute is up. He quickly types out the no-nonsense text—*Departing Louvre*—then shifts into gear. He restrains himself from peeling away from the curb in a scream of burning rubber, and focuses on adding gas incrementally, accelerating slowly, merging into traffic without swerving around too-slow cars, puny Peugeots and effete Fiats, wimpy little cars on their way to nowhere, driven by nobodies, in no rush.

He sure as hell is in a rush.

Remember the money, he tells himself. Remember why you need it.

❖

Even after his discharge—four long years in Afghanistan and Iraq—he'd continued to spend much of his life abroad, three months here, six there, East Africa, Central Asia, places where his skill set was highly valued in the private-contractor environment. He was decently compensated, and for a long time he'd spent all his income freely. Wastefully. A tricked-out Hummer, which he almost never got to drive. Long weekends in Vegas, in Mauritius; full weeks in Jamaica or Bali. Any new weapons that caught his eye. Doing his part to maintain America's 1:1 gun-to-person ratio.

He merges right, into the thick rush hour on the rue de Rivoli, then right again, then takes the first available turn.

Another turn, and another. He can recite this route from memory, starting at any point along the tight streets of the first *arrondissement* and into the second and then the ninth, putting distance between himself and the Arab's drop-off point, away from the confluence of law enforcement and military, from cell-phone cameras and cable-news reporters, from all the potential problems back at the Louvre and the landmarks that surround it, venues where the police are stationed, the army also showing up, erecting roadblocks any minute now, checkpoints, lockdowns.

They'd plotted this out—they'd plotted everything out, beating it to death—but now that it's upon him, the route feels improvised, slapdash. He sticks to the minor streets, the sorts that won't be blockaded. In Paris, minor streets aren't long-distance ones. So the straight line that he's attempting to drive isn't all that straight, the quick escape not terribly quick.

But straight isn't the goal. Fast isn't the goal. Undetected, that's the goal. Unimpeded.

The eyeglasses are distracting him, encroaching on his vision from every direction. There's no prescription to these lenses, yet it still feels like his vision is altered. To acclimate himself, he'd worn these frames a few times around the little apartment, and out in the street, even driving a stolen car along this very route, making all these same turns, at this exact time of day, headed to the same destination.

But practice is practice. Now, in the real moment, the glasses are bothering the shit out of him. Everything is bothering the shit out of him.

The eyeglasses weren't the only thing that had been foisted upon him. He'd been painstakingly wardrobed, precisely haircut and groomed, all choices he would not have made himself.

Wyatt is aware of the figure he normally cuts, buff and bicep'd and heavily inked, jaw muscles twitching in stoic toughness, a lean mean fighting machine, a force to be reckoned with; he thinks of himself in these tough-guy tropes, always has. But this whole getup hides his assets, disguises his bearing, makes him look like any other French fag.

Which he supposes is the point.

He's worried, irrationally, that he's going to run into someone he knows, some hot chick who'll give him a once-over and ask, "Dude, the fuck happened to you?"

Remember the money.

⚜

He did what he could do. He emptied his cash box. He liquidated this and that. When people are selling something to you, they talk about value retention and resale demand; when they're buying back, though, it's all depreciation, it's excess inventory, it's market downturns, global economic conditions. It's fifty cents on the dollar. If you're lucky.

On the other hand: the hospital costs, the specialists, the medications, none of that is discounted. There are no sales on life-saving surgeries.

One minute he was swimming in it—trucks and guns, gambling and liquor and coke and carefree casual sex—and the next, nothing.

Desperate times, they descended in an instant. So he started searching for drastic measures.

⚜

The job was in Paris. Big European cities were not the type of locale with which Wyatt had operational experience, but thanks to the grandparents who raised him, he did speak some French, which was one of the job requirements. And the payday was an awful lot of cake for a few weeks' training and waiting, then one day of actual work.

Today. It would be a long and perilous day, no doubt. Already was, and it was barely nine in the morning. But he'd worked plenty of lengthy dangerous days in his life, and every single one of them had earned him a fuckload less money.

He'd already been paid the first installment. But that moment—seeing proof that fifty K had been transferred to his Cayman Islands account—

turned out to be the saddest of his life. Because it was when he saw that balance that it hit him: the only way he was going to stop paying—ever— was if his little girl died.

And no, not if: when. *When* she died.

In that dark apartment in Paris, laptop in lap, he cried like a baby, tears splatting down onto the trackpad, wiping them away with the bottom of his T-shirt, until a window popped up on his screen, informing him that he was going to be logged out of his account due to inactivity.

"No," he muttered. "I am definitely not fucking inactive."

9

Hunter sees another unmarked sedan pull to a stop, a blue light on its dashboard. Two uniformed patrolmen had emerged from the first car, and now a business-suited man climbs from the second, greets the cops. All three men swivel their heads around, scanning every direction, on alert, looking for something. What? Trouble.

They turn in unison and march to the building's door, their heads still swiveling.

A window has popped up on Hunter's phone: *Unable to connect to server.*

"Colette? I'm having a problem with my phone."

She squints down, then consults her own device. *"Moi aussi."* She shakes her head in disappointment; Colette takes things personally. "Both are not working. I will find out."

"And the police seem to be coming inside."

"Pardon? Coming inside where? *Ici? Maintenant?"*

Hunter nods. He worries that there's a relationship between the two, the phone problem and the police arrival. He certainly hopes not. Any telecom issue that involves law enforcement is much more serious than rebooting the router. He doesn't have time for serious French problems, telecom or otherwise.

His first phone appointment is in ten minutes. His plan is to take this morning easy, slowly, carefully. His jetlag is severe, his nerves are frayed, he's exhausted. So he's going to spend the whole morning here, making calls away from the office, giving himself the space to focus on the conversations, alerting VIPs to the news. Trying to stay calm.

Then he'll have a light lunch and head to the office, where the press conference is scheduled for three P.M., thirty minutes before New York's opening and while London is still trading and the rest of Europe still working, ensuring attention across all the financial institutions and media of the Western Hemisphere, and thus maximal trading volume.

And maximal profit. Today Hunter expects to increase his net worth by hundreds of millions of dollars; today is the day when he finally becomes a billionaire. But it's going to be a hard day; he'll be earning every penny. In fact he has been earning the billions of pennies his whole life, but it's only now that he'll be able to collect them.

The sun never sets on Hunter's empire, thousands of employees in a dozen countries, no time of any day when he does not have active business.

This is something that poor people—and most Democrats of any socioeconomic strata—don't seem to understand about extremely successful businessmen like himself: being this wealthy doesn't mean you can relax. The opposite.

"*Monsieur?* The television, now it also does not work." Colette looks disgusted. "Everything is *en panne*. I am sorry, I—"

Ding.

⚜

What Hunter hopes is that the police are here because of some simple misunderstanding, something that Colette will take care of without even telling him about it. She'll shake her head, not willing to waste even one second of his time explaining it. Hunter relishes the way she shields him; that's part of the whole attraction.

He can hear the guard's voice on the far side of the closed door. Hunter maintains a twenty-four-hour security detail everywhere, and here at the apartment that means a big stoic guy on a barstool in the hall. His global security chief hires local talent in every country, an interchangeable assortment of beefy men who all seem to wear close-cropped beards or goatees, and skulls that are some level of shaved, and automatic pistols strapped into shoulder holsters. It's difficult to tell them apart, to keep track of their names.

At first, the minor *comtesse* who lives in the other penthouse was scandalized by these thugs who were so presumptively occupying their small shared hall. But Madame was also titillated. She still makes the occasional show of complaining, but probably because she thinks these protests will entitle her to some other concession, some favor, at some future point. She's the type who has spent a lifetime trading in favors and obligations. Also the type who believes that surviving till old age entitles you to be a complete asshole whenever you want, a quality that Hunter recognizes from his own mother.

Now he hears heated words from the foyer, an unfamiliar man speaking firmly to Colette, her protests. Then Colette's heels clacking on the wooden floors.

Six months ago, the downstairs neighbor complained about the noise, demanded that carpets be installed to muffle footsteps. But Hunter likes the look of the bare wood. Another problem solved by a timely transfer of a reasonable sum of money.

"*Monsieur,*" Colette says, approaching quickly. "These men, they are insistent. It is one member of the Parisian police, and one man from your embassy."

"The US Embassy?"

In the foyer, the strangers are standing in uneasy poses around the security guard—Guillerme? Gustave?—who's glancing from intruders to Hunter to Colette and back. Hunter's guards have a specific protocol for what to do if the French police ever show up; that's a foreseeable circumstance. But not in conjunction with an American official.

"*Bonjour,*" Hunter says, in French to be polite. Then "I'm Hunter Forsyth" in English, to clarify that this interaction will be on his terms. Everything is on Hunter's terms; he makes that clear to everyone, all the time. "What can I do for you gentlemen?"

"Mr. Forsyth, I'm so sorry to bother you. My name's Tom Simpson." The guy reaches into his pocket, extracts something. "I'm with the Department of State." He extends his hand, an identity card. Hunter looks from ID to person to ID again.

"I'm sorry to inform you, Mr. Forsyth, that we have a, um, situation." The guy is nervous. "Credible terrorist threats against heavily populated landmarks in central Paris."

"You mean the train station?"

"Well, yes. But additional targets as well. The threats are immediate and active."

Hunter instinctively glances toward the windows, the balcony . . . The sirens.

"The police informed us that your regular, um, security detail would be redirected to one of the target sites. The department has assigned two replacements—one has secured the lobby—to come here." Simpson gestures at the Parisian uniform, still at the elevator. It's a crowd of large men in a tight space. "We at the embassy thought it would be prudent to join. And perhaps to wait inside?"

"Inside my apartment? For what?"

"For the situation to be resolved."

There's something Hunter isn't getting. "What does any of this have to do with me?"

The American looks uneasy. "Just a precaution."

Bullshit, Hunter thinks. And speaking of bullshit: there's no way this guy is really from State, is there? No. This must be a CIA officer who's standing in Hunter's foyer. Should that make him feel better? Worse? At this point, hard to tell.

"Okay, I guess. Come on in." He glances at the phone glued to his palm. Still no signal. Still no wifi. "Colette?"

"*Oui Monsieur.* I will try again."

10

"*Bonjour Madame.*" It's one of the morning waiters, in shirt and tie and tightly cinched apron.

"*Bonjour Julien. Comment ça va?*"

Julien shrugs; he's a fatalist. "*Café crème?*" He asks every time, a standing invitation for Kate to change her mind, to order something else. But she never does.

Here on the boulevard St-Germain, waiting tables is not a holding pattern, a job for young people trying to do something else, or figuring out what to try, or for mothers who need to be home in the mornings, or for downsized people, for anyone hoping for something better. At this café, being a waiter is a career, a destination in and of itself.

"You get everything you need?" Dexter indicates the bulging cloth shopping bag, which when empty Kate carries folded into a little packet in the bottom of her handbag.

"Not quite. Could you pick up cocktail napkins?"

"Cocktail napkins?"

"You know. Little square things."

"Where am I supposed to find those?"

"Probably at that place on the rue Jacob."

"Which place?"

"The place with all the paper napkins in the window."

Kate knows where to find things, how to do things, meet people, have a life. Here in Paris, she has made every attempt to fit in. Back in Luxembourg, one of the sources of her discontent was that she hadn't. She'd held herself apart, and not just apart but above, superior to all those other homemakers, their aggressive parenting, fanatical nesting, competitive entertaining. She'd made no secret of her rejection of it all.

Not this time around. Hence the tennis league, the coffees at the café next to school, sitting around, accomplishing nothing more than going to a place for the sake of having a place to go. A concerted campaign to make friends, connections, resources. To be a full human being, complete with all the components of a full life.

She used to invite people out to breakfast—quick, inexpensive, conducive to her late-starting workday—until she realized that breakfast is not a social occasion in Paris; the only defensible breakfast invitation is actually one to have sex the night before. So she stopped doing that.

But despite her best efforts, Kate eventually had to acknowledge that she didn't want to be a stay-at-home parent. It was driving her nuts.

Maybe two years hadn't been sufficient to make the momentous adjustments, the wholesale redefinitions. Maybe in those two years she hadn't been patient enough, dedicated enough, flexible enough. Maybe if she would've stuck it out—another year? two?—she could've found more fulfillment, more joy, less frustration, less resentment. Maybe she could've been happy as a full-time mom, if only she'd tried harder, longer.

She didn't. Instead she found part-time work, like many women in her situation, graphic designers, social-media consultants, the types of positions that accommodate unexpected visits to the pediatrician, and standard workdays that must routinely end in mid-afternoon, and the expanded holiday breaks that correspond with school schedules and amply compensated husbands.

Kate's, though, is different. When she's working, it's sometimes out of town, it's twenty-four hours per day, and occasionally people try to kill her. And it has been going downhill ever since her boss went on a mission to America and disappeared. Presumed, by many, to be dead.

But not by Kate.

When she returned to the working world, Kate no longer had the luxury of frittering away days with three-hour lunches and recreational-retail expeditions to the *grands magasins*. She had become a rarity in her milieu: a working mother, with a working husband. A two-career household.

But she didn't want to withdraw entirely. She'd taken satisfaction in this community, a normal person who drops her kids at school, hosts dinners, meets her husband at the café, everything she's doing today, this regular life, the life she wants, everyone does.

Kate's phone dings: a text-message group chat, a shuffling of responsibilities for a school event next week. Organized, as ever, by Hashtag Mom. Kate can't help but wonder if—hope that—the woman's popularity is illusory, nothing more than a projection of her social ambition, her self-aggrandizing missives punctuated with a barrage of three or four and sometimes as many as ten references, as if the woman dropped a hand grenade into a barrel of hashtags and they came exploding out hither-thither, #Paris #autumn #Saturdays #BlessedLeftBankLiving #matin #fashion, all concluded—always—with #ExpatMom.

Kate occasionally has to remind herself that Hashtag Mom is not the woman's actual name.

It's not really the hashtags that eat at Kate. They're just a symptom. The disease is superior parenting—humble-brags and name-drops and condescending advice that all elicit this stream of positive reinforcement from HM's so-called friends, hollow affirmations and validations, *omg so beautiful!* and *u r the best mum ever!!* and *couldn't agree more!!!*

These posts accuse Kate that she herself is an inadequate #ExpatMom. That she doesn't lay it all out there, her love for her children, her pride in her kids and husband, her rented villas and reupholstered chaises and adventure safaris.

Kate isn't immune—is anyone?—to wanting to be a perfect mom. And all these valedictory hashtags are reminders that she isn't. But Kate reminds herself that this isn't Hashtag Mom's fault. Also that Kate's own priorities are a lot more consequential than social-media likes.

Her phone dings again: *Anyone know why all the police????!!!!*

It's not just hashtags that Hashtag Mom uses with reckless abandon.

"*Merci,*" she says to Julien as he delivers her café.

"*Je vous en prie.*"

The waiters here know everyone in the family, their coffee preferences, evening drinks. They are regulars, just like Sartre and Camus had been, de Beauvoir and Brecht, Picasso and Joyce and Baldwin and Wright, Julia Child. And now Ben and Jake and Dexter and Kate, the Moores. These waiters have watched the kids grow, become fluent in French, Jake now corrects Kate's pronunciation—"No, Mommy, it's *rrhhhobbb-eh*," a guttural *r* sound from deep in his throat, a noise that Kate will never be able to get quite right.

They'd come to Paris licking their wounds, somehow having survived the disaster of Luxembourg and emerging even stronger. Or maybe that's just how they choose to spin it to each other, to themselves. Though not to anyone else, they won't ever be able to explain any of it, to anyone. There were too many illegal aspects, clandestine operations, the CIA and FBI and Interpol, a whole mess.

And maybe the tale they tell themselves is a lie; maybe they're not stronger. Maybe they're just pretending, because that's what you do, that's how marriage works, how life works: you pretend everything is fine. Even in the face of overwhelming evidence to the contrary, a preponderance of evidence. But you convict only if the evidence is beyond all reasonable doubt. The burden of criminal court, not civil.

It's still possible—it will always be possible—that Dexter's past will eventually sneak up and attack him. Or Kate's.

But that hasn't happened, not yet. Their life is placid. So Kate comes to the café with her husband, and she watches Paris stroll by, *les hommes d'affaires* in their slim-silhouette suits and pointy shoes and seven-day stubble, the women in their perfectly tailored skirts and deftly knotted scarves. Kate herself is wearing a scarf, tied the way that Parisian women do, a thing she had to learn.

Kate has grown out of her tourist love of the city, sees this place more plainly for what's wrong with it. She still loves Paris, but now it's a mature love, clear-eyed with no illusions, no misconceptions. No shortage of disappointments, resentments, grievances.

Not unlike her marriage. Not unlike any marriage.

Another flock of police cars comes flying up the boulevard, and everyone watches for a few seconds before returning to their everyday concerns, a little less comfortable.

11

The baby is gurgling, a sound that could be a prelude to crying, or could be harmless. At the moment, no action is required.

She turns her attention back to the computer on the ornate rolltop desk, the barrage of financial-market information bombarding her. She's trying to hear the various squawk boxes of the world at once, her ear attuned to a few specific developments. A handful of bank sites are also loaded onto her screen, plus a dozen brokerage accounts, representing trades she made over the past weeks, all using different aliases, executed at different times of different days for different amounts, eighty here, one-thirty there.

There will be thorough investigations. She's taking thorough precautions.

There are dozens of windows open in front of her.

Each account has its own regimen of security protocols—bot-combating interfaces, triple-encrypted user names, random-character passcodes generated by a battery-powered remote device. A rich tapestry of multilayered defenses against the ever more aggressive, sophisticated, relentless intrusions of hackers.

She of all people is well aware that hacking pays lucratively, and anything that pays lucratively attracts high-caliber talent. Smuggling, drug-trafficking, arms-dealing, bond-trading, hedge-funding, all these legal and illegal methods of skimming, of chiseling a cut between production and consumption. All immensely lucrative. The more original the idea, the more lucrative.

You don't need to have a lot of great ideas to get immensely rich. Just one, really. As long as you also manage to consider all the angles and get there early, preferably first. Plenty of people have great ideas, lying on the couch. The trick is getting up.

She'd already had her one great idea, and she'd executed it with full vigor. But she'd been overconfident, and this hubris had cost her everything. Almost everything.

This is her second great idea, and she probably won't get a third chance. She's not making the same mistakes this time.

She tries to relax. Inhales slowly, deeply, lets her head fall back, stretching out her tense neck muscles.

This living room is huge, with three different seating areas, two fireplaces, French doors to a balcony perched over the *campo*, half-shaded at this hour by the low angle of the sun. She stares up at the coffered ceiling, they're all spectacular in this apartment, different in every room. The master bedroom has a fantastic fresco painted onto a plaster oval, mountains and streams, blue skies and puffy clouds and chubby cheerful cherubim. Lots to look at when you're fucking in missionary position. But recently there'd been precious little of that in the king-size bed with the brocade cover, not with the copulatory consequence in the adjoining bedroom, screaming and shitting up a storm.

Nothing is quite as desexualizing as parenting an infant.

Plus her husband has slept in this bed a grand total of three nights in the past month.

She keeps refreshing one window, keeping herself logged into the account that holds the greatest volume of put options. Waiting for the signal.

This old building is one of many in Venice whose ownership has recently changed hands. The new owner is awaiting permits to renovate, to transition the building from long-term rentals into much more enriching short-term tourist housing. In the meantime everything is falling apart, walls crumbling, electricity fizzling, pipes leaking. At first glance this place looks like luxury, but after ten minutes the decay becomes evident. Just like the entire city, increasingly unable to provide the things that residents need but tourists don't, groceries and hardware and fresh fish.

Venice may have once been a world capital, but that was a thousand years ago, Marco Polo's day. In the past few decades the population has fallen by half, and within another twenty years basically no one will live here anymore, it'll be just tourists who sleep on the main islands, in hotels and hostels and apartments like this one, while every night all the Italians will sleep across the lagoon in Mestre, which is nobody's idea of a pretty place.

The baby's noise has become louder. It's touch-and-go.

For all the fanny-packed visitors discharged from all the mega–cruise ships, for all the rising fetid waters and skyrocketing rents and disappearing services, the beauty is still beyond compare. Venice is a spectacular place to wait it out, to meld into the mass of foreigners, the constant churn of a city whose population turns over every single day, tens of thousands of new faces. A place where familiar faces are noticeable. If someone shows up here, looking for her, she'll know it.

She packed her bag last night, then stopped by Lorenzo's shop just before closing to confirm that he'll be available to give her a ride. Family problems, she said. She might need to leave on short notice. Tonight.

"*Certo*," Lorenzo said. She paid him a hundred euros per month, for various favors. For reliability.

Off to the side, a few prepaid mobiles are plugged into their chargers, lights glowing, awaiting different pieces of information. One of these phones chimes, delivering the expected update. She turns back to her larger screen, the trackpad, the little cursor blinking, winking at her, in on the whole scheme.

She hits EXECUTE, and waits for the screen to refresh. Then she needs to move the cursor to another spot, where she clicks another button: CONFIRM.

She stares at the little animation that signals that something is in the process of happening, but hasn't yet happened . . .

Not yet . . .

Not yet . . .

Then it does. Your transaction is complete, here is the confirmation number, thank you for your business.

That's done. It's not until she exhales that she realizes she'd been holding her breath.

Even in a modest boat like Lorenzo's, you can get to dozens of countries, the Balkans, even North Africa, the Mediterranean Mideast. Down to Sicily or over to Greece. Or instead you could drive up into the Alps, to Switzerland, Liechtenstein, the Black Forest. Or fly anywhere. Venice presents a lot of options, to a lot of destinations. A lot of ways to lose a trail, or create a false one. An easy place from which to escape.

12

The crowd is large at this hour, with the eager hordes who showed up early plus all the people showing up now as the doors open, streaming in from all directions, everybody wants to be here bright and early, go get a glimpse of that famous smile.

Mahmoud walks through the opening in the temporary fence, which is perhaps no longer temporary. Portable, but permanent.

There is no one at this fence to challenge him.

Sculptural-looking concrete blocks are scattered around the central plaza. Tourists stand atop these sturdy forms, balancing themselves in silly positions, or holding up thumbs and forefingers to create a trick of perspective for the benefit of cameras, a novelty shot that is not so novel when thousands of people take it every day.

These protective bollards are another layer of fortification to prevent attack by vehicle, the manner of assault that happened in Nice, in New York. Or to prevent something even more devastating: an armored vehicle delivering a bomb, or an armored vehicle that itself is a bomb. Or a whole fleet of vehicles. Perhaps not even for the purpose of mass killing, but for mass theft, or mass destruction. The treasures here are, literally, priceless. That is why all these people have come. That is why Mahmoud has come.

Yes, these concrete pillars are for protection.

Ha.

⚜

The crowd's collective energy is impatient. Mahmoud feels the humanity thrumming around him, enveloping him, all these heartbeats, all this flesh. He pushes past people, not worried about seeming rude, and suddenly finds himself on the periphery of a large group of children, it is obviously a school group, there must be a hundred little kids, paired off, holding hands.

When he was approaching, this area looked like a depression in the crowd, perhaps a roped-off section, or another big fountain, someplace where it would be impossible for people to be standing. But there are plenty of people standing here, they are just small people, so Mahmoud could not see them.

Back home, he had been an average-size adult male. But here in well-fed Western Europe he is a short man, slight, narrow-shouldered and pencil-armed, even his hair seems thinner here. Everyone in Paris looks like they could beat him up, even the women.

It had not occurred to Mahmoud that there would be little kids here, but of course there are. Probably to see the mummies, overseen by these young women, schoolteachers.

Mahmoud has two little children himself. And his wife, she is a schoolteacher.

He surveys the plaza, the familiar shapes whose most famous incarnations preside over a stretch of desert not far from where he was born, where he lived most of his life, in the southern sprawl of the largest city in the Arab world. Those three immense structures in Giza are made of stone. The four here in Paris are much smaller, and made of glass.

Was, he has to remind himself. *Was* a schoolteacher.

Mahmoud arrives to his assigned destination, the only statue in the courtyard, King Louis XIV on his rearing horse. Mahmoud stops walking and waits, strapped into one bomb and carrying another, in the epicenter of Western civilization.

13

"Dex?"

He doesn't look up from the paper. "Hmm?"

"You're going to remember Ben's present, right?"

An inflexible little-boy birthday request, a much coveted toy—a set of movie tie-in Lego—that has proven hard to find. Dexter should have bought it long ago, or ordered it online; neither the birthday nor the request snuck up. Now he's out of time. A small chore, something he promised to take care of, then didn't. It infuriates her.

"Yes."

"Really, Dex?"

"Trust me."

Kate sighs audibly, a huff of unambiguous displeasure. Dexter chooses to ignore it, and she chooses to leave it at that, unwilling to escalate, at least not at the moment. Maybe later. Especially if it turns out that he'll be unable to find the right box of Danish plastic, which is an outcome that Kate might even be rooting for, it will serve him right, and she will be justified in her sanctimony. There's very little as satisfying as irrefutable spousal self-righteousness.

They sit silently, stewing in the kind of spat that's undetectable if you're not in the marriage, not exhaustively versed in its history, the prior mistakes and misrepresentations and errors of judgment and honesty, the full set of luggage that comes with sharing a life.

Dexter hands the French newspaper to Kate. It's a small gesture, but better than nothing. He moves on to the *International New York Times*.

They sip their coffees, read their papers, in silence. Dexter has never been the most talkative of men, but for the past days he's been especially uncommunicative. Which makes Kate wonder, worry: again?

She tries to brush aside that thought. Again.

But her ire is up, and she refuses to say thanks for the paper. Punishing him, is what she's doing. But he probably doesn't realize he's being punished. In fact—in *fact*—he might even think he's being *rewarded*, afforded a little peace and quiet for once.

Goddamn it.

She flings aside a page without having finished the article she was in the middle of not reading.

Like Kate's, Dexter's workday skews late. Some days they barely overlap. This led to problems back in Luxembourg, where neither had much idea what the other one did all day.

When she took this new position, she tried to be more up-front. There would be travel in this job, she told Dexter, for indefinite duration, to destinations that she wouldn't necessarily be able to divulge. There would be secrets. She couldn't answer most questions, so she'd appreciate it if he wouldn't ask. She didn't want to have to lie to him, she didn't want him to have to pretend to believe her lies. Wouldn't they be better off if they just skipped all the lying?

But he did need to know her cover story. Enough to be able to answer casual questions, or, in a dire situation, noncasual ones. He needed to know enough to be credible.

"You're a consultant?"

"That's right."

Most people in Paris don't talk about work, at least not cocktail-party acquaintances; too *bourge.* But that French anti-bourgeois sentiment doesn't fully penetrate the expat bubble, so Kate needed to be prepared for people to ask her "What do you do for a living?" and not be content with a one-line answer. They might ask Dexter too. And it might not always be casual chitchatters.

"And what is it you consult about?"

"Political-economic issues in France."

"Really?"

It was a ludicrous question. She didn't answer.

"And who are your clients?"

"Large US-based multinationals."

Kate had planned for this conversation. She'd made an occasion of it, a favorite bistro, dark wood and yellow walls and old brass sconces. She sat on the red velvet banquette, the same color as the restaurant's name in extravagant script decorating the china.

"Such as?"

"I'm not at liberty to divulge the identity of my clients."

"Why not?"

"NDAs as a matter of blanket policy. To prevent any misunderstandings."

The menu featured all the greatest hits. Kate was having coq au vin, trying to figure out how to make it herself. Following a recipe wasn't always enough.

"And what is it that these clients expect from your consultancy?"

"That, too, is something I've promised not to dis—"

"Okay, I get it. But just between us."

"Just between us? What does that even mean in this situation? Seriously?"

Dexter looked past her, to the rear wall with floral wallpaper. The tablecloths were white, the silver old and slightly tarnished, the waiters wearing black and white, formal yet discrete and agreeable.

"Listen, Dex, I wouldn't answer that question, so you wouldn't know the answer. Let's just keep it that way. Let's not invent more lies than we need to."

"But do you have an answer?"

"Yes, I obviously know who my clients are, I know what services I provide to them, I know what they pay me, and I keep records to document all this."

"Records." Kate could see it dawn on Dexter: she was advancing the same arguments now as he had, back when they'd moved to Luxembourg, when he'd fabricated his own fake career—fake job, fake office, fake clients.

But unlike Dexter in Luxembourg, Kate in Paris actually generates real reports for real clients—people who could be contacted, files that could be double-checked, verified. The work is not dissimilar to what Kate did as an analyst in Washington, except here she pays anonymous freelancers to do it for her.

This is the difference between Dexter's sham job and Kate's: he's an amateur, and she's a pro.

"Where are these records?"

"My office."

"Where's that?"

"The sixteenth."

"What street?"

"You can't remember."

"I can't? Why not?"

"You don't really go to that neighborhood, the streets are unfamiliar, I told you but you forgot. The street name begins with *M,* maybe. Or *N.*"

Sooner or later, Kate suspected, her husband would try to find out. Just as she had. Back in Luxembourg, she'd succeeded; here in Paris, he would not.

She told herself that these lies of hers were for Dexter's own good. His own safety. The street begins with neither *M* nor *N.*

"So I have to be an idiot."

This was an inane simplification, and he knew it. No reason for Kate to counter the argument, which would only lead to a bigger argument.

"Are all these secrets really any better than lies?"

He was trying to be reasonable, but he didn't have the right to be assertive, and they both knew it. Dexter didn't have the luxury of occupying any moral high ground; the opposite. He was in a low, precarious position, powerless.

"Yes," Kate said, though she didn't have any confidence that this was true, or even if she believed it. But secrets were her métier. She was less comfortable with lies.

"Why do you want to do this?"

That was a valid question. She should have a better answer, but all she had was: "I don't know."

"Do you really think that's good enough?"

"I'm sorry. It's . . ."

She didn't want to explain it, not aloud. That she was worried it was too late for any other options. That she was a mid-forties woman who wasn't educated or trained to do anything else. That she couldn't bear the idea of starting from scratch, she didn't have the humility for it. That it was this or nothing, and she'd already tried nothing, and couldn't handle it.

"This is all I've ever done, Dex. This is what I'm good at."

Some people are able to try a few different careers, hopping around interrelated fields. Not Kate. She'd made her choice long ago, and now it was too late. At a certain point in life, you are what you are.

⚜

"We could also use something for the kids to drink. Orangina."

"Okay."

"Maybe you want to make a list?"

Dexter peers at her over the top of his newspaper. Cocktail napkins and soda. Does he need a fucking list?

"Fine," Kate says, and turns back to speed-reading the paper, a skill she'd developed in her old analyst job, when it had occasionally been necessary to consume imposing volumes of information very quickly. Then when she started living in France, she transferred this habit to scanning the French newspaper—key words, general ideas, proper nouns.

Like this one, right here.

"Oh my God," Kate says, angling the newsprint toward Dexter. "Did you see this?" There's even a picture, a handsome man who's perhaps too well groomed, too smooth looking.

"*Mm-hmm.*" Dexter turns back to his own paper.

"This is a surprise."

He doesn't respond.

"Dex? Are you surprised about this?"

"Um, no."

"Your old friend—"

"We were never friends. You know that, Kate."

"That was sarcasm. Your old *boss* is here in Paris, and you don't care?"

"I'm not saying I don't care. I'm saying I'm not surprised. I've known for a while that some big announcement was coming from him, and that it would involve Europe. So it makes sense that the press conference would be here." Dexter shrugs, trying to dismiss the whole subject, an ineptly feigned indifference. Acting isn't one of Dexter's core competencies.

"How?"

"How what?"

"How did you know about this announcement?"

Dexter screws up his mouth. "It was a while ago. Probably a tech newsletter, or even just the paper . . ."

Kate maintains eye contact with her husband, waits it out . . .

Waits . . .

Dexter breaks his gaze away. He turns back to his newspaper, resumes reading, too studiously.

He's lying.

⚜

She should drop it.

But when Dexter lied to her before, it was a whole series of life-defining lies that almost ruined them, ruined everything. Now he's lying again, she's sure of it. What she doesn't know is why, at what magnitude. She really hopes that it's not his career that Dexter is lying about; the family needs that to be lucrative, and secure.

Because Kate is lying too. She's more and more worried for her job every day, but hasn't mentioned a word of it to her husband. Every day her silence grows harder and harder to defend. Every day she promises to break it, but doesn't.

Another police car goes flying by, this one in a different direction, responding to a different emergency. Just because there's a bomb at a train station doesn't mean all other problems disappear.

14

Hunter looks at his phone again. Still no reception, no wifi.

"Colette."

"*Oui,* I will try again." She heads off to reboot the router.

He should've finished a couple of calls already. He has a list of important staff in Hong Kong, Mumbai, here in Paris; later, after noon, America too. Hunter also has a second call list, this one purely mental, no record of it. People in London, New York, the Bay Area. Two different call lists, using two different phones—

That's the solution. He hurries to the kitchen, through it, to the utility room. "Colette?"

She spins from the electrical panel, startled to find him back here, in the behind-the-scenes mess of wires, meters, fuses, logistics.

"The other phone? Do you have it?"

She looks confused, then realizes. "The Belgian?"

"Yes."

Colette gives him that smile of hers that means no, I am sorry, I am disappointed to need to disappoint you, but I simply must. It's a very expressive smile. "*Non Monsieur.* It is at the office."

Colette had ridden the TGV from Paris to Brussels and back for the express purpose of buying a Belgian burner. Hunter himself has never set foot in Belgium. That was the point.

He returns to the living room. The guy from State, or the CIA, he's facing the window, gazing out at the city. After the initial conversation, the Parisian uniformed cop returned to street level. Now one cop is sitting in the car, the other standing in the lobby. This is not the usual arrangement; there's never an officer inside. This is a change that definitely does not make Hunter feel more secure. But the important thing is not to feel secure; it's to be it.

"Your name is Simpson, right?"

"Please call me Tom."

"You still have no cell service?"

The man looks down at his own phone, presses a button, another. Shakes his head, holds out his hand. "Mind if I take a look?"

Hunter hands his device to this American official, then takes a seat on a velvet sofa that Colette picked out, along with nearly everything else in the apartment except his personal things—a few suits, shirts, ties, toiletries, electronic chargers. He has similar supplies in the other apartments, which is why he prefers them to hotels: so he doesn't need to pack. Doesn't need to wheel a bag through airports. Doesn't need to plan. He always carries his passport, and that's all he needs. At any given moment, he can decide it's more important for him to be somewhere else, and go there.

"What are you doing?" Hunter asks.

He also keeps a couple of Krugerrands in his wallet, always.

"Seeing if I can connect you to another server. Or to someone else's wifi, if there's any other network functioning. Doesn't look like it." Simpson continues to stab his pointer finger at the touch-screen, then finally shakes his head, and hands back the device. "Sorry. Do you think I could take a look at your assistant's phone? Sometimes these problems affect—or don't—different devices in different ways."

"Sure. Colette?"

She exchanges a look with Simpson, something between them. Hostility? Fear? Distrust? *"Oui Monsieur."*

"Could I ask you to unlock your phone, please?"

Colette lets a beat pass. *"Bien sûr."* She taps at a few buttons, then relinquishes her device, and steps away from the American quickly, as if afraid of catching a communicable disease.

"What do you think is going on here, Simpson?"

The guy doesn't look up from Colette's phone. "I don't want to speculate."

"Sure," Hunter says, "I get that. But can you, Simpson? Will you?"

The guy cuts his eyes up to Hunter, then back to the screen, continues pressing and swiping. Then he shakes his head, and walks over to Colette. "Nothing worked."

She doesn't say anything as she accepts her phone, doesn't look at the guy. Just nods curtly. An uncharacteristic lapse in manners.

"Look," Hunter says, taking a conspiratorial tone. Just one guy to another, what can we do about this. "I'm giving a press conference this afternoon. Big announcement. I should be making calls right now. It's going to be a huge problem if I can't get in touch with these people before my announcement."

The guy scrunches up his mouth.

"What does that mean?" Hunter asks. "That face?"

"Um . . . I'm not . . ." The guy trails off, looks away.

"Come on."

"Listen, Mr. Forsyth, you may not be holding any press conference today."

"Why? What do you know?"

"I don't *know* much, Mr. Forsyth, not for certain. I've related to you what I *do* know: there's a widespread attack against Paris. And for the past"—he looks at his watch—"ten minutes, there's been no mobile service here, no electricity. This situation doesn't sound promising, does it?"

No, it certainly doesn't.

"And I suspect it's not a simple problem with a quick solution. Whatever's going on in Paris, I'd be very surprised if everything was resolved by three o'clock."

Hunter doesn't remember telling this guy anything about three o'clock. But that's public knowledge, isn't it? The morning papers. Google.

"Our goal right now—*my* goal—is not to facilitate your business, as important as that may seem to you. My goal is to keep an American citizen safe."

"Safe from what?"

"From getting *blown up*, Mr. Forsyth. From getting shot. *Kid*napped."

"What makes you think I'm in danger of any of those things? What are you not telling me?"

"There's a lot of chatter."

"Chatter? About what? Come on, man. Tell me what the hell is going on."

"Specifically targeting Americans. *American capitalists* is the phrase."

"But not specifically me, right?" Hunter had been threatened before, more than once. He has plenty of enemies, personal ones and professional, corporate, international labor, maybe even organized crime, he isn't completely sure. Hence the bodyguards.

"We're aware of a number of prominent American businessmen currently in Paris."

"*A number.* Like two? Or like a hundred?"

"You know I can't tell you that, Mr. Forsyth."

This conversation has taken a much worse turn than Hunter could've anticipated. This whole day. "It's just two French cops we've got downstairs?" That doesn't seem like sufficient manpower to prevent any professional team intent on—what? On anything.

"Backup should be arriving soon, Mr. Forsyth. Within two hours. Or three."

"Three hours?" A lot of bad things can happen in three hours.

"You have to understand that this is a very fluid situation, an environment that's not under any normal level of control. And as you're well aware, we are not in the United States, we can't just do whatever we want. But I want to assure you that we have procedures for this category of scenario. Protocols."

"Are you armed, Simpson?"

"I understand your concern, Mr. Forsyth, I really do, but sheltering in place is the best option at the moment."

Sheltering in place? What is this, a fucking tornado?

"What about the embassy?" The oldest American diplomatic mission in the world is just a few blocks away. "The embassy has its own networks, right? And secure landlines?"

There have been American diplomats in Paris since Benjamin Franklin arrived in 1776, before there was an American constitution. But the more recent representative doesn't respond.

"The embassy must have its own generators," Hunter continues, his argument building up a head of steam, yes, this is the solution. "And backup generators, it—"

"Mr. Forsyth, let me stop you right there: I can*not* take you to rue Gabriel. The embassy is on total lockdown, even I couldn't get in, and that's where I work. I certainly couldn't bring in a civilian."

I'm not just any civilian, Hunter wants to say, but even in his mounting frustration he realizes this is a dead end. *Don't-you-know-who-I-am?* never gets positive results.

"Is there somewhere else?"

The guy looks away again. He sure is one reticent son-of-a-bitch.

"There is, isn't there? There must be. A safehouse?"

"You've seen too many movies, Mr. Forsyth."

"You're telling me there's no such thing? Come on. All I'm asking for is phone service. Or a wifi signal."

Hunter is a person who's used to getting what he wants, has been getting anything he wants his whole life. His power doesn't derive from his good looks, or his fine clothes, or even his money, it's everything together—the way he holds his body, the way he walks and talks, the way he maintains eye contact and a firm grip, the way he accepts the ministrations of the servant class, the people who do things for him, not merely because they're paid to but sometimes just because they understand, innately, that this is how the world works.

"Mr. Forsyth, I really do want to help you. I'm *here* to help you."

"Then do it."

The guy sighs. Purses his lips. He's really drawing this out.

"Okay," he finally says, followed by a phrase that Hunter hears all the time, the phrase that people always use when confronted by men like Hunter Forsyth who are dissatisfied with something, with anything, men who are not in the habit of accepting their own dissatisfaction. How many times has Hunter heard this phrase? Thousands?

"Let me see what I can do."

15

The sniper rests his elbows on the parapet atop the Richelieu Wing, and sweeps his binoculars across the far side of the cour Napoléon. Dozens of people are milling around in that quadrant, maybe hundreds, doing all the normal things, nothing unusual except perhaps that pair of blondes who are exploding out of their clothing, both wearing T-shirts and miniskirts that do not leave much to the imagination.

Ibrahim Abid adjusts the focus, gets a nice sharp image. Oh, goodness.

He pushes the spyglasses away from this unacceptable distraction, scans back toward the center, where the crowd is denser. It is more difficult to concentrate on one individual at a time, with each person surrounded in close proximity by so many others. But that is what he forces himself to do.

The sniper's great-grandparents both emigrated from Morocco right after the First World War. All of his grandparents were born in Nice, both his parents here in Paris. Himself too, his siblings. Ibrahim is more Parisian than most Parisians, a city bursting with people from somewhere else, from Cairo and Dakar, Saigon and Bangkok, New York and San Francisco, from West London and central Stockholm, sent over from corporate headquarters in Bonn, in Moscow, in Rio de Janeiro, migrating here from the crowded slums of Marseille and the sleepy farmland of the Loire, the gritty industrial towns in Lorraine, Dijon, Pas-de-Calais, people flocking from all over France, all over the world.

Ibrahim is more Parisian than all those carpetbaggers. Though not necessarily as French. But French enough to do six long years of military service, then to join the *préfecture de police,* to become one of the department's top snipers.

He has been assigned to this Louvre posting for only six months. Which is a very long time to do a job in which nothing happens, ever.

Regulations forbid the use of the rifle's sights for routine surveillance. This is Paris, after all, not Tikrit, not Kabul, the ten million annual visitors are not accustomed to being monitored from rooftops through the scopes of high-powered rifles. So Ibrahim continues his sweep with binoculars, pushing the lenses up through the courtyard, back toward the far side of the—

Wait. What was that?

He aims the binoculars back toward the middle, to a densely occupied area, looking for . . .

There.

That man, wearing a windbreaker. He is standing stock-still, arms hanging at his side. Something is not right, but it takes Ibrahim a second to recognize what: his head is at the wrong angle. The man is not scanning the crowd, looking for a friend, a sister. He is not admiring the palace, or staring off at the view. He is facing the sky. And . . . is it . . . ?

Ibrahim adjusts the focus, his fingers spinning nervously.

Yes, the man's eyes: they are closed.

"Command," Ibrahim says into the mic on his headset, "we have a suspicious man in the cour Napoléon."

Ibrahim puts down the binoculars. He picks up his rifle, aligns the sight, locates the man in this different lens just in time to see the guy bend over, deposit a briefcase on the ground. A metal briefcase.

"Position four, precise location of target?"

This lens has crosshairs.

"Five meters north of the Louis XIV statue."

"Patrol is en route." This is the four-man paramilitary team that sweeps the courtyard constantly, one circuit after another, watching everyone from ground level, being visible, a deterrent. At this moment they are as far away from the Louis XIV statue as possible. This, Ibrahim realizes, is not a coincidence. He feels the hairs on the back of his neck stand up.

"Description?"

"Gray jacket, black jeans. He, uh . . ." Damn. Ibrahim does not want to say this part. This is what he wakes up every single day hoping not to have to say: "He appears to be North African. Or Middle Eastern."

"Copy." Pause. Crackle. "Position seven, are you seeing this?"

"One moment . . ." This is the plainclothes officer standing at the café on the terrace, elevated a few feet above the courtyard level, a good angle to see faces. "Yes, got him. I agree, he does look suspicious. Patrol, approach carefully."

"Does anyone see a weapon?"

"Negative."

"Negative."

"Anyone?"

No one says anything.

Ibrahim is growing increasingly anxious. "Awaiting orders, Command."

"Hold."

"He is unzipping his jacket," Ibrahim says.

"Repeat?"

"He just opened his jacket. He is now taking it off . . . Oh *merde*."

"Repeat? Position four, status?"

Ibrahim adjusts his focus, though the image is already sharp enough.

"Position four, please clarify."

Ibrahim is irrationally hoping that maybe refocusing the lens will transform the contents of the vest into something it is not. Into water bottles, perhaps. Fly-fishing lures. Iron-on ski-mountain badges. Anything else, anything whatsoever.

"He is wearing—" Ibrahim's voice catches, and he clears his throat.

"Repeat, please?"

"He is wearing a bomb vest."

16

"Do you know anything that's not in the newspaper, Dex?"

He takes a sip of coffee before answering. "Forsyth is buying his largest European competitor."

"Wow. That must be a big deal."

"I guess."

"You guess?" Kate knows that Dexter isn't guessing any damn thing. He has probably calculated what the deal is worth to a penny. "You participating, Dexter?"

"Uh . . . sort of." He takes another sip. Either buying time or trying to avoid the topic entirely, to wear down his wife with tedious pauses. But he should know better. Kate does not wear down. "I'm shorting it."

Shorting. Dexter had explained this before: betting against a company's performance by borrowing shares, then immediately selling those borrowed shares, then later buying back the same quantity of shares, hopefully at a lower price. Sell first, buy later.

To Kate, stock-market speculation has always seemed more like a game than a legitimate profession. Especially short-selling, which doesn't seem terribly different from poker, or sports wagering, I'll take the Redskins plus points. Is this really the way the world works? Should it be?

Judgments aside, this betting is how her husband earns his comfortable living, and Kate's job has never been lucrative. She can't be sanctimonious about how her good life is provided. Rather: She can't act sanctimonious. She can *be* as high-minded as she wants, within her own high mind.

Hers is not a unique predicament. How many wives volunteer at homeless shelters to atone for their husbands' predatory professions? But then again, Kate doesn't volunteer. And her own career has not exactly been a model of moral rectitude.

❧

A phone is ringing, Dexter's. He glances at the number, hits IGNORE.

"You're not going to answer?"

"It's a robocall. I get them every day."

"Since when?"

"I don't know. A couple of weeks?"

"What are they selling?"

"Car insurance? Life insurance? Some insurance. I listened for only a few seconds, then I blocked the caller. But they keep finding me. What do you care?"

"Just curious. Aren't you?"

He shrugs. There's plenty about modern life that's inconvenient, annoying, offensive. Dexter doesn't seem bothered by most of it. It's one of the things Kate admires about her husband.

"Is this a rational decision?"

"Ignoring robocalls? Why would it not be?"

"No, Dexter. The short-sell." Or maybe he's lying about this too. That's the thing about lying: if you're a liar, when do you not lie? "Is this based on a rational assessment of 4Syte's prospects? Or is this an emotional choice?"

Dexter tilts his head, as if genuinely thinking. "Mostly rational." He obviously doesn't want to discuss this. But he has reluctantly come to accept that silence is not a viable mode of marital communication. He knows he needs to explain himself, sometimes.

"The share price has been inching up for weeks."

He puts down his paper, giving up the hopeful pretense that they're not going to talk about this.

"Immediately after the announcement, I think the share price may rise dramatically. But Hunter is *way* overextending, and I'm sure the acquisition is going to encounter regulatory resistance. A few days from now, a week maybe, the EU is going to start hemming and hawing. Bankers will grow skittish. Then either the deal will fall apart rapidly, and the stock will tank, or the deal will limp through, but with the price slowly eroding. Either way, I'll come out ahead."

And if you're wrong? she wants to ask. But that's a line she shouldn't cross. "How much?"

"How much what?"

She gives him a look, *Are you kidding?*

"Don't worry about it."

"You understand, Dex, that this is a phrase that *ensures* the opposite?"

"Not too much."

"Dexter."

"Two-fifty."

"Two-fifty what? Tell me you're not betting a quarter million dollars on a grudge."

"Euros, not dollars." So it's more. "And it's not a grudge. Plus, wrong tense. I already made the deal."

"Excuse me?"

"This is an exhaustively researched move that I'm in a privileged position to assess."

"What the hell does that mean, *privileged position*?"

"You know: my history with Hunter."

This is so clearly horseshit.

Kate's spirits plummet. For the past couple of years she's been telling herself that she could trust Dexter again, that she should. That the lies he'd told hadn't been so bad. That he was, at heart, a good, trustworthy man. That she loved him. She could tell this to him too; indeed she had. But once trust is destroyed, can it ever be entirely rebuilt?

And now look: he's lying to her again.

"Obviously it's possible to lose money, as with *any* investment," he continues, but Kate doesn't even want to listen. "And, yes, the exposure on a short-sell is far greater. No risk, no reward."

"Don't placate me with platitudes." She's getting angry. What's the good in asking questions if she can't expect truthful answers? "I'm not a moron."

"And I'm not reckless."

She arches an eyebrow, a reminder, enough said.

"And I've learned some important lessons." Sounding apologetic, but not overly, he doesn't want to give an excess of validity to the long-term accusation in that arched eyebrow of hers. "You know that, Kate."

She takes a deep breath.

"Trust me."

"Again, Dexter, you're *completely* misunderstanding the effect of that phrase."

He sighs, clams up, jaw tight. This has always been his response to spats: to shut down. He knows that Kate hates this—all women do—and it's a tactic that has no hope of accomplishing what he wants to accomplish. But he can't seem to help himself.

"Seriously, Dexter: tell me you're not being irrational."

"Seriously: I know what I'm doing here."

She wants to tell him—she *needs* him to know—that now is really not a good time for him to be reckless. Telling him is obviously the responsible thing to do. There are good times to take risks, and bad times.

But she can't bring herself to broach the subject. She'd have to admit too many things that she really does not want to admit.

It's not just Dexter who'd spent a long time lying to his spouse about fundamental facts. It's not just Dexter who'd needed to rebuild trust.

Kate is proud of her career. Of her expertise, her experience, her execution. But that doesn't mean she's free of regrets, of guilt, about the things she has done to other people in the name of professionalism, of patriotism. Plus a different sort of guilt about her personal decisions—about how she treated her sister, how she lied to Dexter so much for so long, how she betrayed Julia.

At the time, Kate had been convinced that it was the right thing to do, the legal thing, the ethical thing. But she eventually realized that it was something else: she'd done it because Julia had lied to her, and had enlisted Dexter too to lie to her. Because Kate had been gullible enough to believe them both. She'd done it because she could; she'd done it out of anger and spite. This wasn't the high road she'd taken. It was low. Petty.

This guilt isn't the worst sort. It's more like the guilt for flying off the handle with the kids. Or for her relationship with Peter. Not a cold-sweat-in-the-middle-of-the-night guilt, just a shiver down her spine in broad daylight, right here, right now, sitting beside her husband in the warm morning sunshine at a famous café in St-Germain-des-Prés.

What she should tell Dexter is this: it could happen any day now. I'll be summoned to a meet, somewhere open and public—a bench in Parc Monceau, maybe, or the Tuileries. A paunchy officious man will arrive, someone I've never met.

This man won't say hello. He'll take a seat and gaze into the mid-distance; he won't say anything for a few seconds, making me wait, making me anxious, a small display of power, wielded by a small man.

Then he'll begin to speak in a slow monotone. The decision has been made—he'll use a passive construction, as if the decision came from a computer—to terminate the operation. To close down this risky, unorthodox initiative. The Paris Substation had been Hayden Grey's project, and Mr. Grey, as you know, has been missing for a long time. There's no reason to think that he will ever reappear. And without Mr. Grey . . . ?

The Agency thanks you for your service. Best of luck in future endeavors.

There will be no apology. No talk of references, of assistance finding a new situation. He'll walk away without saying goodbye. She'll never even be told his fake name.

17

Out past Gare St-Lazare, where traffic grows heavier, Wyatt pulls the van to a stop at a red light. He reaches over to the canvas bag resting on the passenger seat, another prop that had been foisted upon him, along with the clothes, the glasses, the haircut.

He plucks a pair of surgical gloves from the bag. The tight rubber isn't easy to handle, not with his nerves, and he has time to pull on only the left glove before the light changes, and he returns his hands to the wheel. It would be disastrous to crash now, even a fender-bender could be devastating, a rear-end tap, a soft brush against a parked car. He can't afford to interact with anyone, not while associated with this van. Certainly not police.

Only a couple more minutes now. The blue *P* beckons ahead, the final stop of this leg of his journey, thank God—

But what's this?

Fuck.

Stick to the plan. This is just a street cop, preventing street crime, out on patrol, a leisurely stroll. No reason for any patrolman to pay any attention to some tradesman's van pulling into a public garage. And Wyatt shouldn't create one.

He keeps his eyes trained straight ahead, ignoring the cop's gaze. The two men pass within a couple of yards of each other, nearly face-to-face, but Wyatt refuses to glance in the cop's direction. Then he second-guesses himself—maybe he should've met the cop's eye, nodded hello? Would that have been less suspicious?

Too late.

Wyatt turns into the garage, keeps the bill of his cap angled low; he knows where the camera is. He reaches with his rubber-gloved left hand to press the button, collect the ticket. The barrier rises, and he rolls the van down the incline, makes a hairpin turn to descend another level, and another. The bottom.

Down here, most of the parking spaces are available, as expected. His instinct is to pull into the most isolated spot, but he needs light to clean up. He takes a well-illuminated space in the middle, and kills the engine.

He pulls on the second rubber glove. There's a thin plastic film that covers the steering wheel, the gear shift, the directional-signal arm, the door handle, the key—everything he'd needed to touch. He peels off all these car condoms, rolls up the garbage, stuffs this plastic ball into the bag.

It's important not to rush. Not to panic. Not to forget anything.

Wyatt reaches into his pocket, extracts a piece of paper. A checklist. Fourteen items. He scans the lines, mentally ticking off the minor milestones. Parking ticket on seat . . . Key in ignition . . . Wipe down exterior door handles with disinfecting cloth . . .

He reads the checklist one final time, to reassure himself: done. Then he walks away, toward the backlit icon of a man climbing stairs, SORTIE, just thirty yards away, a few seconds' walk. One foot in front of the other, keep breathing.

Remember the money.

Twenty yards.

Everything is fine, everything is going according to—

⚜

Click.

He spins around, eyes darting around the dim-lit space. What the fuck was that?

There, on the other side of the low wide room: a guy is getting out of a car, a little black Cooper. That click? That was the door latch disengaging.

Fuck.

And now a woman too, she's emerging from the passenger side. What have these people been doing in that car? They didn't arrive while he was here, which means they were here before he was. Here the whole time, they saw everything, they watched him wipe down the vehicle, consult his checklist, behavior that's explicable only in the context of the commission of crime. What they saw was a man behaving like a criminal.

He feels the weight in his jacket's pocket, the heaviness, the no-slip grip. It suddenly seems like a hammer, and these people are indistinguishable from nails.

No, he tells himself: They were not watching him. They were not paying attention, they could not have seen much, and what's more they could not have cared. Who are these people? They're no one. They're not police. Not military. Just two randoms, nothing to do with him. Sitting in a car having a marital spat. Or prepping for a meeting. Or fucking—yes, they're having an affair, stealing a few minutes for desperate but uncomfortable early-morning sports-car sex, the shift stick digging into somebody's thigh. If you're planning on using a car for intercourse, a Mini is not the best option. But that's probably not how anyone chooses a car. Not unless you have a pretty serious fucking-in-cars fetish.

Wyatt turns back toward the exit, takes another step away.

That's when he remembers: the bag. It's still on the passenger seat.

Fuck.

He turns back again. He must look like an idiot, back and forth. But an idiot is okay, he's willing to look like an idiot. What he doesn't want to look like is a terrorist.

If he returns to the van now, he'll have to walk right past these people, and the man is going to look him in the face, say *Bonjour.* Not good. Or Wyatt can continue to the stairwell, ascend to a higher level to lurk until these people climb past, then return. Nothing lost except a couple of minutes. No risk, unless he has the bad luck of running into someone else up there, but that's a solvable problem. The trick is to not be startled. To not be stupid.

Yes, that's what he'll do.

He turns back again—he's spinning like a lunatic, isn't he?—and takes a step, and—

"Monsieur?"

Oh fuck. He takes a second step, pretending he didn't hear. A third.

"Monsieur!"

Can he ignore this guy? What would the consequences be?

He glances over his shoulder, but doesn't turn all the way around.

"Vos phares," the man says.

At first Wyatt doesn't understand what this can mean.

"Ils sont allumés."

Phares? He left the headlights on? "Ah," Wyatt says, looking at the van, sure enough. "*Merci.*"

Fuck. Was that on the checklist?

He doesn't have a choice, does he? He can't ignore this. That policeman might still be up on the street, it would be easy for this guy to approach him, almost inevitable. "*Pardonnez-moi, officer, there's a man acting strangely, he left his headlights ignited and then he fled—look! There he is, running!*"

"*Vous êtes très gentil,*" Wyatt says. He starts walking toward the van, which is also in the direction of this couple. Their paths will converge. In three seconds. In two.

The man has stopped walking.

One.

"*Ça va?*" The man looks concerned.

"*Oui,*" Wyatt croaks, a bundle of exploding nerves now, his mind increasingly muddled, looking from Monsieur Cooper's face to Madame's, she too is staring at him with a furrowed brow until she realizes she's staring so looks away, not wanting to maintain eye contact with this possibly crazy or dangerous person in a dark garage three levels underground. She even takes a step away. It's just a tiny step, but not unnoticeable.

These people are scared of him, of course they are. They should be.

These people are going to walk upstairs, they're going to see the policeman, make a report. They will not hesitate, especially if they are aware of the larger situation in the city. Maybe they were sitting in that car listening to the radio, news reports, *Police warn everyone to be on the lookout for a white panel van,* GOUPIL ET FRÈRES ÉLECTRICIENS *on the side—*

"You understand that you cannot allow yourself to be caught?" That's what the man with the big beard asked, the man who has run this op. "Not under any circumstances."

It was a beard that could look like many things, depending on context. A rugged mountain man. Or a hipster. Or an orthodox Jew, maybe a rabbi. Or a devout Muslim. Or a jihadist planning to blow up Paris. A lot of competing types.

Wyatt accepted the familiar handgun.

"But do not use this unless absolutely necessary."

"Sure," Wyatt agreed reflexively, the instinctual response of a trained soldier to an order. But he didn't understand this one, didn't see why he should restrain himself from freely dispensing with witnesses, with obstacles, with challenges, with inconveniences. Many innocent people were going to die anyway. Wasn't that the point?

At the very first meeting, Wyatt suspected that the big beard did signify jihadist. That's the thing that would've made sense, given what it seemed they were planning. But the more he learned, less so.

Wyatt still wants a full explanation of whatever the hell this is, but he doesn't really need one, and doesn't expect one. "That," the man told him, "is what all the money is for."

The man was serious, the type who exudes competence, confidence. A man to be reckoned with. Even in repose, clearly a dangerous man, a lethal man. A man with a scar on his cheekbone that looks like a memento from a knife fight.

Wyatt has spent his life with such dangerous men. His father was one, the sadistic fucker. Wyatt himself is one. You either are or you aren't, and you know it. Though some men turn out to be mistaken, and don't discover their error until it's too late.

But not Wyatt, he's not mistaken: he's definitely a lethal man. An untrustworthy man too, an untrusting one, a man who takes his own precautions. Wyatt is a double-crosser. Which makes him always ready to be double-crossed.

He clears his throat, says "*Oui*" again, trying to sound soft, trying to reassure these scared people. "*Merci, ça va bien.*"

Wyatt musters something that he hopes approximates a smile, aiming his bared teeth in the general direction of M. and Mme. Cooper. He probably looks like a snarling wolf.

He's not going to assuage these people, it's too late for that. All he's trying to do now is prevent them from panicking too early, from running, from making too much noise, too much commotion, before he has time.

18

"Do not engage." This is what Ibrahim hears in his headset, a blanket order delivered to everyone, to Ibrahim and the other sniper atop the opposite wing, to the four-man patrol closing in on the bomber's position, to the plainclothes officers, to the uniformed police.

"Repeat, do not engage."

Nearly every soul has fled the cour Napoléon, except a couple of guards, the guys who manage the crowds at the ticket queues, at the doors, more like ushers than security, empowered to prevent only the most casual of disturbances—line cutters, aggressive panhandlers. This situation is well beyond their pay grade; they do not even wear badges, just laminated ID cards. They exchange looks, a quick conversation—"Should we get the fuck out of here?" "Definitely"—and back away, into the big glass pyramid and down out of view, out of the most obvious harm.

The only other people who are still in the courtyard are the four members of the tactical patrol team, wearing body armor and combat helmets, assault rifles at the ready.

"The target has no visible firearms, but is wearing what appears to be explosives."

The crowd had dispersed quickly, giving these soldiers a clear view of the man before they were anywhere near him. They immediately understood that it was not advisable to simply shoot him, which would neutralize only one part of the threat, a possibly insignificant part compared to that vest, that luggage.

The four soldiers separate from one another, form a staggered line of advancement, different angles. They close in carefully, their target always sighted at the ends of their weapons. Fifty meters away, one of the soldiers holds up a fist, and they all stop.

For a few seconds, they are all absolutely still.

Then the two soldiers on either end begin to move laterally, not getting any nearer to the target, but skirting him. Then the other two also begin to reposition, everyone walking slowly, maintaining ready stances. It takes a couple of minutes before they establish a full containment ring at the four cardinal points.

The bomber is surrounded.

❧

First things first: all the exterior doors are secured, the main doors at the pyramid, the ones under the place du Carrousel, the employee entrances, the supply routes.

Wings are sealed off from one another, rooms locked down, like a ship hit by a torpedo, or crashed into an iceberg: you isolate the compromised sections to prevent water from flooding everywhere, killing everyone.

Guests are instructed to stay calm, take seats on the floor, make themselves comfortable.

The authorities are called, so many different authorities: the army, the national police, the mayor, the president, ministers, senators. Plus museum staff, foreign ambassadors, the director of the Métro, on and on, like a phone tree for an international football league, canceling dozens of games at once, due to natural disaster.

The surrounding streets are closed, the nearest Métro stations too, bus service, river traffic. None of this is simple to effectuate.

The museum's *président directeur–général* leaves his office facing the Seine, and crosses to the other side of the building, to a window that overlooks the courtyard. He stares with wide eyes in broad daylight at his worst nightmare.

They run annual drills. Not just abstract plans that are debated in meetings, modeled on custom-designed software, but real-world real-time simulations using live human beings to test response rates, logistical controls, unanticipated challenges. Some tasks have proven easier than expected; some harder. There is a lot that must be mobilized to secure this capacious site in the middle of the most visited city on the Continent.

No, this right now is not the director's worst nightmare. Just the prelude.

The Palais du Louvre is relatively well protected from attack by vehicle, by car or truck, even armored military vehicles would be thwarted by the layers of hardened bollards. Attackers would need a tank to get through. And if anyone rolls a tank into central Paris, the Louvre is not their target.

But the exercise is like whack-a-mole: you close off one method of ingress and others pop up. There are virtually unlimited locales where crowds gather, and so many options for killing large numbers of people. There is no way to make people safe everywhere. The only thing you can do is make them feel safe, with the metal detectors, the security guards, snipers, enabling everyone to go about their lives believing that every precaution has been taken.

But there has always been this, and always will be: you can never entirely protect against a person who is willing to sacrifice his life in order to kill others.

Ibrahim keeps the target squarely in his sites, finger on the trigger.

19

Dexter steals a glance behind him, the street, the bins, the cars, the hotel on the corner . . . Everything is still, except a small garbage truck passing at the far end of the block, the sanitation workers' outfits in different shades of vibrant green that match the green bins with yellow lids all in a row, looking like the Green Bay Packers offensive line.

Paris is an empty sort of place in the mornings, without people jogging everywhere, scurrying to and from gyms, twenty-four-hour delis and overnight shifts, the morning convergence of enterprise and exercise that you see in American cities. Not here.

He's startled by movement over his shoulder, and spins to see a crow—a huge one—fluttering onto the roof of a parked car. The big black bird seems to stare at Dexter for a second, then herky-jerks its head down to peck at something. That's one scary bird.

Dexter shifts the shopping bag and flowers to his other hand, his tennis bag to his other shoulder, a double-switch.

"Can you take this home?" Kate had asked, in front of the café. She was headed to whatever passes for her office. Dexter doesn't know where it is, or what goes on there.

A few months ago, when curiosity had gotten the best of him, he attempted to follow her; he could no longer live with his failure to even try. Unsurprisingly, Kate was difficult to tail, changing Métro platforms, doubling back on sidewalks, and eventually striding through the wrought-iron door to the Galerie de la Madeleine, one of those marble-floored *passages* that smell of musty old paper, they all do, the covered arcades strewn around the Right Bank, lined with tiny boutiques and artisan workshops and cozy cafés, all with giant plate-glass windows, nowhere to turn, no way to hide.

The *galerie* looked like a trap, set to catch a tail.

Dexter gave up, walked back to his side of the river, dejected. Wondering if he'd ever again know what the hell his wife did for a living. Wondering if it mattered.

He never did find out if Kate realized it was her husband following her that day, or anyone; maybe she went through that evasive rigmarole as a matter of everyday habit. He was too ashamed to ask; she was perhaps too restrained to mention it.

There are some things best left unsaid, even in a marriage. Perhaps especially in a marriage. The dirty things, the shameful things, the taboo sexual fantasies, the fleeting suicidal tendencies, the petty jealousies and juvenile revenge scenarios, things you're more likely to admit to a drunk stranger in an airport lounge, someone you don't have to wake up with for a half-century, don't have to worry if she'll now look at you in a new, horrid light.

Secrets are not unusual. But what is unusual is that "What do you do for a living?" and "Where is your office?" are questions that can't even be asked, much less answered.

Whatever it is that Kate does, at the moment Dexter is thankful for its steadiness, its reliability, the wire-transferred paychecks that replenish their account twice per month.

Dexter thinks of himself as a modern man, a progressive man. He'd be absolutely thrilled for his wife to earn more than he does. But the burden of providing for the family has always sat on his shoulders, and they're not especially macho shoulders—no big muscles, no tattoos, no MBA. It's a heavy weight, uncomfortable. Failure to provide for your family is a pretty big failure. Maybe the biggest.

Kate doesn't know it, but her income is what's keeping them afloat.

Dexter never loops his wife into his trades. Sometimes afterward he'll share wildly positive results, he'll come home with vintage Champagne and a small tin of caviar. He has learned to celebrate, not just the regularly scheduled annual dates, the anniversary, the birthdays.

He was even less inclined than normal to mention this 4Syte position, so reluctant that he stopped talking shop entirely a couple of weeks ago, when he made the decision. Because if he avoided the subject of work entirely, he'd have plausible deniability, later. "Why didn't I mention it? I don't know, Kate. We weren't discussing *any* of my work."

Dexter knows that his wife never, ever stops worrying that it can all be lost in an instant, any instant, tomorrow, today. She grew up with even less than he did, and she can't escape feeling that they don't deserve this life. That it's only temporary, the world will come to its senses and take it away, everything. And the way that Dexter earns his living makes Kate plenty anxious.

It's for her own good that he keeps her in the dark about the details, that he occasionally—very occasionally—needs to lie to her. Mostly lies of omission. Such as: Dexter had been monitoring 4Syte's stock long before Luc's tip. For a decade, in fact.

Also: this short-sell is definitely a hugely risky endeavor, and it is without question an emotional decision. Yes, Dexter has a perhaps unhealthy receptivity to nefarious gossip about Hunter Forsyth, to vicious rumor, to illegal inside information. Some of which have been copious. Because the more success Hunter achieves, the more people want to take him down, want to see him taken down, want to benefit if his take-down eventually happens.

Dexter is one of them.

It's not because there's a sizable population who are so envious that the guy is so successful. No, it's because Hunter Forsyth is an unremitting bastard. There are plenty of successful people who don't step on everyone else as they climb their ladders. And Hunter does it with so little humility, so much arrogance, entitlement. Born on third base, believing he hit a triple.

So many people are defined by their bootstraps, by the lowliness of their origins, people who have no choice but to try to climb out, climb up. Dexter. Kate too. But by the sheer luck of birth, Hunter had been afforded the choice to do absolutely anything. Instead of using that immense good fortune to do something positive for the planet, for mankind—or at least something creative—the guy chose as his goal simply to get richer, to slide through life with the greased ease of an aristocrat.

Dexter hates Hunter's guts.

No, this trade is not entirely rational. It's not unemotional.

Yesterday, in anticipation of today's press conference, 4Syte's stock hit its all-time high. This was exactly what Luc's inside source had predicted. It was real, and it was now.

While the kids did homework and Kate did dishes, Dexter closed himself into his office. He still wasn't entirely comfortable with the information, its circuitous route from somewhere inside 4Syte to that German trader to Luc to Dexter. Not to mention the discomfort endemic to any short position, which entails unlimited downside: if the share price rises dramatically instead of falls, it's even possible to lose more than your original investment, to swing past zero. Way past.

But that's the nature of risk, isn't it? That's when risk is most worthwhile, most profitable: when the outcome is least certain.

This was what Dexter had been working toward for years, this type of move based on this type of info, betting against this particular person. A perfect storm. It was irresistible.

He took a deep breath, then executed the trade. Twice.

Dexter punches in the security code, pushes open the heavy red door. There's always an extra chill in this breezeway, a dampness that clings to the stone walls. He walks past the bicycles into the courtyard, a little garden with a wooden shed that houses the supplies. It's a simple garden, not much in the way of direct sunlight, but well tended by the concierge. Last Christmas, the residents chipped in to buy Madame a chic set of tools from that exorbitant place on the rue du Bac, she was nearly overcome. Madame hasn't been able to bring herself to sully this gift with soil; she gardens with her old tools, while the new ones hang in their canvas belt from a wooden peg on the shed's door, pride of place, like the university graduation picture of a grandchild.

As Dexter hustles through the courtyard, he catches a glimpse of something white peeking from behind a corner of the shed.

He strides over. Peeks around and down, and—*yes*. He kneels, picks up the missing cap from his Luxembourg tennis club. He looks around, hoping his eyes will stumble across some explanation of how it got here. He'll have to ask Madame.

Dexter rides up the slow, loud elevator, clanging and groaning, forever suggesting imminent breakdown. At his apartment door, he pauses, uneasy. He leans over the railing, looks down the stairwell . . .

Nothing.

He stands still, listening for footsteps, for breathing, for anything . . .

Nothing.

He unlocks his front door, and steps into the darkness.

20

K ate has many rules.

One is that she alternates the routes she takes across the river. Some days she'll walk the pont des Arts, other days the pont Royal or pont du Carrousel. Or she'll ride the 68 or 69 bus up the rue du Bac. Or take the number 12 Métro, get off at Madeleine, melt into the maze of *correspondance* tunnels, up and down the stairs, pause at an exit, double back.

Kate had never before been a regular subway rider, it wasn't convenient to her home in DC—saved neither time nor money—and it didn't exist back in Connecticut. But she adores the Paris Métro, the Art Nouveau entryways, the different styles of benches, the manually operated doors. And the subway facilitates extremely effective countersurveillance.

Sometimes she rides her bicycle to work, and very rarely her Vespa, which she keeps parked on the private street in front of her office. She doesn't want the moped to be easily identifiable as hers. When the time comes when she needs it, she wants the scooter to be clean, unidentified, unmonitored.

Kate never takes the family car to work. Their apartment building doesn't have parking in the courtyard, which is instead dominated by a garden—flowers, foliage, a few tomatoes in August, thyme and rosemary for anyone who wants it, limitless mint. When they were looking for a place to live, they didn't realize that courtyard parking was an option. They'd probably do it differently now. They'd probably live in a different neighborhood too, a more livable one, with fewer tourists and students and art galleries. St-Germain is a formal, buttoned-up quarter of *ancienne* nobility who aren't much interested in arriviste expats.

There are many things she'd do differently.

When it's raining, Kate tends to walk. Especially when it's raining hard, because almost no one else does.

The European weather used to get her down, the long months of everyday grayness, it seemed like the sun never shone from September till April, day after day of cloud cover, spitting rain, bone-chilling frost. But Kate got used to it, as you get used to anything. Bad weather couldn't be avoided, it wasn't viable to stay indoors whenever it rained; for half the year you'd never leave home. So she acquired the proper gear, one item at a time—rubberized hat, slicker, comfortable boots—to manage the wetness. Like any other rational adult solution to any other problem. Not ignored, not dodged. Managed.

What drives her crazy about Dexter is that he tries to avoid the unavoidable, ignore the unignorable. It makes her wish she were the kind of wife who could stand in the kitchen and scream at her husband, spewing profanity at high volume, accompanied by projectiles—teacups, produce, hardcover novels. But she isn't.

Another of Kate's rules is that she keeps a log of her routes, to ensure that she doesn't unintentionally fall into a pattern, a predictable sequence. The log is coded—it looks like a list of household reminders, scrawled in a handmade notebook she picked up in Venice—even though there's no danger if this information falls into other hands. It's a record of the past, not a plan for the future. It's nothing.

But using codes is another of Kate's rules, and she adheres to it even when the codes are 99.9 percent superfluous. It's a discipline, she tells herself. It's not the details that matter. What matters is the general state of mind, a state of being: careful. Always.

This is how she was trained, how she has lived. This is her identity, this careful person who maintains coded records of her surveillance-detection routes and countermeasures, of dead-drops and blind passes. This is what Kate knows how to do. This is all.

What could she possibly do next?

During their long year living in Luxembourg, Kate tried having no job; for their first year in Paris too. Then when she finally rooted out the full extent of her husband's duplicities, Kate realized that she had leverage. Leverage with Dexter, who'd nearly wrecked their lives with a combination of ambition, amorality, dishonesty, and gullibility; he owed Kate, they both knew it. She also had leverage with the CIA, courtesy of the huge sum of untraceable money that Dexter had stolen—dirty money, free money that could be used for anything—as well as the prospect of making the FBI look inept, corrupt. And leverage with herself, an argument that Kate could now advance to justify the increasingly uncomfortable feeling that had tainted her first couple of years as an expat: she was not cut out to be a full-time homemaker.

What did Kate want in return for all this leverage? To be young again. But instead she asked for something that was actually possible.

Today she takes the pont des Arts, which affords her her favorite vantage in Paris—the pont Neuf bisected by the Île de la Cité, with the towers of Notre-Dame looming behind, and the grandeur of the Louvre, and the Musée d'Orsay and the Grand Palais, and the top of the Eiffel Tower. You can see it all from one spot, right here.

This city is unrelentingly gorgeous, everywhere Kate turns, the broad boulevards and their neat apartment blocks, the grand *hôtels particuliers* and gothic churches and medieval houses, the wide green river traversed by all these splendid bridges, the quiet little *places* and leafy little parks, the Machine Age railroad terminals and Art Nouveau Métro stations, the incessant materialization of majesty around any corner, a constant barrage of world-famous landmarks. It seems unreasonable, an unfair distribution of assets.

Kate feels the soft give of the wooden walkway beneath her feet, worn and uneven, mossy and damp, the sheen of wetness creating a mirror effect, reflecting the old lampposts and the clouds rushing by in the bright blue sky.

The pont des Arts is a pedestrian bridge, and at this moment nearly all its pedestrians are coming toward Kate, away from the Louvre on the far side. Which is not the typical flow, not in the morning, with the museum just opening, the crowds converging.

The last time Kate was in a museum was a year ago, what she hoped would be a manageable little visit with the kids to the Orsay, an hour tops. Take advantage of the culture; they might not live in Paris forever. She gathered her rosebuds from school, stopped at the bakery for *le goûter*:

a *pain au chocolat* for Jake, a *brioche au sucre* for Ben, who asserts that chocolate croissants are too chocolaty. The same snack every afternoon, no dissatisfaction, no experimentation. Children are creatures of happy habit. Something needs to go awry to sway them to change.

Kate was accustomed to the crowds in central Paris, but they were usually easy to circumnavigate. The multitudes at the Musée d'Orsay, though, were inescapable, unavoidable, holding up their phone cameras, their tablets, amassing in front of each painting to take a photo and then move on, an assembly line. Or—worse—blocking everyone's view to stand directly in front of paintings, facing away, to take selfies with blockbuster backdrops.

Teenage girls were the worst offenders. Posing was second nature for these kids, selfie smiles rehearsed in mirrors, poses perfected after thousands of variations in body angle and head tilt, hair fluff and lip purse and peace sign, a permanent regimen of fine-tuning, akin to practicing piano or laying down a sacrifice bunt, skills never attempted by these kids, who instead know how to do mainly this one thing: look like they're having a great time in social-media photos, exposure and exclamation points compulsory, soliciting other exclamation points, an ouroboros of manufactured enthusiasm.

Kate looks off to one side of the bridge, then the other. The houseboats are sitting there, as ever, but not the *bateaux-mouches* that should be plying the river, laden with tourists on this rarity of a perfect sunny day, thick throngs leaning over the gunwales.

She herself had once been a teenage girl with a water-lily poster thumb-tacked above her dorm-room bed. She understood the attraction, wanting to possess the art. But not the impulse of adding yourself to it. Why? Proving you'd been there? Or something more insidious?

Not only are there no sightseeing barges on the Seine, there are instead police boats.

Kate's little children were too short to see above the packs of autopaparazzi in the Orsay. The only thing her boys could see were other people taking photos, of themselves. It was the opposite of appreciating art. It was unbearable.

Now Kate also notices that there aren't any cars on the far quay's roadway. Traffic must be diverted.

What the hell is happening?

21

"So Mr. Forsyth, I've got good news and bad news."

"Isn't that always the case."

"The radio in my car is working, so I was able to get in touch with the embassy. Which is definitely on complete lockdown. No one in, no exceptions."

"I'm assuming that's not the good news?"

"There *is* a place we can go where the electricity appears to be functional."

"Okay. I guess that is good. What about a phone?"

"It's not plugged in, so I'm not sure if it's working."

That doesn't seem so bad. "Is that the bad news, Mr. Simpson?" Hunter knows that the guy's name isn't Tom Simpson, and he doesn't work for State. But Hunter has decided to let it slide. Proving to everyone how smart you are can be counterproductive.

"Er, no. There are a few bits of bad news. The first is that the cellular networks are all compromised, there's no service anywhere in Paris right now. And it's possible that there won't be any wifi where we're going. We'll have to see once we're there."

"Are there any other places I can go?"

"Not at the moment, no."

"Well then that sounds perfect. Can we get going immediately?"

"There's one other thing, Mr. Forsyth: it'll just be you. Your security can't come with you. And your . . ." He cuts his eyes in the direction of Colette.

"My assistant? She's absolutely coming with me."

"*C'est pas nécessaire,*" Colette protests. But Hunter knows that she really does want to be rescued by him, plucked from her middle-class life as a professor's wife, he'll propose at Le Jules Verne, the ceremony will be on St-Jean-Cap-Ferrat, the honeymoon will be a glamping safari in Kenya. He has planned it all.

It took Hunter a good long while to come around to the idea of marriage, at which point he proposed to a girlfriend who wasn't any more marriage-worthy than the preceding ones; she just happened to be the current one. Since his wedding, he has also become attached to the prospect of fatherhood, which is a much more compelling concept than being a husband. But he has also realized that it's not Jen who he wants to be the mother of his children.

"I'm sorry, Mr. Forsyth. But Mademoiselle, um . . ."

"Benoit. *Madame* Benoit."

"Excuse me, Madame Benoit is not an American citizen. We can't—"

"I'm not going anywhere without her." Hunter is going to bluster his way through this, as he does everything. "Grab your things, Colette. Let's go."

Tom Simpson from State has a quick conversation with the Parisian cops on the sidewalk. Hunter feels like he should hear whatever it is they're discussing, but Simpson told him—ordered him—to wait in the lobby. Hunter understood that there was a dire warning in that instruction, a concern about being in plain sight on the sidewalk. Is it really possible that someone is going to take a shot at him?

Simpson returns, looking serious. "Here's how this is going to work. I'll walk first. Mr. Forsyth, you'll follow immediately behind me. And Mme. Benoit, you'll walk directly behind Mr. Forsyth, flanked by these police officers, with the rear brought up by your security guard . . . ?"

It's something with a G . . . Gérard? . . . Gérome? . . .

"Didier," Colette supplies.

Didier?

"Didier will return upstairs to keep your apartment secure. *Comprenez-vous*, Didier?"

"*Oui.*"

Didier. Hunter never bothered to learn the name of this security guard. Has he really become that asshole? It seems like just yesterday when he accepted the necessity of full-time security. An uncomfortable conversation, like estate planning, contemplating your demise, the different ways that it could—would—come about, and when, and how people would move on afterward.

"*Merci Didier,*" Hunter says, but he's not fooling anyone.

"Please keep your heads down, and walk directly through the car's rear door without slowing. Get yourselves onto the floor quickly. I'll cover you with a tarp."

"A tarp? Is that really necessary?"

"I certainly hope not. But I don't want to discover the contrary due to a bullet in your head."

"Um . . ." Hunter looks over at the sedan. "You don't have bulletproof glass?"

"Or an RPG through the windshield."

How the hell does a role-playing game come through the windshield?

"RPG?"

"Rocket-propelled grenade. We don't want you to get shot, we don't want you to be seen, we don't want anyone to be able to observe that there are any passengers. Just me. And no one knows me, I'm nobody. Okay, are we ready?" Nods all around. "Let's do this."

He's all business, this Simpson character, striding across the narrow sidewalk, just a few steps to the car, the guy's head swiveling left and right, left and right, then he reaches to open the door, fingers on the handle, but something diverts his attention—

He holds up his left hand. His right hand is in his jacket pocket.

"What?" Hunter asks.

Simpson gazes off to the right, the direction from which cars would come down this one-way street. Nothing is moving.

"It's okay. Get in."

Hunter bends into the backseat, scooches across the leather on his knees, and folds himself onto the floor. Colette joins him, limber, flexible. He can't help but watch as her skirt is pushed up, up, high up her thigh . . .

Oh my fucking God: her stockings are held up by *garters.*

How did he not realize at their very first meeting that this was the sexiest woman in the world? Missing that has shattered his faith in his own powers of perception.

Their faces are just inches apart, down here on the floor. It's a new car, very clean carpets. It's possible that there's never been a backseat passenger.

Hunter is plenty used to slipping in and out of car doors that are opened by other people, driven by other people, chauffeurs holding umbrellas, assistants carrying bags, doormen and porters and lawyers and publicists, leading him this way and that, intervening on his behalf. Hunter's is a life set apart, buffered by bodyguards and hired cars, first-class cabins and private jets, three-star restaurants whose astronomical prices segregate the elite like him from the envious masses who want to be.

But he's never been hustled into a car like this. Except that one time in Kuala Lumpur, the political demonstration, who the hell knew what was going to happen, Southeast Asia.

"This is something, isn't it?"

Colette smiles first with her eyes, then the smile migrates to her mouth, her whole face. It's a beautiful smile. "An adventure, *Monsieur. N'est-ce pas?*"

"*Oui,*" Hunter says, "an adventure."

In the end, KL turned out okay. This too will turn out okay.

Hunter would definitely prefer if he had some way of confirming Simpson's identity, his affiliation, their destination, anything. But he doesn't. And he isn't hampered by a dogmatic attachment to certainty. Hunter's competitive advantage has never been fact-based. It's his intuition, and his speed: Hunter acts quicker than everyone else, and has never been proven wrong, not on anything that matters. Except women. But those misjudgments have never really cost him much.

"Maybe for today, Colette, you can stop calling me *Monsieur*? Hunter will be fine."

"*Oui Monsieur,*" she says. They both laugh, and that's when Simpson drapes the tarp over the two of them, a fluttering descent of dark, and the last Hunter sees are Colette's hazel eyes, replaced by the after-burned image of her garters, seared in his memory.

The car pulls away, and his stomach immediately starts to roil. He's going to have to concentrate on not getting sick here. Their romance definitely wouldn't be hastened along by that humiliation.

22

First it was just a single sound of alarm, one woman who said something shrill to her companion, who responded in an urgent tone that was overheard by an adjoining family, and within seconds everyone in Mahmoud's immediate proximity was fleeing in every direction, radiating waves of panic, people dragging each other by their hands, their wrists, falling and trampled and rising with ripped pants and bloody elbows, losing grips on phones and cameras and bottles of water, making a mad dash to nowhere, they had no destination in front, just trying to put distance behind, as much as possible, because no one knew why exactly they were running except those few who had the presence of mind and took the time to look back over their shoulders, to focus through the chaos on the expanding emptiness at the center, and these were the most terrified people of all, these were the ones who understood, who were calculating when exactly all that Semtex was going to be detonated, what magnitude of blast radius, and what in the name of God Almighty was with that briefcase?

"There will then be a long period of waiting," the man had explained. "You will stand there, alone. For a few hours, or all day, into the night."

"Just waiting?"

"We will make demands. There will be negotiations, back and forth. Our demands, theirs, concessions. Lines of communication will be established, credentials confirmed."

"Why will they not simply shoot me immediately?"

"Good question. Two answers. One: it will be obvious from the design of the vest—with the phone—that the detonator is not controlled by you, so even if you are dead, the device can still be detonated. You are not in control; they have nothing to gain by shooting you, and possibly something to lose. Two: the briefcase. At the outset, they will not know exactly what the case is. Why would a man like you have such a thing?"

A man like you.

"They will realize there can be only one reason."

Mahmoud nodded, expecting more of an explanation. He did not get one. But he figured it out, on his own.

After just a few minutes, the soldiers who surrounded him begin to retreat, walking backward, then sideways, until they step through the gap in the fence. Then Mahmoud is all alone.

Except for this earpiece in his ear, and a microphone pinned to his collar. "Everyone is gone," he says into the mic.

"You will have the gratitude of your people," the man says into Mahmoud's ear.

There will be no further instructions for Mahmoud, no updates from him. No decision for him to make, no actions to take.

"Of your family."

There will be nothing.

"You will have the thanks of Allah."

23

She would know if a world leader were in town, a European president, the pope, the type of dignitary whose presence would shut down traffic on the streets and the river too. Those visits are difficult for any run-of-the-mill Parisian to overlook, and impossible for Kate.

So that's not it.

Plenty of large-scale demonstrations occur in Paris. *Jours de grève* pop up regularly; some population of French workers is pretty much always on strike. Large crowds march to support social security, or on the other hand to decry *la sécu*. On any given day, some group is protesting something. But these demonstrations don't arise out of nowhere.

There has been no civil unrest, no overt religious strife, no outrageous incident of police brutality. There's no current, recent, or upcoming election.

This is not a culture inclined toward martial law, nor random displays of military might. Bastille Day is one thing, but the police here don't flex their muscles merely to show off.

There's no volcano within hundreds of miles, earthquakes don't happen here, nor hurricanes, tornadoes, the sorts of natural emergencies that can necessitate large-scale mobilizations of security forces.

No, the sort of catastrophe that happens in Paris is something else. The specifics of each attack have come as a surprise, but not the general fact of them, it's an ever-present possibility. And Kate's job is knowing such things, if not in advance then at least once they've begun, when the circle of secrecy expands to include someone or other in her wide network of paid informants, pink hundred-euro notes handed out liberally across Western Europe. But she has heard of nothing happening today. Is this another failure of hers?

They're mounting. Ever since Copenhagen, from which Hayden fled, chasing a lead to America, where his blood was found on a rocky beach. It wasn't a huge amount of blood, not a lethal volume. And no body. But still.

Then there was the operation in Seville, the missed opportunity. Followed by Palermo, when Kate overcompensated for her failure in the first, and lost an actual person. And not just any person.

Since then, no new assignments, nothing to reassure her that she still directs an active concern. It's hard to avoid the conclusion that she blew it. That after her ongoing ops conclude, the Paris Substation is going to be folded. Which at this point in her career will mean the end of. Like a ballplayer: at a certain point, another surgery is no longer sensible, and there's nothing to be done but hang up the cleats, buy a car dealership.

A few years ago, in Luxembourg, Jake quizzed her about her job. They were in the car, on their way to one of the big playgrounds, three-thirty in the afternoon. The little boy listened to her cover story with no skepticism, nodding along, trying to understand the grown-up world, and his mother's place in it. He considered her explanation for a few seconds, then asked, "Mommy, you're quite young to be retired, aren't you?"

It wasn't until then that she considered the possibility that her unemployment was permanent. "I'm not retired, Sweetie. I'm just taking a break."

While she waits for the hammer to drop, Kate still goes to work most days, even when there's basically nothing to do. Every day might be the day that she can save her career.

In Kate's mind, there are definitely other people who could be blamed. In the ultimate court, she'd be able to call witnesses in her defense, there'd be an argument she could advance, appeals to the judge. But you never do get to defend yourself, explain your decisions, justify your missteps. Certainly not to anyone who can make any difference; the only people who would listen are the people who can't do anything about it.

And in any court there'd be cross-examinations, a solid case could definitely be made against her. "What about Seville?" they'd ask. "What about Palermo? What about Julia MacLean? How do you explain all that?"

✦

Kate plants herself in front of a family of four rushing toward her, parents and a pair of teenagers wearing scandalously short skirts, obscenely tight tees, dance-clubby makeup.

"Excuse me," Kate says. The mother has been crying. The father meets her eye, so Kate addresses him: "What's going on?"

"A man is in the middle of the Louvre, wearing a suicide vest."

They rush past, scurrying back to their hotel where they'll hole up until their flight home, no more museums, no Métro or public places, not with their worst fears about international travel confirmed. Why didn't the CIA see this coming? Isn't that what they're for?

Kate has tried her case herself—over and over, usually in the middle of the night. She knows that in a just world she'd be found not guilty. But that's not the same thing as innocent.

24

This isn't something you know until you've done it: moving dead bodies is extremely awkward. Wyatt hadn't needed to move around any of the previous dead bodies in his life, just let them lie where they fell. These two are also the only completely innocent people he's ever killed, as far as he knows. Maybe the hard work is his penance.

He tries to work quickly, dragging them across the concrete floor, back behind the little Cooper. The man weighs at least two hundred pounds, surprisingly difficult to drag forty yards. When Wyatt finishes he's winded, arms burning, back aching.

He climbs back into the van to catch his breath, gather his wits, collect his bag. This damn bag. If only he hadn't forgotten it.

Though what does that even mean, innocent? Innocent doesn't mean you don't deserve to die. We all die, there's no deserve or don't deserve about it. Just a question of when, and how. His daughter doesn't deserve to die. But she will.

It's possible he's going to vomit. He fights it back, swallows. And again.

Wyatt takes a deep, slow breath, trying to bring his digestive system under control, to halt the reverse peristalsis—

Fuck—he can't help it—he flings open the door, and leans over, and *splat*, it's all coming up, last night's dinner, absolutely disgusting, orange and brown chunks bound up in unctuous slime. He can't stop staring down into this repugnant puddle of sick.

His DNA is all over the goddamned place.

He climbs out of the van, scans the walls, there must be a hose here somewhere, a spigot, a way to clean the pavement, sluice away oil slicks, broken bottles of mango nectar, drunken-relief urine, a long pleasant *aahhhhhh.* He'll hose down this mess, it won't take more than a minute or two, then get—

What's that? Jesus H., will it never end?

Another car is coming down the ramp, he can see the headlights, so he launches himself back into the driver's seat, pulls the door closed, ducks down and leans his body across the gearshift, the side of his head hitting this bag—this *fucking* bag—in the passenger seat, he shoves it to the floor, giving himself room to hide his head.

The new car's wheels squeak around a turn. Wyatt can see headlights flash across his truck's roof, then on the opposite wall, another squeak, then the lights stop strobing, aimed *right here* at the wall in front of him.

Damn.

He can feel the new car pull up just beyond his head, it can be only a few feet that separates him from this other driver.

The new car's engine dies. The click of another door unlatching, a creak as it opens, then slams shut, loudly, echoing. A rustle of movement, clothes, and then nothing. No footsteps. Why? Why no footsteps? Is this fucker looking through the van's window?

Wyatt is lying on his right side, which makes it awkward to shift the angle of his right arm, reach his right hand into his pocket, where the gun is.

Now he notices the glow, it must be a screen, this newly arrived person is standing right here between his car and Wyatt's van, typing a text-message, checking a map, doing something that might seem urgent, with no idea that it might be the biggest—the final—mistake of his life.

Wyatt is going to hyperventilate. He focuses on taking in a breath slowly, carefully, quietly.

This glow persists, right here, just inches from his face.

Wyatt's right hand finds the grip in his pocket. His palm settles, fingers find their positions. He takes another controlled breath.

Then movement—what's this?—it's the light, the phone's glow, the angle shifted, and then the dim light extinguishes.

Footsteps recede.

Another door creaks open, shudders shut, then: silence.

Wyatt counts to ten. Then to ten again. Then he sits up. Looks around, his eyes drawn to the Cooper on the far side. He can just barely make out one of the woman's feet, peeking out from behind a rear wheel.

He can't be here anymore.

⚜

As he hustles down the sidewalk, Wyatt tries to locate the policeman, but can't. The Métro station is right up here, around this corner, which he turns—

Fuck.

Of course that's where the cop is, standing at the top of the steps, in the crisscross shadows of the latticework Métro sign, looking vigilant, alert, like a policeman should during a terrorist siege. *Of course* the patrolman would be dispatched to the subway station. Why didn't anyone think of this? Why didn't Wyatt?

Do not stop walking, he tells himself. Do not slow down. Do not look around. Just one foot in front of the other, step off this curb—

Fuck! What the—?

"Fou!" It's a cyclist screaming at him, cursing. *"Connard!"*

"Désolé!" Wyatt calls out, too late. *"Désolé,"* he repeats the apology, quieter, but that doesn't put the genie back in the bottle: the cop is now staring straight at him.

Wyatt can't turn around now. He continues toward the subway, shaky, God he's nervous. He has to walk right by this policeman, here in broad daylight. Any blood spatters will be clearly visible. The smell of his exertion, his sweat, his fear. And he's carrying this pistol, there's gunshot residue on his clothing, the aroma trapped in his nasal passages.

Stop it, he tells himself. Stop thinking of all that shit. Just put one foot in front of the other, just a few more steps, just one more.

The cop looks him dead in the face, and Wyatt can't help but cut his eyes away from this confrontational gaze, a mistake, what can he do to compensate . . . ?

"Bonjour," he mutters.

"Bonjour."

Now he has passed, and taken one step down the stairs, a second—

"Monsieur?"

Oh my fucking God! What now?

He freezes absolutely still for a second, then turns, looks up at the cop.

"*Votre sac,*" the cop says. His bag? "*Il est ouvert.*"

"*Ah oui?*" Wyatt looks down at his open bag. He zips it closed, and a half-second too late realizes he's still wearing latex gloves. "*Merci.*"

"*Faites attention, aujourd'hui,*" the cop says, already turned away. He didn't notice the gloves, did he?

Be careful today. Indeed.

They're moving at a decent clip on a straightaway, probably one of those broad Right Bank boulevards. At this higher speed the bumps hurt more, the chassis jarring into Hunter's sides, his ribs, shaking the contents of his skull.

Maybe this wasn't such a great idea. What does he really know about this so-called Tom Simpson? What facts did Hunter check? None. He was bullied into blind trust.

"Listen, Mr. Simpson," he says from under the tarp. "Tom."

But what's he going to say? *I'm not having fun, please take me home? Can I speak to your supervisor? Show me your ID again? I want my mommy?*

He almost says *Forget it,* but then chivalry occurs to him as a viable alternative to cowardice. "Could I ask you to slow down? I think you're knocking Colette's marbles loose." Or pretend chivalry. Hunter suspects that all chivalry is pretend, just as he's convinced about all religion. Everyone must know, on some level, that there's no fucking way. But maybe if you pretend long enough, hard enough, you forget that what you're doing is pretending.

The car comes to a stop.

"Just a minute more," Simpson says. "Please remain still."

Hunter hears the driver's door open, but not close. Another noise, a high-pitched creak, a hinge that needs oiling. Then a similar noise, but not exactly the same.

Big doors. Two of them.

The driver plops back into his seat, shifts gears. The car moves forward slowly, then stops again, and the transmission shifts into reverse, turning, then forward again. Hunter realizes what this is: Simpson just turned the car around, so it faces the direction whence they came, the exit.

Hunter congratulates himself on figuring this out. But is it a good thing for them to be ready for a quick getaway? Or bad? What does it suggest about this predicament? About the safety of this location? About the confidence that Simpson has in—

The tarp is yanked off.

"Sorry for the discomfort," Simpson says. "You can get out now." He walks around to open Colette's door, reaches out his hand.

"*Merci.*" She extends her arm, her blouse disheveled, quick glimpse of lace bra, hot pink. Christ. She's got some weapons-grade lingerie under there. Hunter wonders if this is normal, if she wears lace garters and hot-pink bras every day, or if today is an occasion, date night, an anniversary. Or is it possible that she wears special underwear for Hunter's benefit?

"In here." Simpson ushers them toward the building's door, a keypad, a long string of digits that the guy shields from view. "Sorry, there's no elevator."

They trudge up the stairs, one flight, two. They pause on the landing, catch their breath. Then up another long flight.

"I guess we must be in the penthouse," Hunter says. No one responds.

There's a single door up at the top, steel-plated. A few locks, top, bottom, middle.

Something is tugging at the corners of Hunter's consciousness. What? He glances around the short hall. Should there be another door up here? The locks look high-tech, and three seems like a large number of them. But isn't that what you'd expect from a CIA safehouse? The steel reinforcement too?

Simpson unlocks the final mechanism with a loud click, turns the knob, pushes open the fortified door.

It's dark in here, heavy curtains on the windows. Simpson flips a switch that turns on a few floor lamps; there's no overhead. "Come on in."

Hunter allows Colette to step inside first, then follows tentatively.

Simpson reengages the locks, one of which requires a key to secure from the inside. "It's not much to look at, but it's safe." He slips the keys into his pocket.

Maybe nothing's wrong. Maybe Hunter is just nervous. As well he should be. Nothing wimpy about that, just a sensible response to what's obviously a highly fucked-up situation, spirited away by the CIA to protect him from murder, kidnapping. If he weren't nervous, he'd be a moron.

But Hunter is used to trusting his gut. And his gut is telling him that it isn't just nerves.

26

Kate is frozen in the middle of the pont des Arts, a boulder in a stream, people flowing around her like fast-moving currents.

Her first instinct is to spin around, to join the panicked mob fleeing danger, to return to school and reclaim her children, just as it crossed her mind an hour and a half ago, when she heard the first sirens, when the threat was unknown. But then what? Where would the family go? Traffic will be a nightmare, roads closed, maybe train stations, airports. All she'd accomplish would be to panic the children. And the apartment wouldn't be any safer than school. Less so: home is closer to a greater number of higher-value targets. Plus proximity to Kate Moore doesn't necessarily make anyone safer.

Paris is replete with noteworthy terrorist targets—dozens, hundreds, they're everywhere, but the International School of St-Germain is not one. There are no celebrity children there, no presidential daughters, no reason for the school to interest anyone. The kids are as safe as they can be, in that school.

That's the logical assessment. But parenting isn't always logical, and Kate is having a hard time beating back the emotional impulse, convincing herself to do what she knows she needs to do: continue to the Louvre, see this situation firsthand. Kate is the boots on the ground. If she's still a useful intelligence resource, she needs to prove it today.

And if she can't? Well then, that conclusion is inescapable, the sort she wouldn't even need to explain to her younger kid, who'd recently dubbed himself Incompetent Ninja. Like a superhero, but the opposite. "Because, Mommy, I *like* being a ninja, but I'm not *good* at it." Ben executed a wild leg kick and karate chop. "I am! Incompetent!! *Ninja*!!!"

These things are obvious, if you can manage to do what little kids can: suspend your pride, and see yourself clearly.

It was a few years ago when Kate saw clearly what she wanted, at a once-in-a-lifetime moment when she was in a position to get it. She cut a deal with her ex-mentor Hayden Grey, the CIA's chief of Western Europe. She'd hand over to Hayden the bulk of Dexter's stolen fortune, and also facilitate a recorded admission of guilt by the mastermind of the conspiracy, who happened to be an ex-FBI agent. Hayden looked forward to the impending scandal with uncharacteristic glee; the animosity between the Agency and the Bureau was apparently a strong motivator.

What Kate wanted from Hayden in return was two things: immunity for Dexter, and a job for herself. She wanted to be a spy again.

Hayden obliged. He used the 24 million untraceable euros to establish the Paris Substation, a clandestine, agile little outfit whose day-to-day Kate would manage. The fieldwork would be done by freelancers—informants, sources, criminals. The mandate would be the types of extra-curricular activities that the Agency didn't want on their books, or in their meetings, in their reports, their congressional oversight. These were not traditional intelligence-gathering operations, but rather active measures—supporting, undermining, influencing. Sometimes illegal, or close to it: the gray areas of character assassination and scandal manufacture, of destabilizing enemies and propping up friends, the illicit business of interfering in the internal affairs of sovereign governments.

First Kate hired a Paris fixer who could find the strays—plumber, electrician, cat burglar—that you always need. Then a cadre of techs who could hack into police departments, newsrooms, corporate e-mail servers. Bribable low-level officials in customs, in immigration, in tax authorities, people who could be paid modestly to part with modest in-formation, the kind of data Kate could use to extract more meaningful disclosures, an infinite ladder of trading up, each extorted secret building upon another, an edifice of shame.

The irony was not lost on Kate: she had traded her husband's secret criminal enterprise for her own.

This work involved frequent travel for Kate, usually for same-day meetings, away and back between breakfast and dinner, the TGV to

Brussels, a shuttle to Frankfurt, the Eurostar to London. Sometimes an overnight, a week here and there for a cleanup in Capri, or a Basque crisis in San Sebastián, or an extortion of a German industrialist on holiday in Mallorca, as German industrialists do.

She was effective at running her network of journalists, bloggers, influencers, as well as drug dealers, thieves, prostitutes, and cops, plus diplomats and soldiers, maître d's and concierges and bartenders and shopkeepers; it's surprising how much you can learn from the eagle-eyed owner of a well-sited bodega. All these assets, the fabric that holds society together, recruited so Kate could identify weaknesses and exploit them, manipulating reality to one that's a more hospitable environment for the security of the USA and the health of its global corporations, its banks, its exported culture, Coca-Cola, ExxonMobil, the films of Steven Spielberg.

Kate had been thrilled to return to this work, to this world. She got the Paris Substation up and running quickly, ahead of her own self-imposed schedule. Everything was working just fine.

Until Copenhagen.

⚜

Kate's first clue that something was wrong was that Hayden handed her a gun. She'd thought this op was supposed to be a simple stakeout, and there's nothing more boring than a stakeout. Until it isn't.

"What's going on here?" She examined the weapon, the type of locally procured, untraceable gun that means not only that you're expecting trouble, but also more trouble for solving the trouble.

"Kate, I need to explain what steps you'll take, in the event of my, um, *indisposition.*"

"I know the protocols, Hayden. Why are we talking about this?"

He gestured at the building across the street, their operation. He swept his arm: all of this, he was saying. Anything. "Things happen, Kate, you know what the *ifs* are. *If* ever I turn up, um, dead. *If* I'm missing for more than a few days. Or a week. Use your judgment."

Hayden had never before broached the subject of succession plans, and he'd never imposed a weapon upon her. She was worried.

"You'll go to this address."

He scribbled something that she read quickly, then closed her eyes, repeated the address to herself, invented a mnemonic, and repeated that a couple of times too. Then it was done. The Paris address was now, as Jake had been taught to say in math, a known fact.

"It's a travel bureau, not far from your office. You'll see any available representative, and say you're Kathy Anderson, wife of me, Harry Anderson." Hayden took out a cigarette lighter, set the paper afire, dropped it to the floor. "You're collecting my itinerary. The first time, there won't be anything. You'll ask the rep to check with her supervisor. She will. Then she'll assure you that *no*, there's nothing waiting for Monsieur Anderson. You'll leave a phone number—a burner—in case something appears. Sooner or later, it will."

"How long?"

"*I* don't know, Kate. A day? A *month*?" He handed the binoculars back to her. "Looks like another visitor."

Kate raised her binoculars. "The same pizza guy as yesterday."

"Yes. He should get a different drug dealer, one who delivers something else. *Sushi*, maybe. *Falafel*. The guy's going to have a cardiac arrest any second. Keel over."

Kate put down the glasses. "Then what?"

"Then? I guess we'll call an ambulance; it's dialing 112, I think. Is that right?"

Kate shrugged. She didn't know how to dial emergency services in Copenhagen, and she couldn't fathom why Hayden would.

"Or maybe it would be better if we let him die? Then someone else will be forced to show up, and things will clarify?"

She never ceased to be amazed at Hayden's ability to find distorted angles, which is probably what made him such a successful spymaster. "No, Hayden, I mean: what will happen when I eventually get this call?"

"You'll probably be summoned to a meet."

"Probably?"

"Again, Kate, it's hard to say."

"Why not the standard protocols?"

"Listen." He turned to face Kate, held her eye for a few seconds. "It's time for me to level with you, Kate. This operation—me, you, your team—we don't, *technically*, report into Langley. In any way, shape, or form."

She was too surprised to respond.

"Actually, that's not all true: *I* of course do report to Langley."

"But I don't?"

"Your whole substation, Kate, is our little secret, yours and mine. We operate completely outside CIA's chain of command. Our orders don't even come from Langley."

"Then where?"

"The other side of the Potomac."

Kate's mind raced through the possibilities. Secretary of state . . . of defense . . . national security advisor . . .

"Are you going to tell me?"

Vice president . . .

He shook his head. "Sorry."

President.

"It's called the Travelers International Booking Service, and it's affiliated with the American magazine called *The Travelers*. That's where you'll go for assignments."

"You're kidding."

"I'm not."

"It's a real magazine, right? I've heard of it. I've *read* it."

"It even wins awards, I'm told."

"And is it a real travel agency?"

"Yes. The agency is part of the parent company's *revenue* stream. Or a *profit* center." He shrugged. "Whatever they call it."

"And the whole thing is an Agency front?"

"The *whole* thing? No, that's not how fronts work, Kate, you know that. The travel agency is a legitimate business, affiliated with a legitimate magazine, which is a division of a legitimate American conglomerate. But *behind* the front, it's also a couple of other things. One is a clandestine courier service, and that's primarily what you'll be using it for."

"How?"

"Every other week, you'll call in, ask if there are any tickets for me." Hayden didn't need to tell Kate to use pay phones in assorted neighborhoods, to call at different hours on different days, to avoid any pattern, any suggestion of routine. "If the answer is yes, go there yourself. Collect the envelope, like anyone else picking up travel documents. There may be other clients around, you always need to be behaving as if you're one of them."

"Does the staff know?"

"No, not the people in the agency; those people are just travel agents."

"So what's in these envelopes?"

"The names of targets, encrypted using the Berlin code. Usually no other information or instruction. It's completely at our discretion to figure out exactly how, and when. If there's any required timeframe, that too will be obvious. The reasons will also make themselves obvious, once you start looking."

"Such as?"

"Such as an upcoming election. Or a diplomatic summit. A trade deal. But other than the name, there will be no incoming information. And outgoing from you, also nothing. You won't provide any updates, *ever*. If your operation is successful, the necessary reporting will come through other avenues within the Agency, and from the press. Briefs will make their way to the right people. You don't need to worry about reporting successes."

"I'm assuming I also don't need to report failures?"

"You see, Kate? I've always known you're a genius."

"And no specifics about the mission?"

"It's always the same: ruin the target. Discredited. Fired. Arrested."

"Killed?"

Hayden shrugged.

She understood: whatever it took. "And what's the other thing Travelers does?"

Hayden turned back to Kate, and gave her a big smile. "You're going to love this."

"Hi Dex," she says.

"Kate? Everything all right?" It has been only a few minutes since they parted.

"No. There's apparently a suicide bomber at the Louvre. A guy wearing a vest."

"My God."

"Dex, you're planning to stay home all day, right?"

"Well, I still need to go find that Lego. But I guess not if the city blows up."

"Not funny, Dexter."

"You're right. Sorry."

"Listen: please answer any calls, from any phone number, even if you don't recognize it. It might be me calling from another line, or school, or a teacher calling from a mobile, or another parent."

"Gotcha."

"I don't think we should do it right now, but we should be prepared to get the kids."

"And what are you going to do?"

What should Kate say? She wonders where Dexter imagines her office is. Maybe the embassy? Or the American Club? Someplace easily identifiable as American, flag flying out front, a fleet of black Escalades?

"I have work to do."

"Work?"

She doesn't elaborate.

"You're kind of scaring me, Kate. What's going on?"

"I don't know, Dex. But first the bomb threat at the train station, and now . . ." She trails off, pursuing a line of conjecture that she doesn't want to share.

"Should I be worried?" he asks.

"Well, yeah. At least a little."

"About what?"

"I'm not sure exactly."

"Are there other bombs? Let me . . . Oh God, I'm now seeing this on TV. The courtyard has been evacuated, except for one guy. Yes, he's definitely wearing a vest, and he's also got a case. Kate, where exactly are you?"

"On my way there."

"*There*? What the hell do you mean by that? Tell me you're not going to the Louvre."

"Calm down, Dexter."

"*Calm down?* What do you think is *in* that case? The guy didn't detonate immediately, when he was surrounded by victims. And now that the courtyard has been evacuated, what's a bomb going to accomplish? Shatter the windows? Who gives a shit?"

Dexter is right. If it were only a conventional explosive that was going to be detonated, it would make sense only in a big crowd, when there's flesh to pierce, people to injure, maim, murder. But if all the people are gone, there's no one left to kill except the bomber. So what's the briefcase for?

"But even the *tiniest* nuclear detonation? The radiation?"

"There's not really any such thing as a suitcase nuclear bomb," Kate says. "Not one that fits in an actual suitcase." It's a halfhearted objection. She knows that it's only a matter of semantics, and magnitude.

"But a case like that could contain radioactive material. A dirty bomb."

A dirty bomb wouldn't create the same type of blast, no mushroom cloud; downtown Paris wouldn't be leveled. But it could produce plenty of long-term lethal radiation; for all intents and purposes, everything in the Louvre would be destroyed—the Rembrandts and Vermeers, Raphaels and Caravaggios, the artifacts from Greece, Rome, Egypt, the largest repository of art and artifacts in the world.

And it would kill everyone within the primary blast zone, if not immediately from the explosion then within a matter of days from the radiation. Definitely Kate. Dexter too? And the children, are they far enough away to be spared? Every inch might count, when it comes to radiation. Every minute that you get farther away, every second, might save your life.

"Or," Dexter says.

Or. Kate's mind is catching up to other possibilities, worse even than nuclear radiation at the Louvre.

"Biological," Dexter continues.

Worse for whom? she asks herself.

"Chemical."

Worse for her. Worse for her family.

She picks up her pace, breaks into a run, dodging among all the people who are fleeing in the other direction. Kate is the only one who is rushing toward the bomb.

PART II

CHAMPS-ÉLYSÉES

27

I t would be unthinkable, if there still were such a thing. But nothing is unthinkable, not anymore.

There's a suicide bomber at the Louvre.

Kate pushes her way through the chaotic crowd in the plaza, most people still fleeing in terror but some inching forward in curiosity, or milling about in confusion, or inquiry, or simply hovering with smart-phones aloft, citizen-reporters eager to document anything, even if it turns out to be their own demise.

Police are securing a perimeter across all the access points—the *passages* through the palace's ground level, the big open space of the Tuile-ries, the heavily trafficked two-way street that runs through the place du Carrousel, the wide sidewalks, the buses and trucks and abundant vol-ume of pedestrians, a huge space to seal off, requiring a lot of personnel and vehicles, all still in the process of arriving.

The grand U-shaped courtyard itself is relatively easy to secure, with its sole open facet already lined with fencing. Choke points have been closed, checkpoints established. No one in. No one out.

A few uniformed officers are trying to reason with hysterical people—my wife is inside, my grandparents—while also making sure that no one comes bursting through intent on who the hell knows, an accomplice, an unrelated psychopath. There's no accounting for psycho-paths.

Kate finally elbows her way into a position where she can see—

She gasps. She's surprised at her reaction, like an amateur. She has never before seen anything like this. No one here has.

What she sees: a man is standing all alone in the middle of the vast open space, looking tiny. He's wearing a bulky vest, and a briefcase sits at his feet, the sort of luggage that in action-adventure films follows around the president of the United States, a shiny case lugged by a tall square-jawed man wearing a military uniform, a handsome extra with no speaking lines. The nuclear codes.

In real-world non-POTUS life, this case is the sort of thing that can be outfitted with foam insets and thick padding and reinforced super-structure to prevent accidental damage or premature detonation, tidy packets of TNT or nitro or Semtex surrounded by ready-made shrapnel, construction screws or ball bearings, little bits of lethal.

Yes, Dexter was right: that's a suitcase bomb.

Is this an SOS situation?

Kate's cover isn't compromised, her substation isn't blown, her network isn't being rounded up, there's no high-visibility op imploding. Those are the valid reasons for her to send an SOS; those are the potential problems of hers that her superiors might be willing to help solve. Or at least be willing to hear about.

Then again, she doesn't know exactly who her superiors are, so it's hard to tell.

But someone blowing up the Louvre? That doesn't present any immediate risk to Kate's personnel or office or the CIA or the USA. It wouldn't lay bare anyone's diligently covered ass, wouldn't cost anyone a job, a promotion. This attack is not the Agency's failure of intelligence, not its problem to solve. Perhaps even the opposite: this attack could help further the CIA's agenda, could advance a rationale for some action, a policy shift, a realignment of resources. Perhaps it's an opportunity.

Either way, it's not something Kate can ignore, just a bystander, like that truck driver tried to pretend with the dog. He looked like a fool, and Kate would too. No: worse than a fool. She'd look like a neglectful, incompetent fraud. On the heels of her other recent failures, Kate would appear worthless.

She turns her back on the bomber, scans the crowd, the police mobilizing, crowd-controlling, looking for other signs of trouble. This bomber can't be a simple lone-wolf attack; that situation would be over already, the police would have shot him, or he would've blown himself up. There must be a bigger picture, and Kate needs to insert herself into it.

If it turns out that this attack does have something to do with American interests—and at this point in geopolitical history, what doesn't—and Kate has chosen to spend the day watching cable-news coverage? If something preventable is happening in Paris and she fails to prevent it? If there's a plot to crack and she fails to crack it, if American lives are going to be lost and she fails to save them?

Then today will be the last operational day of her career. It won't happen a few weeks from now, with some marginally rude guy on a park bench. No, it'll be immediate, persona non grata. Or worse.

Kate reaches the far end of the *place,* and turns to take one last look at the man who's standing there in the middle of the courtyard, strapped into oblivion.

She knows that this has nothing to do with her. Except that everything in Paris has something to do with her.

Most of the post-Agency options for people like Kate are not available to the actual Kate. Private contracting work in conflict zones, or high-value security details, the types of jobs you can't have if you're a parent, if you need to come home alive every night. Management or consulting jobs in Langley, or in Washington, or on the rural campuses of paramilitary training camps in North Carolina, in Honduras, in Sudan, the types of jobs you can't have if you're married to Dexter Moore, and you've had their shared life experiences, their entanglements, and you live in France.

She could do something completely unrelated, something entrepreneurial, maybe launch one of those businesses like Hashtag Mom, who supposedly designs necklaces, though mostly she seems to make so-called strategic expenditures—the studio in Montparnasse, the personal assistant who's "*so* indispensable," the research trips to India, to Thailand; they're Eastern-inspired, Hashtag Mom's necklaces. #Inspired.

Or she could again try full-time householding, older and wiser, planning the vacations and inspecting the car, paying the bills and filing the taxes, cleaning and cooking and educating and shopping, plus all the personal maintenance, it's like being a professional athlete, constantly training with one exercise obsession after another, plus the manicures, the teeth-whitenings, the haircuts and blowouts and colorings, the depilatorizations, and the fashion—the jeans, the boots, God all the shoes—

amassing the requisite tribal insignia, the logos and patterns and patches and badges that sort you, that identify your clan.

Could Kate do it? Could she compete for firmest ass and strongest triceps and widest gap between her thighs, for the latest this and chicest that, the most original and attractive conversions of the money her husband earns into documentable manifestations of the good life, Instagrammable and Facebookable, eminently enviable, the best of everything, we all want the good life, don't we, and look—I have it! I win.

Could Kate win?

She unlocks a Vélib' bike and pedals away on the rue de Rivoli, completely empty on this section alongside the Tuileries, with squad cars blocking the intersecting streets, traffic jams already formed, drivers standing beside the open doors of their fuel-efficient little *citadines*— Renaults, Citroëns—on the rue de Castiglione, the rue Cambon, smoking cigarettes, complaining into their mobiles. They don't know what exactly the problem is. Rumors are flying.

Kate passes the larger of the English-language bookstores, which reminds her of the other shop, closer to home, another resource developed, just in case.

She glances over her shoulder. It's impossible that any cars are following her, but there are also no mopeds, no motorcycles, no other bicycles. Just streams of pedestrians, some more frantic than others, but none paying any attention to her. No one is following Kate.

She fights the urge to look up into the sky; you can't see the satellites, not with the naked eye in daylight. But they're there, watching. Drones too.

At Concorde she cuts diagonally across the broad expanse of unoccupied lanes, a rare moment of calm in what's usually a madhouse megaroundabout. But now it's just her bicycle headed in one direction, and a trio of cop cars zooming in the other.

She barely glances at the US Embassy on her right; she's not going there. Nor is she going home. Nor school. Nor the musty safehouse out behind Père Lachaise in the *vingtième,* a ground-floor unit with a private street-level entrance in an apartment building occupied mostly by North Africans.

Kate continues onto the Champs-Élysées. The grand boulevard is almost entirely empty, as if the bomb had already detonated.

Suddenly she's facing into a phalanx of police cars with their lights flashing, and behind the cops here comes the army, a few jeeps and a couple of armored personnel carriers and—yes—here they are, a half-dozen of them.

That really didn't take long, something she never thought she'd see in France.

Tanks.

Tanks are rolling down the Champs-Élysées.

28

Shreve looks at his watch. *Fuck.*

He rushes by that awesome sign—PLEASE DON'T WAIL AGAINST THE FLOW—while bounding down the Central–Mid-Levels escalator-walkway that transports pedestrians up and down the steep foothills of Hong Kong Island. Shreve loves that fucking sign—Wail Against the Flow! He wants that on a T-shirt. Or start a band, this could be the title for their debut.

Though the thing is: however you interpret Wail Against the Flow, Shreve doesn't do it. He's more of a wail-*with*-the-flow guy. Maybe that's why he finds the sign so appealing.

Like, what was that band? Rage Against the Machine.

He looks again at his Rolex. Fuck. He's going to be *so* late.

Okay, so, yes, things did get out of hand. It was just supposed to be a quick bite after the gym at that Italian in the Hollywood mall, Dougie and Frenac and the hot arbitrage chick Veronica, they'd already opened a Barolo before he arrived, then Dougie offered a bump, which turned into a few, and soon they were all shuttling back and forth to the unisex as if digging out the final stretch under the prison walls using soupspoons.

So now, yes, he can't deny it: he's pretty fucking high.

But these are *clients;* this is his *job.* Not just chiseling his commission off the intersection where someone else's idea meets another someone's investment, but recruiting and massaging and servicing these clients. They'd all agreed to meet again later, at Kau U Fong, Jell-O shots and beers down in the street, then the elevator up to Ping's, where Dougie could re-up, everyone on sofas, the balcony for cigarettes, Veronica in that skintight skirt, what he'd really love to do is lean down to snort some blow off her back while fucking her from behind, bent over a leather sofa.

Shreve has arrived at the end of the escalator-stairs, and now he's running over a sky-bridge and through the shopping plaza, onto an elevated sidewalk, nothing is on ground level here, you're constantly getting on and off escalators, elevators, even the *sidewalks* are in the sky, like the Jetsons, bars on the fifth floor, restaurants on the tenth, everything in vertical malls built into hillsides, you never know where you are in relation to street level, which isn't even that clear of a concept. Car level.

Even from up here on one-above-car level, Shreve still needs to dash up another escalator to the soaring glass-walled lobby with all the corporate signage, his own bank and a few others, plus media, and that American-based tech company that just expanded onto the fortieth and forty-first, they're obviously growing, maybe he should get in on that, but right now he's frantically searching for the ID card, not there, nor there, patting down his chest, swinging his gym bag off his shoulder, and *fuck* where's my goddamned card?

There. Whew. He looks at his watch again, fourteen minutes late and still in the lobby, Harrison is going to *ream* him.

Shreve drops his corporate-logo'd little duffle—everybody at his gym uses these canvas bags, they're like sports uniforms, they announce what team you play for, HSBC or UBS or BNP, the occasional Morgan or Citi dude—onto the conveyor through the X-ray, and he swipes his key card through the slot and strides into the turnstile, waits to collect his bag, which hasn't come through the belt yet, and the security guards are staring at the monitor, then one of them yells at him—what did that dude say?—while the other jumps off his stool, and draws his gun, and that's when all fucking hell breaks loose.

29

Hunter holds the newly powered-up phone to his ear, depresses the switch hook. Nothing, not even a hiss. Just silence.

"There's no dial tone," he says. Depress and release, depress and release. "Nothing."

"No?" Simpson walks over. "I'm surprised."

Simpson reaches out his hand, and Hunter gives him the landline. Why? Does this CIA guy have a magic touch? Or is he just the kind of man who doesn't trust anyone else to do anything right? Hunter is himself one of those men.

"Huh," Simpson says, depressing the plastic button himself, releasing, depressing. He examines his mobile too. "Nothing. You?"

Hunter already checked. He shakes his head.

"Sorry about that," Simpson says. "I was told—Well, you know what I was told. I bet you don't like hearing excuses. I'll try rebooting."

It's clear that Simpson knows this effort will be purely ceremonial.

Hunter stifles the urge to explode at this guy, who obviously does not understand the magnitude of the shittiness that's confronting Hunter.

You work your whole life for something. You study. You cram. You pull the late nights and early flights, you beg and connive, you plot and scheme, you lie and cheat and maybe even steal, you do *everything,* all to create a specific opportunity at a particular time—your moment. Only to discover that all the things you could control aren't nearly enough, too much is uncontrollable, beyond your influence. The world doesn't give a fuck about your plans. About you.

Okay, Hunter thinks, this is definitely bad on some level. But *bad* is a large, abstract thought. Let's break it down into specific practical considerations.

First, he doesn't need to worry about San Jose, where everyone is still asleep. The people in California won't be a concern for—Hunter checks his watch—another seven hours, maybe eight. And if this whole Paris situation isn't resolved in eight hours? Then the high-level staff in San Jose will be the least of his problems.

So what about Asia? It's the middle of the afternoon in Mumbai, and the business day is almost over in Hong Kong. Both are problems. The people who were awaiting Hunter's call are sitting at their desks, increasingly worried, maybe even panicked, they're calling one another: "Have you heard from Forsyth?," "No. You neither?," "What do you think is going on?" They know that a big announcement is coming, they know Hunter is supposed to be calling, and then *no one* hears from him? *No one* knows where he even *is*?

If it were just internal, that could be managed. His people aren't going to go blabbing; no one in any of his offices would respond to any inquiry by saying, "Sorry, Mr. Forsyth seems to have vanished off the face of the earth. Good luck finding him! If I were you, I'd certainly sell any 4Syte stock you're holding, asap."

But it's not just internal. There are favors owed. A discrete call here and there, using a burner phone with an untraceable number from a country he's never in his life visited, providing a quick update: the merger is on, no regulatory problems, banks committed, all clear. *Guaranteed.*

An hour's head start, or two. For some people, this will mean tens of millions in profit, even hundreds of millions. Not just by the early purchase of 4Syte's and their acquisition's stock, but also by shorting others, their competition's, those companies' suppliers. By making big complicated trades, taking heavy positions, accepting what looks like irresponsible risk in the hope of generating stupendous reward.

These are not the types of investments that these people—that any sane, rational people—would make without assurances. Not just the untrustworthy scripted assurances of blustering from a CEO at a carefully orchestrated press conference. But iron-clad assurances, made by a longtime associate, in a private call.

While speaking obliquely. Because, no, this is not, technically, legal.

But if none of these people hear from Hunter—if this day continues to erode minute by minute, the hours mounting, while he continues to not place call after call—then sooner or later, someone somewhere is going to get worried, and change his mind.

Maybe any minute now, some trader dude who was expecting the call after Hunter's call that doesn't arrive, this dude decides to sell instead of buy.

Maybe this has already happened.

Then someone further up the food chain notices. Does the same thing, in a bigger way.

Then some nerd at a financial news service will catch wind, then mention it to someone else, then the share price will fall infinitesimally, then a cable-news producer will post the activity to the chyron.

Then the share price will inch down further.

Then everyone will notice.

Then calls will be made, increasingly urgent and panicked.

Then it will become clear that no one in the world has seen or heard from CEO Hunter Forsyth all day.

Then the speculation will start, the rumors—drug overdose? kidnapped? hiding in the dark paralyzed with fear because his huge deal is falling apart?—will spread like wildfire.

Then the stock price will fall off a cliff, it'll turn into a fire sale, a bloodbath, and meanwhile Hunter won't even *know* it, because he'll be trapped here in this blackout.

Then when "beleaguered 4Syte CEO Hunter Forsyth"—that's what he'll be called—eventually reemerges, blinking in the daylight, his personal net worth will have reduced by tens of millions, the company billions in valuation, plus he'll have alienated some of the most powerful bankers in the world, he'll have burned his network, ended his friendships.

Then not only will he be broke, he'll also be a pariah. An abject failure.

Then he might as well be dead.

So if some violent death—by assassination, or bombing, or who-the-hell-knows—is what's waiting for him out there on the Paris streets, fuck it, at least he'll die dramatically, while he's still at the height of his success. He'll die famous.

He has worked himself up into a frenzy, sitting here on this musty sofa. He turns to Simpson, tries to wipe the panic from his face, but not the urgency. "Listen," he says, "I have to get to my office. I really do."

Simpson nods. "I can understand why you'd feel that way, Mr. Forsyth, but it's just not a good idea. I'm sure you recognize that."

"Well, good idea or bad"—Hunter stands—"that's what I need to do."

Simpson sighs. This seems to be one of his main methods of communicating. Hunter is really beginning to hate this guy. "I'm sorry, but I have to insist. It's too dangerous out there."

It takes a second for Hunter to understand what Simpson is saying. It's so improbable. "Excuse me?"

"I'm sorry, Mr. Forsyth." Another unapologetic apology. "I can't let you leave."

"Can't *let* me leave? What exactly do you mean?"

The guy doesn't elaborate.

"You're going to forcibly *detain* me here, Simpson?"

"You shouldn't think of it that way."

"By whose authority? In case you haven't noticed, we're in *France*. You don't have any authority here."

Simpson nods, as if in agreement.

"And what about Colette? She's not even American. You, an American—what? What are we calling you? An American diplomat? Or should we dispense with that charade, and say *CIA officer*? An American *spy* is going to detain a French citizen, in France?"

The guy doesn't rise to the bait, doesn't say anything at all.

"Come on, Colette. We're leaving."

Hunter walks past Simpson, brushing him on the shoulder, purposefully but lightly, like a teenage boy in a high-school hall, attempting to start a fight.

He takes only a couple of firm strides before he remembers—

Damn it: for one of the locks, Simpson used a key. From the inside.

"I'm sorry, Mr. Forsyth. It's for your own safety."

Hunter turns around.

"Your own good."

30

Wyatt fumbles in his pocket, locates the Métro ticket, jams it into the turnstile, whisks through with a thump. He collects his validated ticket, pushes through the doors, tries to remember which train in which direction.

He descends to the platform. Looks left, right. Walks to the map, confirms that he's waiting for the correct train, headed in the correct direction, and the stop where he'll get off.

The train arrives in a warm whoosh, packed, newspapers and backpacks and people staring at their phones, earbuds, headphones, everyone in their own private worlds. He wedges himself uncomfortably, arm raised to hold a pole. At the next stop, many people exit, many more board, then the train sits for a long delay. He wouldn't be surprised if the system gets shut down entirely. Wyatt has a contingency plan for that. For everything.

Just a couple more stops.

One more.

Only a few people disembark with him. He walks slowly, allowing the others to outpace him until he's the last on the platform, and the train has pulled out, and the arrivals board refreshes itself: the next train is due in three minutes, the following one in seven.

Three minutes is plenty of time.

He climbs the stairs, turns into an exit-only passage that will remain empty for those three minutes. He checks the photo booth—it's always possible there's a tourist, or a pair of teenagers necking. There isn't.

He drops the bag with a thud, unzips it quickly. He removes a folded-up piece of green nylon, fluffs it open: another duffel bag. He takes off his sport jacket, puts it in this new duffel. Unbuttons his blue shirt, shoves that in too; now he's wearing a white tee. Tosses in the eyeglasses, good riddance. Switches out the brogues for running shoes. He can't help but notice the bloodstains in the treads of the leather shoes.

Almost finished, still more than a minute to spare.

He pulls on a black cap, the bill low over his brow. Places the blue canvas bag into the green nylon one, closes the bigger bag.

Now he's a completely different person, carrying a completely different bag.

He slings the duffel over his shoulder and walks around the corner, where a surveillance camera is mounted from the ceiling. This camera is supposedly disabled, but better safe than sorry: he keeps his head down, face hidden. He descends to the platform for the train heading in the other direction, back toward his origin.

There are more cameras down here, but he knows that if he waits at the front end of the platform, he's out of their range.

Wyatt has a theory about why he came all the way to Odéon just to change his clothes and switch bags, but he doubts it'll ever be confirmed. "You're not going to be told much," the bearded American had told him. "Thus the large bonus. You all right with that?"

"Honestly? I prefer it that way."

⚜

He switches trains at a busy hub, navigates the throngs shuffling through the *correspondance* tunnels, the platforms where everyone listens to the service announcements, moaning and groaning, sending texts and making calls, *Sorry, running late, please don't wait . . .*

He lunges onto the new train, just one more anxious body in a heaving mass of frustrated commuters. A fresh force boards at the following stop, each station more crowded than the last, with different routes converging, all these lines forced to take up the overflow from the suspended line that runs under the rue de Rivoli. The number 1 is closed temporarily, due to a security issue.

Security issue. That is one drastic understatement.

Wyatt checks his watch. This is taking longer than anticipated. But this part of the schedule has built-in padding. It's okay.

After a mass exodus at Opéra, the crowd remains relatively sparse for a couple of stops, then gathers again at Strasbourg–St-Denis, where the subway meets the commuter rail. Then even thicker at the multi-line convergence at République, sardines now, everyone too uncomfortable, too delayed, too scared. It's a buzzing mass of negativity here in this steel cylinder lurching through a burrowed-out tunnel underneath a panic-stricken metropolis.

Wyatt is relieved that there are all these other passengers, the sweaty press around him, the jostling elbows, the inconsiderate backpacks, the roll-aboard bags clogging the aisles, everyone in everyone else's way, short-tempered and impatient and unobservant, lost in their own inconveniences, their own multiplying problems. It's too crowded for anyone to see much, to notice any bags that might be resting down on the floor, or under seats.

As the train slows into the next station, Wyatt nudges the bag under the seat at his feet. He gives it a toe-shove, wedging it far under. He darts his eyes around, but no one seems to have noticed.

The train stops.

"*Pardonnez-moi,*" he says, making his way, "*Pardonnez-moi*" again, a chant on this pilgrimage to the exit, as much to keep himself calm as to be unnoticeable. No one notices normal courtesies. What's noticeable is rudeness.

He mumbles a final "*Pardonnez-moi*" and then he's through the doors, onto the platform, and he forces himself not to glance back to see if anyone has noticed his abandoned bag, calling after him, "*Monsieur, votre—*"

No one would do that. No one would imagine that the green bag was his, no one would have even noticed the thing, not yet, not with so many people surrounding the duffel, so many potential owners. The orphaned luggage won't be remarked upon for at least a half-dozen stops, after the crowd thins as the train heads toward Créteil, it'll be way past city limits before someone in uniform finally takes possession of it, opens the zipper . . .

What will he find? A change of clothes, unremarkable. What will be suspicious is the phone, with a handful of numbers programmed into the contacts. One number is named Gare. Another Vendôme and another Triomphe and another Louvre. Also a contact for PDG—*président-directeur général,* what the French call a CEO. This number is the only one that has ever been called. Every day, in fact. Just a few seconds per call, each made using a special app that disguised the phone number.

How long before investigators compare this bag's contents to the surveillance footage of Wyatt at the bomb sites? Tomorrow? Next week? At that point, they will conclude that the bag was lost, something went wrong, that's why the negotiations never commenced. Criminals are stupid; that's why they're criminals. That will be the moral of the story.

If they ever start to search for the man in the footage, Wyatt will be long gone, back in Louisiana, straightening out McKayla's past-due bills, looking like a completely different person. No one could connect this American military veteran to these surveillance images, this body of evidence, this terrorist plot. If it's an American, it's not terrorism.

31

The convoy rumbles by.

How did the army respond so quickly? Did French intelligence have advance warning of the attacks? Were they already on heightened alert? Battalions pre-deployed in the city?

Or is it possible that the bomb threats are something completely different. A false-flag operation? An excuse to impose martial law, to suspend civil rights, to purge the government, to expel the immigrants, to round up the usual suspects?

When the tanks have passed, Kate cuts across the boulevard. She turns onto a quiet street, then again onto an even quieter one, narrow, tidy.

She deposits her bike at a docking station, looks around, walks away. No one in sight. Kate doubles back to the corner, crosses the street in the other direction.

Still no one.

The entrance to the private street is barred with two gates, one for pedestrians, the other just wide enough for a single car lane, drop-offs and pickups only, no parking allowed, no way for anyone to lurk in a parked car, watching her. No way for anyone to lurk, period.

The lock's code is a number that Kate knows only in French. She memorized the string of digits in French, she tells it to people in French, it's a sequence that's lodged in her brain in this second language of hers, an expanding vocabulary of ideas that she expresses primarily in French, like the backup player who comes off the bench and, sometimes, is stronger. When Kate meets new people, even in English, she says *"Enchantée"* with a straight face. Enchanted to meet you.

There are a few private residences on the short street, but mostly it's professional—a psychoanalyst, a law office, *cabinet de dentiste*. It's both busy and quiet.

Finding this office space had been Kate's first task for the Paris Substation. Someplace where freelancers and sources could come and go without attracting too much attention, somewhere private yet accessible, and convenient for Kate to meet the people she'd need to meet—a quick drink in a café, a blind pass in a park, a discreet encounter in a boutique.

At that point she'd been living in Paris for more than a year, she thought she knew the city well. But looking around for the perfect spot, Kate discovered that she really knew only the same Paris that Dexter knew, the other expats too, a few finite sections of the central *arrondissements* and a couple of select suburbs. She wasn't familiar with the greater city of working-class quarters and commercial ones and the residential *faubourgs* far from her own. She also couldn't have told you the location of the Greek Embassy. Now she can.

Downstairs in the small building, the *rez-de-chaussée* is occupied by an OB-GYN, pregnant women constantly coming and going. Kate is not concerned with pregnant women.

Upstairs, the Paris Substation occupies a couple of rooms, a few desks, computer monitors, a landline that no one uses. Installing all the electronics was not simple, making sure everything was secure and would stay that way.

Thierry, already at his desk, looks up when the boss enters. Kate raises her eyebrows, asking: do you know what the hell is going on? He shakes his head in reply, then turns back to his screen.

More than a dozen items are strewn atop Kate's desk, which at first glance—or second or third—doesn't look particularly neat, keyboard and mouse, in-box and stapler, pencil cup and notepad and tape dispenser, all the normal things you find on a worktop. They're not equidistant from one another, they're not aligned in a grid, they're not arranged in any noticeable fashion.

Except they are.

Moving from the front of the desk to the rear, each item is one centimeter farther away than the distance between the two previous items, as measured at their shortest gaps. Always. Every time Kate takes this seat, the first thing she does is check all the distances, using a tape measure in her top drawer. No one has touched anything, not today, not ever.

Now she can start looking for answers.

Her first call is to a man listed in her app under a different name, with a different address, as the proprietor of a catering outfit. "I cannot talk to you now," he says. No *bonjour*, no nothing. "You know that."

She's not surprised.

Another call, to a supposed hairdresser: this one doesn't even pick up.

Another, another, another, almost no one picks up, and Kate doesn't leave messages. Everyone has caller ID, so it's clear that her sources don't want to talk to Kate now, not on the telephone, not so she can ask questions. On a day like today, the only thing anyone wants from Kate are answers. She has none.

The only people who answer are those who don't know anything; "I don't think" and "I don't know" are how their sentences begin; "Sorry" is how they end.

She's getting nowhere, accomplishing nothing except proving to herself that she's exhausting every possible resource before escalating to the next level. Sometimes that's what you need to do.

Public transportation is going to be unreliable, cars won't be productive, bicycles may not be fast enough. Today is one of those circumstances for which Kate saves the moped, which she now takes down the Chaillot hill, toward the river, where the luxury is a bit louder, the conspicuous-consumption flagships and five-star everything, a neighborhood catering to people who want—who demand—something special, if just anyone can have it they don't want it, their cultural currency is unique experiences. Even though the hotels here, the restaurants, are mostly the generic variety of five-star posh that could be anywhere, menus indistinguishable, linens, obsequious staff, and everyone speaks English, it's all the same, could be Mayfair, could be Madison Avenue.

The old mansion is an imposing pile of blinding white limestone on a quiet side street that's off the path beaten by most tourists. The business plan never anticipated much in the way of walk-in customers, casual browsers, people wandering in to buy group tickets to Versailles. Well-heeled globetrotters come here on purpose, looking for something specific, something special.

One side of the street level is dominated by a plate-glass window,

TRAVELERS INTERNATIONAL BOOKING SERVICE in black lettering with gold outline. Kate puts her hand on the doorknob, turns, pulls. The glass rattles, but the door doesn't budge. She turns the knob the other way. Pushes. Still nothing.

Through the window, Kate meets the eye of the woman sitting at the first of three desks, who reaches down, *buzz,* the door unlocks.

"Bonjour Madame Anderson."

Kate catches a sound bite of news before the young woman mutes her computer's speakers, then turns to Kate wearing a professional smile and a nametag that reads MANON. This office has already been open for a half-hour, but on a day like today Manon probably wasn't expecting any customers yet.

Manon taps on her keyboard, squints at her screen. "I do not believe we have anything for you?" She uses a key to unlock a drawer filled with boarding passes, travel dossiers, long itineraries with contact numbers and addresses and instructions, opera tickets, backstage passes, SIM cards, the occasional passport stamped with foreign visas. And for special clients like Mme. Anderson, the agency is willing to provide extra services that cost the office practically nothing while generating ample goodwill. Like accepting international courier packages, envelopes of various shapes and sizes that are delivered by mail, by messenger, sometimes by the inscrutable woman who works upstairs.

"I want to arrange a new trip," Kate says.

"Très bien Madame. To where, please?"

"Beirut."

The smile remains on the woman's face, but she doesn't say anything. Beirut has not been a popular tourist destination recently. Plus this travel agency is owned by a New York magazine conglomerate, and its mostly American clientele doesn't tend to book trips to Beirut from Paris.

"Do you have a colleague who is familiar with Beirut?"

Manon's smile sags, but doesn't disappear entirely. *"Oui."* She's wearing a headset connected to a keypad, which she jabs using the eraser end of a pencil, protecting her perfectly manicured nails. She rotates in her chair, spinning away so the customer can't hear this in-house interaction, low voice, an economy of words.

"C'est bon," Manon says, rearranging her smile. Everything is very good. *"Un moment."*

⚜

"Madame?" It's another woman standing back there, young and dark-haired and attractive, though not as put-together as Manon, not as blown-out and made-up, not as consumer-facing. This more serious-looking woman assesses Kate from across the room, and Kate in turn sizes her up.

"S'il vous plaît," this woman says, indicating the open door.

They don't shake hands or introduce themselves. It would be impossible for anyone to tell whether or not these two women have met before. Kate steps into a small office, its walls lined with international travel posters—*Afrique, Suède, Brésil, Italie.* No windows. A modern, functional desk.

"How can I help you, Madame Anderson?"

"I would like to arrange a trip to Beirut," Kate repeats. She can smell the woman's cigarettes coming off her hair, her clothes.

"How many people?"

They are still standing, awkwardly, next to the desk. Kate wonders if she's going to be offered a seat. "There are five of us," Kate says. "Myself, my husband, three children." This fabrication—she has only two children—is one part of the code.

"And do you have a preferred hotel?"

"I do. The Kempinski."

And this is the other. The codes are for the benefit of other people who might be in this quasi-public space; you never know. There are no other customers in this room, but the codes are the protocol, and the protocol is sacrosanct.

"Très bien."

This woman opens a deadbolt at another door at the far end of the office, and Kate follows her out of the grim little space into a grand one, the mansion's polished lobby of marble floors, ornate moldings, soaring ceiling, crystal chandelier. Up a sweeping staircase to the *premier étage,* a wide hall lined with glossy black doors. She unlocks the first of these doors using a key card.

This room is extremely large and cluttered, a few desks strewn around, filing cabinets everywhere, screens and keyboards and a dusty typewriter wedged into a corner, maps and posters and corkboards and even a couple of oil paintings, all hung with no apparent plan. It looks like a small-town newsroom run by an eccentric, thirty years ago. Kate had imagined something else, something twenty-first-century, high-tech.

The woman shuts the door behind her, says, *"Je m'appelle Inez."*

"Kate." They shake hands.

It's not just the room that's defying expectations, it's this person too. Is this young Frenchwoman really running the Paris bureau of an American clandestine service? Kate had envisaged a middle-aged man from the East Coast. Then again, Kate too is someone who runs the Paris bureau of an American clandestine service.

Inez turns back to the door, reaches up to the locks. As a matter of habit, Kate glances at the woman's ring finger, and notices that she isn't wearing a wedding band. What Inez is wearing is a shoulder holster, and it isn't empty.

"Please, Kate, take yourself a seat."

A wall-mounted television displays an anchorman sitting at a desk, a crawl that proclaims TERRORISME À PARIS, a screen that's split with video from a helicopter at a great distance, an overhead image of the Louvre that communicates practically nothing, not unless there's a large explosion, which is probably the point of this angle: to record the explosion.

"Okay," Kate says, taking a narrow wooden chair. Inez's own chair is a large curvy plastic-mesh affair that suggests ergonomics, lumbar support, chiropractors, science. "What can you tell me about all this today?"

Inez nods curtly, down to business. "At 8:41, the police received the following telephone call from a mobile." She taps on her keyboard, clicks an icon and then another and another.

A digitally scrambled voice speaks in a monotone: *"A remote-detonated bomb has been placed in the main hall of the Gare de Lyon. If you attempt to disable the bomb, we will detonate. Await further instructions."* The recording ends. "And again, from twenty-four minutes later." Inez cues up the second track: *"A bomb has been placed at the Arc de Triomphe. Await further instructions.* Another on the subject of place Vendôme, and finally Notre-Dame."

"Are there actually bombs at these locations?"

"There are bags confirmed at the locations that could contain explosive devices."

"Or?"

"Or the bags might not contain explosive devices."

"Why would anyone do that?"

"I am not suggesting that anyone has done that. I am saying that it is not yet confirmed that these bags are . . . *comment dit-on?*—weaponized."

This is a very precise woman.

"*Ensuite,* as you know"—Inez indicates the TV—"a man arrived to the Louvre wearing a suicide vest, also carrying what has the appearance of a bomb in a briefcase."

Inez clicks around some more, opens a video feed from a camera that's positioned high above the Louvre, aiming down at the man who's standing between the pyramids. The scene appears unchanged since Kate was there an hour ago.

"This is a livestream?"

"*Oui.* The camera is from the police on the roof of the Louvre. The police are in command of the scene, but I do not doubt that at this moment self-important men are making arguments on the subject of who should make the decisions. *Comme toujours.*"

"No group has claimed responsibility? No demands?"

"Not that I know."

Kate stares at the monitor. She isn't surprised that Inez managed to intercept the phone recordings, which had probably been forwarded to hundreds of people, sprayed out to law enforcement and national intelligence, the mayor and his deputies, local politicians and national ones, foreign embassies, even the CIA. A very wide and hasty distribution, with potential leaks aplenty. No way to keep it all secure.

But this real-time video is not being e-mailed to anyone. This feed represents an impressive level of intrusion into the police's security.

Kate has no idea what size facility is here in this mansion, what resources, what personnel. This office doesn't look like much, but it's a big building, and Kate has seen only a small portion of it. There's more.

"How did you obtain this access?"

"*C'est pas important.*"

Of course it's important. But Kate is a guest here, doesn't have the right to make demands. In this business, everyone deserves to keep their own secrets, and everyone else knows it.

These two strangers have been thrust into a position where they're supposed to trust each other, in the same way that civilians are supposed to trust their bankers, their lawyers. But in Kate's world the blind trust is not with some of your money, or elective surgery, but like trusting someone to catch you when you've made the deliberate choice to fall backward, without a net, off a cliff.

✦

Hayden had let her dangle there in that Copenhagen apartment, grinning while Kate's curiosity mounted.

"*Tell me,*" she pled.

"You're going to *adore* this, Kate."

"Oh for the love of—"

"The Travelers section is, in addition to being a courier service, also a complete parallel intelligence service. With officers, agents, assets, the whole shebang. This cadre occupies a thoroughly separate reporting structure, like us. But unlike us, their bureau chiefs report directly to someone in New York."

"New York? That's nuts. What's in New York?"

"The editor of the magazine. He in turn reports directly to the DCI."

"The director himself? God. And did you say bureau *chiefs,* plural? There's more than one of these bureaus?"

"There are dozens."

Kate was having trouble grasping this. "How long has this been going on?"

"The program began right after World War II, as solely the courier service. It evolved."

"That's incredible. But how is this related to us?"

"It's not, other than our unusual level of independence from Langley. But we both operate out of Paris, so we've agreed to pool resources, in a pinch. If you ever find yourself in one, go there. Say you want to arrange a trip to Beirut . . ."

That's when Hayden explained how to make contact with the head of the Travelers' Paris Bureau. But then he got pulled away by an urgent call, and the next time Kate saw him was when the action was beginning across the street in the hacker's apartment, which spiraled out of control—a shootout followed by a frantic chase, a failed mission and dead bodies. Nørrebro turned out to be the last place Kate ever saw Hayden. He never did get around to telling her who it was back in America who provided Kate with her targets.

In the weeks and months that followed Hayden's disappearance, Kate began to suspect that he'd known exactly what was going to happen across the street, and then across the ocean. She kept remembering a piece of his advice, something he'd taught her when she was new and still figuring out how to make her way in the Agency, how to make things happen in the world: a carefully orchestrated disaster can be the perfect diversion.

3²

She's staring out at the sun-drenched *campo*, trying to appreciate the beautiful surroundings instead of the horrific noise. She's failing.

The boy's midday nap was supposed to begin a half-hour ago, but Matteo is refusing vociferously, going red in the face, then purple. If she didn't know better, she'd think that the baby was suffocating. But she does know better. That's apparently what motherhood is: learning to know better.

The kid doesn't want to eat. He doesn't need a new diaper, doesn't want to be held or rocked. He doesn't want anything that she can provide, and her attempts at soothing him serve only to antagonize.

The decibel level is brutal. Like an enhanced interrogation technique, something outlawed by the Geneva Conventions.

At least she doesn't have to worry about bothering the neighbors. The apartment's walls are thick plaster, the under-flooring solid beneath the elaborate parquet, everything efficiently soundproofed as a side effect of old-fashioned workmanship, a building that dates back at least six hundred years, maybe seven, it's hard to be exact for some of these structures, which have undergone so many transformations over the centuries, transfers of ownership, major renovations, lost records.

You wouldn't think that such a tiny animal could make such a racket.

How many babies have cried in this room? Renaissance babies, Baroque babies, Fascist babies. Thirty generations? Forty? Hundreds of babies have wailed here in this well-constructed room, each and every one of them driving their mothers up a tree.

One of the things she has learned about the child-screaming sound is that it erodes rationality, compromises your ability to make lucid, purposeful choices. An evolutionary mechanism that prevents mothers from ignoring distressed offspring. Like the babies' cuteness, from the other direction. Cuteness is the carrot. This screaming, this is the fucking stick.

The kid screams yet louder, if that's possible.

⚜

She bundles him up into a little pastel packet, a sweater that's beginning to strain at the seams, a matching cap. She binds her own long hair into a ponytail, puts on the oversize sunglasses that she wears for walks regardless of the weather, whenever she's going out in public for a while, visible in the narrow pedestrian lanes of Venice where everyone looks everyone else in the face, at close range. It's easy to be recognized here, if you're recognizable, and if you don't take precautions. If someone is looking for you.

As soon as she moved to Italy, she dyed her hair, her eyebrows too. She can't help but think she looks Italian now, from somewhere in the south. It makes her wonder if her Polish ancestry is more mixed than she'd been led to believe; almost everyone's is. And even after all this time, she's still not accustomed to this raven-haired look, still wonders *Who the hell is that woman?* when she catches sight of herself in a mirror. Not just the hair length and color, but also the big glasses, the absence of makeup, the loose flowing clothing. It would take a vigilant, focused eye for anyone to see under all that, to recognize her as the woman she used to be.

The truth is that she no longer is that same woman, and not just in appearance. The baby changed so much, especially after all she'd been through to carry to term. The husband too, he'd necessitated a lot of changes in her, after so many years without one. And the end of her career, the dissolution of her identity as a respected professional. The setbacks she'd faced—the immense failure, the public disgrace, the hasty relocations, the itinerant lifestyle. Every single aspect of her life.

But in some important respects, she's still exactly the same. Her fingerprints, for example. Her dental records, the bright white mouthful expensively aligned by aggressive American orthodontia. Her ambition, and willingness to bend rules and laws to serve it.

She double-checks that her primary phone has held its charge; now would be a terrible time to be unavailable. She jacks in the headphones, puts a little speaker into one ear, leaves the other free to hear the sounds of the world around her. Pats down her pockets for keys, wallet, the extra pacifier she always carries, diaper, wipes.

She straps the baby into the Swedish baby-carrying contraption, clips clicking, tugging taut.

Finally she pulls open the drawer of the small table next to the front door. She removes the tourism guidebook and the Italian-English dictionary, sets these heavy tomes atop the table, next to the bowl of coins, *vaporetti* tickets, a notepad whose top sheet is usually a shopping list.

With the drawer empty, she runs her fingertip along a seam where the bottom panel meets the side, until she finds the narrow gap, just wide enough for a fingernail.

Retrofitting this drawer was one of the first projects her husband tackled immediately after they moved into this apartment, fresh from their cleansing exile in the Wild West of southern Sicily, where she'd given birth to this baby boy. It was a carpentry job that took him a couple of days—sketching and shopping, sawing and sanding, gluing and clamping.

They have been extremely careful. Every piece of furniture in this apartment came with the lease; the bed linens, the bath towels, the kitchenware, everything. They paid cash for the small additional items they've needed; they established telecom and utility accounts using airtight aliases. They use a rotating assortment of burner phones, replacing them on a regular basis. It's fun, destroying phones. She uses a ball-peen hammer.

Rural Sicily was much more third-world than first, agrarian and analog, sparsely populated and mostly poor and corruptly governed, a place where official favors can be bought from bank clerks, from state ministries, from hospital administrators, favors that can be used to construct new identities with all necessary documentation.

Sicilians had become somewhat inured to illegal migrants, to undocumented people arriving by the literal boatload. But those were North Africans and Middle Easterns, desperate people escaping war-torn hellscapes, risking their lives on treacherous crossings in watercraft of questionable seaworthiness, with unknown prospects on the far shore. It was almost a relief for the Sicilians to be accepting substantial bribes from prosperous-looking Americans, even if these Americans were clearly up to no good. At least there weren't any humanitarian dilemmas to consider, war crimes, genocides.

She'd been gone from America for a half-decade now, except for that scant single year back in Washington when she discovered that while she'd followed her career out of the country, all her unmarried friends back home seemed to have stumbled into long-term relationships, and all her married friends had spawned children. Her college classmates, her work colleagues, her neighbors, everyone procreating all at once. A contagion.

Here in Italy, she gave her own baby an Italian name, a name that might make it less obvious that the adults were a pair of Americans, that might make people wonder if she was of Italian heritage, speculate on some excuse for Americans to be living here, a story they could tell other than the truth.

The drawer's bottom panel pivots upward from a rear hinge. A few items are arranged in the false-bottom recess, each occupying its own carefully proportioned niche, the whole arrangement constructed from balsa strips and crushed velvet to prevent the contents from sliding around and creating noises that might make someone wonder what the hell is in this piece of occasional furniture, and where exactly, and why.

She collects one of the items from its housing, slips it into the big pocket in her jacket, right there with the more usual things that a mom carries.

She pulls the door closed behind her, double-checks that the lock engaged. With this kid screaming in her ear, it's impossible to hear things like the clicking of locks. She squats to pick up a strand of her hair that's resting on the door's saddle. Licks the tips of her forefinger and thumb, and runs these moistened fingertips down the length of hair, which she saliva-sticks against the door and jamb, positioned at exactly the same level as the widest of five separate nicks in the wood.

Every time she leaves the apartment, she uses this discrete privacy seal. Sometimes it's hard to imagine that anyone would still be looking for her, but that's the sort of resigned, exhausted complacency that can lead to disaster.

She walks down the well-worn stone staircase carefully; she doesn't want to tumble herself and her baby headlong into the emergency room. Through the dark damp lobby, where the kid's crying sounds extra-shrill, bouncing off the tall ceilings and stone walls and floors. She pushes open the gigantic slab of door, and bursts into the bright sunlight of the *campo*.

If they ever move back to the United States—an unlikely eventuality—they'd have the option of shortening the kid's name to Matt without the transformation seeming absurd to him, without it being something they'd need to explain with a series of unsustainable lies. Or he could simply remain Matteo, which at that point might be just as common in America.

She still holds out hope that they'll eventually live some version of a normal life, settled in one place, using one set of names consistently, telling mostly the truth to most people, most of the time. But she knows it's a slim hope. Very slim.

33

"*Alors.*" Inez is staring intently at her screen. "Something in Hong Kong. A man was detained attempting to bring a bomb into an office."

"What type of man?"

"What is it you are asking?"

"Does he seem Muslim?"

While Inez turns back to the screen, Kate glances around the cluttered office, paper everywhere. In Kate's office, there's practically none.

"It seems he is American."

"Are you sure?"

Inez gives her a look, *What do you want from me?*

"Anywhere else, besides Hong Kong?"

Inez clicks open a new window, scans line after line of incident reports—street-crime gunfire, a prison break in Kenya, a bank heist in Saigon. It's still too early in the Americas for any law-enforcement alerts, although a hurricane is forming in the Gulf of Mexico. This time of year, a hurricane is almost always forming in the Gulf of Mexico. The opposite of news.

The Frenchwoman leans forward. "*Voilà*: Mumbai, a bomb threat is made to a building."

Another bomb in another office building? "Directed against any specific occupant?"

Click, and click again. "*Non,* it does not appear so."

"You have the Mumbai address?"

"*Oui.*"

"Of the building in Hong Kong also?"

Inez toggles to another window—"*Voilà*"—understanding what to do next, typing both addresses into a search, and it doesn't take even a second for the results page to load, and there at the top, the very first commonality—

✦

Kate feels the air sucked out of her through the hole in her soul that had been blasted open in Luxembourg, decimating the fortifications of truth and honesty and trust that we all rely upon to make it through the day. She'd thought that the hole had been repaired, but maybe it had been shoddy workmanship, bound to fall apart sooner or later.

"This has importance for you?"

Kate nods.

"It is an American company, *n'est-ce pas*?"

"Yes. Listen, would you mind?" She indicates the keyboard, the screen. Inez nods, stands, and the two switch places. Kate's fingers clatter across the keyboard. A new page loads, displaying two hits, one address in La Défense, another in the *huitième,* with map windows. One of the red stars is a kilometer away.

Kate can't wrap her mind around what exactly this means. But it's definitely not nothing.

"Are any of your phone lines clean?" A plan is forming, a way to find answers.

"*Évidemment,*" Inez says. "All of them."

Kate dials the main number of the company, and the line is answered before the first ring is complete. "*Bonjour,* thank you for calling 4Syte Paris, how may I direct your call?"

"I'm trying to reach the public-relations department."

"Hold one minute, please." But Kate has to wait only seconds before someone new comes on the line. "*Bonjour!* This is Schuyler Franks in community engagement?"

Kate's fingers fly, typing in *Schuyler Franks* and *4Syte* and *Paris,* and the young woman's photo pops up, her contact info, hits for a LinkedIn profile, Facebook, a college young-alumni association and a volleyball team and a high-school graduating class, an article in a local newspaper about where the graduates will attend college. There's so much information about everyone, so available, requiring so little effort.

"Hi Schuyler. I'm looking for Hunter Forsyth."

"I'm sorry, Mr. Forsyth isn't available? What's this regarding?"

"Is he in the office?"

"I'm sorry, may I ask who's calling?"

"Is Hunter Forsyth on your premises at this moment?"

"I'm sorry, ma'am, but that information isn't something I can just, y'know, *give out* to anyone? But if you help me understand why you're asking? That would be *super*-helpful?"

So: the staff are still in their offices, not evacuated; these women both sound calm, business as normal. Which means the Paris office is not under attack, no violent threat has been made against 4Syte's European headquarters. At least not yet. Or not in the same way.

Hayden had been right: after a few weeks, Kate was summoned to a meet. For the only time since the Paris Substation was established.

She spotted her contact right away, limping his way through the park, sidestepping the children darting about, smiling indulgently at the little ones flinging sand, their mothers gossiping on benches. This man was clearly a father himself, accustomed to the constant disarray, always prepared for crisis.

The place des Vosges was a well-chosen venue, large enough to be anonymous but small enough that from the right vantage you can see nearly everyone scattered around the park's well-groomed foliage, the square-cut trees, the conical shrubs.

The man collapsed onto one of those uncomfortable-looking high-backed wooden benches near a fountain. He didn't seem old enough to be so exhausted, so tottering. Injury, Kate guessed, maybe he'd blown out his knee in the weekly pickup game with guys from law school. He looked like he could've been from New York, as Hayden suspected. But then again he could've been from Washington, or Langley, or Moscow via an intensive English-language immersion program in New Hampshire. He could've been from anywhere. If someone makes a concerted, professional effort, it's impossible to tell.

Clusters of teenagers were nearby, sitting cross-legged, smoking cigarettes. A grade-school girl was doing a tumbling routine on one patch of grass, while on another a couple of boys were kicking a ball. Neither field was quite big enough for its activity, but the kids were making do. City kids, city life.

The American man unfolded a newspaper, crossed his legs gingerly. He lit a cigarette. After just a single drag, he tossed the butt, ground it out on the dirt path littered with leaves, with twigs, but with surprisingly few cigarette butts.

Despite appearances, those high-backed benches are surprisingly comfortable. Kate rose from hers, and made her approach.

"Bonjour?" Dexter answers tentatively. He doesn't recognize the number; Kate has placed this call on a Travelers' secure line.

"Hi Dex."

"Hello my wife. This is a lot of phone calls for us, isn't it?"

"Listen: where'd you get your information about 4Syte?"

"My information?"

"You know what I'm asking."

He pauses, then admits: "Luc."

"And where'd he get it?"

"We shouldn't be talking about this on the phone, should we?"

"Why not?"

He doesn't answer, which is all the answer she needs. Then he says, "An investor named Reinhard Jeckelmann. I think you met him, at Luc's party?"

A louche affair with an ill-conceived guest list, an embarrassing imbalance of single women, free radicals floating around the party, gravitating toward the men, many of them married. Kate remembers Jeckelmann as a disagreeable German, angular eyeglasses and poor manners, a general brusqueness.

"And where did Jeckelmann get *his* info?"

"Someone inside 4Syte, but I don't know who exactly. Jeckelmann didn't tell Luc, or Luc didn't tell me, and I didn't feel like I could press him. Or should."

"Why'd this person come forward to Jeckelmann with this leak?"

"They knew each other somehow. Earlier in life."

"But you don't know how?"

"That's not something anyone would share. To protect everyone else."

That makes sense. But that doesn't make it true. "And you just accepted this?"

"No, I didn't just accept this. I did exhaustive due diligence. I made dozens of calls, full days of research."

She sighs loudly enough for him to hear, on purpose.

"This information is not slam-dunk true, Kate, but I've executed far more speculative trades based on far less convincing intel, successfully. Profitably."

Profitability is no longer Kate's primary concern. But she doesn't want to share her suspicions with Dexter, at least not yet. She doesn't want him to flip out. "Has anyone ever given you info like this before?"

"Sure. Some people have shared tips with me. And vice versa."

"Anything illegal, Dex?"

A second of silence, two. "It's not always black-and-white."

Kate had been in command of the Paris Substation, temporarily, until Hayden returned; but he never did. So Kate was in command until a replacement was found; but a replacement was never found. So this man had come to Paris to tell Kate that she was now in command, full stop.

"This substation is yours," he said. "Are you ready for it?"

"I am," Kate answered quickly, trying to manufacture self-confidence by projecting it. She had no idea if she was really ready. But she definitely wanted it.

"I guess we'll find out," he said, pushing himself up with a wince and a low groan.

When she was young, Kate imagined that these moves happened by careful design, with exhaustive interviews and committee meetings and long training periods. But she'd come to understand that life doesn't work that way. So much is haphazard, one short-term problem solved after another, with scarcely a sideways glance at any big picture.

That's how someone like her can be thrust from a part-time position to full-time, from freelancer to manager of a secret substation that's subject to no chain of command, no oversight. Which unfortunately also meant no access to Agency resources, assets, networks, files, personnel.

Nothing except a tenuous connection to this other clandestine bureau, managed by a Frenchwoman, hiding above a high-end travel bureau.

This isn't the way anyone would deliberately design anything, but here it was, here Kate was, suddenly abuzz, more excited than she would've expected. She'd come to the place des Vosges fully prepared to be fired, she was already considering options on how to console herself. But instead she was leaving with a giant promotion bestowed by this man from New York, who despite the creaky limbs was sexy, and the thought of him flickered in her brain, a fleeting fantasy, or maybe it wasn't exactly her brain that generated this idea that propelled her homeward as fast as possible, pedaling across the Île St-Louis and then along the actual bank of the Left Bank, ditching the bike, rushing upstairs.

"Hey?" Dexter said, turning away from his computer, surprised to see his wife in the middle of the afternoon. "What are you doing here?"

"Let's make this quick." Kate unfurled her panties, dropped them to the floor. She was planning to keep everything else on, even her boots. Especially her boots. "I need to get back to work."

She stands at the mirror in the Travelers' small bathroom. She unzips an interior pocket of her handbag, removes a nylon packet. She extracts a couple of hairpins, and secures her hair tightly to her scalp. Then she pulls out a blond wig, a messy mop of coif, a distraction of a hairstyle. She tugs here, pushes there, good enough. She adds a set of thick-framed eyeglasses.

"Okay," she says to Inez. "Let's go. I'll explain on the way."

34

"... and stocks are down *across* the board due to *massive* uncertainty regarding the ongoing terror attack in Paris, which is about to enter the *third* hour of a standoff between an apparent *suicide* bomber at the Louvre and the authorities."

Dexter looks out the dormer window, past the shutters that hang on hinges topped with finials that are little cast-bronze statuettes of men, tiny servants whose job it is to preside over hinges.

"We also have *unconfirmed* reports—and let me stress, these reports have been neither confirmed *nor* denied by *any* officials—of *other* threats against high-visibility targets in Paris, beyond the Louvre and the Gare de Lyon. And we *just* learned, only moments ago, that there might be a threat in *Mumbai,* and that's where we go now, to our ..."

Dexter listens to the Indian reporter for only a minute before he understands that she doesn't know anything. This is the sort of report that didn't exist until the advent of twenty-four-hour so-called news stations that need to fill every moment of every day with something, preferably alarming, to prevent viewers from changing the channel.

He lowers the volume of this report in one of the windows on his large screen, the one he uses to monitor the international broadcast-news stations to which he pays varying degrees of attention, plus the home-pages of a few media outlets that continue to be known as newspapers, despite the increasing irrelevancy of the actual paper.

Otherwise, Dexter's vision is filled with numbers, almost entirely red. Over the past hour, the share price of nearly everything to do with Europe has dropped, at least incrementally, and some of it dramatically. It's not a general panic, but it's getting close. And if the Louvre situation doesn't get resolved soon, who the hell knows.

This is both good and bad. Dexter obviously wants one particular stock to tank, but he's extremely motivated for some others to turn it around. Just thinking about it makes his chest tighten. He stands, stretches, takes a few purposeful breaths . . .

That's not enough; he needs a real break.

Some days Dexter doesn't even emerge from the apartment for lunch. He keeps the refrigerator stocked with yogurt, little glass jars of different combinations of fruits and spices and sweeteners. The nearby *supérette*'s largest section is yogurt, everyone in Paris seems to eat it with every meal. Yogurt or Nutella, sometimes both.

Something is tugging vaguely at his consciousness, pulling his concentration into some murky corner where he can't recognize what it is that his mind's eye is trying to look at.

Is it something he just learned, or should have? Or . . . ?

Dexter showers, dresses himself like a grown-up Frenchman. He's still a nerd, and will be forevermore, but he can no longer be identified as one as quickly, from as far away. Dexter is of that generation who embraced nerdiness as a badge of so-called authenticity, contriving to be uncool by exaggerating their awkwardness, shuffling their feet and slouching their shoulders and stammering, wearing shirts that didn't fit in colors that didn't flatter, a uniform of antifashion.

Then he turned forty-five, and realized he looked like an idiot. He stopped wearing sneakers except for exercise. Started wearing jackets—actually, *jacket* in the singular, the same navy canvas every day. Button-down shirts in a finite assortment of light blue or white, no more T-shirts. He has forsaken the geeky rimless Bill Gates look for tortoiseshell eyeglasses, and every six weeks he endures a proper haircut from a stylist, a concession to his wife, who had grown tired of looking at his walk-in-barbershop hatchet jobs.

He has even begun to clasp his hands behind his back, like any other middle-aged-plus Frenchman walking down the boulevard. Trying it out.

It wasn't just the bad haircuts that Kate had grown tired of. And she'd grown tired of keeping it all to herself. They'd had a tumultuous few years. It would be a mistake to pretend that the rough patch was over. Maybe it never would be. Maybe that's not how marriage works.

❧

When the realization makes a sneak-attack on his consciousness, Dexter runs back down the hall wearing only one shoe, rushing toward his computer, trying to figure out what this could mean . . .

He'd been taken advantage of before, exploited, while he'd been utterly convinced that he was being the genius, that he'd anticipated every possible problem. Afterward, he told himself: never again.

So now he sits at his terminal, staring at the news reporter, a stand-up shot in a busy city on another continent, trying to figure out if there can be any connection among terror threats here in Paris, and terror threats there in Mumbai, and himself.

Yes.

❧

For such a long time, Dexter and Kate had lived so responsibly, and he'd disdained the rampant profligacy he saw everywhere in America, consumerism amok, all the fossil-fueled toys—the SUVs and ATVs, the speedboats and Jet Skis—and the double-height foyers and picture-windowed great rooms and slate-surrounded swimming pools, every house twice as big as anyone needed, wall-mounted plasma TVs everywhere.

Even as Dexter scorned all this acquisitiveness, he also envied these people. Not their stuff, but the freedom they enjoyed to be so irresponsible.

Then his own money started to flow in. His trades were predominantly positive, and his confidence grew each week as he tallied the results on his obsessively maintained spreadsheet of realized gains and losses, of current valuations against purchase prices. So one decision at a time, they took on this increasingly expensive life: Paris, the international school, the apartment, matching luggage and Michelin stars, an incremental accumulation of comfort, restaurants three or four nights a week, Tuesday-night family suppers of nothing special—roast chicken, wood-oven pizzas—whose bill comes to a hundred euros.

Dexter had allowed himself to fall victim to the excess of confidence that can come with an insufficiency of experience. Something he'd been quick to notice in other people, but was awfully slow to recognize in himself. This isn't so hard, you tell yourself. That nincompoop over there can do it, so can I.

So perhaps this is what he has coming to him, like any other over-extended entitled American who thought he deserved everything.

There are so many awful aspects. The constant sense of dread, the nightmares, the panic attacks. The shame and embarrassment of having been so wrong; not only of being such a rank amateur, but of being unwilling to acknowledge it, even to himself. The intense loneliness, unable to share his problems with anyone, especially with his wife, who's not only the single person who'd care the most, the one person most affected, but also the only person with whom he'd want to discuss it.

He's reminded of Hemingway's line from *The Sun Also Rises*, Mike explaining how he went bankrupt: "Gradually, then suddenly." Dexter used to think it was funny.

He knows there have to be many commonalities between Mumbai and Paris, but at the moment he can think of only the one, and only one reason for it.

35

Kate examines another of those huge doors that are everywhere in Paris, big enough for horse and carriage, doors that open up to schools, to courtyards, to private mews, to that surprisingly large segment of the city that isn't visible to the public. This set is wide open, and the broad archway between is barricaded with magnetic-card turnstiles, and a small hut where a guard sits, looking bored. It's an unusual level of security for a Paris office building, but Kate isn't surprised. Inside is an American tech company, and almost no one is more paranoid, except absolutely everyone in Kate's line of work.

Inez pulls up on her own Vespa, parks a few meters beyond Kate's.

A small crowd of young people is clustered on the sidewalk for their *pause clope,* each wearing an ID badge hanging from a lanyard, or clipped to a lapel. Everybody under thirty in Paris seems to smoke. It's like America a hundred years ago.

"Do you have any credentials?" Kate asks as Inez stows her helmet.

"Credentials?"

Kate cuts her eyes across the street.

"Ah," Inez says, seeing the security guard, understanding. *"Non."*

Kate herself doesn't have any authority here, no reason for anyone to let her in anywhere, to provide her with any information about anything. "Can you make a distraction?"

Inez cocks her head, running through the imaginary interaction, her line of dialogue, his. "Yes." She glances down at herself, her blouse. Unclasps a button. "I will have the guard open his door. It will be three, four seconds after, that is when you should be at the gate. *Ça marche?"*

"Yes."

"The mark will be when I sneeze. Then sixty seconds precisely. *D'accord?*"

Kate nods. She glances around, searching for any apparent problem, any reason not to do this right now—

Oh my God, look at that.

"One moment," Kate says. "I'll be right back."

Kate was the one who'd done everything. The research, the specialists, the pharmacies, the follow-ups, every medical assessment of her shirtless little boy, his bony shoulders and hollowed-out chest, he looked so fragile, so vulnerable, so quiet, so scared. This was the boy who used to laugh so easily, not just at the joke in front of him in the book or the movie, but at all the jokes in the world, the joke of life itself. Now he went entire days without even smiling.

And all the while, Dexter hung back, a dispirited spectator in the endeavor of keeping their child alive, like at a ballgame that wasn't going his team's way.

"Why aren't you doing any of this, Dexter?"

He looked confused, as if he didn't understand the point of the question, as if she'd asked, *What shape is the earth?* Everyone knows that, even the kids.

"Why is it me who has to take care of all of this? How did that become the default?" This wasn't about merely doctor's visits.

"Because you're the one who's best at this stuff," he said, matter-of-factly, as if this were a matter of actual fact, two plus two equals four. "You're in charge, Kate." Plain as day. "You've always been in charge."

But I never asked for that, she thought; we never agreed to that. And it wasn't even true! If Kate was in charge, why was it she who always did all the work? That's not what it means to be in charge.

Back when Kate didn't have a paying job, it made sense for her to assume all the household responsibilities. And when she first rejoined the workplace it was piecemeal, half-time, so they never reassigned the chores. That was her fault as well as his, this imbalance.

"You have to do more, Dexter. You have to care more."

"I care."

"Then you have to show it."

"I care plenty. That's a terrible thing to say. A terrible thing to think."

"I can't continue to do all this on my own. I can't come home from work trips to find actual litter on our floor. I can't collect every single prescription. I can't be the only one who ever serves the children a vegetable or puts away laundry or buys toilet paper or—"

"I buy—"

Her glare cut him off. "I don't know where the fuck you got the idea that this is how marriage works. But it's not, Dexter. Not one to me."

Is this how a marriage ends? Maybe it doesn't need to be a life-shattering betrayal, nothing explosive or dramatic, nothing cinematic, nothing filmable. Just an absence.

And that was exactly when Peter reentered her life. When Kate allowed him—invited him—back in.

That fault, that was hers, and hers alone.

The coveted box of Lego is right there in the *vitrine*. She could send a text to Dexter, letting him know it's here, saving him the trouble of searching. Or she could ignore it, leave her husband to fend for himself, and possibly fail, and suffer the boy's disappointment. Or she could walk into this store and buy it, solve her husband's problem for him, as usual.

It's not even really a decision. Ben needs something good to happen to him, and here it is.

"*Tout va bien?*" Inez asks.

"*Oui.*" Kate is wedging the box into her bag.

She composes a text to her husband. *Pls make sure bathrooms and bedrooms tidy.* She's not going to let him off the hook.

Then she turns to Inez. "*On y va.*"

Kate walks a few steps farther up the street, putting distance between herself and Inez, creating the appearance that they're not together. Just strangers who happen to be crossing the same street.

There's a gap in the traffic, a large truck that's lagging far behind a speeding taxi. Both women cross the street at different paces, alighting at different points on the opposite shore, where Kate comes to an immediate stop and watches Inez continue up the street, then turn into the archway, pause, push a button on her watch, and sneeze.

Kate starts a stopwatch on her phone.

Inez begins digging through her bag. She removes a wallet, sunglasses, a coin pouch. Kate can see the woman mutter to herself, shake her head, let out a frustrated huff. She drops her glasses, picks them up. Walks to the security hut, taps on the window.

Twenty seconds.

The guard looks up. Inez's mouth is moving, but Kate can't hear what she's saying.

Thirty seconds.

Inez makes a helpless gesture, palms up, please. The guard shakes his head, unmoved. *Non.*

Thirty-five.

Inez slips something out of her wallet, extends it toward the guard, who frowns, skeptical.

Forty.

Kate starts walking.

Inez extends her hand, shoving this thing at him, some irrelevancy.

Forty-five.

Kate is now close enough to hear him say, "*Désolé, Mademoiselle, mais c'est pas possible,*" the unremitting chorus of nay-saying that you hear whenever you try to get anything done, from every single representative of *l'administration,* the vast network of bureaucracies that underpins French society. *Sorry, but it's not possible.*

Fifty.

Inez beseeches, "*S'il vous plaît, Monsieur. C'est très important.*"

Now Kate is just a few steps away, perhaps getting too close too fast—

The guard relents, pushes open his glass door, and Inez steps toward him, and that's when her bag slips from her shoulder, slides down the length of her arm, past her elbow, her wrist, crashing to the floor—

"*Putain!*"

—fifty-five seconds—

—and as Inez kneels to collect her spilled belongings, her blouse billows, and the guard stares at the fabric's gape while Kate turns into the arch, and he steps forward toward this woman in distress, this attractive mess, while Kate slides behind him—

"*Oh, merci bien Monsieur . . .*"

—and hops the turnstile in one fluid motion, and strides forward as if she has every right in the world—

"*Merci*," Inez repeats, gathering her things, tossing them back into the bag, then cutting her eyes up to the helpful man, giving him a small thankful smile.

"*De rien*," the guard says with his own smile.

—and Kate disappears around the corner.

✦

The elevator opens onto a smoothly impersonal waiting room, right-angled and hard-edged, glass and chrome and large expanses of cold dark stone.

"*Bonjour*," Kate says to the receptionist. "I'm here to see Schuyler Franks."

"*Bonjour.* Your name, please, Madame?"

"Lindsay Davis."

"*Un moment, Madame Davis.*"

The receptionist is wearing a headset, so Kate can't hear a thing, but from the woman's response it seems as if Schuyler is denying this appointment. It's taking longer than a quick dismissive "I don't have any appointment with any Lindsay Davis," so maybe Schuyler is searching her calendar, looking for this name, double-checking that she hasn't made some horrible mistake, because any mistake of any sort can be horrible when you work in PR, anyone you insult, any information you neglect to forward, any call you forget to return, any tiny thing can turn out to be a career-wrecking epic fail, this has been ingrained, the public-relations Hippocratic oath: first, do not offend.

"*Donc*, what do you want me to do?" The receptionist whispers. Then she turns back to Kate. "*S'il vous plaît*, Madame Davis. Mademoiselle Franks will be one minute."

There's already another woman waiting on a firm, uncomfortable-looking sofa, between end tables adorned with small stacks of magazines, tech and business, and a few of today's international newspapers. A security camera is suspended in one corner; Kate noticed a seeing eye in the elevator, and a pair of them at the security gates in the breezeway. Her presence here is being amply documented, she registers that now. But it won't be until later that she understands the magnitude of the threat this presents.

Pls get 6 candles, she types. *Plain white, no scent.* If there's one thing Kate hates, it's scented candles at the dinner table.

The other woman waiting is a middle-aged suit-wearing executive type, serious eyeglasses and sensible hair and a dour expression, constantly fidgeting with her collar, her neckline, as if worried that too much breast might be visible. She has smile-lines and crow's-feet and deep-set wrinkles across her forehead, the unmistakable look of someone who consumes a daily diet of recirculated office air and salad-bar lunches, too much work and too much stress, too little sleep and too little fun and far, far too little sex.

For a couple of years back in DC, Kate worried that she was on a path to becoming one of these women, officious and humorless, no room to project anything except hyper-competent professionalism, as if any chink in that armor would be fatal, the gap that would allow sexism and ageism to sneak in, to infect her career, lay ruin to it. Nursing the bunions from high heels and the hangovers from office parties, harboring deep resentments that her work kept her away from her children, and her children away from her work, everything always tugging in the other direction.

Her Washington office had even looked a bit like this one, the absence of personality its own kind of personality, institutional gray walls, loudly patterned wall-to-wall to hide soil and stains, chest-high cubicle dividers and glass-walled offices, women's room down this hall and men's down that one with the kitchen in between, decaf in the orange-handled pot and a plastic platter with leftover cake from a conference-room birthday celebration, the bulletin board with sign-up sheets for the potluck picnic and the softball squad, a list of the names and numbers of the fire-safety monitors, a long-ignored memo about recycling sent by an office manager who quit years ago.

This caught Kate by surprise. It's not what she'd imagined back when she'd first applied to the Agency, senior year of college, looking for a job that would take her far from her decaying hometown, far from the ghosts of her dead parents, from the mounting problems of her dysfunctional disaster of a sister. Far from a life she didn't want.

The CIA was Kate's first escape, her first reinvention. It would not be her last.

❖

"Madame Davis?" It's Schuyler, twenty-five and slender, pencil-skirted and long-haired. Her cell phone is in her palm, facing up; this is a woman who never misses a call, an e-mail, a text-message, a tweet, the alerts flashing constantly, the light igniting every few seconds, and never, ever failing to catch her attention.

"*Bonjour.*" Kate stands, extends her hand. Ready to head back to Schuyler's office, or a conference room. Ready for their meeting.

"I'm sorry, I don't *think* I have any appointment now? Are you sure it's me you're here to see?"

Kate does her best to look worried. "Oh crap, do I have the time wrong?"

She takes out her phone, brings up her calendar, into which she has entered a meeting with this woman—her address, phone number, job title. Kate extends this screen in front of her, here, look, I'll prove it to you, we have a meeting.

Schuyler glances at Kate's phone. Yes indeed, that's her name, right there. "I'm sorry, I see *you* have a record of it, but I don't? Maybe you can tell me what this is about?"

Kate takes a deep breath, as if bringing herself under the barest tether of control.

"Yes, of course." She glances at the receptionist. "But not out here, okay?" Kate leans in. "It's, um, sensitive," she says in a near-whisper, and places her hand on Schuyler's forearm. *"Please?"*

36

"We are getting a much more full picture of this man." It is someone new speaking, a voice that Ibrahim does not recognize. "Mahmoud Khalid."

"Finally."

"Oh give me a fucking break, François. Using nothing more than the long-distance visual, this has been an extremely fast response. And it must be said—"

"Do not—"

"—that I have not seen an *abundance* of information being supplied by military—"

"Oh go to hell."

"That *suffices*, you two."

"—intelligence."

"You are like children."

Ibrahim can imagine the bickering men behind him, glaring at each other, the third one standing there, shaking his head in disgust. The pissing contests are endless, it is just one after another, dicks hanging out all over the place.

"Everything we have learned so far indicates that Mahmoud Khalid is a secular Egyptian. No ties to radical Islam. Not him, not his relatives. He migrated here immediately after the Arab Spring. Accompanied by his wife and children. They were two and three when they moved here."

"And the wife?"

"Neela Khalid. A schoolteacher in Egypt, worked at a crèche here, not far from their home in the eighteenth. She appears to have died last year. Then a month ago, the children flew to Cairo, and it appears that they have not returned to Paris."

"The children traveled to Egypt by themselves?"

"No. They were accompanied by what looks like the wife's father."

"And what does Mahmoud Khalid do when not a suicide bomber?"

"For the past two years, he has worked full-time in a *quincaillerie*."

Ibrahim almost drops his gun. He fights the urge to spin around, to see who offered this bit of information, to ask for details. Is it possible . . . ?

He needs to know.

"Sir?" Ibrahim has not spoken in a while, his voice is croaky. He clears it. Then starts anew, "Sir, permission to ask a question?"

This is a surprise to everyone. A long pause. "Yes, Officer Abid. Go ahead."

"Could I ask, where exactly is this shop?"

"This is a strange question, Officer Abid."

"My parents, they are proprietors of a *quincaillerie*."

The hardware store is where Ibrahim worked his very first job, after school, stocking shelves, reorganizing the storeroom. Price-stickering was the first gun he ever used, back when guns were a completely different idea, when guns meant fun, games. You wore a smile on your face when you held a gun.

His parents limited his working to just a few hours per week; token employment. They said he needed time to do his schoolwork. But school was easy, homework minimal, he had plenty of time. It was not until years later when he understood that they were trying to give him a normal schoolboy's life—friends, football, girls. They did not want him stuck in a hardware-store basement. They were not immigrants, they did not want to live like immigrants, with the children working in the family shop.

Ibrahim often wonders if his parents would make the same decisions today. And his great-grandparents, would they still leave Morocco for France? Would they still be as eager to raise their families here, to make their lives in a country that is increasingly hostile toward people like them, increasingly intolerant? Or maybe this tendency is merely how it looks to Ibrahim now, because when he was a child, things seemed to be headed in the other direction.

He worries sometimes that he is living in a variation of Germany, 1932. That in five years, or ten, he will look back on this moment from a jail cell, or from an internment camp, or from some newly invented horror, and he will be furious at himself for his failure to anticipate what is so clearly the logical extension of everything that is coalescing around him now, and not just in France but in England too, in Russia, even in the United States, which is perhaps most terrifying of all. It is supposed to be the United States that prevents this from happening elsewhere. But then what do the Americans go and do?

Is that what today is about? Is that why this man is standing here, clad in explosives? This Muslim man from North Africa, this family man who works in a *quincaillerie,* this man who could be Ibrahim himself.

It is hard to understand what could bring a man to this. But Ibrahim is sure that it is not as simple as evil. Almost nothing is. Evil, in his experience, is a temporary subjective condition, not a permanent objective fact.

"Where is your family's shop, Officer Abid?"

Ibrahim wonders why the man is responding this way, then he understands. "In the sixth, sir. The rue du Cherche-Midi."

It is the man named François who answers: "It is not the same store."

"Thank you, sir."

Ibrahim returns his focus to the target, to the man who works in a hardware store that is not owned by Ibrahim's parents. Mahmoud Khalil is not a man whom Ibrahim has met. If Ibrahim needs to kill Khalil, it will not mean anything personally to him.

But if the opposite were true? What would François have said? He would, of course, have lied. Maybe he just did.

"Oh, here is something interesting. A new-patient record for a Mahmoud Khalid was opened at the University Hospital eight months ago. One guess: which department?"

A whole crowd has gathered on the Richelieu Wing's rooftop, men who had been arriving over the past couple of hours, one by one and some in twos. There is Ibrahim's commanding officer, who runs the Louvre detail, and his commanding officer, plus a couple of other serious-looking men from the police department, management types. There is a deputy mayor. A pair of uniformed military men. A couple of guys in suits who must be from intelligence; Ibrahim did not catch their names, their affiliations, or maybe they did not say.

Not one of these men has introduced himself to Ibrahim. The sniper is not here to give any input, discuss any options, make any decisions. He is here for one purpose.

"What do we have to lose, Édouard?"

"You mean if we take him right now?"

He is here to pull the trigger.

"That is a good question. Jean-Paul, what do you think?"

"Well . . ." Jean-Paul either does not have an opinion or does not want to share it. Instead he makes a noise like a harrumph. It is when all the options are bad that true cowardice reveals itself. "There is no evidence that he has been radicalized."

Ibrahim hears one of the men snort at the absurdity of that statement. *Evidence.* Ibrahim cannot turn around, but he does not need his eyes to see it clearly, the man pointing at the center of the *cour,* at the terrorist in a bomb vest. Evidence? There is your fucking evidence.

"You have to be firm with these people."

"These people?"

"You cannot just let them get away with this, cannot let them hold a whole city—a whole nation—hostage. Every minute that we wait serves only to embolden them, to legitimize this tactic. *Every* minute. I strongly urge we take action right now."

"Yves?"

"No. An unprovoked assassination could trigger a disproportionate response."

"Unprovoked? Assassination? What the hell are you talking about?"

"I am just trying to put myself in their position. If what they are trying to do is open a negotiation, and we preemptively end the negotiation before even *any* communication—"

"But there has been no communication, has there? And it has been three hours. So we have to consider the possibility that this is not a negotiation."

"It must be. Do we know anything more about the other devices?"

"The sites have been cleared, wide perimeters established around maximum blast radii. The explosive-ordnance disposal devices—"

"Eh? What does that mean?"

"Robots. The robots are in position to approach and investigate, which should take between thirty and sixty minutes. Each location presents different challenges."

"But that has not commenced? Why not?"

"Awaiting the final order."

"Really? Whose order?"

"Um . . . at this point, Édouard . . . ?"

"I believe we are waiting for the president of the republic."

"The *president*? That does not make sense."

"No, it does not, but who is going to tell him that? You?"

"I still say we shoot this bastard right now. Even if this is supposed to be the opening move of a negotiation, eliminating him establishes our position. Displays our strength. Our willingness to make a hard choice, even at high risk."

Ibrahim can feel the posturing behind him, like a cloud of indignation: we in *la police*, our hands are always tied, we never get to arrest anyone anymore, much less shoot the bad guys, everything is so PC, all the criminals are owed all the understanding, the immigrants too, one must have sympathy, *n'est-ce pas*?

No, damn it, and it would feel awfully good to just shoot one, blow his fucking head off.

Sometimes Ibrahim feels himself agreeing with this sentiment, with the frustration behind it, probably shared all across the world wherever the impartial rule of law butts against respect for human rights and civil liberties. On the other hand, most of the heads that get blown off look a lot like Ibrahim's, while the people who do the shooting do not.

"You are a lunatic, do you know that? An irresponsible lunatic. Does your wife know she married a lunatic?"

"And what if they call our bluff? If they are willing to detonate just because we shoot the messenger, then they are planning to detonate anyway. By waiting we are simply putting ourselves into a weaker position."

"Listen: is there any way to *prevent* the detonation from occurring?"

"Are you kidding? And we would have chosen *not* to do that yet?"

"Frankly, it is not even the suicide vest I am worried about. It is that briefcase. Yves, do we have the readings yet?"

"That team is still setting up the equipment. I am told that it is not so simple. Another few minutes."

Then they are all silent, perhaps waiting for those few minutes to pass.

"There are cell phones out there, you know. Look at all those people. News cameras too. It would be throughout the world, instantly. A cold-blooded assassination."

"Of a *terrorist*."

"Of one scared man who is standing still, putting no one in imminent danger."

"*Everyone* is in imminent danger. He is wearing a suicide vest! He has a suitcase bomb!"

"Maybe what they are *trying* to do is provoke us into shooting him. Have you considered that? Cameras everywhere, footage, they will be able to say, *Look what these French savages did*. And for all we know, this man is completely innocent."

"*Innocent*? What in the name of . . . ? How could he be *innocent*?"

"His family is being held at gunpoint. His children are huddled in some dark room at the business end of AK-47s. This poor sap here, he has been forced to walk into the cour Napoléon wearing this suicide vest or his kids are going to be beheaded by machetes."

"You have a fucked-up imagination, do you know that?"

"And if we blow this patsy's head off for eight billion people to see? Then they will be able to say that we forced their hands, they had no choice, so look, everyone, watch as we saw off all these little heads with a scythe?"

"A *scythe*?"

"They are barbarians."

"Who are you even talking about? We have no idea who is responsible for this."

"They are *all* barbarians."

Sudden silence. Ibrahim suspects that someone just realized that the sniper is one of the *they*, and probably held up a finger to lips, maybe inclined his head toward the man at the edge of the roof, creating a silent standoff.

"Gentlemen. Look at this."

"What is this?"

"A screen-grab from footage of the van that delivered the bomber here. We now know the vehicle make and model, the license plate. And, here, this image is a clear shot of the driver getting out of the van at place Vendôme. Depositing one of the bombs."

"He does not look, um . . ."

"Arab?"

A phone rings. One of the men answers tersely, listens for a few seconds, says thanks. "That was the tech team: the briefcase is definitely emitting radiation."

"Fuck."

"But that cannot really be a nuclear *bomb,* can it?"

"No. It is too small to be a fission device. I am pretty sure."

"*Pretty* sure?"

"But what it could be—in fact, what it *must* be—is a dirty bomb."

"Dirty. That could be nuclear dirt, right? What would we be looking at?"

"Depends on many factors. Too many. I cannot speculate about the likely extent of damage."

"What about minimum?"

"Without question it would make this immediate area a kill zone due to radiation poisoning. Radius of one thousand meters, at the absolute minimum. Possibly much more."

"Not to mention the contents of the Louvre contaminated for decades."

"A minimum of one thousand meters, you say? The radiation could reach l'Élysée?"

"Oh yes."

Everyone lets that sink in.

"Is he there today?"

"Yes."

"Someone needs to tell him."

Silence. No one wants to make this call.

"Yves?"

"*What*? Why me?"

"You know why. And it has to happen right now, this minute. The president needs to evacuate."

37

Kate pulls Schuyler's door closed.

"So, I'm sorry, but what's this all about?" Schuyler is still standing behind her desk, looking affronted.

"Listen carefully." Kate needs to put this woman on notice, to scare the shit out of her from the get-go. "You're having the hardest day of your career."

"Excuse me?"

"It may turn out to be the worst day of your entire life."

Now Schuyler has grown outraged, but speechless. And getting scared.

"Your company is under attack. *Physical* attack. Mortal, physical attack."

The woman's eyes dart to the closed door.

"Not by me, don't worry about me, I'm here to help."

"So says everyone who's not."

Schuyler Franks is a woman whose profession is to manipulate the public's perceptions of reality, to construct narratives, alternative facts. She probably confronts everyone else's narratives with a strong dose of skepticism.

"You're completely right, you don't have any reason to trust me," Kate says. "So I'm not asking for you to simply believe some woman—some possibly crazy woman—who has lied her way into your office."

"So let me get this straight: we don't have an appointment?"

"What I'm telling you is to check this out for yourself. Make a couple of calls."

"I'm sorry, who *are* you?"

"My identity matters a lot less than you might think."

"I'm sorry?" Shaking her head. "I'm going to need to call security?"

"No." Kate grabs the woman by the forearm, not gently.

"*Ow.*"

"You're not."

Kate doesn't like doing this, intimidating a woman who has done nothing wrong except appear accidentally in Kate's path. Getting bullied herself is something Kate still remembers intensely, viscerally. The CIA halls were suffused with the miasma of testosterone, and Kate was under a more or less constant threat of getting dismissed, getting ignored, getting rejected. She felt the sting well before it even happened, the aggression, the condescension, the subtle slights and hostile body language and flippant smirks.

She remembers how effective it was. How it kept her on the constant defensive, willing to do practically anything to avoid confrontation.

"Sit the fuck down," Kate says. "And for the love of God *stop* apologizing to me."

Schuyler Franks is not one hundred percent willing to accept Kate's authority, but she's awfully close.

"Right *now.*"

There, that does it. Just as effective as ever. The young woman takes a seat at the edge of her chair, back rigid, eyes wide. She doesn't know what defense is available to her—should she call security? Call her boss? Or should she hear out this intruder?

"Hong Kong and Mumbai, your offices there—those office buildings—both have bomb threats against them, at this minute. Please go ahead, check it out yourself."

"I'm sorry, what? How?"

"*Stop* apologizing. Just *call* someone over there. Anyone you want."

Schuyler nods, seems almost relieved to be told to do something so concrete, so straightforward. She looks at her screen, then down at her keyboard, her forefingers finding their positions at *F* and *J*. She types in a password, then clicks around with her mouse.

The speakerphone answers, "Hello, 4Syte Hong Kong, how may I direct your call?"

"Hi! This is Schuyler Franks in the Paris office? Do you work in reception?"

"Yes I do." This call to the other side of the world is very clear, to a woman with a very British accent. "How may I be of assistance?"

Schuyler is staring at nothingness, concentrating. Kate uses the opportunity to unlock her own phone and launch an app. Then she puts her device on the desk, just inches from Schuyler's cell. The process should take less than a minute.

"Sorry, may I ask you a strange question?"

"Erm . . ."

"Is there a *bomb* threat to your building?"

"Uh . . . One moment please."

Schuyler is put on hold with ambient music, or maybe this sound doesn't qualify as music, just a series of oscillating tones, hypnotizing—

"Yes." The Hong Kong receptionist says.

"Yes? Yes what?"

No answer.

"I'm sorry, I don't want to harass you?" Schuyler says. "But you just put me on hold to ask for permission to answer my question, right? You called someone in public relations? *I'm* in PR, check me out if you need to? Do you want me to spell out my name?"

"No, I've already verified you, your phone number."

"Awesome. Well, I received a query from the press, and my plan is to phone back and say I don't know anything? But that's not going to cut it forever, we're going to need a real response? So I'm sorry, but I have to know what's actually going on over there?"

That's a good story; Kate nods her encouragement.

Hong Kong pauses, then says. "Right. One moment please." Hold again, another half-minute. Then: "Right. Building management alerted all tenants that someone attempted entry with a potentially explosive device."

Schuyler's eyebrows shoot up her forehead, her mouth hangs open. She doesn't know where to go from here. Then she gathers her wits, says, "I'm sorry, may I have the name of the building management? A contact number?"

"Very well."

The Hong Kong woman rattles off some information, which Schuyler dutifully writes down, ends the call. Then she just sits there.

"Are you going to check with Mumbai?" Kate asks.

"Is it the same thing?"

"Similar, probably. Have you heard anything about this building? Evacuations, threats, anything?"

"No. Do you think *this* building is under attack?"

"I don't have any reason to," Kate says. "But other parts of Paris are. I understand that your CEO is holding a press conference this afternoon. Will that take place here?"

"Um . . . I'm sor—" Schuyler stops herself. "Listen: you need to tell me who you are, and what you're doing here, or I'm going to have to call security? I don't . . . I can't . . ."

Kate pushes past this. "Is Hunter Forsyth here right now? In the building?"

Schuyler doesn't answer.

"If this office is going to be attacked, Schuyler—if your boss is going to be attacked, abducted, *assassinated*—"

"*What?*"

"—do you really want to be the one who's responsible for *failing* to prevent it?"

"Why *me*? Why did you come to me?"

"You answered the phone."

"Wait, what? You're the one who called earlier?"

"Listen, I didn't choose you, that was just luck. But we're here now, you and I, and it's possible that something *very* bad is going on in your company today. Right now. You can either be a hero, and help me figure out what it is and how to prevent it, or you can be a villain, an obstacle. I'm sure we don't have an excess of spare time, so for fuck's sake tell me right now: is Hunter Forsyth here in this goddamned building?"

"I don't know."

"Well, can you find out? *Now?*"

A long second passes while the young woman makes her calculations, weighing one unpleasant possibility against another. She nods again, then stares down into her lap, thinking. Nods once more, this time agreeing with herself, with the plan she just hatched. She clicks her mouse again, and another speakerphone call goes through.

"*Allô* Schuyler."

"Hi?" She furrows her brow. "Colette?"

"*Non, c'est Dominique.*"

Kate leans forward, plants her elbows on the desk, listening carefully.

"Oh, okay? Has Colette stepped away?"

"Colette, she is not here."

"Sorry? Where is she?"

"She is with Monsieur Forsyth, at his home."

"Okay, well . . . um . . . I want to check if Hunter needs anything last-minute for the press conference?"

Dominique doesn't answer.

"Sorry, can I ask you to check for me? With Hunter?"

Dominique pauses before answering, "*Oui.* I will try."

Schuyler is put on hold again. It takes longer than expected, while Schuyler stares down at her desk, avoiding Kate's gaze.

Dominique comes back on the line. "Monsieur Forsyth, he does not answer."

"Can you try Col—"

"*Oui,* she also does not answer her mobile. And no one answers the telephone at the apartment. *Personne* answer *rien.*"

"That's strange, isn't it? When is Monsieur Forsyth expected to the office?"

"Another hour."

"Aren't you worried?"

"Worried? *Non.* Why should I be worried?"

"Because no one answers the phone?"

The other woman laughs, a humorless staccato burst.

"What's funny?"

"What do you think, Schuyler?" Pronounced *skee-LAIR.*

"Sorry, I really don't know? Please, what are you talking about?"

Dominique sighs. "Why would a man and a woman together in an apartment not answer their phones? Can you imagine a reason?"

Kate knows how it can happen: an everyday relationship that exerts pressure, builds toward something, momentum without friction, acceleration. Like physics.

Part of the appeal was her growing resentments at home, a long-term amalgamation of little slights, minor inconsiderations. Dexter's parental neglects, educational, social, recreational, spousal. Kate could group them on a spreadsheet, sorted by category, ranked by orders of magnitude.

This is apparently how you can get to a spot where you can't stand your spouse.

The title of the spreadsheet would be: GRIEVANCES.

That was the push. The pull happened in Seville, the way these things happen. Kate and Peter had a typically late Andalusian dinner accompanied by vermouth and then *tinto* and then sherry—all told, perhaps too much to drink, though it didn't look that way at the time. It never looks that way at the time, especially when you're having great fun, sharing jokes, smiles, intimacies, a long slow walk through the sexy Spanish streets, the tapas bars spilling tipsy patrons onto the sidewalks, an air of permissiveness.

It was the type of night that looks a lot like a romantic date, one that ends in bed.

"So," she said to him in the hotel lobby, "what now?" Peter seemed like a man with something on his mind, a man who wanted to unburden himself, but needed to be given permission. Kate wanted to give him that permission, wanted him to open up, she wanted to be that sort of boss, that sort of friend, that sort of woman. She wanted to hear what it was he needed to say.

What else did she want? Yes, she did: she wanted him to make a pass. She didn't want to accept it, no, she was sure of that. But she wanted him to try.

Kate already knew the risks people could take, the damage these risks could do. Her career in exploiting people often hinged on the discovery of extramarital affairs, or the invention of them, which could happen even when—especially when—they could be most damaging. There are so many ways it can turn out badly.

And badly is the only way it can turn out, isn't it? In the end—and there's always an end—it's just a question of who ends up most hurt. But make no mistake about it: everyone ends up hurt.

"What," he said, "are my options?"

She'd asked for that, hadn't she? Kate turned away, fought a smile, felt herself blushing. She hated blushing; it made her feel exposed.

"Okay, I'll tell you what I want," Peter said. He took a step closer.

She kept her eyes averted, down at the floor, over by the door, anywhere else.

"I want you to come upstairs with me."

That's when she looked up. His eye was firm, he was absolutely sure of himself. This didn't come as a surprise to her, neither his desire nor his declaration. She knew him pretty well at this point.

"I want you to come to bed with me." He smiled. "Again."

Absolutely sure of her.

It has to be admitted: at that point in her life, Kate preferred a good flossing to having sex with Dexter. She'd been doing everything possible to avoid him short of saying no point-blank; she didn't want to create that rift in her marriage, possibly irreparable, a wife who denies sex to her husband. It was temporary, and she didn't want to impose a permanent solution onto a temporary problem. This is what she told herself, staring in the mirror, wearing her most matronly nightgown, shapeless plaid flannel.

"I want you," Peter said. "That's what I want."

38

Two knocks in quick succession. Pause. Then three knocks. Pause. Four. Then Simpson unlocks the various mechanisms, pulls the heavy door open just wide enough to collect a bag from the uniformed policeman. "*Merci*," he says, and shuts the door quickly. Re-engages all three locks.

They have a code, this CIA dude and a local cop? That's odd. Is this something they worked out just today? Or is it a standard spook-cop thing? If so, wouldn't all the bad guys also know the code?

Bad guys. Did he really just form that phrase in his mind? Jesus.

"Sandwiches," Simpson says. "And coffee. Water too." He sets the bag on the table, begins unloading little wax-paper packets. "*Jambon-beurre*, I hope that's okay with everyone."

Hunter doesn't want any damn ham-and-butter sandwich. He remains in his seat, dejected, slouched in this lumpy futon, with an out-of-date American gossip magazine in his lap. He has already leafed through all the more substantive publications; next is going to be fashion. Which will at least have the benefit of plentiful pictures of pretty women.

He watches his own pretty woman walk across the room. Though *walk* isn't the right word for what Colette does. *Saunter.*

She picks up a bottle of water, sparkling. Hunter has been making an effort to catalog Colette's preferences—whites from Burgundy, grilled *loup de mer*, triple-crème cheeses, swimming in the Mediterranean, Prada shoes. Sparkling, not still. He's laying the groundwork to be an attentive, considerate husband.

It's true that at this moment Colette already has a different husband, a guy—named Guy!—whom Hunter has researched exhaustively, exhaustingly. This Guy guy, a professor, apparently wrote the definitive biography of some long-dead French novelist—not Balzac, but another dude with a *z*—which makes him a writer who writes about other dead writers, which: for fuck's sake. Guy's headshot—turtleneck, long wavy hair, staring off into the distance—has Sensitive Guy written all over it, like a watermark in stationery.

Other than their mutual affection for the same woman, Hunter and Guy don't seem to have anything in common. Hopefully Colette's taste in men isn't completely consistent.

Hunter has considered different strategies for wrecking her marriage, a few very different schemes. Weighing practicalities, challenges, likelihoods of success. He always comes back to his first, most obvious concept: entrap Guy into having an affair, and make absolutely sure he gets caught.

The main stumbling block to this scenario is super-ironic: the person Hunter would entrust to find the right seductress? Colette. She solves all the problems that aren't the express domain of someone with a different specialty, and no one has this specialty.

In whatever way Hunter is going to ruin Colette's marriage, he'd better start soon. It's not as if he has forever. His sperm is fine—he had himself checked, that's not the concern—but the rest of his body is definitely aging, and he wants to be able to play catch with his son, hit fungoes, toss a football. Who knows how many more years he'll be able to rely on his body? Hunter's own dad tore an ACL at age forty-eight, and never skied again; never did much of anything physical again. By that point, Hunter was sixteen and no longer wanted to do anything with Dad, except that one trip to the brothel near Tahoe, which he'd never before realized was an option as a father-son activity. And it turned out to be just the one time, not an ongoing hobby.

Hunter watches as Colette unscrews the water-bottle cap and tips the bottle into her mouth, her lips open and pursed, barely touching the plastic, certainly not engulfing it, not wrapping her mouth around the shaft of it—

Oh, *God*, it's a physical ache he has for her, an actual generalized pain.

It really wasn't supposed to be this way. For this Paris assistant, he'd made a special point of asking HR to send over an older woman. Not *old*, per se, but at least well into her thirties. Labor laws being what they are, sexual harassment suits, who knows about French customs; Hunter didn't want to run any risks. This is a country in which every employee is guaranteed the right to *not respond* to work e-mails on vacation, of which everyone is guaranteed at least *five weeks per year.* Everyone! It's insane.

He was already well aware of his own predilection for French women, and for twenty-five-year-olds. He was, frankly, terrified to combine the two.

For her job interview, Colette had worn a roomy pantsuit, her hair strangled up in a bun, thick eyeglasses. She barely smiled. She was clearly a good-looking woman, but not in any distracting way, nothing to worry about. And she was obviously a hyper-competent, super-efficient person. Maybe a bit of a pill, but that was okay. Hunter wasn't trying to hire a friend. He'd learned that lesson already, more than once.

But it slowly became clear how obscenely clever Colette is. She's unfailingly pleasant to everyone, without ever seeming insincere. Every once in a while she even displays a flash of a sense of humor, which Hunter never could've anticipated from that brittle, joyless interviewee.

Then that night last year.

It came out of the blue: Colette accompanied him for the short walk over to his drinks date, as she does. The street in front of the hotel was lined with luxury cars, including a matching pair of cherry-red Lamborghinis with Qatar plates, an ostentatious display of wealth that made Hunter feel downright middle-class. He'd heard that a sultan rented out the presidential suite for an entire month on the mere chance that his family would want to come to Paris for a few days. *And then never did.*

Boss move.

That's the sort of money Hunter wants. The sort that makes it okay to throw away hundreds of thousands of dollars for basically no reason.

He made his way to the terrace while Colette stepped inside to check for his guest. As she was reemerging, she came face-to-face with a friend—*Mon Dieu,* big hugs, big smiles.

Hunter was sitting at a table under the red awnings that matched the red blooms that cascaded from the flower boxes of every red-awninged window. At the next table, a Pakistani guy wearing a bright-pink jacket was reading a London paper. That type of crowd, of place, exuding money. Across the wide tree-lined street, exorbitant fashion boutiques beckoned. Come over here, they called. You belong here.

In places like this, Hunter hated staring at his phone. So instead he watched Colette, who was only thirty feet away but hadn't seen Hunter sit, didn't know how close he was. So she was interacting with this person from her private life as if out of her boss's sight.

She was a completely different person. Her face was lit up in a wonderful smile, one that Hunter had never before seen. Those deep dimples, the rosy glow of her cheeks, the affectionate way she caressed her friend's arm. Her eyes were twinkling. She pushed a wisp of errant hair away from the side of her neck. Her long, incredibly sexy neck.

It was like a flash of lightning, the immediacy of this epiphany, the drama of it, the irrefutability of this violent bolt of electricity exploding in the sky, making everything else look minor, irrelevant: Colette was the most beautiful woman he'd ever met. His assistant! How had it taken him three years to realize this?

Now it was like looking back on a time when he believed that the world was flat, that politicians were honest: inconceivable, from this vantage, to fathom how he'd been so completely wrong, for so very long.

"Can we get some light in here?" Hunter asks, flinging aside the heavy drapery—

He freezes, staring. Turns back to face Simpson. "What the hell?"

Simpson holds up a finger while he finishes chewing his ham sandwich, swallows. "Sorry," he says. "I told you this place wasn't much to look at."

"But boarded-up windows?"

"For safety."

Hunter's first thought is about fire safety; there was an issue last year with inaccessible windows at the plant in Guangdong Province, six people died, or maybe it was eight? Some small, even number of dead Chinese people.

But this wasn't the type of safety Simpson was talking about. "In today's age of electronic intrusion, Mr. Forsyth, windows are too porous.

With directional microphones, portable telescopes, night-vision goggles. Not to mention high-powered sniper's rifles."

Hunter's mind roams to the bathroom, the small window there. Is that one boarded up too? The bedroom? "This is a super-cheerful place, isn't it?"

"It's not meant to be cheerful, Mr. Forsyth. It's meant to be safe."

Hunter has given up asking Simpson to call him by his first name. He prefers Mr. Forsyth anyway.

"Is there anything I can get for you? *Try* to get for you? To make you more comfortable while we're here?"

Hunter fingers a section of sandwich, but doesn't pick it up. "Can you please find out what's going on out there?"

"The police who accompanied us have instructions to bring me any news immediately." He shrugs. "They haven't brought any news."

Hunter examines this so-called Tom Simpson, a guy wearing a forgettable outfit, an unflattering suit and oxford shirt with repp tie, cap-toes that could use a shine, like a bureaucrat's uniform. Maybe it is an actual uniform, guidelines in some handbook. But any guidelines would probably prohibit these grooming choices—the big beard, the large square eyeglass frames with amber lenses. Like a character from an old cop show, *Kojak* maybe, *Columbo*.

Plus there's that scar on his cheek. Maybe the beard is there to hide others.

Barney Miller.

"You don't seem particularly concerned. Or interested."

"I'm concerned, Mr. Forsyth. And plenty interested. I understand that this situation is inconvenient for you, I really do. Today is not going how you planned, and it's an important day. That's true for lots of people. I hope for everyone's sake—including my own—that we can normalize as soon as possible. But my job right now is to keep you out of harm's way. In the meantime, we have to accept that everything else about the situation is out of our control."

Do we? Acceptance is not Hunter's style.

He looks around again, the boarded-up windows, the triple-locked steel-reinforced door, the magazines, the TV hooked up to a DVD player, the small stack of American movies, the shelf's worth of paperback books.

The bathroom has a bare-bones supply of toiletries, the single bedroom a queen-size bed. And that landline, plugged into the beige plastic box of a wall jack. It looks like an old piece of hardware, that box. Something from ten years ago, maybe more. Fifteen. Pre–fiber optic.

The phone unit also looks like it's not especially new. He walks over to the console table, picks up the handset, checks that there's still no dial tone. There isn't.

It's a model with two lines, an integrated digital answering machine. The kind of outdated phone you find in a mom-and-pop roadside motel, neither mom nor pop willing to invest in the latest communications systems, their clientele not in a position to care. Hunter has used a couple of those motels, once or twice.

This device is something that was bought from a consumer-electronics retailer, for your home office, for your kitchen counter. This handset wasn't one element of a big network buy with a purchase order, a complex install sequence, coordination between IT and HR, a temporary outgoing message for everyone, memos, complaints . . .

It never ceases to amaze Hunter how *anything* can become a royal pain in the ass.

But this phone wasn't. This was a quick inexpensive purchase, a one-minute install. He turns the base over, where MADE IN CHINA is die-cut into the beige plastic. He puts this down, walks away.

China . . .

Made in China . . . ?

This phone was made in *China*?

39

"Schuyler? Is Forsyth married?"

Schuyler is staring off at nothing, in stunned shock. She nods.

Kate retrieves her phone from the desk, glances at the screen. Yes, her intrusion has been successful.

"Happily?"

The woman looks at Kate. "Are you kidding me? How would I know?"

It's certainly not unheard-of, especially in France, where extramarital affairs are practically a requirement, especially for powerful men. Perhaps Schuyler thought her boss was different—a visionary, a genius, a whatever, above all that. No one is above all that.

So, yes, that could be a possibility: an affair plus blackmail. But how could this garden-variety shakedown fit into a coordinated terrorist attack on multiple continents?

Though there haven't been any *actual* attacks so far. No hostages taken. No networks breached, no systems crashed. No violence of any sort, physical or cyber. Although explosives have been planted at the Gare de Lyon, Arc de Triomphe, place Vendôme, and Notre-Dame, plus a suicide bomber in the middle of the Louvre, there have been no detonations. No trucks plowing through crowds. No deaths. No demands. No claims of responsibility. Just threats, strung like a necklace of menace across the city's neck.

Kate brings to mind a map of Paris, and drops mental pins at the bomb sites. They surround this office.

"Where's Forsyth's apartment?"

The young woman doesn't answer.

"Listen, I know you don't want to—"

"No, that's not it: I actually don't know where it is?"

"You need to find out."

"Sorry, and then what? *Go* there?" The young woman shakes her head. "No way."

"You have to."

"I *have* to? I don't think so."

"Then get me the address, and I'll go."

"*That's* out of the question. Listen, Miss ... What *is* your name anyway?"

"Lindsay."

"Well, *Lindsay,* I have no clue who you are? Or what you're doing here? Or what business this is—*any* of this—of yours? Seriously, who *are* you? A reporter?"

Kate doesn't answer.

"Are you CIA?"

Kate remains silent.

"For all I know, maybe *you're* involved in these attacks? Maybe you're a Trojan horse? Maybe this whole thing is orchestrated to trick me into taking you to Mr. Forsyth's apartment? Maybe *you're* the enemy?"

Kate opens her mouth to explain how wrong this is, but then changes her mind. This young woman is better off not knowing Kate's theory.

"Okay." Schuyler gets up. "I'm going to have to ask you to wait in reception?"

"Come on," Kate says. "What do you think I'm going to do in here? Steal your press releases?"

Kate holds up her phone, pretending to read messages so she can surreptitiously take a photo of the young woman.

"I can't guess what you want to steal? But if you're not planning on stealing anything, you'll be just as happy to wait out in reception?"

She follows Kate like a prison guard back down the gray hall. Kate sends Schuyler's photo to Inez, with instructions to follow her to Forsyth's apartment.

"This woman is going to wait for me here? I'll be back in fifteen minutes?"

"*D'accord.*"

"Hey," Kate says. "Take my phone number. In case you need help."

"What help am I going to need that you can provide?"

"You never know."

Schuyler seems to consider what possible threat it might be to take possession of this strange woman's number. "Write it down?"

"Let me call you, then you'll have it in your phone."

"No, I don't want your number in my phone? And I certainly don't want you to have mine?"

"Why not?"

"*Why not?* Because I don't trust you?"

Good for her. Kate scribbles down her number.

"Don't follow me?"

"Of course not."

Schuyler smiles at Kate's naked display of disingenuousness, turns to the receptionist. "If this woman leaves, please call me immediately? And then call security too?"

Did Kate debate it? Not really. As soon as Peter said it, she knew how she was going to respond. It just took her a few seconds to do it.

"I'm sorry," she said.

He didn't argue. He just left it there, hanging between them in the hotel lobby, the invitation, reiterated in his silent stare.

"I can't."

She could. And she wanted to. The one night they'd shared fifteen years ago had been spectacular. But at the time, neither was in a position to pursue a relationship with the other. The next time Kate saw Peter, they were both married to other people.

"I'm sorry," she said again, and before she changed her mind she aimed her good-night kiss unmistakably at the air beside his cheek, with her face angled away, for the avoidance of doubt. She marched to the elevator, to her room, she flung herself on the bed, her fingers working manically, her fantasies exceptionally vivid—this bed, now, me, him—and she came quickly and then again, fantasies intermingling with memories of that night in Morelia in the cheap hotel room where everything was done up in red and black and Gothic typefaces, Peter's tight taut body, a clump of soft threadbare sheet in her mouth—

Then she lay sprawled in the bed, panting, one hand on a breast and the other between her legs, sticky thighs, the cool of the soft sheet on her hot skin. She gathered her breath, then her phone.

She was still debating, still had time to change her mind . . .

Kate typed quickly, paused. Should she say something more? Or something else? Or just keep it simple?

Yes, simpler is better.

Good night. Wish you were here.

She hit SEND, and waited for a reply, which came quickly:

Miss you too.

Then the symbol that meant he was still typing . . . more to come . . .

Come home soon. D.

Kate felt a bit righteous, then felt guilty for feeling righteous about something that shouldn't even have been a question, taking candy from a baby, stealing from the collection jar, it goes without saying that you don't do it, and you don't congratulate yourself for not doing it.

Then she heard the knock on her door.

40

"Okay, listen, seriously: why would I do this?"

The policeman doesn't respond.

"It doesn't make any sense, surely you see that, I mean . . . Look." He takes a deep breath. Slow down, Shreve. Sound rational. "I'm successful here. I'm well-compensated, believe me. I have no debts. I'm loyal."

"Loyal? Interesting word to use in this situation. You are an American citizen. Born in America. Correct? You are loyal to America?"

"Sure."

"Yet you choose to work for a German bank? Why?"

"*Why?* What do you mean?"

"Why work for Germans, not Americans?"

"That's a crazy question. Because it's a good job. Because they pay me a lot."

"Do you *hate* Germans, Mr. Shreve? Perhaps you are Jewish?"

"I'm not."

"You hold grudges against the Nazis?"

"I'm not a *fan,* but seriously? Are you suggesting—"

"Do you have another reason to be anti-German?"

"I don't have *any* reason to be anti-German. *I'm not anti-German.*"

"Then you are angry at another business in this building? Which is it?"

With each passing question, Shreve feels more and more like he has fallen into the twilight zone, an increasing sense of disorientation that began when he was lying on the marble floor, hands behind his head, someone's foot in his back.

"The French bank? Or the expanding company?" The cop glances at his notepad. "4Syte?"

Shreve can't handle this conversation. He's crashing. "I want to speak to a lawyer." Didn't he say that already? "Didn't I say that already?"

"A solicitor? Mr. Shreve: are you . . . how shall I put this? Are you *altered*?"

Oh, wow, no, Shreve really doesn't want to go there. He's not sure, *precisely*, what crime it is, in Hong Kong, cocaine use, possession, though he's not in actual possession of any blow—is he?—no, so that doesn't matter. But could the Hong Kong police forcibly drug-test him? And is *using* cocaine an actual crime? Or buying it? Selling it, obviously, sure. But he doesn't do that. Almost ever. Never professionally.

Regardless of the criminal status of cocaine use, it obviously wouldn't *look* good, not from a law-enforcement perspective, not from an employment one. Nor for that matter from a personal one.

Christ: his mother.

But embarrassment aside, how much of a legit disaster is this? Is it possible that Shreve is going to *jail*? In Hong Kong?

The police have gotten a lot less understanding with young Anglo-expat finance guys ever since Occupy Hong Kong, and that call-girl incident with the super-disturbed Brit dude. For the entire time Shreve has lived here, local law has sadly been a lot less willing to turn the traditional blind eye toward expats' debauchery.

Shreve is sweating something fierce. The thing about Hong Kong that he didn't realize beforehand: it's tropical. Not just like South Florida, it's not Miami Beach tropical, not San Diego. It's Costa Rica tropical, equatorial. Here in this police station, it's hot as fuck.

"Lawyer," he repeats. He wouldn't be surprised if a goddamned tarantula appeared, crawled across the table. A scorpion. "Or embassy." He doesn't know which. He wants the cop to choose. "Listen," Shreve says, trying again to adopt a reasonable tone. "Listen." He has to focus here. "That thing—whatever it is, I never even *saw* it—was *not* in my bag when I left the gym. Someone must have put it in my bag when I was at the restaurant."

"Yes, you asserted that before. Why would anyone do such a thing? Explain that to me. Please. I want to understand."

"*I* don't know. I guess to get it into the building?"

"But the X-ray machines are not a secret, Mr. Shreve. The failure was foreseeable."

It's true, it doesn't make any fucking sense, nothing does, Shreve hasn't been able to come up with any plausible explanation since those first seconds lying on the lobby floor with his face pressed against the marble, an entirely new perspective on the space, the architecture, on the whole world, when your eyes are just inches off the ground, from there absolutely everything is up. Shreve was accustomed to looking down on things.

He inhabits that lobby for a few minutes every day, yet could not until today have been able to tell you what color the floor was.

"I don't know, man." Is this a *Midnight Express* scenario he's facing?

It's a peachy, rosy marble streaked with brown and magenta veins, the lobby floor.

Shreve sniffles—of course he sniffles, he's been sniffling for hours. "I really don't." And he realizes that this sniffle is a different sort, not the sniffle of someone who'd ingested eight fatties of high-grade blow, but the sniffle of someone who's being interrogated by the police halfway around the world from home, without his passport, without a lawyer, without any understanding of why someone—why anyone—would plant a bomb in his gym bag, would leave him literally holding the bag. The sniffle of someone who's crying.

41

It's good to be outside, in the semi-fresh air, surrounded by the ambient noise of Venetian life, drowning Matteo's sobbing into the purring of the *vaporetti* motors, and the water glurping in its currents and eddies, splashing against the canal banks, and the low-pitched rumble of the tradesmen's wheelbarrows laden with mortar and bricks and big bags of sand, and the tinkle-rattles of hand-trucks delivering cases of beer to the *tabaccheria,* and the scratch-scratch of a wide wicker broom against stone as the woman in the blue work-shirt sweeps the plaza, she's here every day, greeting all the other municipal workers and shopkeepers and waiters, the collective staff of the *campo.*

Around the corner, the stonemason keeps a soprano beat, chiseling away at a façade, another structure undergoing prettification. Nearly every surface in this city is visibly damaged, or eroded, chipping, falling apart, plaster giving way to the brick underneath, the brick to wood, cracks in everything, iron welts fastened to marble plinths to forestall expansion, mottled paint jobs, weeds growing from walls, peeling paint and water stains and soot streaks, the accumulated grunge of centuries, of millennia, all these blemishes somehow appealing, shabby chic.

A stroller is counterproductive here, with all the steps of all the bridges, up and down, up and down, every bridge an opportunity to jostle a child out of sleep, which is often her point in being outdoors in the first place. This is exactly why she's wandering these narrow streets now, with the baby harnessed to her chest, trying to get the little fucker to nap.

The only time she ever brings the stroller is to go to the Coop, using the thing as a dual-purpose baby carrier and shopping cart. It's a five-minute walk with two bridges to cross, six steps times two at the first, seven times two at the second, not easy, but easier than lugging groceries with the dead-weight of a child hanging off her shoulders, straining her lower back, which hasn't completely recovered from the strain of being pregnant. One of the many strains of being pregnant.

She is no whiner, no stranger to difficulty. She has done a lot of hard things. But until this baby, none of the difficulties had been surprises. She'd had no illusions about what she was attempting in her career, what adversities she'd be facing. She was prepared for all of it, she diligently managed her expectations, she always erred on the side of over-preparation, anticipating that things would be harder than they turned out to be.

There, she always thought: *that wasn't so bad.* Until this baby.

She turns off the street into a *sotoportego,* one of those low dark passageways burrowed through buildings' street levels. This one ends at a quiet narrow canal, alongside which she walks for a minute before it too ends at a small bridge, where she crosses to the other side of the canal, turns another corner.

It's quiet here, off the main *calle,* away from the tourists thronged on the banks of the Grand Canal, hanging off the Rialto. There are no landmarks here, none of Venice's top-ten must-see attractions, just normal life, small churches and modest *piazzi,* grocery stores and this *tabaccheria* here, whose owner Lorenzo lives in the neighborhood, she has met his wife, he has met her husband, they all shared a drink in the *campo* a few months ago.

Lorenzo is the type of shopkeeper who knows everyone in the neighborhood, who keeps a watchful eye on everything; the type of local who can be a real asset. He collects packages for her, important mail—her apartment's mailbox is insecure, she explained. This is one of the favors she pays him for, but mostly it's an arrangement whose main purpose is merely to have an arrangement, for the eventuality when she will really need someone to rely upon. Tonight.

"*Ciao* Susanna!" Lorenzo calls out. She waves back.

Susanna. Not exactly the name she was given at birth, but it's close, the Italian version. It's what she has been going by, here. It's her new name, part of her new life, her new plan.

What do you do when none of your schemes pan out? When everything comes crashing down—when you lose a fortune, a career, and a baby all within forty-eight hours? How do you come back from that?

Here is what she told herself: coming back is what makes you you. Coming back is how you get to deserve it. Coming back is everything. So stop your whining, get off the couch, and get the fuck back to work.

Two weeks ago, in a moment of what she now realizes was fatigue-induced delirium, she started researching babysitters, nannies, options that they'd already discussed and dismissed, decided they shouldn't pursue, couldn't do. But she was falling apart, losing confidence in her certainties.

It was then, at her weakest point, when her faith in humanity was restored, because the kid finally relented: Matteo fell asleep quickly, then slept soundly for eight hours straight. And so did she.

She awoke refreshed, amazed that it was past dawn, double-checking her clock against her watch against her phone, unwilling to believe that it was really seven-thirty in the morning.

Yes, she could make it. No need for babysitters, no strangers in this household, no way, no how. It won't be long now, and then her husband will be back, this time for good. And they will, finally, be rich.

Today is it. If all goes well, he'll be back with her tomorrow. And at this moment all seems to be going well. There's still plenty of time for everything to go sideways, but she's prepared for that too. She's prepared for everything, even the things she doesn't know to be prepared for.

She sometimes has trouble identifying what it is that she actually wants, versus what she believes she's supposed to want. In an ideal world, they'd be the same. But she doesn't live in an ideal world. No one does, though some people choose to pretend. She has never been one of them. Which is why she's walking through the streets of Venice, with her new-born snuggled against her chest, and a semiautomatic handgun in her pocket.

42

Kate waits. Office workers are pouring out on their way to lunch, the three-course prix fixe, out and back within an hour.

It shouldn't be long before Schuyler returns with the CEO himself, a guy who thinks he'll be making a fortune today. Not if Kate is right about what's going on here.

She sends another request to Dexter: *Also check to see if we have bday candles.*

He responds quickly: *Yup.* Is that snarky? Is he tired of the to-do list she's scattershooting into his day? Well, she thinks, fuck you too.

She can feel the receptionist appraising her. Kate is increasingly aware that she's illegitimate here, exposed, sitting alone with this suspicious sentinel, in an office that any second now may discover that they're being assailed, and she may look a lot like an assailant.

A new message, this one from Inez: *She is ringing bell.*

It had taken nine minutes for Schuyler to get to the apartment.

Still outside. With a woman, I believe concierge.

The previous text in Kate's stream is from school, a wordy one; the head of school is new to texting, doesn't make any attempt at brevity. *Despite today's events, we are trying to have a normal day. However, we do understand if any family would be more comfortable collecting their children, so as to be together during this stressful time. If so, please be sure to ring the main office before arriving, to facilitate a minimum of disruption. Thank you so very much.*

Normal school day.

Another ding: *She went inside.*

The kids are scratching away at math problems, they're memorizing verb conjugations, they're doing all the normal things, running around the courtyard at recess, kicking a ball, playing tag. Not huddled around screens watching footage of an ongoing terrorism event, freaking them out about a danger that's looming outside the high stone walls. It was the right decision, leaving them at school.

Kate's phone buzzes. She picks it up, listens.

"Hi Dominique, it's Schuyler?"

This is an intercept of Schuyler's phone, transmitted to Kate's line. As if Kate is on a conference call, muted: she can hear the connection, but can't participate in the conversation.

"Schuyler, ça va?"

The other call participants don't know she's listening in. This was what Kate accomplished in Schuyler's office: cloning the young woman's cellular line. You think your phone is safe, just sitting there in plain sight, home-screen locked, password-protected? You're wrong.

"No. I'm at Mr. Forsyth's apartment, talking to the security guard? He says that at a quarter after nine, a man from the US Department of State showed up, with a pair of Parisian police? The official stayed in the apartment for a half-hour, then they all left? Mr. Forsyth told the guard—his name is Didier—that they were taking him someplace secure? For his protection?"

Protection? Is that possible? Would the embassy send someone to retrieve an American executive during a terrorist attack? Maybe. But not solely because of a generalized threat. At any given moment there are tens of thousands of Americans in Paris.

"Et Colette?"

"Elle aussi, she went with Mr. Forsyth." The assistant who might be fucking him. That makes sense. *"Didier says that his instructions were to remain at the apartment, to keep it secure, for Mr. Forsyth's return? Once the attack is over?"*

If this purported protection guy isn't really State, but is actually Agency, that's more plausible. Especially if the CIA has a particular interest in Hunter Forsyth. Why would they? Maybe Forsyth's business dealings are a matter of national security. Or maybe there's a specific threat against Forsyth.

"Dominique, has anyone from the American government called Mr. Forsyth's office?"

"Non."

Or maybe Forsyth is an asset.

"Anyone unusual at all?"

"Ah . . . non."

Or maybe there's no truth whatsoever to this cockamamie-sounding explanation.

The line is silent for a few seconds, while the two 4Syte employees try to figure out what each should do next.

"We have to loop in legal, don't we?"

Kate wasn't going to answer his knock. Peter knew, obviously, that she was in the hotel room. She couldn't pretend that she wasn't there, nor that she was asleep, nor that she didn't hear it, nor that she couldn't get to the door. She was just going to not answer.

That's what she should have done; that's what she tried to do.

She failed.

Kate rose from the bed. She crossed the room. She leaned against the door, put her hand on the knob, debating, wavering . . .

She opened the door.

Peter didn't look surprised, not even relieved, it was simply what he expected. He glanced at her disarrayed blouse, her mussed-up hair, her smeared lipstick. He could see it all, the past five minutes; he could smell it.

She didn't say anything. Neither did he.

He leaned toward her, and she couldn't stop it, wouldn't, his tongue was in her mouth and hers in his, and he leaned into her, she could feel him firm against her thigh, and she grew hot again, he was pressing against her harder, and then his hand was on her leg, he had snuck up her skirt, and she felt a finger slip inside, they were standing *in the hallway,* and she thought, no, we can't do this here, not in public like this, and then she thought—no!—it's not the location that's the problem, you idiot, it's the whole thing, you can't do this—

"I can't." She pushed down her skirt, expelling his fingers, his hand. "I'm sorry."

How long were they kissing? A minute? Two?

She kept trying to give herself over to it completely, but all these other scenes came rushing at her like a collage, the stolen afternoons in out-of-the-way hotels, and the coded messages on encrypted apps, and secretly holding hands under restaurant tables, kissing in elevators and tears in taxis and ignored phone calls, cover stories about the account being hacked, *No I don't know who that is . . .*

Kate could see it all so clearly. Even though she'd never done it, and never will.

She left Seville the next day. It was a few weeks before Kate and Peter had an opportunity to be alone, truly alone, with a chance to discuss what had happened. What hadn't happened. Kate wondered if they ever would get around to talking about it, or if instead it would hang there undiscussed, uncommented upon, a sexual sword of Damocles, ready in perpetuity to fall.

Then Palermo put them in a car together, alone. They arrived two hours before the meet, to ensure that no one could get the drop, also to give them—to give Kate—plenty of time to vocalize her myriad objections. Saying them aloud made the reasons more real, transformed the solo ideas into a shared reality, this discussion building a consensus, a bulwark for a state of no-ness. Though it wasn't a discussion so much as a monologue.

"This is not a rejection of *you*," she said.

"I don't think I could live with myself," she said.

"I couldn't have you working for me," she said.

"I don't think I'd be able to talk to you ever again, or even to see you," she said.

"I couldn't do that to my husband," she said.

"I've already done too many things that were wrong," she said.

"That's not the person I want to be," she said.

"I don't think I could live with myself," she said again.

She had a lot of reasons. Some were so compelling she counted them twice.

"I *know* that this is the right path for us," she concluded. "You see that, don't you?"

"I do," he said. "You're completely right. About all of it."

And she chose to believe him, although she knew he was lying. Because so was she.

It's impossible to be certain that she didn't put Peter in harm's way purposefully. Maybe, subconsciously, she wanted to prove that she wasn't playing favorites. That this man was not her lover, just another operative, expendable, no special treatment.

Maybe it was worse. Maybe she actively hoped for something bad, something that would remove this temptation, would bury this secret forever, from everyone.

She was parked a half-block from the café where Peter would meet the asset. It was a busy street, mid-afternoon, broad daylight, plenty of witnesses. There was even a policeman at the far end of the block, staring at his phone. A safe environment.

The first thing that happened was a beat-up Skoda double-parked next to her, trapping her. The driver killed the ignition and jumped out.

"Hey!" she called, but the man ran across the street, into a shop.

Not only couldn't she pull the car out of the spot, she couldn't even open her door.

This could've been benign, but Kate knew it wasn't.

She strained her neck to see through the sidewalk crowd. Peter was in front of the café now, about to turn, but then there was fast movement from a minivan parked at the curb, its door flew open and a man emerged, and Peter turned to confront this potential menace, unaware that another man was closing in rapidly from the other direction—

"*Fuck*," Kate muttered, trying to climb over the gear shaft, into the passenger seat—

What *is* a thought? An infinitesimally small electrical charge jumping among synapses in the brain's frontal lobe. What the hell is that? Plenty of these electrical charges were hopping around Kate's brain in the space of the second it took for her to cross to the other side of the car. Intervention scenarios, rescues, shootouts on the streets of Palermo.

Plus this: maybe it's not such a bad thing, for me—for my marriage, for my life—if Peter disappears forever.

—and she reached for the door handle while this second man shoved Peter from the side, knocking him off-balance, allowing the first man to easily grab Peter from beside the van's door, and these were both big men, Kate could see they were businesslike and calm, these weren't panicked irrational hotheads, these were professionals, and it took at most two seconds before the door slid closed and the van was pulling away, while the policeman was still staring at his phone, and Kate had never even gotten herself out of the car.

This is what haunts her the most. Not the things she did, but this thing she didn't, this inaction. This shot she didn't take. This life she didn't save.

What does *deserve* mean? Who does the measuring, the meting out? What does Kate's scorecard look like?

What is she? She's a woman who has killed people, and at least one of them was innocent. She has ruined lives because it was her job. She has destroyed marriages, she has taken husbands from wives, parents from children, money and security and peace-of-mind from dozens of people. All over the world there are people who can't sleep at night because of what Kate did. Because someone told her to, and she didn't say no.

Has she been a good worker, using her employer's resources for her own agenda? A good parent, actively choosing not to stay home with her children, perhaps even putting them in peril because of her professional choices? A good wife, standing in a hotel hall, another man's fingers bringing her to the brink?

Kate had stayed in Seville for too long—longer than had strictly been necessary. By the time she came home to Paris on a Sunday night, Ben had fallen sick again, his medications run out. She hadn't been around to prevent it.

She took her little boy straightaway to the hospital, and sat there in the waiting room, wondering: what does a person like Kate Moore deserve?

Kate shifts the phone to her other ear. She has noticed that her hearing is no longer as strong in one ear, but sometimes she forgets which.

A double-whammy of hearing loss exacerbated by memory loss. It's humiliating, and no one even knows about it. She almost told Dexter, but something held her back.

She wishes some doctor would present her with a chart, or a timeline: which bodily functions she can expect to fail, with what speed and level of discomfort and inconvenience, beginning when, lasting for what duration, and ending with what level of incapacitation.

"*Sans doute, we must cancel the press conference, Schuyler.*" This is a new call that Schuyler is on, with the lawyer.

Eyesight, hearing, knees, lower back, libido, hips, hair loss, menopause, breast cancer. It's all just a matter of time, isn't it?

"*We cannot have la presse here and Monsieur Forsyth does not arrive. Even if it would be possible to keep the fact of his disappearance secret— which I do not think would be possible—it would still be a large problem to cancel when reporters are here, asking their questions, with their recording devices.*"

"*Agreed, Aurélie.*"

"*We must inform the board of directors, immédiatement.*" The woman sighs. "*Mon Dieu.*"

There are legal ramifications to a situation like this, a missing CEO during a terrorism event. Responsibilities that employees have to their boards, to shareholders, perhaps to police, to other authorities.

"*When the stock market opens in New York—*"

The ramifications are immense, for 4Syte's employees, its investors, shareholders.

"*—ça sera une catastrophe.*"

Yes, it certainly will be a catastrophe.

But that's when Kate realizes: not for everyone.

She has to get the hell out of here—

43

Think, Hunter tells himself: is it possible that the CIA would use a phone that had been manufactured in China, embedded with who knows what hidden technologies, or compromised microchips, or surreptitious recording mechanisms, or remote-activation triggers, or fiber-optic splices?

It seems so unlikely. But that's not the same as impossible.

He looks around at the curtains that hide the boarded-up windows, at the triple-locked door, at the American sitting at the small dining table, leafing through a newspaper. The guy looks like he knows his way around a fistfight. That cheap hopsack suit isn't hiding a spare-tire belly, his hands look like they've never met a manicure.

Think this through again.

Okay, yes: it does make sense that a CIA babysitter wouldn't allow a man like Hunter Forsyth to walk out this door, into a dangerous environment, when the Agency has been tasked with keeping him safe. If something awful happened, the babysitter would lose his job. Maybe end up investigated by the Senate, his own Benghazi, a public outcry, talk-show humiliations, criminal charges.

But what could be the excuse for detaining Colette? She's not a kidnapping target. Sure, the CIA would be worried about her blowing the location, but how important is that? Couldn't they just shut down this safehouse? Or hustle Colette out the same way they hustled her in?

She shouldn't be here. Hunter shouldn't have insisted that she come, that was selfish of him, greedy. He put her in harm's way.

But then again, he can't help thinking: Colette makes it two against one.

And: Hunter will have the element of surprise on his side.

And: Hunter is a strong man, he's fit, he has fast reflexes. Plus he knows how to throw a punch. Or at least he did, twenty years ago. Twenty-five.

And: maybe Colette can be useful, at the very least a distraction. She sure as hell distracts Hunter. She could distract any man, couldn't she?

But, on the other hand: Simpson is probably armed, and the cops outside too.

But, without a doubt: Simpson is trained in hand-to-hand combat.

But: if the CIA wouldn't buy a Chinese-made phone, that means that Simpson is not CIA, so what the fuck is he?

Every answer is more terrifying than the last, all variations on the same theme: Hunter has not really been taken under the protective embrace of an American diplomat or intelligence officer.

Hunter's pulse is racing, brain growing fuzzy with increasing panic.

What has happened to him is something much less outlandish, much more predictable, a contingency that he has foreseen, for which he has planned. His security chief, his international bodyguard teams, the motion-detector alarms, the armored cars, the whole thing, hundreds of thousands of dollars per year that Hunter Forsyth spends to try to prevent this very thing from happening.

He's almost sure of it now. Because he just realized what it was that was bothering him three hours ago, when they first arrived at this ostensible safe-house: how the fuck did Simpson get its keys?

PART III

PALAIS-ROYAL

44

"*M*adame?"

Kate pretends to be startled. "*Oui?*"

"I am *directeur* of communications. Can I be of some assistance?"

"I'm waiting for Schuyler Franks."

"*Oui.* And you are who, please?"

"My name is Lindsay Davis." Behind Kate, in the hall, the elevator door dings. She should've left already, when it was easy. Now it's going to be harder.

"Please, what is it you are doing here?"

"I told you, I'm—"

"Yes, *mais pourquoi?* Why, Madame, are you here to see Schuyler Franks? *Why?*"

Kate can feel the air pressure change as the glass door is opened. She doesn't need to look over her shoulder to know who has arrived. "It's personal."

"Sandrine?" The woman cuts her eyes toward the receptionist. "*Appelle la police.*"

"I'm sorry." Kate turns toward the door, which a security guard is now blocking. "There must be some confusion."

The guard takes a lumbering step forward, asserting his presence. He's a big guy, but not a hard-looking one. He's big and soft and slow moving, the type of large animal that looks a lot like prey to a smaller, agile, more vicious species.

"Perhaps I should leave," Kate says, smiling at the guard. He doesn't smile back. She reaches down to collect her bag, filled with sunglasses and wallet and lipstick and keys, and this box of Lego, and a packet of the biscuits that Ben likes, because you never know.

The guard is holding a walkie-talkie in one hand, a phone in the other, neither hand anywhere near his holster, both engaged in something that's not protecting himself. Maybe he's too dim-witted to think Kate could be a threat, or too dim-witted to do anything about it. Either way, his wits are not luminous. Kate feels sorry for him. It's possible that she really does have an enemy out there, intent on doing her and her family grievous harm, but this security guard isn't him. Or her.

"Please tell Mademoiselle Franks that I'll return when it's more convenient."

Kate can't allow herself to be detained by this rent-a-cop, to be questioned by the genuine police. She has a cover story, of course, a legend that will stand up to casual questioning, a set of rehearsed answers that paint a perfectly credible picture, as long as there's no compelling reason to believe otherwise, no conflicting evidence. But if the police and intelligence coordinate on a deep-dive into her life? Dexter's? On a matter of terrorism? Her legend might be able to withstand that level of scrutiny, but her husband would not be able to withstand that sort of interrogation.

Kate takes another step toward the guard, slowly, nonthreatening, continuing to wear a placid smile.

What at first looked like a holster is on second glance just a tool belt. A place to hang a walkie-talkie, a flashlight, a nylon pouch that holds whatever, but not a gun. Probably snacks. He's a potbellied man who seems to push out his stomach purposefully, accentuating his roundness, proclaiming, *That's right, I'm fat. What's it to you?*

And she's just a woman! The guard doesn't sense any challenge here, he's a big man in uniform, an authority, there's no way that she'd—

Kate lands her punch directly on the front of the nose, and he never even twitches a muscle to defend himself. After the fact, he now raises both hands to the pain in the middle of his face, protecting against a further onslaught of the same. But this is a counterproductive instinct, because not only does he conk himself in the middle of the forehead with his walkie-talkie, he also leaves his entire body exposed.

She now has her choice of unmissable targets, an embarrassment of riches. But this one's a no-brainer, the blow that she knows has zero chance of failure.

The noise he makes is subhuman.

The reassuring thing about perpetrating violence with your hard knee against someone's soft crotch is that you're in no danger of injuring yourself. Punching is risky; people break their fingers all the time. Kicking too, if you don't know what you're doing, an unrehearsed swift kick could land you on your own ass.

The guard doubles over, totters, then collapses.

Kate is coiled, her whole body tingling with tensed muscles, with adrenaline. She looms above the writhing pile of a person, ready to strike again. But it's clear that this guy isn't getting up anytime soon, he can barely breathe. Kate doesn't want to kill this innocent sap by mistake, doesn't want to send him to the hospital, doesn't want to give the police any additional motivation to go looking for her too hard, tomorrow.

So that's enough.

Kate realizes that she's disappointed. It has been a while since she hit anyone. This felt good. She wants to do more of it.

The director of communications is standing a few feet away, hand held up to her aghast mouth; the receptionist too is frozen. Kate doesn't want to hit either of these women. But there is a specific woman Kate suddenly wants to punch in the face.

"*Désolée*," she mutters at the guard, then rushes to the elevator, hits the call button, thinking that if the elevator isn't waiting here she'll take the stairs, but the door does open immediately, because the guard arrived only thirty seconds ago.

Life would be a lot easier if the things that felt good were also the right things. But Kate is pretty sure that the truth is closer to the contrary.

45

Hunter's stomach sinks with a whoosh, as if in a roller coaster's front car that has crested the apex and is now free-falling, and you're wondering if the descent is going to continue to accelerate forever, or if you'll discover some alternative explanation, backing up from terminal velocity, some other answer to this question, an answer that doesn't mean that something horrible is going on here.

Simpson should not have the keys to this apartment. If this guy really is from State, or CIA, the only reason he'd already be in possession of these keys—on their own key ring—is if he knew he'd be using this safehouse today. Yet it was supposedly only after Hunter's pressure that he reluctantly agreed to come here. Which meant he'd been dishonest to Hunter. Which in the abstract is fine with Hunter, he's not anti-lie, there are plenty of legitimate reasons for dishonesty. He himself lies often. But always for a clear purpose. What purpose did Simpson's misrepresentation serve? Why did he pretend to need to search for a safehouse, when he was already carrying the keys to one?

If it were just the keys, or just the Chinese-manufactured phone, Hunter could discount it. One misgiving could be a fluke, paranoia, misunderstanding. Two is a legitimate suspicion. Three pieces of corroborating evidence? That's not a coincidence; that's a conspiracy. That's what he needs to test, right now.

⚜

He runs through it again, his rationale, the rebuttal, the counterargument for one or another of Simpson's responses, the credibility of Hunter's replies, the viability of the whole plan. It's like a logic problem, a chess match.

He certainly hopes he's wrong, he has never in his life hoped so fervently to be so wrong.

Hunter's phone is still useless as a communication device to the outside world. Is it really possible that there's no cell service anywhere in Paris? All carriers? For hours on end?

Maybe. All the towers could be somehow compromised. Or all the networks breached, disabled. Or all the signals scrambled by some EMP. Hunter is looking for reasons, he wants to believe in them. Because if not? What are the other possibilities?

One: there is no Paris-wide telecom outage, but just something specific to him—to his phone, or to his physical environment. What? An exterior signal-jamming device could have been used at the apartment, and another here in the safehouse.

Two: his phone has been disabled from within. Simpson did take possession of Hunter's device, back at the apartment, supposedly trying to help. But he could have been installing malware, disabling cellular, he could have done so many things that would render the phone inoperable in ways that Hunter wouldn't be able to observe.

And yes, the guy did something with Colette's phone too.

And yes, of course—*of course*—the wifi service here would not work. Nor would this landline, this piece of consumer electronics manufactured in China, of all the unlikely origins for telecommunications equipment procured by an American intelligence service.

So, okay, let's say that this is what did happen: it's specifically Hunter and Colette whose communications have been cut off. With no way to find out what's going on in the world. No way to tell anyone where he is. No way to reassure anyone. Why?

Is there more than the one obvious explanation?

Hunter's chest grows tight again, this panicky feeling, this unfamiliar sensation. Hunter is not a panicky person, never has been. That's the essence of him: *not* panicky. Ask anyone, that's what they'll tell you: Hunter Forsyth, dude has balls of brass.

He tries to take a deep breath, but it doesn't work, he's not getting enough oxygen.

"*Monsieur?*" Colette is standing over him, concerned. She puts a hand on his shoulder, a soft touch.

"I'm okay," he says, even though he isn't, and she didn't ask. "How are you doing?"

"*Pas mal,*" she says. That's the worst that Colette would ever admit: not bad. And when the French say "not bad," what they usually mean is: pretty damn good. Colette is not a complainer. She's a pillar of strength, Colette is.

Christ, he loves her so much.

He wonders what she thinks is going on here, if she's imagining the same scenarios he is. Maybe she got there long ago, even before Hunter. Maybe she has known all along, and has somehow remained poised, placid, unpanicked—

Wait a second—

No. There's no way. That's a ridiculous thought.

But is it? Is it *really* impossible?

No.

Okay, what if she is? What if Colette is in on this whole thing? And he tries to enlist her in this plan to escape? Then what?

Then, obviously, Hunter will be fucked. But will he be any more fucked than he is already?

No, he literally shakes his head at himself: she can't be, not Colette.

Get your shit together. This is your company that's in danger, your future. Maybe even your life, and the woman you love. *Everything* is at stake. Now is not the time to start being a wimp, not the time to devolve into stress-induced paranoia. Now is the time to man up, as Forsyth men have always done.

Hunter's grandfather went to law school after Korea, then joined the same firm where his own father had worked, then moved to in-house counsel at a multinational, where he eventually rose to CEO. Albert Forsyth had chosen the right path in the 1950s and '60s.

Hunter's dad Thatcher embarked on his career in the early '70s in the fledgling investment-banking sector, a wave he rode through the obscene '80s to its residential apogee in Greenwich, Connecticut, where his cohort of robber barons headquartered their hedge funds, built their trophy houses where trophy wives raised trophy children, trophy cars in the driveway, trophy everything.

Trophy son Hunter Forsyth was vaguely aware of the tech boom even before it existed. After Yale he went West to business school and then one startup after another until pay-dirt. Just a matter of time. Not a question of if, but simply when.

All the Forsyth men had been in the right places for their times. They'd all made their own fortunes in their own ways, and though none would deny that they were helped by the successes of their forebears, they'd all deem that help to be incremental, incidental.

They all learned, as boys, to box. Hunter remembers his first lessons at Grandpa's greenhouse, which had been transformed into a gymnasium, with a rowing tank and a lap pool, a weight room and a basketball half-court and the leather-scented boxing corner with a speed bag, a heavy bag, a canvas ring, pairs of red-and-white gloves in various sizes hanging from wooden pegs.

How old was he? Six? Seven? He remembers not being able to reach the speed bag, Grandma helping get the gloves on and off. He remembers it was fun.

As a teenager, Hunter boxed in a gym out in White Plains; boxing was no longer something that went on in the types of schools he attended, no longer a gentleman's sport. Everyone else he met at Power Boxing was a minority or poor, mostly both. These guys were—still are—Hunter's main exposure to ethnic and economic diversity.

When he was a teenager, Hunter used to have fantasies that boxing would one day be real-world useful. That he'd find himself cornered by bullies at school—never happened—or confronted by muggers in a dark alleyway—ditto—or he'd be a senator, or maybe even president, and they'd kidnap him—the Soviets, the Colombian cartels—and they'd never suspect that he possessed this secret lethal skill, which is what he would use to save himself, and the beautiful woman too.

In this fantasy, there was always a beautiful woman. In every fantasy.

"Colette?"

"Oui Monsieur?"

"May I borrow your phone? I'd like to give you some notes on calls for you to make, when we're finally finished here. We're going to have a lot of catching up to do."

"Calls?" This is not really what Colette does.

Hunter meets her eye, trying to communicate that this isn't a debate, she just needs to obey. "That's right." His gaze is level and unwavering, and he hopes she understands what he's communicating.

"*Très bien.*"

He sees her cut her eyes to Simpson, then back. She unlocks her phone, hands it over.

"*Merci,*" he says, with a gentle nod, trying to soften the exchange.

He tells himself again that this is a smart thing to do. He starts to type, using more words than normal, being less economical. He needs to be clear more than he needs to be quick.

"Here." He extends the device. "Why don't you look this over now? Let me know if you have any questions."

At the very bottom, he'd typed, *DO NOT ask any questions. If you have not understood something, type your question, then hand back to me.*

Hunter stands above Colette. After she has read the opening lines, she's going to look at him with a question in her eyes, and he's going to nod in confirmation.

Do not panic, his note begins. *I think we may have been kidnapped.*

46

They tried, using a bullhorn, first in French, then English, then Arabic and Farsi and maybe Urdu, he stopped paying full attention. It could not matter, anything they were saying. Later, they tried Arabic again. He never responded to any of it.

There is no way to be ready for this, Mahmoud knows that. He might have told himself that he would be prepared, convinced himself that he knew what it would eventually feel like. But he always understood, on some level, that he had been deceiving himself.

He has now been standing here for four hours. He has taken thousands of breaths in this courtyard, with so many weapons pointing at him, the long-range rifles on the rooftops, the assault weapons, the automatic handguns. He is just a split-second from being blown to smithereens by the twitch of some stranger's finger. Then again, so is everyone.

Any of these breaths may have been his last, but turned out to not be. Maybe the next will be.

Or the next.

Or the next.

He tries again to focus on the good that will come. On the bad that will be avoided. Both sides helped make his decision, that late afternoon, sitting in the quiet room alone with the bearded American.

"A boy and a girl," Mahmoud said. "As I indicated on your questionnaire."

The man nodded, looking sympathetic, saying nothing, as usual. This was their fifth meeting.

The paperwork was something Mahmoud had been handed in front of the hospital, where an attractive woman stood near the entrance that was used by his ward's patients. She was offering fifty euros for nothing really, just an initial survey, it would take only a few minutes. Then another five hundred—five hundred euros!—for participating in the full study, long-term.

Or as long-term as possible. Given the obvious limitations.

The survey was highly personal: physical questions, medical history, even religious beliefs, philosophical, sexual. It was being conducted by an American institute, an organization that Mahmoud researched for a few minutes to satisfy himself that it was not an identity-theft scam. Mahmoud could not imagine why anyone would want to steal his identity, or what such a theft would entail. But this had become a subject people discussed, without knowing what they were talking about. As with many things.

The institute was headquartered in Boston; the European outpost was in Geneva.

"How old?"

"Four and six."

"So, after . . . what is going to happen to your children?"

"My wife's family, in Egypt. We have already made the arrangements."

"Do your in-laws have money?"

Mahmoud was sure that this man already knew the answer. He did not like this type of question, this conversational game. He did not answer.

"No, I do not suppose they do." The man sighed, as if disappointed in the answer that he himself provided. "But they could, Mahmoud."

"They could what?"

"They could have money, your in-laws. Plenty of money. Enough to ensure that they will be comfortable. That your children will be educated, have opportunities."

Their previous meetings had focused on Mahmoud's illness, his prospects. But the conversations had also veered into politics, into religion. It was an unusual relationship they had been developing for a few weeks.

Then one day the man had a proposition. Something Mahmoud could do, before he died, that would benefit his family immensely, after he was gone. The man had not explained immediately, had left Mahmoud wondering for a week. Dreaming. Wanting. Trying to guess what this man could possibly want that Mahmoud might be able to provide. There were not many explanations.

"Could my children live in America?"

"Perhaps. But that is not something we can arrange. We cannot offer papers. What we can offer is money."

Mahmoud was becoming increasingly convinced that this man was going to propose something illegal, something immoral, something horrible. But Mahmoud was reluctant to confront that obstacle head-on.

"How much?"

"Well, that depends. How much do you think you need?"

Mahmoud did not want to commit to anything—he did not even want to frame the negotiation—until he had a better idea of what was going on. "What is it that I would have to do?"

"As I have said, it will be only one day's work. Some training beforehand, but that will be incidental." The man made a dismissive face. "It is not a complicated job, physically. There is nothing you need to know how to do. Nothing you need to learn."

That was when Mahmoud began to understand. The most obvious answer is usually correct. Occam's razor, he had learned about it in school.

"You will not suffer a long, painful decline. Your children will not watch you wither away. You will not spend all your family's money buying yourself tortured extra days. You will not lose control of your body. You will not endure one sleepless night after another. You will not spend months in and out of hospitals, and hospice. You will not leave behind a mountain of debt."

Those were very compelling points.

"Instead what you will leave behind, Mahmoud, is a fortune."

"That sounds too easy. Too good to be true."

"Well, yes. It is not all going to be easy."

They sat in silence for a moment. This man was comfortable with silence.

"I am not a violent person," Mahmoud said, eventually.

The American nodded.

"I do not believe in violence."

The American remained silent.

"How many?" Mahmoud asked.

"How many what?"

"How many people would I need to kill?"

47

At the foot of a bridge she comes to a sudden stop, and spins around, starts walking back quickly in the other direction, as if she'd just realized something urgent, she left the stove on, the door open.

Susanna scans the faces in front of her, but doesn't see him. He's gone, the man she thought might be following her. She's relieved, but also a bit frustrated. If someone were following her, she could elude him, solve the problem. But if there's no one there, the problem is simply her nerves, her mind. Less easy to solve.

She has no one to blame but herself, not even her husband, and she has come to understand that being able to easily assign blame is one of the chief advantages of having a husband. But she knows that all this is her own doing. She's the one who desperately wanted to have a child; he was ambivalent about parenthood. She's the one who thought they should settle here, live this life. She's the one who came up with the new complicated plan, not to mention the old complicated plan. She's the one who put everything at risk, again.

For a while it looked as if childbearing was going to pass her by. That too was her own fault. She hadn't taken any of her relationships seriously, hadn't been attuned to the ticking of her clock. It turns out that if you wait until your career is fully established, your window is small, and it was nearly shut by the time she found the right man, almost by mistake.

And, being completely honest: he isn't necessarily the right man. Plus: they didn't find each other so much as they were thrust together by happenstance. Theirs was a professional partnership, arranged by management. They lived together, they shared a home, meals, vacations, sometimes they even shared a bed, though not conjugally; they both knew that sex would be a mistake. All the while, he was more than happy to find his outlets elsewhere—other men's wives, or young women in bars, one-night stands that didn't even last a whole night, stumbling home at two A.M., smelling like women who weren't her. But what did she care.

Except she did, a little bit.

She couldn't bring herself to behave the same way. She told herself that it could compromise her cover, jeopardize her mission, but that was only partially true, and became less true over time, until the night when she crept into his bed in the middle of the night, when their mission was near its end, at its most exciting, and she just couldn't help herself anymore. She knew he'd be good in bed; she didn't know how much she'd enjoy it.

She slows her pace. Is it? Yes, it's silence that she hears. Golden silence, silken silence, the warm-bath embrace of silence, better than Champagne and caviar, better than the famous duck at La Tour d'Argent, better than the very best sex. Nothing compares to the onset of silence from a crying baby.

Three years ago, if you'd have asked her what she'd be doing today, she'd never in her wildest dreams have predicted this. Married to that hopefully reformed cad, wandering the streets of Venice with their napping baby. The handgun in her pocket was the only predictable element.

She stopped walking in the middle of a narrow lane, became one of those pedestrian obstructions that makes her want to throttle heedless tourists.

With the baby asleep, and currently no crisis, she should eat, take care of her own physical needs while she has this chance. Another lesson from parenthood. There have been many teachable moments.

"*Ciao Susanna.*"

"*Ciao Guido.*"

"*Aperol spritz?*"

She would love to have her regular drink, sitting here in the Campo de la Pescaria, facing the Grand Canal, sun in her face, beautiful baby sleeping in her lap, net worth skyrocketing by the second.

"*No, grazie.*" No alcohol today, not even a sip. There still might be plenty of action in front of her. She orders mineral water, seafood risotto.

Her phone buzzes, an incoming text: *All ok?*

Richie Fucking Benedetti. Who'd have thought he'd turn out to be a pussy?

She's had enough of him, and his ilk. She's been interacting with scum for her whole life, she can feel the film of it coating her, she can't wash it off, it has seeped into her bloodstream, infected her, she recognizes this, an awareness that has heightened since Matteo was born, after so much effort, so many tears.

It's amazing that there's any path from being this innocent baby to becoming a Richie Benedetti. Or to becoming herself. She can't let either happen. This has become her primary goal, the organizing principle of her life from now on.

Starting tomorrow.

Yes, she types her reply, *all ok,* and hopes it's true.

When everything had been figured out, the final hurdle was securing the investment capital. If they landed just one big fish, others would fall into place, buoyed by someone else's confidence. That was the way these things worked.

This wasn't an opportunity they could take wide. The opposite. There was a very finite population of individuals who'd be willing to participate in this endeavor, and an even smaller subset she'd be willing to trust with it.

For better or worse, both her and her husband's careers had afforded a broad acquaintance with exactly the sorts of people who'd be interested in this investment. But the first candidates had declined, and she was losing confidence.

"Are you sure about this guy?" her husband asked, just steps from the hotel's revolving door.

They were running out of money, which is the same as running out of time, living on an ever thinner cushion of savings. Sicily had been an inexpensive place to live, and they'd been comfortable enough there, and for logistical reasons they'd wanted their kid to be born there. But they didn't want to raise a child there; they didn't want Sicily to be their permanent home.

"Am I *sure*? No. Obviously."

"It's not too late. We could . . ." He raised a hand to indicate the network of canals, boats, escape to other places, other possibilities. Her husband wore the cloak of a supremely confident man, a handsome man, a man who was good at everything; he had no doubts about his abilities to ski a steep bumpy slope, repair simple machinery, get a woman into bed. Trivial matters. It was the larger challenges that made him doubt himself.

"This is going to work," she reassured him. That was one of her roles in their relationship. Their partnership.

That was all he needed. He nodded, turned to the revolving door, which a navy-suited man had already launched into motion. Guests here didn't even need to push a door, the staff would do anything you wanted, fetch anything, arrange anything.

Upstairs, Richie Benedetti sat in a wingback chair, facing the terrace over the Grand Canal. He'd draped himself in a big British newspaper, and crossed his legs the tough-guy way, displaying every contour of his ball sack in his tight custom-tailored suit pants, a long expanse of brightly patterned socks, suede loafers with a garish logo.

Richie was small-time wiseguy from South Philly who'd turned into a halfway-connected mobster, then he stumbled first into a fortune and then into a quagmire and subsequently into the witness-protection program in North Carolina, from which he grew bored and skipped out to reunite himself with the money he'd squirreled away in a diverse portfolio of Italian real estate, Swiss numbered accounts, and Monacan safety deposit boxes. Richie wasn't a devotee of traditional market-based securities. This was going to make the pitch both easier and harder. Because this opportunity was both a traditional security and the complete opposite.

"Hi Richie," she said. "Long time."

Richie looked her up and down, took in her distended belly, her new hair. "A pleasure. Who's your friend?"

"This friend is my husband Chris."

Richie didn't stand to shake the new man's hand. "That's quite a beard you're sporting. What are you, some kinda hipster?"

"Something like that."

Richie turned back to her. "You won't mind if I have Gianna check you both out, will you?"

Susanna glanced at Gianna, bee-stung lips and jet-black hair and gravity-defying tits.

"No problem," Susanna said. "But we're going to have to check you too."

"You're fuckin' kiddin' me."

"Nope."

Richie contemplated the situation, shrugged. He wasn't wearing a wire, wasn't carrying, there was nothing to find. He didn't love the prospect of sacrificing his dignity by submitting to a pat-down, not at this stage in his life, but he understood the necessity. No one could trust anyone, not in his line of work. Not in anyone's. And he'd long ago relinquished his dignity to this woman. He no longer gave much of a shit.

"Phones?"

Everyone handed their mobiles to the bodyguard, who left the room.

"How's life treating you, Richie?"

Benedetti adjusted his heavy silk tie, one of those unmistakable patterns that certain men recognize, it's like a secret handshake, hey, look, we're both guys who spend a couple of hundred dollars on neckties.

"Can't complain."

He looked like part of the décor, decorated in that maximalist Italian fashion of velvet and silk, gold-leaf and marble.

"You enjoying life on Lake Como?"

Richie was a fourth-generation Italian-American whose ma cooked tuna casserole and meatloaf, not Sunday gravy. He learned everything he needed about being a guinea gangster from *The Godfather* and *The Sopranos,* and spent four decades fake-rhapsodizing about the old country that he'd always avoided visiting, too worried that reality would disappoint, that he'd be mocked for not speaking the language.

When he needed to start a new life, he finally made good on his supposed fantasy. He bought a modest villa on the lake, probably thinking he'd be hanging out with George Clooney.

"Sure, it's a nice place. But what are we doin' here?"

"No pleasantries, Richie?"

"You know I ain't that pleasant a guy. And you were never that pleasant to me, were you? So." He turned up one corner of his mouth, a sneering smile that's laughing at you, not with you. She really despised assholes like Richie. But that's how the world works, isn't it? For anything involving big money, you have to deal with big-money assholes.

"Okay, Richie." She was about to launch into it, but just then the bodyguard reentered, delivering their *espressi,* swiping lemon peels across the rims of the glasses, one, two, three of them. Then the factotum retreated.

"How much money do you have?"

Richie sneered again. "You fuckin' kiddin' me?"

"I'm going to guess somewhere between twenty and thirty mil." She used to have surreptitious access to Richie's financial situation. Not recently. "Am I right?"

He shrugged.

"That's certainly enough to live on for the rest of your life, I guess. As long as you don't go doing anything stupid like buying jets." She knew for a fact that he'd recently bought a jet. "But you're continuing to hustle, aren't you? Putting your neck out. Juggling this, juggling that, exposing yourself to people you don't—"

"We here to go over my whole, what, résumé? That's not so interestin' to me. I'm already familiar with the particulars. So why don't you tell me the fuck you want?"

She leaned forward. "How'd you like to double your money, Richie?"

He rolled his eyes. "Sure, I'd like that very much."

"In a couple of months."

His eyebrows shot up.

"Without hurting anyone. Or lifting a finger."

Go through it chronologically, she reminded herself. Richie was a guy who needed a story to be linear. Visual too.

"At eight in the morning, we call in a bomb threat to the police. A single device, deposited in a train station. The police radios will crackle with reassignments, calls to action. Units will rush to the scene, drawing forces from elsewhere. Trains will be canceled. Media will gather."

Richie could see this. He nodded.

"This bomb will be a few sticks of TNT in a backpack, a detonator wired to a disposable mobile. But this bomb isn't there to explode. It's to draw the police. And to establish an aura of terror, first thing in the morning. During the next half-hour, while the police are swarming the train station, we plant a handful of other devices at high-visibility sites. To cap it all off, a man walks into the middle of the museum's courtyard, wearing a suicide vest, which draws every last cop from their normal assignments."

"So, what? You robbin' a bank?" Richie needs to prove how smart he is, which is actually not that smart. "This a heist?"

"One of these normal assignments is to guard the home of an

American CEO who spends time in Europe. This police escort is a privilege he pays for under the table."

This was something Richie could respect. He'd paid for more than his fair share of cops over the years. But sadly there was no buying off feds, at least not American ones. That's what got him exiled.

"The threats will be all over, alerts will be popping up on everyone's phones, coverage will blanket the media, there will be video of this backpack sitting in the station, being approached by a bomb-dismantling robot. Sharing a split-screen with an aerial view of the museum, a suicide bomber standing in the center. Utter terror."

Richie was nodding again.

"So the CEO understands it when his police escort abandons its post. Just minutes later, reinforcements arrive—policemen in one car, an American official in another, a middle-aged guy from the State Department, sent on a crucial mission to protect a prominent American citizen during a moment of extreme peril. Because not only is the city under attack, but a threat has been made against Americans. Specifically against prominent American businessmen. This is a man who always thinks of himself as the smartest guy in the room. So he's proud of figuring out that a person like this bureaucrat, claiming to be from State and showing up in this situation, is lying. And because he's so damn smart, he knows what the lie is."

Richie leaned back, trying himself to be that damn smart too. "CIA."

"Exactly. At the same time that the police escort is called away, the CEO's cell service disappears. Because the trunk of the police car contains a powerful mobile device that jams any and all mobile-phone and data service."

"How do you get the squad car?"

"We don't. We're using an unmarked car. If we need to explain this, it's because all the cruisers have been deployed to the sites of the bombs. Extra personnel have been called in for the emergencies, more bodies than vehicles, et cetera. But we have the siren, a couple of other official-looking accessories."

"What about the CEO's landline?"

"One of the cops heads to the basement to cut the wires, taking out cable and Internet and landline telephone. This complete comms blackout, combined with the citywide attack, makes the CEO very anxious, impatient. Our State-slash-CIA official offers to try to fix the CEO's cell phone, but fails. Sorry, he says, I couldn't help."

"He doesn't really try?"

"He disables everything, including all geo-location services. So as the minutes tick by, the CEO grows increasingly frustrated. He demands a solution."

"The embassy?"

"That's his first request. Not possible, our guy says, embassy in total lockdown. So the CEO demands other options. Our guy hems and haws, doesn't want to offer the thing that everyone knows he can offer. But eventually he relents, says he'll look into finding a situation. After an understandable delay, he does find a secure location that has working telecom."

"A CIA safehouse."

"Exactly right, Richie. Though that's not the phrase our guy uses, because a CIA officer wouldn't. But this CEO, he's a man of the world, he knows what's what. This appeals to his sense of his own importance. Plus to everyone's romance about the Agency. A CIA safehouse! He wants to see this."

"So you're saying that the CEO *demands* his own kidnapping?" He was nodding appreciatively. "Jeez."

"And that, Richie, is how you kidnap a high-value, high-net-worth target who maintains twenty-four-hour, three-sixty-five armed guards, without hurting anyone."

It was beginning to make sense to Richie, but he saw some holes, wanted to poke at them, see how big they'd grow.

"This is a very complicated plan for a kidnapping. Why don't you just kill the guard, snatch your hostage by force?"

"That's a good question, Richie. Why do you think?"

The guy squinted again, mouth hanging open, like the illustrated-dictionary picture of a dunce trying hard to figure out something. "Afraid of drawing attention?"

"Not especially. I think we could discretely effectuate a quiet abduction in a simpler fashion. We'd still have to draw away the police, but we could do that without a terrorist attack against an entire city."

She could see Richie thinking, his eyes darting around. Then they opened wide, and refocused on her. "You don't want anyone to know that he's been kidnapped."

She smiled. "Not even *he* will know he's been kidnapped."

"Then why doesn't he just walk out the door?"

"Remember, this escape to a safehouse, that's his own suggestion. The city is under attack! And he specifically has been targeted. The CIA has received direct orders—from the highest level—to keep this VIP off the streets, safe from abduction, from assassination, from all sorts of terrifying possibilities. Even if the CEO demands his freedom, our guy simply cannot let him go. For his own good."

"But what if he refuses to kidnap himself from the get-go? What if he *doesn't* demand to be taken someplace else?"

"Unlikely. He'll be desperate to resume communications. To explain his disappearance. To be in touch. To run the empire that he believes only he can run."

"Sure. *But.*"

"In that unlikely case, our man will claim to receive new info from the police radio. The situation out in the streets has deteriorated, there are now explicit orders from the DCI to remove the high-value target to a secure location."

"DCI?"

"Director of Central Intelligence."

"And if he still doesn't agree to this?"

"He'll be forced to. For his own good."

"By just this one fake CIA guy?"

"Also the pair of cops. In uniform. Armed."

"Why cops? Why not American army?"

"The local-law look might come in handy if the team ends up interacting with citizens out in the streets. No one is going to challenge a local cop during a terror attack."

"What about the CEO's security? Why doesn't he bring along his muscle?"

"That's one of the benefits of making it the CEO's idea to leave the apartment: his only option is to go to a safehouse, so it's on the CIA's terms. And his guard is local, not an American citizen, so he can't be allowed into any secure Agency facility."

"Is that true?"

"None of these people will know it isn't."

"Once this guy is at this facility, what if he asks to leave?"

"We tell him he can't."

"If he disagrees?"

"We have three armed men on-site. Our holding area—the safe-house—is an unoccupied building; condemned, scheduled for demolition."

"If he tries to escape?"

"We'll subdue him."

"If that fails?"

"At the end of the day, Richie, I really don't give a shit what happens to this guy."

"But you're not going to *kill* him?"

"Ideally, no."

Richie had been following along more or less successfully to this point, but now he became lost. "I don't understand."

"What part?"

Richie looked exasperated; his short fuse was burning quickly. "If you kill him, how the fuck are you gonna get a ransom?"

She leaned back, let her hands rest on her protruding belly. She used to be annoyed by all those pregnant women who couldn't stop cradling their bellies, something self-satisfied about it. Now look.

"Who said anything"—she allowed a smile to spread across her lips, she couldn't help it—"about a ransom?"

48

As soon as the elevator doors begin to open, Kate can see that a security team is crossing the courtyard, headed in her direction— She flattens herself against the wall, out of view, and reaches over to hit the door-close button, again, *again*—

Closing . . . closing . . .

Finally.

She presses −2, which is neither the next level down nor the lowest, both too obvious.

This building must have an exit other than the front door, a place for loading bays, service elevators, delivery entrances, fire exits, all accessible from the *sous-sols* levels, the garage, mechanicals, a warren of tunnels, of corridors that connect one wing to another. Kate has been beneath plenty of these old European buildings, and they're all similar in their lack of similarity, their wildly disparate layouts and the incomprehensibility of their floor-plans, no rhyme or reason to what's where, spaces that have been repurposed again and again for centuries.

Kate could easily find a place to hide down here, wait out the security team's search. But there's often no mobile signal in those deep levels; she'd be cut off from Inez, from Dexter, from school, from her kids. She wouldn't be able to access any useful apps, any maps. She wouldn't be able to accomplish anything.

So, no: Kate can't afford to waste time hiding out down here.

She looks right, left. Right would be toward the front of the building. She turns left.

The rough-hewn stone walls are whitewashed, but that doesn't totally disguise the dankness. At the end of the hall Kate turns onto another long stretch, plenty of doors on either side, but none of them marked for exit.

The police aren't going to drop a dragnet on Kate today, but tomorrow might be different. There are the cameras in the elevator, at the security hut, in the waiting room. There will be a surfeit of footage of Kate gaining illicit entry to this building, sneaking through these halls. There's also the beaten-up security guard, the receptionist, Schuyler. They'll all be shown this footage.

Under close scrutiny, the wig will not help, nor the eyeglasses. Not if the investigators are diligent, not if they press these witnesses, not if they use software to remove these eyeglasses, to change this hair, to provide alternative superficialities to help focus on the bone structure, the shape of the face, the jawline, the eyes.

"Yes," Schuyler will say, looking at a picture of Kate Moore. "That's definitely her."

⚜

SORTIE.

Kate opens the door gingerly, as if it's an injured limb that she doesn't want to move too quickly, it might hurt. She listens . . . listens . . .

Nothing.

The door closes behind her. She's in an institutional stairwell, cinder-block walls, steel-tube handrails, emergency lights. Empty. Silent.

She drops her bag. Removes her jacket, throws it to the floor. Yanks her blouse over her head, rolls it up into a tight cylinder. She leans over, shoves the blouse—

What's that?

Voices. A tinkle of laughter. Two people, up a few flights. The unmistakable click of a Zippo being opened, the scrape of the flint wheel, the *whuff* of the flame igniting.

"*Merci.*"

The lid clicks closed.

"*De rien.*"

Surreptitious cigarettes. They're going to stand up there for five minutes, smoking.

Kate moves more carefully now, silently. Reaches into her bag, pulls out a different cloth cylinder, rolled up with a rubber band. She pulls this T-shirt over her head, shimmies in, tugs down the bottom.

Now she takes off the blond wig, the bobby pins, the clunky eyeglasses.

She pushes her hands through her real hair, shakes her head. Runs bright lipstick across her mouth.

There: now she's a Frenchwoman. No middle-aged American woman would wear this T-shirt proclaiming VIE DE MERDE, the Shitty Life, which encompasses so much disappointment in so many things, the way young people feel, always have, everywhere. But not well-off middle-aged American #expats; they want to message the opposite of VDM.

Kate tiptoes up to the next landing, another fire door with a narrow vertical panel of safety glass to provide a view out to a hall, a way to check for flames, smoke, assailants.

Nothing.

This door squeaks on its hinges, but there's no one to hear it except Kate and the surreptitious smokers, and they're not going to come investigating—

But damn, here comes another woman, turning at the far end of the corridor.

Kate doesn't slow down. She smiles at this woman, says *"Bonjour"* while making firm eye contact, a preemptive attack of collegiality. Kate is a person who belongs here, who's hiding nothing.

"Good afternoon," the woman responds in English. The lingua franca here isn't franca, it's another place where English has taken over, another domino, one office at a time, city by city, country by country.

This woman doesn't even think of challenging Kate.

Bluffing: it always works. Almost always. And if it hadn't? Kate was ready—maybe eager—to use other means. One of the things Kate has learned over the past couple of years is that being the manager of other ass-kickers is not nearly as satisfying as doing the ass-kicking yourself. Not remotely.

The rear exit leads to a narrow side street lined with cluttered shops whose windows display ribbons and buttons and bolts of fabric, cash registers at the front, worktables in the middle. A specialty commercial strip that's visited by the same people all the time, it's a community that congregates here, coffee and gossip, draping saddle bags onto motorbikes or hopping into those little three-wheeled mini-trucks with a boxful of supplies, headed back to the dry-cleaner's, the seamstress shop. Their day is going on, mostly as normal.

Kate is darting through the thick mid-afternoon crowds on the busy street, dodging businessmen whose eyes are taking in her VDM T-shirt stretched tight across her breasts, a double-distraction.

At one end of this street: police.

Kate heads in the other direction, past salons offering cheap haircuts, Chinese restaurants offering cheap lunches, eight euros for the *menu rapide.* She slows when she notices a trio of soldiers up ahead, olive-drab camouflage fatigues, blue berets. They're scanning faces, body language, looking for something wrong, someone wrong.

But they're not looking for her. It's the Paris police whom the 4Syte receptionist called, not the French army. The army is looking for terrorists, and Kate isn't one, and none of this has anything to do with her.

Though Kate is beginning to suspect that maybe this isn't true.

She'd been blind before. She'd refused to be suspicious back when Dexter moved the family to Europe on short notice for a big new job—big client, big money, a big adventure. She'd been seduced by it all, by the prospect of living a different kind of life, of reinventing herself. As with all seductions, she chose not to see the inconvenient, the insincere, the incredible.

Dexter had no client. There was no job.

The real reason they'd come to Luxembourg was for Dexter to orchestrate a complex cyber-intrusion, to steal a fortune—fifty million euros—that he would split with his partner, an FBI agent who was investigating this massive theft in order to ensure, with absolutely certainty, that the crime would not be solved. That agent had followed Dexter to Luxembourg, where she was calling herself Julia MacLean; her bogus husband was Bill. The MacLeans infiltrated themselves into the Moores' lives—Julia fashioned herself into Kate's best friend; Bill, Dexter's. Dinner dates and tennis matches, dancing in Paris and skiing the Alps, the fast friendship of fellow expats.

All four of them were pretending to be something they weren't, someone they weren't, each lying to everyone else.

Those memories of Luxembourg are dimming. Time is speeding up, the kids are growing so quickly, details are beginning to dissolve—the wallpaper in the Luxembourg hall, the route Kate drove to the international school, her first meal with Julia.

Although some edges of memory have become dull rounded corners, other details are sharper than ever. If only Kate could choose which she would remember, and which she could forget.

A clear picture is forming in her mind, but Kate knows she's painting with a strong bias, a suspicion based on previous events, which may have no objective connection to today. Facts, she tells herself. Focus on facts.

Fact: Hunter Forsyth is not at his office, where he really ought to be.

Fact: nor is he at his apartment, where he might have reason to be.

Fact: an American who claimed to be from the State Department escorted Forsyth somewhere that's supposedly secure.

Fact: Forsyth brought along his assistant, who'd been with him since early morning. They'd had plenty of time for a quickie, if that's what was going on, before Forsyth got down to the business of CEO'ing, preparing for an important press conference at which he's going to announce a huge deal. It didn't even need to be quick. A longie.

Fact: Forsyth has now been out of pocket for nearly five hours, and it looks like no one from his company has any idea what has happened to him, and they are beginning to panic.

So: who could have caused that? And why?

A few suspects come immediately to mind.

One: this assistant-concubine, the last person to see him on this day when his company is being assailed internationally, and the city engulfed in terror.

Two: the purported State official. The more Kate thinks about this, the more it's clearly a lie. But just because the guy's identity is false doesn't point Kate in the direction of any particular truth.

One plus two: it's possible that the State imposter and the assistant are in league.

Three: Forsyth himself. Is his disappearance connected to his press conference? His big deal? Is this a last-minute bargaining tactic? Has he orchestrated his own disappearance? As a response to the terror threats?

There's a fourth suspect too. And a fifth. Both of them connected to each other. Both connected, intimately, to Kate.

⚜

She has to consider abandoning him, doesn't she? And doing it right now, before a net can fall. Taking the kids, driving out of Paris into the rolling farmland, the yellow mustard fields and long rows of vineyards, stands of cypress trees along property lines, the monumental wind turbines presiding atop the ridges, the occasional castle clinging to a hillside, its keep crumbling, tumbling down to the red-tile roofs of the village below.

Out of France then, into Luxembourg, no border to cross but clean passports in the glove box anyway, a million euros in getaway cash stashed in the farmhouse. Just a couple hundred miles away, they'd be there by dinnertime, schnitzel and spaetzle at the quiet inn the next town over, she'd light a fire while the old radiators took their time.

Dexter would have to fend for himself. He'd come and join them when he could. If he could. And if he couldn't? That would be because he's guilty, and Kate and the kids will be better off without him.

She feels like a monster for admitting this into her consciousness. It's deplorable. But she'd have no choice, if for no other reason than to protect the children.

Kate knows that Dexter isn't guilty—she *knows* this, doesn't she? He wouldn't get himself involved in anything that would put the family at such risk, not again, not after Luxembourg. Would he?

She needs to get back across the river quickly, get to her husband. And she's beginning to worry about what she's going to find over there.

Favor? she types into her phone.

Inez responds almost instantaneously: *Oui?*

Meet at Palais-Royal?

OK. I am at the office. Dix minutes.

Kate locates the financial app on her phone, way back on the fourth screen; she consults it roughly never. So it takes her a bit longer than it would take most people to find what she's looking for, but hoping not to find.

She does.

⚜

It won't be difficult for the police to put it together.

Yes, Schuyler will say, nodding. That's the woman who lied her way into our offices, then brutalized a security guard so she could escape.

Which that woman did just hours after 4Syte's CEO was kidnapped.

Which combined with these international threats in Hong Kong and Mumbai—and this widespread attack across Paris—has caused 4Syte's stock to crash.

Which was precisely the unlikely development on which this woman's husband had wagered a substantial sum of money.

Which this husband just did after decades of a widely known, easily documented grudge against that very same kidnapped CEO.

Which is all an overwhelming volume of evidence.

49

"*Monsieur*, I do not think this is a good idea." Colette stares into his eyes. What is it she's looking for? His resolve?

"I understand," Hunter says, as quietly as possible without whispering; he doesn't want to seem to be plotting anything. "But we have to try before it's too late."

"Too late? For what?"

"To survive."

Colette is taken aback, but not convinced, at least not as immediately and unequivocally as she usually accepts his orders. Because they're not at work, and if they're not at work, then Hunter is not her boss, he's just the guy whose fault it is that she has been kidnapped. He's not necessarily part of the solution. He's part of the problem, is what he is. Not just part of it, he's the whole goddamned problem. Is that what Colette is thinking?

"Are you ready?" he asks. This is his subtle way of opening the door just a crack, enough for her to rush through with her strenuous objections, *No, Monsieur, I am not ready, I am not going to participate in this horrible plan . . .*

But she doesn't, thankfully. She nods.

Hunter walks over to where Simpson sits, too far away to hear, but still observing with well-warranted suspicion.

"Listen, Simpson. My assistant has to go to her kid's school. An important meeting with a teacher."

Colette has a seven-year-old, or maybe it's six, or five, Hunter can't keep track; he doesn't pay attention to any information about any children. Even though he wants to be a father, he can't bring himself to get interested in other people's kids. He doesn't even pretend to try.

Simpson turns to Colette, standing a few meters away. "Son or daughter?"

"*Fille,*" Colette answers. "Séverine is nine years old."

Nine? Okay, he was off by a couple of years.

"And you scheduled an appointment for a day that you knew was going to be very busy?"

That's a good point.

"My husband Guy, he is the one who is planning to go. But I fear he will not arrive."

Hunter is impressed with Colette's on-the-feet thinking. As always.

"Why's that?" Simpson asks.

"Guy is returning from Dubai on a flight that will arrive midday. But I believe that all flights will be diverted, *n'est-ce pas*? Certainly all flights from *les pays arabes.* And as you know, I have no way to contact him."

Simpson considers this. "I can't imagine that any schools in Paris will be having normal meetings this afternoon."

"The school is outside of the city, *Monsieur.* We do not live in Paris."

Simpson has no rebuttal to this.

"I cannot simply abandon my child, *Monsieur*!" Colette is growing self-righteous, angry, loud. "It is a very important appointment."

Simpson sees that he's trapped. He has no rational, humane reason to prevent this agitated mother from moving on with her life. Yes, Hunter realizes, this was a good plan; he's proud of himself for thinking of it.

Hunter would be so happy to be wrong, for Simpson to relent, allow Colette to leave. Because if not, this guy will be acknowledging something else, and Hunter and Colette will have to initiate the only plan he has been able to come up with.

"I have sympathy, Madame Benoit. I really do—"

Hunter's heart sinks while his adrenaline spikes. He knows that a minute from now, he might very well be dead.

"—but I'm sure your daughter won't be the only such child, on an extraordinary day like today, plenty of parents will have trouble with transportation. The school will make arrangements."

They are staring at each other, Simpson and Colette, both of them fuming, both of them lying to the other. Colette's husband isn't in Dubai, he isn't flying back to Paris today, there's no school appointment.

"It is necessary for me to leave."

"I'm sorry, but I can't allow it."

Colette glances quickly at Hunter, and he blinks once at her, a long blink. This is their signal. No turning back now.

❧

She takes a deep breath, girding herself, and turns her eyes back to Simpson. "I will," she says.

"No," Simpson says firmly, "you will not."

Colette starts walking toward the door, stomping. Everyone knows full and well that the door is locked, that Simpson holds the key, that she will not be able to open the door. But nevertheless both men watch to see what she's going to do when she reaches the threshold.

Which is: bang with her fists, one, two, three times.

Then she screams, *"À l'aide!"*

Simpson stands, pushes his chair away from the table. It's a heavy wooden desk chair, the type you find in a library, or a bookstore, the seat worn into butt-cheek buckets by generations of occupants sitting down, sliding around.

"Stop it," Simpson says and takes a step toward Colette, his back now completely turned to Hunter.

"S'il vous plaît!!" She bangs again, with both fists.

Simpson takes another long stride, and that's when Hunter makes his move, rushes up to grab the two rear legs of Simpson's sturdy chair, keeping his wrists firm, his forearms flexed, maintaining his balance with all his core muscles engaged, everything straining to stay in control, as Colette continues to bang on the door, and Hunter pushes up from his quads, lifting the chair aloft, holding it above his head now, taking quick steps to catch up behind Simpson, with Colette's racket providing aural cover for his footsteps, and Simpson helping the effort by yelling, "Stop!"

Hunter squeezes his grip even tighter, and raises his arms higher, his muscles burning, everything straining as he begins the swing while he's still hustling up to his target, just one more stride will do it—

The chair-back meets Simpson firmly on the top of his head, and Hunter continues to power through with a full swing, the wood now hitting the guy in his upper back, he's buckling, collapsing to his knees, and Hunter is losing his grip, he doesn't fight it, he lets the heavy piece of furniture fall onto the guy, another insult to the injury, and now all this wood is in the way, so Hunter shoves it aside with his knee, and yanks Simpson by the hair, spinning the guy's face around so Hunter can punch him once, twice, the guy's nose bleeding and his upper lip split—

Colette drops to her knees and reaches inside the guy's jacket and finds the holster and removes the gun and leaps back to her feet, fumbling with the weapon, which almost slips from her hand once, now twice, and she steadies her hands with both fists encircling the grip, aiming the weapon at the man who's lying on the floor, not moving, not at all.

"Okay," Hunter says, breathing heavy. "Good. We're good."

His hands are already hurting, possibly broken bones in both of them. Fuck. This is why you wear boxing gloves.

"Are you okay?"

Colette doesn't answer. She's entirely focused on her white-knuckled death grip of the pistol, hands shaking, eyes wide.

"Okay," he says again. "We're good." Trying to convince himself as much as her.

He finds the keys in Simpson's jacket pocket. "I'll take that gun now." Hunter needs to pry Colette's fingers off the weapon, then fills her empty palm with the keys. "Here. You're going to unlock the door, and turn the knob, and pull open the door while you step away in that direction." He points to the far side of the door. "Understand?"

"*Oui.*"

"I'm going to be over there, lying on the floor, aiming the gun at the opening of the door. If anyone is waiting for us on the far side, I'm going to shoot."

"*Oui.*"

"If no one is there, we will wait one minute in case someone arrives. We will wait in the same position, you there, me there, hidden, unmoving, until I get up. Then we will leave, me in the lead. In front. *D'accord?*"

She nods.

"You did good, Colette." He rubs her upper arm. "You did great."

"*Merci.*"

"Are you ready? We should not wait long." How long has it been since she started banging and screaming? Sixty seconds? Is that enough time for someone downstairs to rush up here?

"*Oui.*"

Hunter crosses the room, and drops to his knees, then stretches himself flat on his stomach. He extends his arms, grips the semiautomatic with both hands, aiming at the edge of the door, up at an imaginary spot that's four feet high: center of mass for a man at the door.

"Okay," Hunter says. "Now."

Colette turns to the door. The first key she tries doesn't fit, nor the second. She looks over at him.

"It's okay," he says, "one of them will work."

The third does. Colette turns the key slowly, trying to minimize the noise. Then she leaves the key in the lock, the whole ring hanging there, and places her hand on the knob. She glances at Hunter again, and he nods.

She turns the knob—

50

"The license plate of the van?"

"Van? What van?"

Ibrahim has been on an extended break. He went to the bathroom, ate a sandwich, called his parents. They know what is going on in Paris, they know that their son is at the scene. They know he cannot talk about it on the phone.

Now he is back in position, along with all these other men who have been up here for four hours.

"The van that delivered the bomber here."

"Ah. That van."

"Its license plate was reported stolen three weeks ago, from a car park in Reims."

"Naturally. If the name painted on the side of the vehicle is a fiction . . ." The speaker trails off, probably shrugs, what do you expect.

"Maybe the bomber was visiting for the harvest."

"Muslims do not tend to be Champagne connoisseurs, you know. They—"

"I was kidding."

"Ah, I see. Very amusing. It was a public car park with a security camera at the entrance. The vehicle whose plate was stolen—a farmer's truck—was parked for forty minutes, during which ninety-two other vehicles were in the building."

"Ninety-two, okay, we can work with that."

"Of those, only seventeen exited while the *camionette* was parked."

"Seventeen? That is a much more manageable number."

"Of those seventeen, two are registered here in Paris."

"Only two?" An appreciative whistle. "We should send teams."

"They are already en route."

Ibrahim can feel the satisfied silence all around him, these men congratulating themselves, in their minds, for the solid, industrious work of their underlings.

"This is how we find them, you know. Every plot has its holes, blind spots that even the author cannot see. One tiny mistake, that could make all the difference."

✤

"Is this Dr. Féraud?"

"Yes."

"My name is a Colonel Étienne Desmarchais. You are on speaker-phone with a number of military, law-enforcement, and political personnel."

"That is unusual."

"You have a patient named Mahmoud Khalid."

Silence on the phone.

"Doctor? Mahmoud Khalid is the name of the man standing in the middle of the Louvre, wearing a suicide vest."

More silence.

"Doctor, did you hear me? Do you understand?"

Finally: "How is it that you think I can help you, Colonel . . . ?"

"Colonel Desmarchais. Please, tell me, what is wrong with Mahmoud Khalil?"

"Well, Colonel, if what you say is true, then what is wrong with Mr. Khalid is that he is standing in the middle of the Louvre, wearing a suicide vest."

"Are you trying to joke with me?"

"Unsuccessfully?"

"Listen, Doctor Fér—"

"I am sorry, but I simply cannot share a patient's confidential records with someone who calls without a proper medical reference. I am sure you understand."

"Reference? No, I certainly do not understand."

"Doctor. This is now the deputy chief of police speaking."

"Hello deputy chief."

"We can get a court order."

"Then I look forward to examining it, and I will respond as quickly as circumstances allow. Now, if you will excuse—"

"This is not finished."

"I do not doubt it. But I am simply following the *law*, which, as a law-enforcement officer, I am sure you can appreciate."

⚜

"The back-trace is now complete. Here, look . . ."

"What? What is this? I do not understand what I am looking at."

"This is a map of Paris, sir."

"Am I stupid?"

"Of course not, no sir, I was . . . er . . . Using the surveillance-camera network, we have traced the van's route back to its first movements of the day, at seven this morning."

"Good. This is quite good. And this is it, here, this big red dot in Clignancourt? Okay. We should breach as soon as possible."

"Yes, the teams have already been dispatched. Arrival in five minutes."

"But the driver will not be there now, will he? Have we traced his route?"

"We are still trying. It appears that he entered the parking garage here at this spot, then entered the Métro system here. It is likely that he walked right past a patrolman who was stationed at the entrance."

Ibrahim is beginning to fatigue of holding this position, this level of concentration, this preparedness. Also of listening to these men, and saying nothing.

"It does not really make a difference, does it? The type of cancer. The treatment."

"Well . . ."

"There is obviously a very large difference between Stage I carcinoma and Stage IV lung. In terms of his thought processes. His motivations."

"Yes, obviously, I understand, but does any of that matter to *us*? To our decision-making? Listen. Perhaps Mahmoud Khalil is a very sick man, a dying man, so he has nothing to lose by dying here today, because he may very well die tomorrow."

"Exactly."

"But still, the fact is that he is standing here *today*, ready to die *today*, and perhaps ready to take half the population of Paris with him—"

"Oh, let us not exaggerate—"

"—and create a crater of the Louvre that will be radioactive for a century. Regardless of his own prospects for a tomorrow, this man is a threat to Paris, to all of us, *today*. And I assert that regardless of the severity of his illness, it is time for us to blow his brains out all over the cour Napoléon."

"What a surprise! The police want to shoot a Muslim man. I am shocked."

"Everyone, calm down. Keep this rational. And *civil*. I am talking to you, Yves."

Hrumph.

"What precisely do we have to lose by waiting?"

"*Control.*"

"Control? Are you out of your mind? We already do not have control. We cannot lose what we do not have."

Ibrahim knows that sooner or later everyone will accede, and his long period of inaction will come to an end; that might happen any moment.

"If it *looks* like we have control, Bertrand, then we *do* have control. And at this moment, there is only one way for us to create that perception."

It will be such a small motion, a nearly imperceptible physical exertion, it will last less than a second. Then his role will be finished.

"*Fils de pute.* The van driver, we lost him. We have him all the way to this Métro platform, there, do you see? But then we lose him in the station. Three of the cameras are broken, which was noticed yesterday, and a work order was created immediately. The repairs are scheduled for Friday."

"*Hmm.* Suspicious. And surface cameras?"

"None seem to have captured him."

"Are there any other exits from the station? Service tunnels? He could have used the unmonitored station to disguise himself."

"Yes, that is possible."

"Then he could have returned to the platform. Or to the platform of the other direction. Or he could have changed platforms to another line. Or he could have fled through the tunnels."

"Yes, those are all possibilities. Where is this station?"

"Odéon."

"Odéon? In St-Germain."

"Obviously."

"That is where one of the cars is registered."

"Cars? What are you talking about?"

"The cars that were in Reims at the same time the license plate that was on the van that delivered this bomber to the Louvre was stolen. Those cars."

⚜

"This is bad."

"What?"

"The wife: she was killed during a police action in Belleville."

Belleville. This time, Ibrahim holds his tongue.

"I remember that. It was the roundup after the arrests at Bastille, yes?"

"Yes. But Neela Khalid was completely innocent."

"That is what they all say."

"*They all*? You really are a racist son of—"

"No, truly, she was walking to the station after visiting her colleague, who was just home from hospital."

Ibrahim remembers this. How could he not? Belleville is where he lives.

"Oh yes. This woman was a complete bystander."

"That is right. She was hit by a stray bullet."

"And it was not just any stray bullet, was it?"

"No."

Ibrahim feels a hand on his shoulder. He flinches, almost screams, *Do not fucking touch a man whose finger is on a trigger.*

"Officer, is everything okay?"

"Yes sir," Ibrahim says.

"Good. Can I ask, what is your confidence in this shot?"

"My confidence?"

"Yes. What are the odds of an instantaneous kill?"

When the bullet exits the muzzle, it will be traveling at 900 meters per second. During flight, the bullet will slow due to air friction, but the target is only about 400 meters away, so the speed diminution will be negligible, and will not compromise the trajectory. The wind is practically nonexistent, and there is no sun in Ibrahim's eyes. He is in a comfortable, stable position, not overly fatigued. The sightline is clear. The target is surrounded by nothing distracting, nothing that might move at the last second.

The conditions could not be more perfect.

The flight of the bullet will last a half-second, and it will make contact with the target somewhere inside a zone that is about the size of a mobile phone. A small mobile phone.

"One hundred percent."

51

Colette yanks the handle, and the door flies open.

Nothing.

There's no one on the other side, nothing but the dim quiet space, the dingy dinged-up walls, the chipped-paint floorboards.

Colette is standing behind the open door, flat against the wall. Hunter is still lying on the floor, twenty feet from the door, obscured from view by furniture but not totally hidden, aiming the gun at the now-open doorway, waiting for someone to arrive.

Will he shoot absolutely anyone who appears? He hopes he wouldn't shoot an innocent old lady, a curious little kid. But he's not confident that he'll have the poise to tell the difference.

He's really fucking terrified. And he has only the vaguest idea of how to handle this gun.

Ten seconds have gone by, and no one has appeared.

Twenty seconds.

Hunter once had a shotgun pressed upon him for the purpose of shooting skeet. Making a sport, a casual pastime, out of hurling high-speed bullets at things. Whooping it up with those guys, wearing the ludicrous outfits, the glasses, the padded-shoulder vests, it's always about the accessories, the toys. He abhorred it. He was disappointed in himself for allowing anyone to talk him into it.

He has never before held a handgun. Handguns aren't for sport. Handguns are for only one purpose: killing other humans.

Thirty seconds.

Colette is still behind the open door, trembling.

Hunter shifts his weight slightly, so less of it is pressing down on his right elbow, which is beginning to hurt.

Forty.

New York still won't be open for another hour and a half, if he can get out of here now, get himself to a working phone, make a couple of reassuring calls, let people know he's alive, push back the press conference a few hours . . .

Fifty.

He's relieved that he hasn't yet needed to shoot anyone. But he's also disappointed that he hasn't yet shot anyone, because that means his captors are still out there, unshot. And now he needs to get up, walk out of here, and either get by them or confront them.

Hunter tiptoes toward the door, toward Colette. He nods at her, she nods back. He steps through the doorway first, into the short hall with the stairwell opposite. Just a single light, a bare bulb hanging from a cloth cord. Are there neighbors at home, people who heard this commotion, peering through peepholes, peeking through cracked doors? Is someone going to intervene? Call the police? If the police show up, he doesn't particularly want to be a man creeping around holding a gun. But if they don't, he does.

He creeps to the stairs, which turn back upon themselves in all four directions, a narrow shaft in the middle, he can see all the way down to the bottom, it looks like fifty feet. He tries to carry the gun like guys do in films, which is how we all learn to hold guns: actors, in movies, where the good guys shoot the bad guys. In real life, though, it's almost always the other way around.

Hunter takes one tentative step down. Another. Another and another until the first landing, the first turn, affording a different angle on this stairwell, on the openings to the other floors. Still no sign of anyone.

Colette follows a half-dozen steps behind.

Hunter picks up his pace, descends all the way to the floor below without pausing. Should he peek his head into this hallway? What might he find? Nothing useful. Just a way to get himself shot.

He keeps moving as quietly as possible, but that's not silently, because his leather soles are clicking on the wooden stairs, which is not a loud noise but it's definitely enough to hear, bouncing off all these hard surfaces. He looks up and sees that Colette is carrying her heels, she's padding down the stairs in her stockinged feed, stealthy silent.

Hunter looks down again to the bottom, still no sign of anyone. He's approaching another doorway to another hall. He slows, moving more quietly, the gun aimed at the opening, tiptoeing past . . . one more step to the next stair . . .

Still nothing. He takes a step down onto a loose floorboard that squeals like a pig, an extremely loud noise, an alarming noise, and he spins to see if that has attracted any attention, just in time to—

5²

If there's one principle everyone agrees upon, it's this: markets hate uncertainty. When confronted with uncertainty, people are quick to panic about their money. When they panic, they sell whatever it is they can sell. Everyone knows this. It's right up there with buy low, sell high, kill or be killed: panic begets more panic. Panicked selling leads to falling prices, and falling prices leads to more panicked selling, accelerated sell-offs. Panic consumes wealth, wolfing it down, poof, gone.

The uncertainty engendered by the attacks in Paris has been making prices fall broadly all day. Dexter hits UPDATE. The algorithm loads the latest share prices of his various positions, and compares all the current sell prices against his initial buys, and deducts transaction costs and taxes, and calculates his bottom-line aggregate delta, which appears at the very top of the screen instead of at the bottom, so Dexter doesn't have to scan down the page to see, at a quick glance, the so-called bottom line—

Still red.

But because of the falling value of 4Syte's single stock futures, Dexter's overall position is heading steadily toward zero. Today's goal, though, is not merely a mitigation of red numbers, it's a transition well into black.

His attention is suddenly drawn to one of his screens where 4Syte's logo is split with a pair of talking heads. Dexter turns on this broadcast's volume—

". . . in Mum*bai,* where the office building has been com*pletely* evacuated on the credible threat of a bomb."

The anchorman considers his response for longer than normal. The inclination, on these shows, is to bluster ahead.

"To be sure," he finally says, "it's *far* too early to say for certain that

there's a *definitive* connection between these ongoing attacks and 4Syte."
He's trying to sound reassuring; he could get in well-deserved trouble for
igniting an unwarranted panic, a sell-off, hundreds of millions at stake,
billions.

"That's true: so far there is no *proven* correlation among the three cities, other than what very well may be the completely *coincidental* locations of the attacks."

"Indeed."

"And in Paris, as you know, the bomb threats are *not* against the 4Syte
offices, which are I believe in *two* locations, one in the center and one in
the outlying business district of La Défense. But it *is* in Paris, later today,
where 4Syte founder and CEO Hunter Forsyth is meant to give a press
conference, in what is expected to be the announcement of a *major* deal."

"And have we received any comment from 4Syte?"

"No, not as of this moment."

No comment? This is a company that's nothing if not PR-friendly,
with an international army of polished spokespeople, well-armed with
facts, figures, carefully worded press releases. Dexter searches the web for
their counternarrative, but finds nothing.

He checks 4Syte PR's social postings, in the US, in France, in Asia.
Nothing.

He finds Hunter Forsyth's social feed: the last post was 7:55 this morning, a photo of sunrise over the city, *Good morning Paris! Looking fwd to
a great day ahead.* Six hours ago. This is a man who normally posts every
few hours, no matter how anodyne. And this silence is on a day when he
wants everyone in the world to pay attention to him, closely, constantly.

Dexter checks for 4Syte in other trends. There's no hard information,
anywhere, about Hunter Forsyth. Dexter's initial reaction is joy—what
could be better, really?

But on second thought?

They met two decades ago, two young tech guys who'd arrived in the Bay
Area at what would later prove to be the exact right moment, for some of
them.

Hunter had skipped the whole shared-house-in-Mountain-View
pupae stage, moved directly from Stanford B-school into full-fledged

adulthood in Nob Hill, where he hung his diplomas from Groton, from Yale, lined his built-in bookshelves with tennis trophies, a preppy Wall of Fame, this guy *owned* it. There are people who are born to rule the world, and Hunter Forsyth was one of them.

Dexter is reminded of Jake's misunderstanding, back in Luxembourg, about the palace guards: "Epaulets," the little boy asserted, with the supreme confidence of misinformed little boys, "are so people know you're in charge." Which was not at all true. But epaulets did let everyone know something, that was for sure. Hunter wore his proudly.

Dexter was an early hire in Hunter's first startup. But Dexter didn't have the competitive instinct, didn't have office-politics savvy, didn't understand how to flatter and pander, to dissemble and cajole. He was a hard worker, a great engineer, but that wasn't enough. That wasn't even required.

He eventually left in a huff, burning a bridge with a rising star, not doing himself any favors in the community, which was soon filled with old friends and colleagues who'd been hit by one filthy-rich lightning bolt or another, VC infusion or IPO or corporate buyout, a constant churn of liquidity events generating Gulfstreams, weekend houses in Cabo, Ferraris. Dexter was still driving a Honda.

You get to make only so many bets in a lifetime, and the things you choose not to do may be just as consequential as the things you choose to do. What Dexter chose not to do was stay in Silicon Valley. A college buddy had a spare bedroom in DC, where Dexter met his future wife. Also where he ran into that old friend from college, the one who cooked up the scheme that led to Luxembourg, to Paris, to this career, this moment—

⚜

"Holy crap."

The banner running across Dexter's screen announces: *Breaking News! 4Syte announcement postponed.*

"—now have *confirmation*, Robert, that the 4Syte press conference, which was meant to start less than two hours from now, has been postponed."

"Has it been rescheduled?" Re-*shed*-yuled.

Dexter feels himself hunched forward, mouth hanging open, he must look simian. But who cares, he's alone, as usual. Sometimes when not alone, Dexter has to force himself to maintain awareness of that, to chew quietly, keep his pants buttoned. He spends more time with his children than with anyone else, and they're rubbing off. He's modeling the kids' behavior. It's supposed to be the other way around.

"No, Robert, not at this time."

"Has any reason been given?"

"None. But spokesperson Schuyler Franks advises that a statement *will* be released by the end of business today, if not earlier."

Dexter refreshes his screen again, hitting the button compulsively, a new addiction.

"Thank you for that report, Tessa." Robert the anchor turns back to face the camera. "So. Still no *official* word from 4Syte or its CEO, Hunter Forsyth, on the possible threats against 4Syte's international offices, and the ongoing situation in Paris, where the announcement was to be held. Nor any connection these events might have to this *very* surprising postponement of a *major* announcement."

In the past minute alone, 4Syte has lost 2 percent of its value, a rapid acceleration of the slow slide that started this morning.

The top, the bottom, these are not fixed points, they are fluid positions, and there's never any definitive moment when either is completely clear to anyone. It's only in hindsight that you can see if you held too long, or sold too early. Timing is everything.

The situation looks promising. But things often look promising and turn out not to be. That's how he found himself in this predicament in the first place, and how he got himself into his original European fiasco: by choosing to see the things he wanted to see, and ignoring those he didn't.

He knows he shouldn't have left Ben's present to the last minute, *of course* he knows that, he's not a moron. No excuse, it just slipped his mind, again and again.

Like the inhaler. Which was Kate's last straw.

It was a Sunday. The boys spent the entire day at a birthday party in Passy, driven out by the overbearing woman whom Kate calls Hashtag Mom. Dexter stayed behind in St-Germain, read even the soft sections of the newspapers, took a long walk, indulged in a decadent lunch, self-rewards for his grueling weeks of solo-parenting. Kate had been away longer than anticipated, a work trip that kept getting extended, "I'll be home in a couple of days," over and over.

The kids came home just before bedtime. Ben was coughing, pale, short of breath.

"Okay, kiddo, let's get your inhaler." Dexter walked into the bathroom, and collected the little canister. It felt light, and a stab of worry shot through him. He didn't want to test the device in case that test squeeze turned out to be the final dose.

So Ben was the one who squeezed the little pump into his mouth; it was Ben who discovered that the final dose had been inhaled yesterday. The canister was empty.

Sunday nights, nearly all pharmacies are closed. Something would be open somewhere; Dexter was pretty sure there was a twenty-four-hour drugstore over in the fifteenth, perhaps another down in the thirteenth, neither particularly nearby, and both no doubt mobbed with sick people, whimpering children, waiting for hours—

That's exactly when Kate walked in the door, wheeling her luggage full of dirty laundry, looking like she'd just been dragged through something awful.

Dexter was standing there, holding the inhaler. "We just realized it's empty."

Kate barely glanced at her husband before turning to her obviously ill boy, you could see it in one glance. "Let's go, Sweetie," she said, holding out her hand.

"Where, Mommy?"

"To the hospital."

Kate didn't talk to Dexter for the better part of the next week, nothing but monosyllables and hostile glares and cold shoulders; she literally turned her back on her husband, repeatedly. He apologized a hundred times, uncountable times. To his wife, to his son.

"It's okay, Daddy," the boy said. "It wasn't your fault. It was mine. I should have been keeping track of the counter."

Dexter hugged this beautiful boy, so grateful for this kid, so disappointed in himself.

"I'm sorry," Dexter told Kate. He bought her an extravagant watch, a belated anniversary gift. A bribe. And an action figure for Ben. "It won't happen again. I promise."

And he meant it: he would never again neglect the inhaler, the nose spray, any of the boy's meds. Dexter checked these supplies daily, it had become an OCD tic, took up a disproportionate share of his consciousness, so much that there wasn't sufficient space for all the other chores he was supposed to remember. Like this birthday present.

That's what he told himself.

⚜

Dexter steps out into the world, in search of Lego and lunch and sanity. He needs to calm the fuck down or he's going to have a stroke.

He can see that people are unsure how to behave today, is it the end of the world or just a single-news-cycle blip, or something in the broad spectrum between. Waiters huddle in conspiratorial clumps, shopkeepers are conferring on sidewalks. Some businesses are shuttered, while the *quincaillerie* is packed with people buying flashlights and batteries, and others are lugging home bottled water, canned beans, jars of cassoulet, full-scale Armageddon panic.

Dexter doesn't know where he falls on this continuum. It's a choice, it's controllable, and he's trying to choose to occupy the less hysterical end. It will all be okay. Perhaps bombs will take some lives today, but that's true every day, somewhere. Today it will not be his life, nor his kids', nor his wife's. They will still host their dinner party, and the TV will remain on during cocktail hour with the volume muted, tracking the latest developments, the investigation, the police will be raiding mosques while expats sit around discussing the events between bites of chicken stew, putting their bread directly on the tablecloth, the French way, though none of them is French.

In the hours before then, Dexter will, hopefully, make a fortune.

And he'll find this Lego. There are two stores within striking distance that are likely to have the thing in stock. He tried calling ahead. At the nearest store, the clerk confirmed their inventory, but she did it quickly, dismissively, like someone who hadn't checked anything. The other store's clerk put Dexter on hold, supposedly to go look for the item, and never returned. Dexter has grown accustomed to this type of customer service, more take-it-or-leave-it than in America, where nothing is worse than losing a sale.

It's cool on the shady side of the street. In Paris, in Luxembourg, in this general part of the world where Dexter has been living, the seasons skew early. By late August it already feels like autumn; early November is full-on winter.

He buttons his jacket, turns up his collar against the wind. Maybe it's time to switch out this navy cotton jacket for the gray wool, suede gloves in the pocket, a cashmere scarf.

Dexter is a creature of habit, he wears a uniform, he eats the same things in the same restaurants and cafés, a salad here and a sandwich there, the Tuesday special fish. He keeps to a regular schedule of tennis matches and gym routines, of morning newspapers and online research, Asian and European trading, late lunch followed by New York's markets.

He has always wanted this life, a life of predictable regimen, the same satisfying thing day in, day out. He takes comfort in the certainty, in the daily consistencies and the predictable variations, school pickup three days per week, cooking dinner on Wednesday nights, sex on Saturdays.

But it's not as consistent as it looks, nor as permanent. Kate travels often. Her trips arise quickly, last an uncertain duration, and end with no warning, with unexpected interruptions while she pops home for a day or two—or ten—before heading out again, to Palermo or Lisbon, Copenhagen or Marseille, or wherever the hell she actually goes when she claims to be in these places.

School holidays intervene. American bank holidays. The weather makes outdoor tennis unpredictable, the kids get sick, dinner parties, birthdays, birthday-present shopping.

Even if Dexter doesn't succeed in finding this Lego, Ben is not going to fall apart, the boy is not that sort of child. It's not the fear of meltdown that's motivating Dexter. It's that the kid would be quietly, sullenly disappointed, and this would break Dexter's heart.

And Kate would be apoplectic. Dexter has used up every one of his free passes. His wife has been awfully mad at him lately, morose, hostile. Her response to his next offense might be cataclysmic.

As he passes the entrance to his garage, it occurs to him that perhaps he should drive. Maybe on a normal day, yes. But today, who knows what traffic will be like, which streets will be open and which closed, which bridges passable.

No, the car would be a mistake. He'd end up caught in a closure, penned in, trapped for hours. He'd have to abandon the Audi somewhere, parking on the street, which he avoids like the plague. Parisians don't think they've parked successfully until they've used both front and rear fenders to expand the dimensions of their space, a push forward here, another push back, forward and back, like bumper cars, which may have made sense in the days when cars had actual bumpers, but they don't anymore.

He resumes walking, faster now, rushing. Glances at his watch—

"*Pardonnez-moi, Monsieur.*"

Dexter turns. It's two cops approaching him. Where did they come from?

"*Oui?*"

"*Un moment, s'il vous plaît.*"

53

Kate races up to the street, then spins around the corner and guides the moped through the bollards into the pedestrian-only sector. Here she putters slowly, not wanting to draw attention, nor the ire of shopkeepers, waiters, customers.

At the next corner she exits the Montorgueil car-free zone, back out to another traffic-clogged street, but Kate doesn't need a lane, she's zooming past buses, weaving between taxis, a dangerous but critical component of her most aggressive surveillance-detection route: make it physically impossible to follow her.

Kate is no longer concerned merely with being tailed by counterespionage, by intelligence, by a curious husband. Now she also has to worry about counterterrorism, about French police, Interpol, anyone, everyone. The stakes have become much higher than the security of her legend, than the secrecy of the Paris Substation. It was just a couple of hours ago when those were her primary concerns.

She pulls to a stop, looks around at all the open space that surrounds la Bourse, a broad hulk of building that opened two centuries ago as the stock exchange, now obsolete, a victim of automation and internationalism, merging with Brussels and Amsterdam and Lisbon, capitals of colonial empires that for centuries had been global trading centers. The *bourse* became fallow, lolling here in the middle of the city, hosting temporary exhibitions, expositions, waiting for a new purpose to present itself. Stocks these days are all traded elsewhere, anywhere, everywhere, men sitting at home wearing sweatpants and T-shirts, in between tennis matches and birthday-present shopping, eating sliced apples and Nutella sandwiches—

That *bastard.*

How is she going to keep him out of the grasp of French authorities? Should she try the US Embassy? Or go directly to the Paris Substation's safehouse? Or would they be better off completely DIY? Kate could take him to that other location, much closer to home, with less of a connection to anyone else, completely unknown to anyone in any intelligence service.

She doesn't want to have to trust anyone. Because it's definitely possible—it's likely—that there's hard evidence against Dexter, beyond the mere circumstantial. His phone records, browsing history, e-mails, who knows what. There could be plenty that makes him look guilty, creating ample incentive for people to turn him in.

But could Dexter actually *be* guilty?

It was much easier to be an intelligence operative when it wasn't her husband in her crosshairs.

Back in Luxembourg, when Kate finally confronted Dexter with her suspicions, he explained the rationale for his conspiracy: he was a vigilante, not a mere thief; he was meting out justice on a global scale, taking a monster's money and his life, making the world a better place; he was avenging the murder of his brother, who'd been an American peacekeeper in the Serbian civil war. The money was beside the point, mostly.

His arguments were not without merit.

Kate's counterargument was simple, moral: even if it was true that the man Dexter robbed was a horrible person—an arms dealer, a murderer—and even if this man did deserve the harshest possible sentence, Dexter himself did not deserve to benefit from it. Certainly not with a stolen twenty-five million euros. That wasn't justice, that was opportunism; it was illegal, and unethical. Dexter couldn't keep this blood money, not if he wanted to keep his wife.

He didn't put up a fight.

And, Kate added, one other thing: he had to give up his partner, the person who'd lured him into the whole plot, who'd used him, who'd ruthlessly put Dexter and Kate and their kids—their lives—at mortal risk.

She realized that she was lashing out in anger, but she did it anyway. Kate was the one who made the immunity deal, who set up the CIA sting. Kate was the one who lured the woman called Julia MacLean to collect

the account number for her share of the heist, with the Agency van waiting around the corner, ready to take her into custody. It was all set up.

But at the last moment, in an unexpected burst of sympathy, Kate had
a change of heart. She allowed Julia to go free, to escape the clutches of
prosecution, to avoid the worst consequences of her crimes.

Not, though, with her twenty-five million euros. Just with her husband and her freedom, or some semblance of it.

A framed map of Europe hangs in Kate's office, and behind the map is
a safe mounted in the wall. This is where Kate keeps a few thousand in
cash—walking-around money for bribes, payouts, secret salaries. Also
an expensive wristwatch that she ended up possessing after a series of
boneheaded missteps on the part of an asset; Kate didn't know what else
to do with this tacky piece of jewelry.

If anyone ever has the temerity to break into the office, to crack the
safe, they will be excited—hey, look what we found, it's the secret stash.

It isn't.

In the kitchenette, the small microwave's back panel can be removed
in less than thirty seconds with a Phillips-head screwdriver. That's where
Kate stores another hundred thousand euros, plus a few passports with
her picture but different names and nationalities. She also used to keep
an untraceable SIG Sauer in there, but she brought it along for Peter, and
hasn't gotten around to replacing it. It's been a few years since Kate has
needed a gun.

She keeps hoping that her days of shooting people are behind her.
After Oaxaca, she'd told herself that it had been a fluke, an extraordinary
confluence of circumstances, something she'd never need to repeat. But
then she did, and not just once. Oaxaca was nearly two decades ago.

She never imagined that she'd kill a person, that she'd be a cold-
blooded killer—of course she wasn't, that was so obvious, wasn't it? Look
at her, with her station wagon, her coq au vin, her little-kid birthday-
party favors. This isn't what cold-blooded killers look like.

Kate descends the stairs from the rue des Petits Champs, and walks
through the *passage* out into the airy gardens of Palais-Royal, one of

Kate's favorite places in Paris, where the Moores attend a semi-regular weeknight picnic with other families, chilled rosé and good pâté, kids inventing games while adults play progressively more vigorous rounds of pétanque, surrounded by other people everywhere, packed into the cafés in the colonnades, reclined in the green metal chairs, strollers and loners and smitten lovers.

Kate hopes she doesn't have to leave Paris, now. Not like this.

Inez arrives, kisses her on one cheek. "*Ça va?*" she asks, and kisses the other. Just like any other pair of friends.

How's it going? Terrible, that's how. "Inez, I'm in a bad situation. Dangerous. I can't get to my weapon, and I think I might need one."

Inez nods, understanding. She reaches her right hand inside her jacket while leaning forward, all the way into Kate, and brings her left hand up to Kate's shoulder, around it, a close embrace. Inez gives a squeeze, as if in support—it's so good to see you after so long, I'm so sorry about your mother, your job, your problems—then leans away. "*Bonne chance,*" she says.

Somewhere in the middle of that, Kate felt the handgun fall into her pocket.

❧

One ring.

No answer.

Two rings.

Her unanswered call isn't going straight to voice-mail, which means the device isn't powered off, isn't out of range. The phone is ringing. Just not being answered.

Three.

And then that's it, voice-mail: *Bonjour, it's Dexter, please leave a message.*

"Hi," she says, "it's me." As a rule Kate doesn't leave messages, just ends the call; Dexter knows to ring back. That's how life works now.

She doesn't want to say anything too specific. In fact she hasn't wanted to make this call at all, she's almost certain that his phone is compromised, not just the meta-data but probably the actual content of the communications too, the location, everything. But she needs him to get out of their apartment, and get rid of his phone.

"Call as soon as you can, okay? It's important."

Kate still remembers her parents' first answering machine, a Sony the size of a dictionary, it sat on the kitchen counter next to the phone books, white pages stacked under the more frequently consulted yellows, life used to be easily divided, social contacts here and commercial there, dog-eared corners and circled numbers for mechanics and doctors, plumbers and pizza, take-out menus tucked inside, bills of service too, business cards. Phone books served as filing cabinets, booster seats, leaf presses, paperweights, weapons. She hasn't seen a phone book in years.

Why is he not calling her back? Dexter isn't a husband who doesn't answer, not one of those guys who's always in meetings, on conference calls, at business lunches, you know how it is, crazy-busy, I can barely come up for air. Dexter is a reliably available person. Even in the midst of his big trades, he always has thirty seconds to talk to his wife.

What Dexter is also—inconveniently, at this moment—is a guy who refuses to enable location services on his smartphone, a guy who's a zealot for maintaining the most private settings on his device, who refuses to install apps that could track him, apps whose systems could be hacked. Dexter is ultra-paranoid about electronic intrusions, about hacks. Because Dexter is a hacker.

There are plenty of good reasons why he wouldn't answer his phone. He could be on the Métro, in one of the tunnels with no cellular service, on his way to buy Lego. He could be in the middle of a complex trade, can't distract himself. He could be standing on the street, talking to a neighbor, doesn't want to be rude. He could be watching extremely compelling porn, concentrating hard.

Maybe she'd believe any of those reasons, on any other day.

⚜

Her phone buzzes, another intercept of Schuyler's line.

"Hi, sorry to bother you so early? My name is Schuyler Franks, I'm calling from the Paris office?"

"It's . . . what time is . . . Jesus. Why are you calling me at home at five A.M.? Who are you?"

"We have a, um, situation here? Can you gather the board of directors for a conference call as soon as possible?"

❖

It was an immense favor that Kate did, allowing Julia and Bill to escape the clutches of the CIA, of arrest, humiliation, prosecution, prison. Julia deserved so much worse.

That was one point of view.

As that final encounter faded into the past, Kate began to accept that there was another possible point of view: that she'd deprived Julia of a fortune the woman had spent the entirety of her adult life pursuing, money stolen from a despicable criminal who didn't in any way deserve it, money that was now sitting in a numbered account, unrecoverable, forever. Kate had sentenced someone who'd once been her closest friend to a life on the run, a life of aliases and temporary homes, of fleeting friendships using fictional identities. Half a life, at best.

Perhaps Kate had been too punitive, like the Allied powers in the aftermath of World War I, engendering fascism from their own vindictiveness.

From this point of view, Kate's final encounter with Julia in that café may not turn out to be final. And gratitude was not what Kate should expect. Not at all.

Revenge was. Another world war.

PART IV

NOTRE-DAME

54

"Would you prefer English?"

"Yes," Dexter says, "thanks."

"You are a tourist, *Monsieur*?"

"No, I live near here."

"*Ah oui?*" Eyebrows raised.

One policeman is doing the talking, while the other lags behind, silent, waiting.

"I see that you look into this parking. Could I ask, *Monsieur*, why?"

"I keep a car there."

"*Une voiture? Ici?*" The cop purses his lips to expel a burst of air, a French gesture that can connote a wide breadth of emotions—exasperation, surprise, disappointment, frustration. Dexter understands what it means here, coming from this policeman: you must be plenty wealthy, *Monsieur*, to house a car here in the middle of St-Germain-des-Prés.

"I was thinking of using the car. To run an errand."

"Errant?"

Errand. How do you say this? "*Je dois faire une course.*"

The cop looks confused. Dexter doesn't know if he got the vocabulary wrong, or the grammar, or just the pronunciation. There are a lot of ways to be wrong.

"But I decided against it."

"No? Why?"

"With what's going on at the *gare,* and the Louvre, I thought traffic would be bad. Streets closed. Bridges."

"You are correct, *Monsieur*. It is not a good day to drive a car in Paris. You keep the car here all the days?"

"Yes." Dexter glances at his watch. He really has to get moving. "Is there something I can help you with?"

"If you please, yes: could I ask you to admit us to *le parking*? There is no attendant. And no person answers the telephone."

Dexter doesn't respond immediately; he doesn't want to get involved in whatever this is.

"Are you in a rush? I do not want to . . . er . . . *detain*? Is this the correct word?"

"Yes," Dexter says, but he isn't so sure. *Detain* has a couple of different meanings, especially in the context of police.

"*Bon, merci,* I do not want to detain you."

"I am, actually, in a hurry."

"Oh yes? Why?"

"I have to buy a toy. A birthday present."

The cop smiles indulgently. Or maybe ironically. Toy shopping during a terrorist attack.

"This will not take long, *Monsieur.* If you please."

"*D'accord.*" Dexter starts walking, it's just a few steps back to the garage entrance, the ubiquitous keypad that confronts Parisians at every door, a code to punch, then the overhead light begins to flash red, the door starts to rise, slowly, loudly.

"When you want to exit, press this button." Dexter points to the big SORTIE, realizing too late that this is a completely unnecessary instruction. Insulting.

"*Oui.* Could I ask, what car do you drive?"

Why the hell is he asking? This cop is starting to make Dexter nervous.

He feels his phone buzz a half-second before the ringing commences. He reaches into his pocket—

It's Kate again. He hits IGNORE.

"Is it necessary for you to answer?"

"No."

"You are sure?"

"Yes, it's fine."

"Thank you. *Donc,* your car?"

"It is an old car, a *break.*" French for station wagon. "Good for the family."

"Family? You have children?"

"Yes. Two boys."

"*Ah, c'est bon.* They are at school now?"

"Yes." Why the fuck is this cop asking him all these questions? "Officer, if you don't mind, I really must . . . I have to . . ."

"Yes, I understand, just one more moment." The cop reaches into his pocket, takes out his notepad, continues to rummage around in there. "It is necessary . . . for our records, do you understand? Ah!" He has found what he was looking for, a pen. "Your name, if you please? And your address? Phone number?" He extends the pad, the pen too.

Dexter doesn't want to provide this information. But nor does he want to refuse, to get into an antagonistic relationship with this cop. He has that immigrant's innate fear of law enforcement, you don't know what they can do to you. Keep your head down, do what you're told.

He's getting a queasy feeling about everything here. A fake name, fake address, fake phone number: these are what he's going to give the cop.

Dexter reaches for the pad, eager to get this over with, and his nerves about the cop, plus the general anxiety of today's make-or-break trade, not to mention the terrorist siege of the city, all this is enough to make Dexter jittery enough to fumble the handoff, and he drops the pen to the pavement with a tinny little clatter, and stumbles slightly as he bends to collect it, and mutters an apology, and comes up flustered and a little lightheaded.

The policeman stares at him.

Dexter starts to write, and can't help but notice that his hand is trembling.

55

Hunter's vision is blurry, but nevertheless yes, he can tell that it's the same place. He's now sitting in a chair, and he can't move his arms, nor his legs. He is tied up. And gagged.

"Ah, you're conscious." Simpson is applying ice to his own skull. "Good."

Hunter can't respond.

"That wasn't very smart of you, Mr. Forsyth. I'm disappointed and frankly surprised. I would've thought, a man like you, a business genius, a master of the universe. But don't you remember how that ended?"

Hunter furrows his brow.

"*Bonfire of the Vanities*? Tom Wolfe? Never read it? But surely you saw the movie, Forsyth. No?"

Colette is on the other side of the room, also tied up. By the ankles and wrists only, and she's sitting on the couch. She's not the one being punished.

"If I were as stupid as you, Mr. Forsyth, I'd be punching you in the face right now, getting revenge, *pow pow pow*. But I'm not. Because I have foresight. Foresight!" The guy laughs. "Ironic, isn't it? But I don't want it to look like you were *recreationally* beaten. If you end up dead, that's one thing. Honestly that's an outcome I wouldn't mind. But tortured? Very different implications."

Simpson looks over at Colette, then back at Hunter.

"Speaking of: you probably need water. But listen, Forsyth: if you start making a racket, annoying me? I'm going to beat the living shit out of you, and—full disclosure—I'm going to enjoy it. It's true that I'd rather it not look like you were tortured, but that's just a slight preference, not a requirement. You understand me?"

Hunter nods, and Simpson retrieves one of the water bottles that had been delivered earlier, along with ham sandwiches, back when hunger was relevant, when Hunter's biggest problem was lack of a cell signal.

The guy yanks out the gag. Tips water into Hunter's mouth, waits for a swallow, tips again.

"You all right?"

"Yes," Hunter says, a raspy sound. He coughs. "You've *kidnapped* me?"

"*Kidnapped?* I don't know about that. You came voluntarily, in fact it was your idea. And we're not seeking ransom. So I think *false imprisonment* would be more accurate."

"No ransom? Then what the hell do you want?"

"Merely the pleasure of your company, Mr. Forsyth."

"Oh come on."

"Believe it, don't believe it, I don't give a rat's ass." The guy shrugs. "Actually, to clarify: the *pleasure* part, that's a lie. Your company is not enjoyable. You're a prick. You know that, right? I can't be the first person to have told you."

"How much?"

Simpson raises his eyebrows, says nothing.

"What would my freedom cost?"

The guy still doesn't respond. His face is hard to read, with the big beard and tinted glasses and wavy hair draped across his forehead. Which must be the purpose of the whole getup: disguise.

"A million dollars?" Hunter starts, leaving plenty of room.

He'd flirted briefly with the prepper culture in the Valley, guys like him who were buying tracts of land in New Zealand, hardened bunkers in Nebraska, helicopters and motorcycles and private islands, stockpiling canned foods, water, fuel, ammunition. Like other guys with their hunting, their fishing: excuses to drink beer and talk gear.

Hunter himself wasn't going to build any bomb shelter, he didn't go in for that level of alarmism; he was too confident in the durability of the world order, and his place in it. But this burgeoning panic did have an effect, along with less apocalypse-themed horror stories of people who'd confronted problematic situations with prostitutes, with drugs, with cops, with legitimate mistakes of their own doing as well as setups, entrapments, frame-ups. And then to exacerbate matters there'd been the election of that unqualified unprepared irresponsible lunatic as president, a man who's capable of Lord knows what irrational behavior that could produce life-threatening conditions at any given moment, anywhere in the world.

Hunter sent Colette out to find a gold dealer on the rue Vivienne to buy the Krugerrands, then a leather-craftsman to retrofit his wallet with special slits that are snug enough so the coins won't slip out without requiring a bulky snap or zipper, but loose enough that the gold can be removed without destroying the wallet. Hunter never travels without this gold—anonymous, untraceable, universal liquidity, the sort of thing you can slip to a police officer, a prison guard, an immigrations official. "Look," Hunter could say to anyone, anywhere in the world. "Google it."

He is always prepared to purchase his safety, to negotiate for his release. Everyone has a price, and Hunter is willing to pay it. But the Krugerrands are not the right order of magnitude for this situation.

"Two million," he counteroffers himself.

"You think you can buy your way out of this?"

"Why not? This is about money, isn't it? Everything is."

"Okay, that's valid. But if you're really trying to buy your freedom, stop fucking around."

"Two million dollars is fucking around?"

"We both know, Forsyth, that it is."

"So this is a negotiation?"

"Not really. But maybe you'll blow me away. Shift my paradigm, as they say. So go ahead, Forsyth: your very best number."

What should Hunter say? Should he offer everything he could possibly get his hands on? There's no such definitive number, not without a timeframe. "How long do I have?"

The guy thinks about it. "Forty-eight hours."

One of Hunter's takeaways from those prepper dudes was that he needed to assess how much cash he could raise on short notice. Turned out it was only a couple hundred thousand, which wasn't going to get him very far, not in a bona fide cataclysm. So he began shifting things around until he could reasonably expect to be able to walk out of a bank branch with a million cash on any given day. If he has a few days' warning, a lot more; on the weekend, much less. He hopes the apocalypse doesn't begin on a Friday night.

"Okay: four million."

"Really? You're telling me that's your best number?"

"Five?"

"You disappoint me, Fors—"

Pounding at the door startles both men. Colette too, who has been completely silent, sitting in the corner, bound but not gagged, her big eyes moving from one man to the other, both of them probably looking to her a lot like different varieties of enemies.

Simpson undoes the locks and admits one of the French cops, with whom he confers at close range, low voices, then turns back to Hunter. "Listen: I need to run out for a few minutes. We'll pick this up when I return. Meantime, if you make any trouble, Claude is fully empowered to pinch-hit for me. *C'est vrai*, Claude?"

⚜

Just the pleasure of your company—what can that mean? It must have some meaning, it's not a random lie, it has a ring of truth, or partial truth, or—

Yes.

Hunter gets it all at once, the whole thing bum-rushes his brain—the early-morning terror attacks to draw away his police guard, to divert all police, and the telecom outage, the timing of it, and naturally there'd be no ransom, no interaction with the company or the family, with the police, with any authorities, with anyone at all, much safer without any communications, just remove Hunter from the office, from the press conference, from the multibillion-dollar merger, which will thus appear to be collapsing, speculation that the whole company is imploding, so inevitably the share price—

Fuck.

There is no transfer of any practical level of ransom that could possibly compare, no amount of cash inducement that Hunter could offer. Three million, five, ten: drops in the bucket. If his captors have access to real investment money—and they obviously do—they could make hundreds of millions today. Just like Hunter was going to.

Yes, he can see the whole ploy now.

Except one component. One not-at-all-minor detail that he can't see clearly, perhaps because he really does not want to: how does it all end for him?

56

Wyatt walks quickly. The street is quiet but not completely un-occupied, with most but not all of the shutters closed. Some-one might be observing him from any one of those apartment windows above, or from the stores below, the cleaning ladies who are mopping the bar's floor, the café waiters cleaning up after lunch service, the attentive owner of the cramped little *tabac*.

About a hundred meters up ahead, another pedestrian is walking away. Farther along, a lone man stands in a doorway, wearing a baseball cap, a bulky hoodie, sunglasses, though it isn't sunny on this close stretch of street.

Wyatt rubs his hand through his brand-new buzz-cut, self-administered fifteen minutes ago in the tiny bathroom of a brasserie that faced off against a *bar-tabac* on the far side of the intersection, the Métro station in between. The same setup everywhere. Wyatt is sick of Paris.

Remember the money.

He flushed his hair down the toilet, dropped the electric shaver in the trash. He took one final look in the dingy scratched-up mirror, nodded in appreciation: if anyone did a police sketch of the driver of the van, that sketch would not match the dude in the mirror. That driver doesn't exist anymore, that guy who'd scouted sites all over Paris, taking notes on the number and location of police and military, on the positions of security cameras and anti-ramming bollards and steel-toothed wedge barriers.

"Shouldn't I be worried about being noticed?" he'd asked. "While I'm taking all these notes?"

"No." The bearded guy was not concerned at all. "These are busy places, tens of thousands of people pass through every day, everyone typing into phones, taking pictures. No one will think you're doing anything unusual. Taking pictures of Notre-Dame? Please."

"But afterward? There are surveillance cameras."

"That's why you'll be wearing the eyeglasses, this hairstyle, these clothes."

It had been the same outfit on every recon mission, the same as this morning, this daily uniform. Except the few times when he'd been told to wear the athletic clothes with the cap, to carry the same canvas bag as he'd done this morning, that fucking bag.

"After you change your clothes and cut your hair and throw away the glasses, everything about the surveillance footage will look like someone who's not you."

As part of his interview process for this job, he'd needed to provide documentation that included a photo of himself. Which didn't seem odd at the time.

"Someone in particular?"

"No. Just not you."

"But facial recognition soft—"

"You're an *American*. That's not where they're going to look. No one looks at white American men as terrorism suspects. Not even in America, where practically all terrorism is perpetrated by white American men. Plus it's not as if you're going to be staring into the cameras, smiling for headshots."

Wyatt hadn't been convinced.

"Seriously," the guy said, "I know what I'm talking about here."

"Isn't that what everyone says who doesn't know what the fuck they're talking about? What makes you different?"

The man nodded, respecting the question, the challenge. Then he leaned forward, elbows on the table, eyes boring into Wyatt. "Because," he finally said, "I spent two decades working for the FBI."

Wyatt turns into the *passage,* which is divided into two lanes. One lane is a narrow street, one of those ridiculously long Parisian blocks that can really piss you off if you discover yourself at the wrong end of it. The other lane is a tall, slim tunnel carved out of the ground floor of a concrete-clad hulk of a building, spray-painted graffiti and glued-on concert posters, chunks missing from the exterior to reveal the cinder block underneath and the brick under that, with cauterized electrical wires and a capped-off plumbing pipe, piles of dogshit and a chained-up bicycle that has been stripped of most of its parts, one flat tire resting in a pool of what smells like urine. Somebody pissed on this poor abandoned bicycle.

This tunnel had once been the drive-through loading area for the building when it was a small factory, or a warehouse. The loading bays are now covered in plywood, the ground in trash: empty beer bottles, cigarette butts, a few hypodermics, condom wrappers, the full assortment.

There's no light in there.

Wyatt doesn't spook easily, he even relishes extracurricular violent encounters, muggers, panhandlers, junkies, he's more than happy to kick anyone's ass who even remotely merits an ass-kicking, plus plenty of people who don't.

Even for him, this is one scary-ass tunnel.

Wyatt won't be surprised if someday he ends up getting murdered. Hopefully he won't see it coming, won't feel a thing. One minute he'll be minding his own business, and the next someone will have shot him in the back of the head. That would probably happen in a place like this. This is where he himself would kill a guy like him.

He's glad he still has the weapon. He'll have to get rid of it soon, a firearm is not something he can take to the airport, and he probably shouldn't even bring it to the train station. Maybe after the transaction he'll leave it here in this tunnel.

Wyatt is also glad he'd arranged for backup. A side deal that the boss wouldn't know a damn thing about.

"I don't trust this dude," Wyatt had said to Blake, in that nearly empty bar in the eleventh. They knew each other from Afghanistan, then both had migrated into similar private-sector arrangements. "I need someone to watch my back."

"No doubt," Blake said sagely, then took a sip of beer. "You got it, brah."

"You'll need a gun."

"Already have one."

"Don't hesitate to use it."

"Dude."

They had a good laugh at that, both pretending it was funnier than it was, exaggerating their own heartlessness, their recklessness. In their line of work, it was worth actual money, this reputation, it was a bankable asset, like a hundred-mile-per-hour fastball, or a close friendship with a Trump. Things that could be relied upon to get you paid.

Wyatt stands in the tunnel entrance, peers into the darkness. Then he glances up the street, where the man in the hoodie has started walking in this direction, closing the distance. But there's no sign of anyone in the dark tunnel. Wyatt takes out his phone, composes another short text: *Here.* His finger hovers above the SEND button for a few seconds while he looks around, then his fingertip meets the touch screen—

The flash of light is almost immediate, preceding the sound by a split-second, the unmistakable ding of an incoming message, just twenty meters ahead, the device's light dimmed by a pillar but its sound amplified, bouncing off all the hard surfaces here, not quite an echo but something like it, an elongation, the psychological effect of sound in darkness.

The bearded American is already here.

Wyatt slides the phone back into his pocket, and replaces his grip around the handle of his pistol. He takes another step forward, deeper into the dark.

Remember the money.

57

Kate accelerates, weaving through traffic once again, cars are stopped everywhere, complete impasses at major intersections, police redirecting this way and that. She wends a path between cars, up on sidewalks, through a pedestrian plaza, the police aren't going to bother with some woman puttering around on a scooter, pleading about retrieving her children from school.

Kate alights on the Left Bank where the Gare d'Austerlitz borders the Jardin des Plantes. The first time the family visited Paris from Luxembourg, they drove up to this very stretch of street, and Ben exclaimed from the backseat, "Mommy, look! There's an ostrick over there!"

"An ostrich?"

"Yah! Right there!"

She didn't see anything except trees. "I don't see it, Sweetie. Are you sure?"

"Yah. But it went away."

She didn't believe him; there weren't ostriches roaming the streets of Paris. But Ben was four, alternative facts were still excusable, an understandably hazy line between real-life and make-believe. A year later, when they finally made a visit over to the *ménagerie,* there it was, an ostrich enclosure, right here abutting the quay.

"You were right," she said to Ben. She felt terrible for not having believed him in the first place. "There *are* ostriches here."

"Yah," he said. "I know. Let's go back to the baboons."

⚜

Kate tried harder here. She became more patient, more present, more competent than she'd been in Luxembourg. Most days she could convince herself that it was fine—no, more: it was good, maybe great, yes, this was definitely what she should be doing with her life. Late at night, though?

Yes, she had learned how to be an expat, friendly with strangers in cafés, in bookstores, at school, accepting every invitation, open to new people, to new experiences, the default position was yes. But what she had not mastered was how to be a full-time stay-at-home mom. Even on the days when she found it satisfying—and there were more of them as the children grew more manageable, and her existence more comfortable— she was also aware that this stage was so finite. In the blink of an eye, the kids would be grown. Then what would she do? And when would she do it?

When she figured out what had really gone on in Luxembourg, she was able to come up with at least one of the answers: now. She would go back to work. Start fresh, wiser this time, better equipped to handle the problems, to attain the balance. This time, it would all work out.

Now she understands that she was wrong. That she'd allowed herself to be deceived by selfishness, by vanity, by the delusional charade that she could have everything, that maybe she even deserves everything— the husband and kids and career and money.

No.

❦

There are two distinct possibilities, and Kate can't quite decide which is worse.

One: Dexter is part of—the architect behind?—an international con- spiracy to kidnap 4Syte's CEO while manufacturing terror threats at the company's global offices and general terror in Paris to obscure the spe- cifics while causing a widespread dip in securities valuation throughout the world's markets and in particular an extreme loss of value in 4Syte's stock, ensuring immense profitability for his 4Syte short-sell.

Two: Dexter is being framed for all that. And there's only one person in the world who'd be doing the framing.

❦

Kate is almost home, taking a corner at high speed, when the Peugeot in front of her slams on the brakes, and she's forced to slow down. She cranes her neck to peer up ahead, where a police car is parked partially on the curb, half-obstructing the traffic lane. The Peugeot overreacted, prematurely: the obstruction is still a couple hundred meters ahead.

"*Connard!*" Kate curses, loudly.

The profanities that Kate mutters to herself, that she sputters at strangers, these are mostly in French, like the numbers of the access code to her office building. This isn't purposeful; it's evolutionary. She can't even say the word *coffee* anymore, it sounds ridiculous to her.

She re-angles the scooter, trying to get a better view of what the cops are doing, why they're blocking the street. There, she can see a pair of them at the entrance to a garage, it's her own garage actually, and—

Oh God no.

Her stomach falls away.

What the hell can she do about this?

The simplest solution is impossible: she can't just walk up to a pair of Parisian cops and shoot them. Not here in broad daylight. There's a pedestrian halfway between the corner and the garage, a witness—

Christ, did she really just formulate that thought? That she's not going to shoot policemen because she's *afraid of getting caught*?

No, she needs to divert them, and she sees how immediately. She spins the Vespa back onto the cross street, just out of the police's sight, then around again, ready to return. She has no time to waste; it could be too late already.

Earlier this morning, Kate worried that at some point today, any given second might end up counting. This wasn't what she was envisaging.

She draws Inez's gun out of her pocket. Kate glances around, there are a few people walking on these sidewalks, but no one is paying attention to her. Afterward they will. And then . . . ?

And then: fuck the consequences.

She releases the safety, aims, and squeezes the trigger, twice, *pop-pop*.

A pedestrian is screaming as Kate tears around the corner as fast as possible, trying to look like a woman fleeing in sheer terror who pretends to notice the police and comes to a screeching, swerving stop.

"*S'il vous plaît!*" she yells at the cops, pointing back up the street. "*Un homme—*"

She doesn't want to say more than necessary, doesn't want her accent to betray her. She's wearing a VDM shirt and riding a Vespa, she might very well be French, nothing whatsoever to do with any American man the police are questioning here.

"*Restez ici,*" one of the cops says to the civilian, who answers immediately, "*Bien sûr.*"

Both police jump in the car, and the driver starts reversing before the passenger has closed his door, backs up violently to the end of the block. The car fishtails to a stop, then shifts, and speeds through the intersection—

"Get on," Kate says to her husband. Saving him, yet again, from his own stupidity. "Let's go."

It was such a complex web of dishonesties and betrayals in which Dexter had gotten caught, long-term entanglements with savage criminals and international law enforcement, with stolen Russian fighter jets and ruthless African warlords, cutting-edge electronic intrusions and high-class hookers, bank break-ins and heartless torture, a townhouse in Belgravia and a farmhouse in the Ardennes and fifty million stolen euros divided in half, in two separate numbered accounts for two separate people, both planning to never work again, to never want for anything.

This was a plot that doesn't come to a definitive finish, not until everyone involved is dead. Maybe not even then.

Kate has never stopped looking over her shoulder, never stopped watching, waiting, planning. Never stopped expecting that one day, it would catch up to Dexter. To her too.

58

C hris steps from behind the pillar, makes himself visible. His hands hang at his side, empty. He doesn't want to look threatening, he wants to put Wyatt at ease, and the guy is obviously in a state of high anxiety, you can see it at a glance, even from a distance: a danger-ous armed man with adrenaline coursing through him. It wouldn't take much to push him over the edge.

"Hello?" Wyatt takes another step into the tunnel, straining to see through the darkness. Chris can't see Wyatt's gun, but he can tell by the guy's stance.

"Yeah. I'm back here."

Wyatt takes another slow step, looking around side to side.

"Everything okay? Any problems?"

Wyatt continues to approach, but doesn't answer. Chris instinctively shifts his weight to his right, toward the safety of the concrete pillar.

"Affirmative," Wyatt says. He takes another couple of steps, stops. "There actually was a problem. A pretty fucking big one."

"And that was?"

"When I abandoned the van, there were two people . . ."

Wyatt looks around again, nervous about . . . what?

"They saw you? These people?"

"Affirmative."

"And?"

"Well . . . You know."

"No, I don't. It's just me here, Wyatt. No one's listening, I'm not re-cording. So tell me what happened."

"I took care of it."

"Okay, that's good. But I need to be one hundred percent sure I understand what it is we're talking about."

"I. Took. Care. Of. It."

"You mean you killed them? Two people in the garage?"

Wyatt nods. He seems to be avoiding saying anything specific aloud, maybe worried about creating recorded evidence. That's a surprising level of paranoia to adopt at this stage of the game, considering what they've already discussed aloud, in circumstances in which a recording would've been far easier.

But that was all before the fact. Plotting is not the same as executing. Plotting can always fail to coalesce, plotting can fall apart, plotting is just words, plotting can turn out to be bullshit.

In this general type of situation, Wyatt is probably right: paranoia is an asset, a survival mechanism. But in this particular situation, he happens to be paranoid about the wrong thing.

"Does that, um, event present any further threat to you? To the op?"

"Negative."

"Okay. Any other issues?"

Wyatt shakes his head.

"So everything else went as planned?"

"Affirmative."

"You went to the Odéon station to change clothes, swap bags? No problems?"

"None."

"You changed trains and ditched the bag on the Métro? Which line did you end up on?"

"Does it matter?"

It doesn't. Maybe he shouldn't push too much, should leave well enough alone, end this interaction before anything goes awry.

Then again: no. He can't show any weakness. He can't give Wyatt any idea that he's a man who can be taken advantage of. Even though this is the final time these two will meet, it's important to maintain the balance of power. Wyatt needs to understand that he can't simply decide unilaterally to turn this final encounter into something more adversarial, more profitable. He needs to remember who's boss, and why. And if he doesn't remember, he needs to be reminded.

Which is why Chris says, "It matters because I'm asking." Quietly, but firmly. "So tell me, what fucking Métro did you leave the bag on?"

Wyatt seems to wince at this quiet tirade, but it's hard to tell. "The 8."

"Thank you." The two men stare at each other across the divide of darkness, of wariness. They'd needed to trust each other until today, but now that Wyatt's job is finished, everything has changed. "Anything else I need to know?"

"No sir." Unmistakable hostility in that *sir.* Ironic obedience, like a petulant teenager addressing a gym teacher.

"Now I'm going to put my hand into my breast pocket. Get your envelope."

"Slowly. If you don't mind."

"You're the one with the gun." Chris had been halfway expecting Wyatt to pat him down, had planned for that.

"Thank you. You've done good work."

"Uh-huh." Wyatt takes the envelope, glances inside. A chunk of cash, an RER ticket to Charles de Gaulle, a boarding pass to Miami.

"So are you gonna tell me now what any of this has been about?"

"Sorry, that's not how this works." He knows Wyatt doesn't care, at least not much. Doesn't care whom he killed directly, whom he might kill indirectly, whom he killed in the past. Wyatt is willing to kill anyone for a price, and it's not even that high of a price.

Which makes this so much easier.

The guy actually boasted, in his interview. At least eighteen confirmed kills. In Afghanistan on behalf of the government, that was defensible, though the glee in it was not. But then in Sudan, Kenya, Syria. Not just a mercenary, a murderer; also a human trafficker.

The world is going to be a better place.

He does feel bad about the guy's sick kid. When he first heard Wyatt's story, he thought it was horseshit, exactly the kind of sad-sack fiction that an unimaginative asshole would invent to make himself appear sympathetic, to cloak the selfishness of his motivations. Parental love of a sick child: who can argue with that?

So Chris checked out the story, and was surprised to discover it was true. That's one of the reasons you check out stories, even the unlikely ones.

He was sympathetic. Chris too had his own familial responsibilities to consider, as a husband, as a father. Also as a son, that whole fucked-up fiasco with his mother. He was completely surprised by it; he'd ignored the signs. He's forever surprised by people's ability to surprise him.

"Okay then." Wyatt nods once more, this time a final goodbye. He turns away.

Chris won't waste a second now. He raises his right hand, back behind the concrete pillar, where his fingers immediately find the pair of bolts that he himself drilled into this wall at waist height. Similar to what some guys have in their garages with pegboards, to hold tools, except this is just the one tool, which he now swings in front of his body, the thing longer and heavier because of the bulky sound suppressor attached to the end.

He steadies his arm, taking careful aim through the darkness at the silhouette's center, now five yards away.

Chris has practiced this countless times, but that was decades ago, back in training. The physical motion is easier than tying your shoe, turning a doorknob. Mentally, though?

He has spent so much of his life pretending to be hard as nails, but he isn't, not at all. He has never even meted out a serious beat-down, much less killed anyone. But from an early age he learned to act, as many boys do, then as he grew older he took the acting more seriously—acting for football, for law enforcement, for high-stakes international crime.

The disguise helps. Looking like a different sort of man while behaving that way, fake it till you make it. Till you become a guy who can do this.

It's possible that at the very last instant Wyatt hesitates, slows his step, something of a syncopated beat of a stutter step, maybe suspecting what's going on, maybe considering his options—should he break into a run, should he fall to the ground, should he leap to the side, should he draw his own weapon while dropping to a knee and spinning, the things you can do to make it harder for someone to shoot you—but in the end he doesn't have time to do any of those things, or even to come to a decision, before the first bullet hits him square in the middle of his back, an immediate blinding wave of pain, and perhaps he's aware that he's beginning to sink to his knees, but he's unable to will his body into any other movement, any evasion, and it's just a half-second at most before that thought is obliterated, along with any other thoughts, as the second bullet explodes through the back of his head.

This is not exactly how Wyatt imagined it would happen. But it's pretty damn close.

❧

Chris stands over the inert body, gives a kick, an abundance of caution. The dead man's arm moves against the shoe, but nothing in the lump of flesh responds.

He drops the bulky gun into his pocket, adjusts the angle so the grip isn't sticking out. He kneels, reaches into Wyatt's jacket, extracts the cash and travel paperwork.

What about Wyatt's gun? Chris had been planning on leaving the weapon with the dead man. But now this gun has become a ballistics match to a double-murder, bodies with the toxic van in a parking garage, and that's not something that should be associated with this corpse. He should take it, dispose of it. Which will entail first walking around with it. A gun in each pocket, double-fisted, like the psychopath villain in an action-adventure movie.

The smell of gunpowder hangs in the air. He glances around, sees nothing. He listens, hears nothing.

He takes one final look at Wyatt. Ex-Wyatt. A man who long ago seceded from the brotherhood of man, and now has finally been erased as a further threat to humanity.

Chris starts to walk away, his mind moving onto what's next, when, where—

❧

"Not so fast."

He freezes, staring ahead at a man who has appeared in the tunnel's entrance, a silhouette backlit by daylight, wearing a hoodie and a baseball cap, holding something in front of him. Chris can't confirm with absolutely certainty what it is, but he certainly has his goddamned suspicions.

59

"Tell me what the hard parts will be," Mahmoud said.

"For one, you would have to send your children away in advance. Back to Egypt. Your kids cannot be here when you do this job."

"That sounds ominous."

"Yes." The bearded American looked grave. "It is."

"I will never see my children again?"

The man did not answer.

"Because I will not be able to leave France?" Mahmoud realized that he sounded irrationally hopeful.

"No, that is not it."

"My children, they will be okay?"

"Yes."

"I see." Mahmoud realized that he had known, even before this meeting. "I will not." This was the obvious explanation for all the solemnity. But it was not until this moment that he allowed himself to articulate it. "My job will be to die."

"Yes."

"How?"

"Painlessly."

Mahmoud let out a short snort of mirthless laughter. "One hopes. What does that mean, in effect?"

"Are you sure you want to know?"

"Yes." Though was that true? "I think so."

"It is your choice."

Mahmoud gave it a few seconds' thought. Wild, disorganized thought, ideas shooting off in every direction. *Thought* was perhaps not the activity that was going on in his brain.

He nodded.

"Okay. It will be—" The man cut himself off. "Are you sure?"

"Please."

"Okay. One possibility is that you will be shot by the French police, or army, using a high-powered sniper's rifle."

"That is horrible."

"It will be painless."

"And what is the other way?"

"You will be wearing a vest packed with explosives. That vest will detonate."

"A suicide vest?"

"Either way, the end of your life will be instantaneous."

"How will I know which?"

"Does it matter?"

Did it?

"You will not know. *I* will not know. There will be no warning. No alarm bell will tell you that you have one minute left, or ten seconds, nothing like that. One moment you will be standing on this earth, and the next you will be in paradise."

A better world for him, that is the promise. And a better life here in this world, for those he leaves behind. For his children. That was the only conceivable motivation, and that was exactly what was being offered.

He had not thought it was possible, that a moment could be worse than receiving your death sentence, with the doctor's hand on his shoulder.

"There is nothing to be done?"

The doctor shook his head, looking very sympathetic. It must be horrible, telling people they are going to die, there is no hope, you have twelve months, you have four, one.

"Surgery?"

"It is too widespread."

Mahmoud was about to ask about chemotherapy, radiation; he had been educating himself. But when the moment came, he did not want to make this conversation worse for Dr. Féraud, who was a very nice man. This was not an argument Mahmoud could win by trying harder.

He nodded his acceptance to the doctor, to himself. *I am going to die very soon.*

That had been the worst moment of his life. Until this one: kneeling in the airport, with his children gathered in his arms. The awfulness of it grew and grew, expanding outward like an explosion, a nuclear detonation.

"I love you," he said to the boy.

The infinite awfulness of it, of knowing that he was seeing his son and daughter for the very last time. He tried desperately not to cry—he did not want to make the children cry, he did not want to alarm them—but he failed, it was so far beyond his control.

"And I love you," to the girl. "You are in the heart of my heart." He pressed both fists to his chest. "Here."

He had told all of them—his children, his in-laws—that he wanted to save as much money as possible, that he would forward it to them in Egypt, that he would rejoin them soon. He would be working all the time, he said, he would not be able to care for the children properly, he did not want their education to suffer, he did not want to neglect small children who needed attention. It would be only a few months. He would save so much money that when they did reunite, they would live well.

Today is when his wife's parents will discover the truth. But hopefully his children will never know every detail. Hopefully the money will help, if they do.

Mahmoud had already accessed the numbered account. He had changed the password, he had verified that the first payment had been transferred; it was so much money. He had sent the necessary details to his in-laws. He had done everything there was for him to do.

"I wish I could tell you something different." Dr. Féraud took Mahmoud's hands. "But you will be dead within the year. There is no question about it."

"You can leave your children poor, Mr. Khalil."

Mahmoud wishes he could control it, pull the trigger himself, put himself out of today's version of misery, after many months of living with a different misery, and a year with another. More than his share.

"Or you can leave them rich."

He had not wanted to ask the final question, because he knew he did not want the answer. But it was unacceptable to leave it unasked. He had to know.

"None," the man answered.

Mahmoud was confused. "Excuse me?"

"You will not kill anyone."

How was this possible?

"Only one person will die."

Perhaps this strange American man was lying to him. Mahmoud accepted that he might never know the truth. Not in this life.

"You."

60

"Don't move," the guy says.

This new arrival must be some confederate of Wyatt's, backup, a bodyguard against the possibility that Chris would turn out to be a double-crosser. Which he was. So as a bodyguard, this guy has been a profound failure, what with the dead body he was tasked to guard lying right there. Maybe he was supposed to be a bodyguard, but decided to play it different. More lucratively.

Chris should've seen something like this coming. What would he have done different?

"I don't wanna hurt you." The drawl is Deep South. Alabama, maybe. Mississippi.

"I appreciate that," Chris says. "I don't want to get hurt."

He can see that this guy is gripping his weapon firmly with both hands, sighting just below eye level, arms extended rigidly in front, with one leg slightly ahead of the other, his torso half-turned to the side. A trained pose. This is no mugger.

"You're gonna lie on the ground." Of course—the accent is Louisiana. Just like Wyatt. "Facedown, legs spread, hands behind your head."

Chris looks down at the disgusting filth. "Come on, man, is that necessary? Let's—"

"Do *not* move. Not a fuckin' muscle."

"Okay, let's stay calm."

"I'm plenty calm, don't you worry about my level of calm. You worry about your level of obedience."

"Okay."

"When you're lyin' down, I'm gonna walk over to you, reach into your pockets. Relieve you of your weapon. Your cash. Then I'm gonna walk away. You're gonna remain lyin' on that ground for a count-a hundred. You understand?"

"Sure do."

"If you, um, *deviate* from these instructions, you know what's gonna happen?"

It's apparently not a rhetorical question, so Chris nods.

"I'm glad we understand one another."

Chris doesn't give a damn about this cash, he'll be making so much money today that this couple hundred grand will amount to a rounding error. But the money isn't the only thing this guy is planning to take. This is not a guy who simply showed up here, noticed an opportunity, and seized it. This is not a crime of opportunity. And this guy is not going to let any witnesses walk out of here.

This whole thing was a horrible plan. A greedy plan. An *insane* plan. Chris shouldn't have agreed to this, he has known it all along. And now his child will grow up without a father, his wife without a husband. Although knowing Susanna, she may solve that problem quickly.

He has always just gone along with other people's schemes. Sometimes midstream he'd try to take ownership of a plan—a frat prank, a ski trip, a sting operation—by being confident and competent, by being a leader, he was all those things. But he was never the one with the ideas. He worries that this means he's stupid, a self-awareness that's arriving—among others—with the onset of middle age. And, as self-realizations tend to be, after their utility.

"You waitin' for somethin' in particular?"

"I guess not."

He wishes he'd had the chance to remove the various components of his disguise. Shaved off the ludicrous beard, cut away the long wavy hair, peeled off the cosmetic facial scar and the fake forearm tattoos, removed the colored contact lenses. If he's going to die here, he wants his corpse to be identified as himself, an innocent American. Not as the mastermind behind today's citywide terror siege and kidnapping.

The primary witnesses, the most important actors, will be dead: Wyatt is dead already, and maybe even Mahmoud too. But there are also the bit players, the people who deposited the bomb-filled bags around town, and the ersatz cops waiting for him back in the condemned building, and

Forsyth and his assistant, and the stray freelancers whose jobs had been to construct alternate narratives, starting conversations on street corners, planting physical evidence in residential courtyards.

It was more than one narrative that they constructed: one to implicate their target, another to exonerate him.

Any of these piecework freelancers will be able to identify the black-eyed heavily bearded American with the cheek scar and the tattoo sleeve, if this incarnation of him is what they're shown by police.

"Go ahead, then. On your knees."

Chris knows he's out of time. He takes a deep breath, getting ready. "Okay."

He begins to kneel, but instead flings his body to the side, falling, meeting the ground with his right shoulder, rolling toward the dark wall—

⚜

The unmuffled gunshots sound like sonic booms in this tunnel, once, twice, the explosions echoing off the hard surfaces. A third shot strikes something metal, a loud ping, a ricochet.

Chris has been hit, he knows this instantaneously, but he can't yet assess the severity, can't tell if he has absorbed a bullet into a fleshy part of his arm or if an artery has been severed, a vital organ punctured, his life slipping away in the next minutes or even seconds.

He continues another rotation of roll, and as he comes to a stop he reaches into his pocket to grasp his own weapon, yanks it out with a tear of cloth—

Another shot explodes from the other man's muzzle—

The source of the pain is somewhere on the upper left of his thorax, the chest or the shoulder, it's a deep burning, it could be very bad, but he can't afford to dwell on that as he lies in a puddle of urine, with the angle of his prone body presenting the smallest possible target, the only thing that could be shot now is his face, he has no time to spare, he squeezes the trigger once and shifts his aim and squeezes again and shifts again and squeezes again and once more, a cluster in the other man's direction.

He can't hear the body hit the pavement. But Chris does see the man fall, completely limp. Is it possible that he's playing possum? No, why would he do that, he had the drop, the upper hand, every advantage. And he has the most to lose by drawing out the duration of this exchange.

No, this isn't a ruse. The guy is down. Definitely. Permanently.

The pain is now flooding through Chris, radiating from his shoulder in pulsating waves.

His breaths are quick and shallow and extremely painful. Oh this hurts.

Okay, what now, what now, what now . . . ?

He can hear voices beyond the tunnel's entrance, in the street. This is a grubby neighborhood but not a violent slum, people here aren't going to ignore gunfire, pretend they saw nothing, heard nothing. No sane person is going to come into this darkness to investigate an ongoing gunfight, but someone will call the police, very soon. Maybe already has.

Would that be terrible? At least he'd get medical attention, have a chance to survive this gunshot, which is definitely not an incidental flesh wound.

Then what? How could he explain this shootout? He's in possession of all this cash, what can his story be? The passport in his pocket is fake, but his real identity will be confirmed quickly. Then what?

Jail, that's what. In France. Or America. Or worse: a black site in the mountains of Romania, in eastern Poland. No lawyer, no trial. No exit.

Is he thinking clearly? He can't tell. Can you tell when you're not? Or is part of not thinking clearly not knowing that you're not thinking clearly?

Jesus, it hurts so much. But he needs to get up. And he needs to do it right now, or he never will again.

61

"Come on." Kate hops off the scooter. She looks across the small spit of river that separates the Île de la Cité from the Left Bank, at the flashing lights of police cars surrounding Notre-Dame, an army truck as well. This is such a big production, today's terror threats.

"What happened back there?" Dexter is hustling to catch up.

"I fired into the air. To divert the police."

There's a good-size crowd in the small plaza here, as usual, mostly American tourists—loud bachelorettes in matching berets asking strangers to take group photos, middle-aged American men wearing golf-brand caps, teenagers in flip-flops staring at phones, Chinese-character tattoos on characters who aren't Chinese.

The attached café is packed, mostly coffee drinkers but also a few glasses of wine have appeared. Paris may be besieged by terror threats, but the afternoon is creeping along without any detonations, without any fatalities, and *l'apéro* hour is approaching.

"Why do I need to be gotten away from the police?"

Kate glares at Dexter, but doesn't say anything.

"What are we doing here?" he asks.

English speakers come to this bookshop from all over the city to buy current magazines, or the latest bestsellers from New York and London, or the Lost Generation classics, paperbacks of *The Little Prince*. Or just to hear English, to interact in their native tongue with other college students, other expats. All Americans seem to find their way here, which means no one would remark upon another one or two showing up on a late afternoon, walking past the register and through the warren of low ceilings and uneven floors, books jammed onto every surface, shelves above your head when you pass through one room after another all the way to the very back, where they find the proprietor bent over a counter, peering at paperwork, presenting to the world a violent explosion of blond curls that emanate every which way, like a small-town Fourth of July fireworks display, the grand finale, streamers shooting willy-nilly, the point not art but just light and noise and—if everyone is being honest—more than a little bit of danger.

"*Bonjour*," Kate says. "I'm wondering if you can help me?"

The woman looks up at Kate and smiles, then notices Dexter. "Delighted to." She's a younger woman than you'd imagine would own an old shop like this.

"I'm looking for a gift. Could I ask you to show me some first editions?"

Big smile. This is something booksellers love to hear. "Please, follow me."

Dexter leans toward his wife's ear. "What the hell are we doing?"

Kate still doesn't answer. They follow the owner back the way they came, out the shop's front entrance, and through an adjoining door, propped open by a workman's pile of bricks. These stairs are rickety, uneven, and men are working on an elevator shaft, which is shored up with wood planks. They climb, and climb, then come to a stop. The woman flips through a big key ring, finds what she's looking for. Turns a couple of locks.

This is another book-lined room, with a dining table and chairs, a table with a printer and office supplies, a window that looks out onto the Petit Pont, the Seine, Notre-Dame.

"This way." Through the narrow kitchen, boxes of biscuits, tea, mismatched plates, old dishrags. Up a couple of steps into a utility room, washing machine, bathroom sink, linen cabinets. She unlocks another door, and they all step into a bedroom, blue walls, vintage posters, more bookshelves packed with old hardbacks, a small desk with a bright red typewriter. This window faces onto nothing, just another window whose curtains are drawn.

Kate shuts the door behind them. "Thanks so much," she says. "This is Dexter."

The two shake hands.

"I'm sorry but I don't have much time," the woman says, turning to an armoire. "Look." She pulls the armoire's door open, there are a few things hanging, a rain slicker, a windbreaker, a cable-knit cardigan. She pushes the hangers to the side, revealing the furniture's back panel.

"You put your hand here, like this. And push."

There's a soft click as she presses into a section of wood, and the panel releases on a hinge. It's a small door, two feet wide and four tall, carved out of the wall behind the armoire.

"There's no light switch back here, so you'll have to use your phone. There, you can see now. Come, have a look. We built this hatch during the Occupation."

Dexter peers in. It's the landing of another staircase, not the one they ascended.

"You follow this down to a short hall that leads to the backdoor, which lets out onto the other street. There's an old bicycle hanging on the wall next to the door, if you need it."

Now she fumbles again with the keys, removes a couple. "Here." She presses the keys into Dexter's palm. "There's a toilet across the hall, a shower round the corner, I'm sure a bit to eat in the kitchen."

She scans a bookshelf, yanks down a clothbound volume, opens to the endpapers, and scrawls a price with a pencil that she yanked from the hidden depths of her hair. "When you leave, pay at the front." She thrusts the book at Kate. "I hope one day you'll explain all this to me. Good luck Dexter." She kisses Kate on both cheeks. "Kate, you too."

"What the hell is going on?" Dexter asks.

Kate watches her husband closely as she says, "Hunter Forsyth is missing." It certainly looks like genuine surprise on his face. But then again, he'd be prepared for this.

"Missing? I guess that's why the press conference was canceled. You think he was kidnapped?"

"I'm almost positive of it. Listen, Dex: how much money have you made today?"

His eyes cut away. "I don't kn—"

"*Dexter.*"

He winces at her tone. She's pissed, and wants him to know it.

"Last I checked, it was about two hundred K."

A lot more than she would've thought possible. "That's just from shorting two-fifty worth of 4Syte?"

He cuts his eyes away again.

"Jesus, Dexter. What else?"

He doesn't answer. She's fed up, and without really thinking about it she punches her husband in the arm.

"Hey. What the fuck?"

"Tell me right now, goddamn it."

"Okay, I also used funds from a Swiss account. Another two-fifty."

She shakes her head. "I can't even . . ."

He'd lied to her, again. But at the moment that's not what's important. Which is that Dexter invested a total of five hundred, and so far has made a profit of two hundred. And although that's certainly a profitable one-day return, it's not anywhere near a sufficient order of magnitude to justify today's conspiracy. Dexter is a man who once stole fifty million euros; he wouldn't do something like this for two hundred thousand.

Which means that Dexter can't be one of the conspirators; he must be innocent, relatively. That's a relief. But there's still a conspiracy, and he's in the middle of it.

"Dexter, did anyone see you this morning, between say eight and nine-thirty? This is when I think Forsyth was being kidnapped."

"You're asking for my alibi? Jesus, Kate."

She glares at him.

"Okay: Luc, as you know."

His friend, tennis partner, and guy who served as the conduit for the insider-trading information to begin with. Luc is not an alibi. He'll look like an accomplice. He'll be arrested too, if he hasn't been already. Maybe that's what he deserves.

"How exactly did you meet Luc?"

"Message board."

"Were you identifiable as you?"

"Um, not really. I guess."

"No? Or not really?"

"No, I don't think so."

"What's your handle?"

"LuxDayTrader."

"Really? A Luxembourg day trader who now lives in Paris? You don't think that's identifiable as you? Are you an idiot?"

So that's a possibility: Luc was a plant, used to lure Dexter. In which case Luc would definitely not be an alibi. He would no longer even be findable.

"Okay, anyone else?"

"Julien." Their everyday waiter. A guy who'd probably be willing to lie for a high-tipping regular customer; another non-airtight alibi.

"What about people you don't know? Did you stop somewhere to buy water? Wave to a baker?"

"Yes, there was an old man waiting at a street corner with me—just *Bonjour, comment ça va,* chitchat while we waited for the light. And a woman too."

"At the same light?" That would be an awfully friendly corner.

"No, she was right after tennis ended at nine. I kind of crashed into her, at the park. Spilled her groceries everywhere. I helped her pick up, and I apologized, but . . ."

"What?"

"I got the sense that I'd seen her before."

He'd seen her before. "She attractive, Dexter?"

He looks like he's about to say no, but changes his mind. "Yes."

What does this mean? Two alibis, at either end of the hour when he played tennis in the Luxembourg Gardens? That's not a coincidence. But there's no way to find these alibis, they're just strangers on streets, no connection to anything. They're useless.

"Why are you asking about this?"

"Because you're being framed, Dexter."

"Framed for what?"

"What the hell do you think?"

"But there's no way . . . how could . . . ?" He shakes his head. "Why would I kidnap someone I'm well known to hate? No one would believe I'd be that stupid."

It's true. Not at a trial, with lawyers, a jury, judge. But at first glance, he looks too guilty not to investigate, and the investigation wouldn't even need to get anywhere near trial to ruin their lives. That, Kate now realizes, is exactly the point: not jail, just ruin. An eye for an eye.

"Who's framing me?"

Kate turns back to her husband. "You know damn well."

"*Bonjour?*"

"Hi, it's Kate."

"Kate! We're *so* looking forward to tonight."

"Yeah. About that."

"Oh dear. Is something wrong?"

"I'm afraid so."

Kate promises herself this: you will never, ever again use that nickname, not even in your head. If this woman does this enormous favor for you, forevermore you must call her by her real name, even in—especially in—your mind.

This will be hard.

For a split-second it escapes Kate, she uses it so infrequently, but then she remembers Hashtag Mom's real name: "Hailie, could I ask for a *huge* favor?"

Kate looks around this small room, exactly how a place like this should look, a refuge for visiting writers above a Left Bank bookshop. How long will Dexter hide out in here? Where will he go next? And will Kate—will the kids—go with him?

"I'm going to leave you," she says.

Dexter's jaw drops open, devastated. Misunderstanding.

"Not permanently," Kate clarifies. "But I have to go."

She arranged for Hailie to pick up the kids, and to call around to the other families to cancel dinner.

"So, what?" Dexter asks. "I'm just supposed to hide here? Above a bookstore?"

"We can't risk you being seen by any police. We'll need to get you new clothes, a shave, a haircut, a new everything. Did you give the cops your name?"

"Fake name, address, phone number. But they do know that I keep a car in the garage."

It won't be hard for the police to find Dexter, if they try. Will they?

That depends on what else the investigators find in the coming hours, and what clues or evidence or anonymous tips are provided to help them. But if the police are hunting for an American in connection to terrorism, this bookstore refuge will last only so long. Dexter would be in custody within a day, and he might never be released. Who knows what would happen to a man like him, in a French jail, facing the sorts of charges that could be trumped up against him.

Kate will need help getting the police called off, intervention from a legitimate authority. That will have to come from America; that will have to be part of the cleanup. Tomorrow. The day after.

But maybe that won't be necessary. Maybe there's another solution, one built into the problem itself. Kate thinks she knows what it is, but not how to find it. And she's running out of time.

62

He pushes himself up from his right side, his uninjured side, but it's not as if the right is unconnected to the left, and the pain is immense, it's overwhelming, and his arm buckles, and the pavement rushes up—

⚜

How long was he unconscious? It couldn't have been for more than a few seconds, a minute, the light seems the same, the noise beyond the entrance to the tunnel, everything. No one has yet joined him here in the darkness. He's still alone. Still shot. Still bleeding.

He has to get up, get out of here. He braces himself for the pain, he knows it's going to be horrible, he doesn't want to be caught by surprise again, that was his mistake the first time.

Use your lower body, he tells himself. He twists onto his stomach, and pain explodes from his shoulder. He pushes his weight into his knees and from there into the ground, and rolls onto his toes, and with every movement the pain continues to mount, it's getting worse, and worse—

Don't pass out . . . *Don't* . . .

He pushes, and pushes, and—

He's standing. He did it. He's dizzy, he's out of breath. He can feel the blood trickling down his chest and stomach, warm and sticky, his shirt is already soaked, cool against his skin.

He starts to walk. Stumbles past Wyatt's corpse, it seems like a lifetime ago when he shot the guy.

The gun slips from his grasp, clatters to the pavement. Damn. He starts to bend but realizes that's a mistake, blood will rush into his wound and to his head, he'll lose his balance, he'll pitch over, crack his head—

Instead he squats. Reaches for his weapon, manages to retrieve it without losing consciousness.

He can hear the voices gathering out on the street, he can't go out there, a crowd will be amassing. He walks in the other direction, toward the far end of the tunnel where it merges with the parallel street.

The voices behind him grow louder. He walks faster.

Open daylight, blinding bright. He raises his hand to shield his eyes, surveys this very long block, maybe a quarter-mile to the next intersection. There are a couple of people near the far end walking in his way, but they don't seem to be in any rush, they're not investigating gunshots, they're not coming for him.

A car turns the distant corner, also heading his way.

He takes a quick glance down at his shoulder. It's pretty clear there's a bullet hole in his jacket, but there's no blood visible, or at least very little blood, it's hard to say because the whole front of his clothing is soaking wet from lying in that pool of urine, and now that he's giving himself the once-over he sees that he's a complete fucking mess. He can't stumble around the streets looking like this.

The car is fifty yards away, decelerating as it approaches the split with the tunnel. As it approaches him.

He sidesteps off the sidewalk, into the gutter, and takes another step and another, he's in the middle of the roadway, it's a narrow street with no room for parking on either side, no room for this car to swerve around him.

Through the windshield he can see that the driver looks confused, then angry, then worried as he gets near enough to clearly see the state of this man who's blocking the street. The driver seems to debate his options, whether to get out and help, or to roll down the window and inquire, or to throw the thing in reverse and get the hell out of there.

Chris staggers sideways toward the car, keeping his right side shielded from the driver's view, the uninjured side of his body, the side whose pocket holds the gun, which he slowly draws until he arrives at the window, places the muzzle directly against the glass, just inches from the guy's face—

"*Sortez!*" Chris screams. "Get the fuck out! *Maintenant!*"

The guy's hands are raised, as if he's being held up, eager to show that he isn't armed, please take my wallet, there's no reason to shoot. He slowly lowers his left hand to the door handle.

Chris takes a half-step backward, away from the door, in case the driver grows bold and tries to fling it open as an attack. The car is a beat-up old Renault the color of rust, like it came from the factory pre-shitty. The owner of a car like this shouldn't take heroic measures to prevent its theft. Better off with the insurance settlement. But you never know, maybe there's a bag of cash in the trunk.

The door opens. One foot emerges, a running shoe, planted on the pavement. Then the other. The driver hoists himself up, then returns his hands to the *please-don't-shoot* pose.

Chris uses the gun to motion the guy away from his car, to the sidewalk. *"Asseyez-vous!"*

The man obeys, sits at the curb.

Chris tumbles into the seat. He realizes, a split-second too late, that it's going to hurt like a motherfucker when he attempts to close the door with his left hand, and he screams out in pain, squeezes his eyes shut, shakes his head back and forth . . .

The driver looks worried. *"Monsieur? Si vous voulez . . ."* He mimes pushing. Is this guy actually volunteering to help someone steal his car? Maybe what's in the trunk is a dead body.

Chris nods, then warns, *"Attention."*

"Bien sûr." The driver approaches tentatively, shuts the door gently, backs away.

"Merci." Chris shifts into gear—it's an automatic, thank God—and executes a jagged six-point U-turn while the driver watches, getting a better and better look at him, this guy will be able to help the police draw a sketch, he'll be able to identify a photo, he'll be able to provide a positive ID if he's confronted with something to compare . . .

But who he'll be able to identify is an American with a mountain-man beard and unruly hair and eyeglasses and a long scar on the side of his face. A version of a person that has only ever existed here, in this city, over the last few months. There is no long-term past tense of this person, no match to be made.

Unfortunately, this wound suggests there won't be a future tense either.

Chris wishes it were true that he's too young to die, that he doesn't deserve it. But he knows that neither is true.

Excruciating pain shoots through him, and he barely manages to extend his arm to the machine, to pull the ticket out of the slot. The parking garage's barrier raises, and he rolls the car slowly down the ramp, finds an empty space in a quiet corner. He's panting, shaking, his vision blurry.

He needs to think. And he needs to attend to his wound. He needs to think about attending to his wound.

The trunk. Maybe there's a first-aid kit in the trunk.

No such luck. What does he find back there? A neon nylon emergency vest, a warning triangle, the things you're legally required to keep in the trunk to pass safety inspection. Also a soccer ball and a pair of cleats, a plastic jug of motor oil, a half-full bottle of cheap vodka, an old sweatshirt, a roll of duct tape.

A plan forms.

With no small amount of effort and pain, he removes his shirt. He uses a window as a mirror to examine his wound: the bullet passed through. That's the good news. The bad news is that these gunshot holes are seeping a lot of blood, and have been exposed to a surfeit of bacteria. He needs to disinfect.

This is definitely going to hurt something fierce, maybe too much to stay conscious. He doesn't want to soak the driver's seat in vodka, in case he needs to drive again, so he walks to the passenger side, opens the door.

He rips a few long strips of musty fleece from the sweatshirt. Tears lengths of duct tape, hangs them from the car's roof.

He sits. If he passes out, he wants to already be in a sitting position, no way to fall and crack his skull open.

Okay, now there's nothing left to do but to do it.

Okay.

He really doesn't want to do this. But he has to. Now.

Now.

Now—

He splashes vodka on his front entry wound, and it hurts so immediately and so much that his vision goes dark, and his whole body seizes.

He feels a fresh wound appear on his lower lip, where his top teeth have dug into his flesh.

The pain recedes, barely, from the brink of unbearable. He sits there, panting.

That was bad. But he made it.

The back will be worse, but fuck it, this time he doesn't delay, doesn't indulge in any pep talk, just throws a splash over his shoulder, which lands in the wrong spot—no pain—so he does it again, and then again, alcohol streaming down his back until—oh, God—there it is, and this time it's the same sensations as with the front wound but doubled, trebled, it's too much, it's—

He comes to with a start.

The vodka bottle has fallen from his hand. The glass remained intact, but most of the liquid spilled out.

He wraps a few strips of sweatshirt around his shoulder, looping under his armpit, then secures the cloth with duct tape. He adds more strips at a different angle, more duct tape . . .

Is this going to make any difference? Is this going to keep him alive? Maybe not. But it's all he can do right now.

He and his wife had discussed a wide variety of foreseeable problems, including this one. He knows what he's supposed to do next.

If only she'd listened to him—if he could've convinced her—then he wouldn't be sitting here in this stolen Renault, shot, dying. He'd tried. But there was never any convincing her of anything.

It had taken him a while to come around to the big-picture viability of the scheme. At first it seemed so utterly outlandish, so completely unfeasible. Then she explained one element at a time, gambit after gambit, how the whole thing would coalesce. At the end, there was only one facet he still wasn't sold on: framing Dexter.

"It's an unnecessary level of complexity," he said. "It'll make it that much harder to pull off, it adds challenges to every other component. We'll need to choose our primary operative based on his looks, which is obviously not the best determinant for finding talent. We'll need to re-search Dexter's wardrobe, eyeglasses, sunglasses, everything, then we'll need to buy all that, which will leave a trail—"

"Not if we're careful."

"*Yes,* even if we're careful. The trail may be faint, but it will be there. And we'll need to steal that ridiculous hat? Then replace it?"

"The hat is the nail in the coffin."

"We'll need to disable the security camera in the Métro station so our asset can change wardrobes. We'll need to run the risks of the guy actually doing that."

"Please, it doesn't even matter if someone—"

"Yes, I know, I know: you can dismiss any one of these as quibbles. But as a whole, framing Dexter will add a lot of unnecessary risks to what's already a very long list of necessary ones. You can't deny it."

She didn't, so he pressed his advantage. "Plus it's an irrational choice. You *know* this, Susanna: the scheme is not stronger by framing Dexter. It's weaker."

She shook her head, closed her eyes, trying to be patient. "If we don't frame Dexter, we can't get the fifty million."

"*So what?* So we make only five million euros? Ten?"

She snorted, as if ten million were chump change, not worth getting out of bed.

"It's a good scheme," he continued. "No: it's brilliant. We can get rich *and* play it safe. *If* we leave Kate and Dexter out of it."

She shook her head again.

"For fuck's sake, why not?"

"Because they're *the whole reason.* Don't you see that, Chris?"

They hadn't used their real names in years. Back when they were living in Luxembourg, they'd played characters called Bill and Julia MacLean. When they were forced by Kate to run, to hide, they adopted new names, variations on the names given to them by their parents: Craig Malloy and Susan Pognowski. He became Chris; she, Susanna. These were the only names they'd used for the past two years. That's how new identities become real.

"I worked *so* hard," she said. "I planned for *so* long. Then she made a fool of me."

"A fool? No, that's not what happened."

"They sat around, the two of them, and discussed how to screw me out of my fortune. I was going to be rich! And now look."

"Yes, exactly, *now look*: is this really so bad?"

"That's not the point."

"No? Then what *is* the point?"

"That she *took* it all from me."

"But she didn't. All she took was the money."

"Don't give me that shit." Gritted teeth. "You know it wasn't only the money."

Susanna was right. Kate Moore had taken much more than the money.

"Just because we managed to get some things back, that doesn't mean she didn't take everything. Plus, we won't be hurting anyone who doesn't deserve to be hurt."

"Deserve to be hurt? What does that mean?"

"You know exactly what that means. Our primary investor is a life-long criminal, a rat, an informer. Our driver is a psychopathic murderer. A random douchebag amoral trader-bro in Hong—"

"Is this really what you want?" he asked. "To put *Dexter* in jail? He didn't do anything to you. Not really."

She snorted. "Dexter will never go anywhere near jail."

"Then why the hell do you want to do all this?"

"Because I want her to fear for her freedom, for her life, her home, her precious kids. It's that terror I want Kate to feel. To live with."

This wasn't surprising. His wife was charming; she was intelligent; she was clever, witty, sexy; she was beautiful. But she was not nice.

"She didn't *need* to ruin my life, Chris. She *chose* to do that."

He'd known this all along, well before they became a couple, he'd known this back when they were casual colleagues at the Bureau, sitting in the same meetings in the same conference rooms, everyone was impressed with her, but also at least a little bit scared.

"So now I'm going to make her pay. Force her to make a horrible choice."

His eyes had been wide open, no one else to blame. Life is compromises.

"Give me the fifty million euros, or I'll ruin her fucking life."

❧

He has to put distance between himself and this car, which the police could be tracking this instant, surrounding the block, weapons drawn.

Chris staggers up the ramp.

He can't type this out in a text-message, or an e-mail. It needs to be a conversation. And it needs to happen right now, before he gets caught. Or dies.

She answers after one ring. "Hi."

"Hi." He's approaching the street, nervous about exiting, what could be out there. He stops, peeks around a wall: looks normal. He continues walking, and talking. "Things have . . . um . . . deteriorated."

She doesn't respond.

"I'm injured." This type of voice communication—it's not exactly a phone call—is supposed to be secure, but who knows anymore. "It's bad."

Pause. "I'm very sorry to hear that."

"I can't travel the way I planned. Not sure I can travel at all." The pain is making him dizzy. "I need medical attention."

He wants her to say: do whatever you need, get to a hospital, save yourself, don't worry about me. But that's not what he expects, nor what he gets.

"You're prepared for that, right?"

This is one of the contingencies they'd discussed: avoiding hospitals, their records, the police that can often be found in emergency rooms.

He swallows back the nausea that accompanies his intense pain and dizziness. He has already thrown up, which hurt so much that he almost passed out again. "Yuh."

"Is there something I can do for you?"

There isn't, is there? "Don't think so."

"Okay then." She pauses. "Good luck."

He's pretty sure this is the last conversation they'll ever have, which makes this the last thing he'll ever say to her: "I love you."

He hopes his wife makes the same choice. He waits, and waits, and wonders if the connection has been dropped.

Then he hears: "I love you too." And the line goes dead.

63

Kate rides past her building without slowing, searching for signs of surveillance, men sitting in cars, leaning in doorways, loitering in the lobby of the hotel at the end of the street.

No one.

She doubles back and parks the Vespa. Inside, she takes the stairs, creeping up, peeking down each hall, her hand in her pocket, resting on Inez's gun. It's a long climb to the top.

Still no one.

Her apartment door appears to be undisturbed. These are hard locks to pick, but not impossible. She opens the door slowly, just halfway, until right before the point in the arc where it squeaks.

A few months ago, Dexter said, "I'll fix that now. Just needs some oil."

"No, leave it."

He looked at her with furrowed brow.

"It's a good alarm." Which she doesn't want to trip now, in case someone is waiting inside. She tiptoes through the hall, skirting the creaky floorboard near the boys' bedroom, down to the end, the office. She looks around carefully. No one has been here.

She sets to work quickly, removing the screws from Dexter's CPU, setting aside the panel. Then her phone rings.

"Gunshots are reported," Inez says by way of hello. "Witnesses say that the men who are shooting, they speak English. Two are dead. Another is injured, and he stole a car."

Kate isn't sure exactly what this means, but it's definitely not nothing. "Where?"

"*Le onzième.*"

"Exactly where?"

"I will send the position to you."

During Kate's first months working for Hayden's new Paris Substation, it slowly dawned on her that her manager wasn't really monitoring almost anything she did, and neither was anyone else. She was, in effect, completely unsupervised.

Maybe, she thought, this was a test. Of her dedication. Of her responsibility. Of her maturity. Doing what you're supposed to do, even when no one could know if you're not.

Sometimes Kate believed that Hayden's hands-off management style was because he liked to give his subordinates the freedom to make their own decisions, to succeed or fail based on their own actions and the ensuing consequences, enough rope. But in darker moments it occurred to her that Hayden's scarcity reflected a more nefarious motivation: a deliberate attempt to maintain his own plausible deniability.

Little by little, she began to act on the presumption of complete autonomy. She recruited assets that had nothing whatsoever to do with any of her active operations, nor any reasonable expectation of future ops. She pursued her own private interests, cautiously, always ready to get caught, to get called out—what the hell do you think you're doing?

It never happened.

Her personal agenda was modest. It wasn't as if Kate was trying to overthrow a democratically elected president. All she wanted was a single discrete piece of information.

Kate's search was both broad and narrow. Broad, because she could be looking almost anywhere in the world. Narrow, because she was looking for something very specific.

And although in the abstract her target could be anywhere on the planet, Kate was confident that the effective search range could be much smaller. There were language considerations; Romance countries were most likely. And the quality of life, the rule of law, the general level of medical care, these were not irrelevant. There had also been a previous lifetime of living in the pampered plush of the United States, and now there would be a child too. A certain standard of living.

These factors made Kate feel safe ruling out large swaths of the planet.

Europe was by far the most likely, especially the Mediterranean. France, though, was unlikely. Luxembourg completely out of the question.

Kate added one piece at a time. She recruited a functionary in the Turkish border control, a federal bureaucrat in Madrid, another in Switzerland. A Portuguese diplomat living in Brussels, a German police chief, a Greek mayor, an Italian minister's assistant. She gained access to real-estate transfers, visa applications, immigration rosters, birth records. She hired a freelancer named Henri to sort through all of it. He came in one day per week, like the cleaning lady.

It used to be easy to disappear; the main challenge was resisting the temptation to make contact with your old life. But the digital age shrunk the world exponentially, with every new database, every app, every electronic intrusion to which we voluntarily submit ourselves in exchange for the promise of a more convenient life, while in the meantime dragging everyone else into a global surveillance state.

It's impossible to completely hide. Not if you want to live any version of modern life, with a family, with the Internet, with bank accounts and airline tickets and healthcare records. There are cameras everywhere, digital footprints, satellite images, centrally collected phone records, all searchable and sortable. There are informants, hackers, leaks, spies. Any data can be bought, or stolen, every interaction that anyone has, every purchase, every e-mail, every phone—

Yes. That's the solution.

Kate calls Inez again. "Can you access mobile meta-data?"

"Oui, c'est possible."

"Sometime right after the gunfight, a telephone call was placed from that vicinity. Or soon will be."

"I am sure many."

"Can you get records of all of them?"

Kate can hear Inez take a drag on a cigarette. Kate has never been a smoker, but she has always envied this thing smokers have, this tension release, this dramatic pause, this purchase of small bits of time, this thing to do after orgasm, when there's otherwise nothing left to do.

"Mais oui. You are looking for something specific?"

"Yes. A call from that immediate area to one particular city."

⚜

Kate continues to destroy evidence—disassembling Dexter's computers, removing hard drives—with her phone on speaker. She can hear Inez barking commands, rapid-fire instructions—*maintenant, vite,* the voices of a couple of men responding.

"*Alors,*" Inez says. "There has been none."

That doesn't make sense. "She must be using more than one phone."

Kate can hear fresh commands being issued, gruff voices responding, *non, désolée.*

"I am sorry," Inez says. "We find nothing. But the records, they are not, how do you say, instantaneous? It is taking ten, twenty, maybe thirty minutes to appear in the database."

⚜

Kate's phone dings with a new text stream, an update. She responds quickly: *Grazie. I will wire payment immediately.*

She dumps Dexter's hard drives into her bag. She opens the bottom desk drawer, the combination-locked strongbox, and begins to transfer the contents to her bag: an extra burner, and all eight passports—the four real ones and the corresponding fakes—and small bundles of various currencies.

Her phone rings again.

"It happened."

"The call?"

"*Oui.* And then the phone in Paris, it is immediately dead. Powered down."

Who turns off a mobile on a day like today? Only someone trying to be invisible.

"Do you have the last location of the Paris phone?"

"I send it to you. Also, bad news. The police, I believe they are looking for you."

"For me?"

"A woman of your description, who is riding a black Vespa, last seen in St-Germain-des-Prés, who is firing a gun."

The last item Kate retrieves from the strongbox is her own handgun. Now she has two.

"This is you, *n'est-ce pas?*"

64

So. This is not the outcome for which she'd been hoping. Obviously. But it is one for which she'd planned.

She stares at the phone, now a useless piece of garbage. No: worse than useless, this cheap electronic device has become a piece of damning physical evidence. She pops out the SIM card, cuts it in half. Opens a desk drawer and removes the ball-peen hammer, which she uses to pummel the phone into shards. She opens the window and tosses this shattered plastic into the narrow canal forty feet below.

Don't cry, she tells herself. You have things to do.

She turns back to the computer, all those red numbers, all those downward-facing arrows. And in particular 4Syte, whose rate of decrease is continuing to accelerate. Perhaps trading will be suspended, any minute now.

Goddamn it: Do. Not. Cry.

This moment may not be perfect, but it's more than good enough. An injured Chris could be taken into custody any second now, and you never know what someone is going to do when hurt and desperate. She doesn't actually expect him to throw her under the bus, but she needs to be prepared for the worst case.

She's continuing to tell herself not to cry, like a mantra running in the background of her brain. But it's futile, it's counterproductive—

Okay, she tells herself: go ahead, cry.

For ten seconds.

Then get your fucking money back.

⚜

"But . . . I don't understand . . ."

Richie looked at her like she was an idiot, or insane, how could she not understand what he doesn't understand, the whole point of this whole endeavor, of every endeavor: "If there's no ransom, how do we make any money?"

That's the question, isn't it. That's everyone's question, what we all do, the paths we take, the decisions we make, the choices: what will I do, and who will I be, and how much will people pay me?

She doesn't know what level of deliberateness other people bring to bear while making their lives' most important choices. For example, Richie Benedetti: did he sit in his childhood room, assess his skills and predilections, weigh his options, and come to the rational conclusion that, yes, I will become a professional hoodlum? Or did he stumble into a life of crime one half-assed ill-considered decision at a time?

Not Susanna. Her choices were not a series of spur-of-the-moment schemes, not some opportunistic lark. She had a carefully considered, meticulously constructed life plan.

At first she didn't know exactly which exit she'd end up taking, but she did decide that the road to her destination would be the FBI. After a couple of years working at the Bureau, poking into one corner and another, it became clear that she should specialize in something with a very high barrier to entry, a niche that could endow her with an impenetrable cloak of specialized technical knowledge: cyber-crime.

How long would the whole thing take? Five years, ten, thirty? She wouldn't rush it. This was the work of a career, and as with any career she took the necessary steps—to pay her dues, to establish her reputation, to prove her work ethic, to develop her expertise, to rise to a position of authority, of independence, of unassailable integrity.

She recruited a wide network of experts to help her identify money-laundering operations, illegal transfers to offshore entities, the kind of financial activities that have practically no legal justification, the proceeds of exactly the sorts of crimes, perpetrated by exactly the sorts of criminals, that she eventually intended to use: drug cartels, arms dealers, human traffickers, merchants of one type of death or another.

Someday, she knew, the perfect situation would present itself, the culmination of this career-within-a-career. Her own version of partnership, corner office, golden parachute: she would get immensely rich by robbing a criminal kingpin.

This was admittedly not exactly what the FBI was invented to do, but when it comes right down to it, it's not that different.

She'd probably have only one shot, but she was confident that she'd need only one.

She was wrong.

⚜

It's time to tie off the loose ends.

She opens the messaging app on another mobile, finds the contact, types the short message.

After this, she'll walk out the door, lock it, leave the keys in the stairway's light fixture. She'll drop this phone into the water from the back of Lorenzo's speedboat as they bump across the lagoon, on the first leg of her journey to a new life.

She hits SEND.

Events will now unfold quickly, and will mostly be out of her control. So far, she has been the one orchestrating the action, but as of this moment she'll become just another private citizen, responsible for only herself and her baby.

She bundles up Matteo again, straps him to her chest.

Before the kid was born, she couldn't have fathomed the extent to which parenting meant ceding control. For a long while, especially when you're a child yourself, it looks like the opposite: parenthood *is* control. Untrue. So much of a parent's life is determined by the biological imperatives and whims of this tiny inchoate animal. Trying to control it is an exercise in frustration.

It's one thing to learn this, another to live with it, to accept it. In general, Susanna has trouble accepting lack of control. She knows this makes her a difficult person to live with, and for a long time she didn't give a damn. Then she realized that she wanted this man to be her husband; then she realized that if she wanted to keep this husband, she had to make some accommodations. More than none. That's what it means to be married.

She stands at the desk, leans over the keyboard to execute the trades, first one, another, another, dozens of them, small transactions and big ones and a number of midsize, nothing unusual, nothing noteworthy, using brokerage accounts connected to banks all over Europe, with untraceable aliases and shielded identities, LLCs and SARLs.

As she waits for the confirmations to arrive, she rocks from one foot to the other, trying to keep the baby in his soothed state. There is no excuse for disturbing a contented baby.

Secure messages begin to arrive to her in-boxes, confirmation numbers, amounts in US dollars, in euros, in British pounds, transferring funds from all these disparate sources into a single account at a Swiss bank whose originating branch is just over the Alps, a few hours' drive.

This whole process takes ten minutes.

Almost finished.

Finally she double-clicks the large black *X* icon on the bottom of her screen. The program launches, a dialog box opens, and she initiates a three-stage protocol that requires three different passwords, until at last:

Are you sure you want to destroy this device?

Her finger pauses for a second. The default answer—the button you'd hit by mistake—is NO.

She clicks YES.

Nothing happens. Her heart sinks, she can feel anxiety welling up, what if this doesn't—

The screen goes blank.

Then she hears a soft fizzing noise, like a fresh soda bottle being opened, slowly. A wisp of smoke appears from the side of the CPU, another from the bottom.

The smell is acrid.

The blank screen flashes, then goes dark again. Then darker.

A loud pop, and it's done.

⚜

The bulk of their belongings have already been packed, picked up by a moving company, sitting in a warehouse outside of Treviso, awaiting delivery instructions, which she will provide tomorrow. The ultimate destination depends on what else happens today and tonight.

She'd picked out two different locations, in two different countries.

The preferred scenario is that she'll head east to a busy tourist town on the Croatian coast, just across the Gulf of Venice, a few hours away in Lorenzo's speedboat, if the weather cooperates. Croatia is the option if everything has gone okay in Paris, and her husband escapes unscathed, hops a TGV to Nice tonight, then tomorrow morning a short flight to Zagreb.

Happily ever after.

The other option is to fly west to Spain, to a White Village in the sparsely populated Sierra de Grazalema Mountains of Andalusia, where she made a week-long reservation in a modest hotel in an area where vacation properties abound, month-long stays, year-long leases, she won't have a problem finding a comfortable place to live. Her Italian will help her learn Spanish, and she will have an immense amount of money to help with everything else.

What she won't have in Spain is a husband. She'll be a single mother of a young child. Life will be challenging, but people will have sympathy.

Her husband doesn't know anything about the Andalusian option. The White Village is in case of his capture, or his compromise, or his demise; it's the option if she needs to cut connections. She has a pretty clear set of guidelines in her head, different scenarios, different levels of risk she's willing to tolerate. If he's detained by the police. If he's questioned, but let go. If he's identified, being hunted. If he's dead.

And if he's seriously injured. She can't be weighed down by that, can't subject herself and Matteo to the risks attendant with traveling with someone who has wounds to treat, someone seeking medical attention, undergoing surgeries, removing bullets whose ballistics might be traced, administrative records that are fed into centralized databases, blood types, fingerprints, dental records.

If he's seriously injured, she knows what she needs to do.

"Okay." Richie picked an imaginary piece of lint off the hammy thigh of his tight pants, then turned back to face her. "I've got some concerns."

She had just finished explaining what needed explanation, but that left ample room for questions, of which anyone in their right mind would ask plenty. Richie may not have been the sharpest tool in the shed, but he wasn't crazy.

"First, obviously: how do we not get caught?"

"To begin with, you don't need to worry about yourself. You're completely in the clear. No one knows we're here, we barely even exist."

Richie understood.

"Most important, Richie: no Internet for any communications, ever. We need to use the Internet for research, but we do everything that's necessary using a single computer set to a masked IP address, at a physical location that will not be traceable to us. Before the day itself we destroy the computer and scrub the apartment."

"How do we communicate?"

"Burner phones, using code. Nothing complicated, just enough to avoid key-word recognition."

"How many people are involved?"

"A couple of handfuls."

"Tell me about them."

"Okay. Chronologically, it's *one,* a woman posing as a scientific researcher at the cancer ward, to buffer the recruitment process of *two,* the suicide bomber. *Three,* the driver who delivers a couple of the bombs and the bomber. For the kidnapping, a pair of fake cops, that's *four* and *five.* Plus *six* and *seven,* a couple of freelancers to deposit additional bombs. *Eight* and *nine,* incidentals doing small piecework, completely firewalled from the rest."

"Piecework?"

"Just some advance intel." She doesn't want to explain this legwork, which veers into territory that she intends to keep from Richie, for the benefit of everyone.

"What about the State-slash-CIA guy?"

She pointed at Chris.

Richie turned to examine him. "Interesting."

"To generate the other international panics, two people—number *ten* in one country, *eleven* in another."

"How much you paying all these people?"

"Wildly varying compensation, for very different responsibilities and risk levels. Only two will be large. Most will be small, not enough for anyone to think they're doing anything serious. A few hundred euros, leave this backpack over there, that kind of thing. By the time any of these people realize what's really going on, they'll have no way of changing their minds, no way of contacting us, no way of ID'ing anyone."

"So what's the grand total?"

"In sum the freelancers will cost about four hundred thousand."

Richie mugged an exaggerated frown, wise-guy for *not bad.* "Other expenses?"

"Another two hundred K for flights and apartments, hotel rooms and meals and wardrobe and living expenses, plus the van, other supplies. And another couple hundred for the bomb materials." She'd budgeted every single item, line by line. The nuclear waste had been particularly expensive. "Overall, it's just over three-quarters of a million of non-recoupable expenses."

A drop in the bucket, considering the upside. But that upside will be worthwhile only if they raise copious quantities of additional investments. With a couple of million, they'll break even. One or two high-net-worth investors, that's all they need.

"So who's managing all this on the ground? I'm assuming not you." He indicated Susanna's swollen stomach. By the time everything had come together sufficiently to seek investors, she was visibly pregnant. She'd been pregnant a few times before in the past couple of years, but this was the only one that had advanced to viability, to visibility. Every day that she didn't miscarry felt like a miracle.

"I am."

Richie turned to Chris. "You know what you're doin', huh?"

"I'm not incompetent."

"Oh no? What sorta jobs you work?"

"I have the same professional background as my wife."

"That right?" This tickled Richie. "You two meet on the job?"

Neither answered. Richie didn't press it. "So, you gonna tell me who this CEO is who you're gonna kidnap? And where this is all gonna happen?"

"Eventually."

"What exactly are you waiting for?"

"For you to commit."

"Why this particular guy? You have something against him?"

"Probably."

"The fuck does that mean?"

"It means that although I don't personally know the CEO, every indicator suggests that he's a jackass. But his jackassery is beside the point."

"Which is?"

"Pure opportunity, Richie. This scenario would work with any number of targets. This particular individual is simply the one who's most available."

This was the first significant lie she'd told Richie. She didn't want to loop him into that component of the plan, the real reason that the target needed to be Hunter Forsyth. Because that would smack of revenge-driven motivation, which everyone, even Richie Benedetti, knows is bad for business.

"Here's something I don't understand."

"Shoot."

"If there are never any negotiations, never any demands, how is this gonna make sense to the cops? How will they believe they've solved the mystery, stop looking for us?"

"They'll find a duffel bag on the subway containing burner phones that connect to the bombs. They'll understand that something went very wrong with the attack, and that's why the bombs were never detonated, communications never established, a negotiation never initiated. The police will think that the duffel and its owner got separated somehow. Or he got cold feet, he got arrested, he got killed by a double-crossing confederate. They will have many theories."

"Won't they look for him?"

"Of course they will. It will be an extremely bad day to be a Muslim man in this city."

"But they won't find anyone?"

"Oh, they'll find someone. Someone who looks very guilty."

"And what's to prevent that guy from talking?"

"What do you think?"

Richie got it. In his line of business, there are always bodies. "And this is a guy who'll look like the brains behind the operation?"

"No, this is a guy who'll look like a mercenary bagman. It will literally be his bag that the police find. With his change of clothes, his fingerprints, hairs, everything."

"Won't law enforcement be able to back-trace his steps?"

"Yes they will. Which will lead to an empty apartment. To a stolen van with stolen plates and no connection to us. To electronic communications with someone who doesn't exist."

Richie looked skeptical.

"Listen, Richie." She leaned forward. "We have a huge amount of experience in things like this. We know what investigators look for, obviously. We know what they find, how they find it. We have a combined half-century of experience here."

Richie didn't seem completely satisfied, but he was willing to move past it, at least temporarily. "When does this go down?"

Ah, good: he was thinking about the practicalities from his own point of view. First schedule. Then he'll have another, larger question.

"Two to four months from now. After we have all the pieces in place, and the right moment presents itself."

He nodded, then leveled his gaze at her. Here it comes.

"So."

"Yes, Richie?"

"What's your ask?"

She met his eye. "This is for winners only. Like everything else in life, right? You get to make a lot of money if you have a lot to begin with."

"But you don't, do you? That's why you're here."

"Exactly. That's why I'm here, giving you this chance to exploit me."

"Yeah, exploit you. To what tune?"

Don't blink, she told herself. "It's a ten-million-dollar buy-in."

Richie whistled. He had a good whistle, a clean sound, the whistle of a guy who'd spent his whole life whistling.

"What if something goes wrong?"

"I'd be surprised if a variety of things didn't go wrong. That's why this plan is replete with redundancies. Verifiable threats in the company's international locations, a handful in the city. Global terrorism on global TV. Is there any way whatsoever that this doesn't trigger a generalized sell-off?"

He made an *I'm-reluctantly-satisfied* face.

"And if you want to hedge your bets, by all means spread your short positions around to various sectors. That's definitely the safe move, and that's what I'd do if I were you. A couple diversified million will be enough to guarantee profit. Everything is going to be down three, five percent intraday. Except maybe defense-industry companies."

She leaned forward.

"But the guaranteed big money, Richie? That comes from shorting the CEO's company."

"Sure. And what if its trading is suspended?"

"Why would it be? Because some exec is on a bender? Or run off with his secretary? There's no reason to suspect anything more nefarious, no reason to suspend trade. That's why we're not manufacturing any events in London or New York: to keep the markets open. And that's why the abduction is secret: to keep trading open."

She could see that Richie got it, he had dollar signs in his eyes, he understood how an investor like him could clean up. It's all about privileged access to actionable information.

But that wasn't how Chris and Susanna were going to make their fortune. Which would not be dependent on the markets. And would be much more lucrative than Richie's five or ten or fifteen million euros in profit.

"It's time for a decision, Richie. You in?"

"I'm definitely intrigued. I need some time."

"I definitely understand. You've got five minutes."

"Fuck you."

She didn't respond.

He didn't flinch.

They stared at each other for ten seconds. Twenty. Thirty—

"Okay," he said. "Sure. I'm in."

"Thanks. I'm glad. But that, in and of itself, is not quite good enough."

"The fuck you want from me?"

"A gesture of good faith, Richie."

"Oh yeah? How good?"

She took a sip of her water—the relentless hydration of pregnancy—then put down her glass deliberately. She wiped her lips with the small napkin, placed the linen back on the mirror-topped table. Then she looked back up at him.

PART V

TOUR EIFFEL

65

K ate is climbing off her moped when her phone buzzes again. What did people do before smartphones? She can barely remember. It seems like historical fiction, in her memory.

It's another message from her Italian source, an alphanumeric string— tail numbers—and an originating airport code. But no destination.

Grazie, she replies.

Prego.

Kate barges into a shop, inexpensive clothing targeted at teens, blaring the English-language pop that harasses you everywhere across the Continent. Like bad pizza, and Zara.

In the changing room, she puts on her wig again; better to look like the intruder at 4Syte than the woman who discharged a gun in the street and then abducted a person-of-interest from a police interview. She buys a lightweight motorcycle jacket, rips off the tags, zips it closed to cover her shirt. She retrieves a handful of magnetic bumper stickers from the Vespa's helmet case, slaps them onto the metal.

A different person, yet again, riding what now looks like a different moped.

The last-known location of the mobile phone is a half-mile away from the shooting, which is unfortunately nowhere near here. Then the phone was powered down. Anyone who's careful enough to power down a phone is also going to be careful enough to move afterward.

Kate isn't confident that she's going to find the person she's looking for. But you do what you can do, use what you have. Sometimes things work out, just because you tried.

During Kate's long-term global search, what made her task appreciably easier was that she wasn't asking her sources for much. She wasn't looking for missile blueprints or troop movements or the aliases of double agents, she wasn't looking for classified information, she wasn't looking for anything that was going to get anyone fired, or jailed, or killed. In fact, the thing she was looking for wasn't a state secret—it wasn't even a secret—and no one had any special interest in preventing her from getting the information.

It didn't take very long.

"*Madame?*" Henri said one day, standing in her doorway, big smile on his face. "I found her."

This did not completely solve the problem, but now it could be managed. Monitored. Contained. At least that's what Kate had thought.

Before she gets on her moped, she phones Inez again. "Another favor, I'm afraid. Are you in your office?"

"*Oui.*"

"Can you access international flight plans?"

Kate parks a hundred yards past the address, and across the street. She needs to be extra-careful here.

She takes in her surroundings, the pedestrians, the parked cars, the idling taxi whose driver is talking on the phone, the store selling African clothing wholesale, front door wide open. Not a particularly busy stretch of street, nor quiet.

Kate scans the building. He's probably gone. But he could also still be in there, or maybe in the buildings to either side; GPS coordinates for mobiles are not always reliable. The only thing remarkable about the five-story structure is that its ground floor is a public garage entrance.

Yes, that must be it. He wouldn't want to drive long distances in a stolen vehicle, he'd want to get that car off the streets asap, perhaps trade it for another, one for which the police aren't already searching.

Yes, he's in this garage. Or was.

Her pulse races.

Kate descends the ramp slowly. She fights the urge to retrieve Inez's gun; she shouldn't be walking around with a gun drawn.

It's a clean, well-lit garage. There are, no doubt, surveillance cameras.

Kate sees it immediately, the rust-colored Renault, parked along the far side. She approaches slowly, obliquely, her feet falling almost silently, while her heart hammers loudly in her ears.

Twenty meters away from the car, she stops. She's shielded by a tall SUV, whose windshield she peers around.

The Renault appears to be empty.

Kate continues to creep toward the passenger side. She reaches her hand into her pocket, grasps the gun, but doesn't draw it out. Not yet.

Another step.

Now she's separated from the Renault by just a single car, alongside which she crouches, still shielded from the most direct view, but not completely hidden. If there's someone in the stolen car, and he's paying attention, he'll be able to see her now.

But he doesn't, because he's not there.

The Renault is empty.

Kate catches a strong whiff of alcohol. There's a big jug of vodka lying on the ground near the passenger door; some liquid remains in the bottle. Also what appears to be a strip of cloth and a roll of duct tape.

She comes closer. She sees blood splatters on the floor, fresh ones, still wet, still red, not yet oxidized—

Kate spins, her eyes scanning everywhere quickly. It has been a matter of minutes, at most. She kneels, peering under all the cars, looking for someone lying there, hiding, or maybe dying.

He's injured; she knew that already. He dressed his wound here, he tried to sanitize it with alcohol, he used cloth and duct tape as a bandage. Then he put distance between himself and the car he stole.

It's a lot of blood on the ground. Now she sees blood smeared along the door too, the trunk. He's hurt badly. What would he do now?

What would she do?

66

He tries to tell himself that he's lucky, shot in the shoulder. At least he's able to walk. If he had the same wound but in the leg, he never would've gotten out of that alley.

Chris climbs the steps between the streets, up the hill, the old streetlamps, the wrought-iron banisters, people taking pictures, walking dogs, schoolchildren headed home, mothers carrying grocery bags with baguettes poking out. Normal life continues to swirl around him. He continues to bleed.

The suit jacket does a nearly acceptable job of hiding his wound, but not entirely. At least one person has noticed, probably more. He has to get off the street. He has to get treatment.

The doctor's office is at the top of these stairs, around the corner. He pauses, leans against the banister. Looks back down the hill, Paris spread out there, the domes, the spires, the Juliet balconies and mansard roofs and dormer windows, the sinking sun, the late-afternoon golden light. It's a beautiful world.

Now is not the time to quit. Quitting now is quitting forever.

He turns back up the hill, and keeps climbing.

The *cabinet médical* is just off the lobby, mere steps from the front door. But this door is locked. He rings the buzzer.

Please answer.

Please be open.

Please let me in.

Nothing.

He rings again, then hears—

Bzzzzzz . . .

He pushes the buzzing door open. There's one person sitting in the small waiting area, an old man, dozing, plus the doctor who's standing behind a desk; there's no receptionist. The doctor looks at Chris with obvious concern.

He turns away from her, toward the door that he pulls closed behind him. He locks it.

"*Monsieur?*" she asks.

He turns back, and her eyes go wide.

"*On y va,*" he says, walking toward her and the old man, gun in hand.

The doctor pauses, considering her options, then nods. She takes the drowsy old man by the elbow, helps him stand, leads him to the examining room.

"*Parlez-vous anglais?*"

"Yes," she answers. She plants the old man in an upright chair—he doesn't seem to mind this change of routine—then turns back to the armed invader, who's trying to take off his jacket, but failing. He can't move his shoulder.

"I can do it," she says, and slides it off, very gently, but still the pain is excruciating.

"*Mon Dieu,*" she says. "Gunshot?"

"Yes."

He can see that she understands his predicament. He's here to get whatever level of medical treatment he can, then get the hell out, as quickly as possible. This is not going to be a permanent solution to his serious injury, but it will buy time, and time will buy distance, and distance will buy safety.

He notices a framed photo on the wall, the doctor is in the middle of the image, standing between a young girl who looks like her and an old woman who also looks like her, all of them wearing surgical scrubs.

"This," the doctor says, holding up a pair of scissors, "is going to hurt."

67

Insistent banging. The Parisian cop strides to the door, unlocks it, pulls it open. He leans in to listen as the other policeman whispers, urgently. Hunter thinks one of them says, "So what the fuck do *you* think we should do?" and the two have what looks like a heated debate. Then they appear to come to an agreement, nodding.

"Okay," the talkative cop says, turning quickly back to Hunter and Colette. He yanks a knife—a big one—from his back pocket.

"Hey, what are—"

"Oh shut up." The guy stands in front of Hunter, brandishes the knife. "Don't be foolish."

"Never," Hunter says.

The cop glares at him, then drops to one knee and saws the knife quickly through the rope that binds Hunter's ankles, then again at his thighs. He walks around to the back of the chair, and Hunter can hear the soft whoosh as the knife releases his arms too.

Hunter shakes out his numb hands.

"Get up."

Hunter suspects that he shouldn't obey. Maybe it's because it wasn't that long ago when he heard the sound of gunfire nearby. He imagined it was Simpson out there, shooting someone. Perhaps shooting someone who'd come to rescue Hunter and Colette, and failed. Then Simpson hadn't returned.

"Come. The two of you." This cop looks like he's on the edge of panic. Something is wrong. Something new, beyond the plenty of things that were already very wrong.

"Why?"

"We're leaving."

Is this good? Or is this very, very bad?

"Why?"

The cop returns the knife to his back pocket, and withdraws his gun again. "Why do you think?"

Well that's exactly the problem, isn't it? Hunter glances at Colette, who also seems uncertain, scared. This man's suddenness, his brusqueness, the debate between the two cops; none of it seems right.

"Now. We don't have time."

Why not? Hunter is too scared to ask any questions; he's afraid of the answers. He knows he'll be lied to, and he'll recognize the lies for what they obviously are, and he'll no longer be able to deny what's really about to happen to him.

He struggles up from the chair, legs trembling. He glances at the cop's hand, at the gun resting there, almost like a cell phone, the way some people are always holding their phones, absentmindedly, permanently planted in their palms. People like Hunter.

He glances down at the floor, sure enough, it's his own necktie that had bound his wrists. Now it's a piece of two-hundred-dollar silk garbage.

The four of them walk out the door; Hunter notices that no one locks up. They hustle down the tall flights of steps, one cop in the lead, the other sweeping up the rear, both holding their weapons, neither brooking any further nonsense from their captives.

"Get in the car. Same as before."

Is this the time to object? To scream? To flee? To fight?

Hunter glances around. He doesn't see any signs of life in this court-yard. He doesn't see any way of getting out, other than the big door through which the car is going to drive. This is not where Hunter is going to make his escape, not where he's going to prevail in any confrontation. This is not the time to take his stand. He can only hope that another chance will present itself.

The car comes to a stop, and the driver shifts into PARK. This was a quick trip. How long was the ride out this morning? Hunter can barely remember it. When was that? Six hours ago? Seven? That had been a much longer drive.

"Get up."

The tarp is yanked off again, the darkness is replaced with light, with Colette's face just inches from his. He tries to give her a small reassuring smile, which, after an uncertain pause, she returns.

He hoists himself off the floor, looks out the window. It's an outdoor parking lot they're in. But no, that's not it, there's something wrong with all these cars, missing wheels, broken windows, flat tires.

"Get out."

He doesn't want to get out here. "Why?"

This is a mechanic's yard. A junkyard.

"Out." The talkative cop turns around, brandishing his gun. "Now."

This is the sort of place you bring people to kill them.

68

"*Maintenant, c'est fini.*"

"Now? What do you mean?"

"Now is when we end this."

Ibrahim has been listening to the men behind him all day, having their debates, making their arguments, covering their asses. He knows where this has been leading, it was just a matter of time, and the time appears to be now.

"I have received the order."

"From?"

"Directly from the chief. And he received *his* order directly from *le Président de la République.*"

The last time Ibrahim looked, there were a dozen men arrayed on the roof. All of these men are, for a moment, silent.

"It is final."

Ibrahim feels a presence at his back. He turns slightly, just enough to confirm who it is.

"Officer Abid?"

"Yes sir."

"There are many officials here, but only one who is your commanding officer," the man says. "That is completely clear to you, correct?"

"Yes sir."

"So if I give you an order, you are obligated to follow it. Everything else . . ." He indicates the other people here, taking in their uniforms, their communications, their chains of command. "Everything else is not your concern."

Ibrahim does not answer; it was not a question. But it is ludicrous. Not his concern?

What will happen after he squeezes the trigger? Yes, the *préfecture* will try to keep his name private, or at least they will claim to try. But will they succeed? Even if they do, will Ibrahim himself be able to keep this secret? Not a word, even to his parents?

Perhaps he will. Then what? Will he drive himself crazy with doubt, with guilt, with self-loathing?

Or will he admit his role to his parents, in quiet confidence? Maybe to his brother? Will these relatives of his remain completely silent? Or will one confide in a friend at the café, a colleague at the store, a schoolmate, the greengrocer, a cousin? How long will it take for this information to spread around the neighborhood? Will the community shun him? Will people hiss at him, spit on him? Will some fanatic exact misguided retribution for the wrong crime? Sneak up behind Ibrahim on a dark sidewalk?

Not his concern?

No, perhaps he is not the one who will face internal criticism, a disciplinary hearing, a formal reprimand on his record, maybe even be forced out of the police force, spend a few months on extended holiday in Corsica before settling into a new job, something more lucrative in private security.

None of that is what will happen to him. Instead he will be shot in the back of the head. Payback in kind.

Who *is* this man about to be put down like a rabid dog? This hardware-store clerk whose wife was murdered by the police? This widower with the two small children and terminal cancer? What exactly is this man doing, and why?

Perhaps he is just another man being used for someone else's agenda. By French nationalists, manufacturing an excuse. By American spies, manipulating public opinion. A cheap life, easily expended. By Ibrahim.

"With all respect, sir, that is simply not true."

"Excuse me? What is not true?"

"That the concern is not mine."

The commander takes a few seconds to consider his response. All these other powerful men around, a story that will be told many times, up and down the corridors of power, in well-appointed offices and exclusive clubs, in casual cafés and formal-dress soirees, whispered among other powerful men while their elegant women stand by, *It was a tense moment,* they will confide, *and then the lieutenant calmly said—*

"I understand that this is difficult. I do." He places his hand on Ibrahim's shoulder. "But it is a difficult act, not a difficult decision. You do not have a decision here."

This is true, Ibrahim knows it. All he could hope for is to change this man's mind. But he has heard what he has heard, and he knows this is not possible.

"Now is the time, Officer Abid."

Ibrahim's face has been turned halfway between his captain and his target, looking at neither, but instead facing the direction of the Tuileries Gardens and Concorde and, beyond, the Arc de Triomphe, the Eiffel Tower. It is a spectacular vista from up here; he should have appreciated it more. In a minute he will be escorted away to begin the debriefing. Then he will be ordered to take a few days off. Then he will be reassigned. This is Ibrahim's last moment up on this roof.

"Yes sir."

He settles over his weapon. His finger finds the trigger.

"You are making a big mistake, Marcel. I urge you to reconsider." This is just for the record, for the stories he will be able to tell. Everyone here knows that Marcel is not going to reconsider.

The suicide-vested man has not moved, nor has Ibrahim's weapon moved, so the target is still in the middle of his sight. Center of mass in the center of crosshairs.

Then Ibrahim hears, "It is necessary, you understand, for it to be the head."

His breath catches.

"You know this, yes? That vest, it is an impediment."

The head.

"A single thorax shot might not be lethal. At least not immediately. There is the vest, its contents. We cannot have him writhing on the ground. Yelling, bleeding. Dying slowly."

Yes, Ibrahim can see this image clearly, a film playing in his imagination. It would constitute torture. Inhumane.

"We do not want you to need to take multiple shots."

The head is a smaller target, a less certain shot. And a much more awful thing to do in this context. A more awful thing to be videotaped, to be broadcast around the world. It will not be a body slumping over, suddenly dead, a dark pool spreading beneath, smooth red streams in the little grout canals between the paving stones. Instead a head will explode, there will be blood and bones and brains expelled from a gory crater on the far side of the skull, pink mist sprayed into the air, gray matter everywhere.

It will be horrific.

People at the periphery of the courtyard will scream, the sound will bounce around the stone surfaces even as the rifle's report is still echoing. People in their homes will gasp when they see it on their televisions, on their smartphones, they will be screaming in the streets of Paris, they will be screaming in London and Brussels, in Istanbul and Beirut, in Tehran and Baghdad and Damascus and Riyadh, in Rabat and Tripoli and Khartoum and Addis Ababa, in Kabul and Islamabad and Karachi and Jakarta. A billion and a half Muslims, a quarter of the world's population.

"Also, hitting the vest might risk detonation."

And the other three-quarters, they will see it too.

Ibrahim does not argue. There is nothing for him to say except "Yes sir." Then he returns his eye to the sight. Adjusts his aim. It is just the tiniest movement on his end, four hundred meters away from the target.

The head.

"Fire when ready."

When ready! How will he ever be ready?

It is his job to always be ready, more so than it is to actually make the shot. His job is to be prepared to take a life, every time he arrives to work. But he has never before done it, not while wearing this police uniform. Not in Paris.

Ibrahim takes a deep breath in, exhales slowly.

Another breath, another exhale.

Now—

69

As soon as she stepped out of the garage, Kate sent another text to Inez: *Flight plan?*

While she waited for an answer, she searched for nearby doctors. The closest was two blocks away, but that was a pediatrician's; not a first choice. Another quarter-mile farther afield was a general practitioner, with a name that suggested it might be a father-and-son operation. That's where Kate would go—more than one doctor, more chance of more supplies, more expertise, pain medications, perhaps surgical experience, maybe even familiarity with gunshot wounds.

Or maybe it was a mother and daughter. Two sisters.

Inez replied: *Still waiting.*

Kate drove away from the garage, from the surrounding commercial clutter, headed up the Montmartre hill, Sacré-Cœur looming off to the side, high up on its commanding perch, surveying the city below.

The doctor's office should have been right around the next corner.

It wasn't.

According to her map it was *right here* damn it, but somehow this was not the correct spot, the real-life street did not match the virtual one on her screen, she was supposed to be on an adjoining street, one farther up the hill, separated from this one by—what? Here it was: a long staircase.

She couldn't drive the moped up that.

This is the problem with GPS-powered maps: they make you believe that they're showing everything, that they're infallible. But their fallibility is the same one that maps have always had: limited to two dimensions.

The street dead-ended. This was taking too long. She was running out of time, she could feel it.

She spun the bike around, tried another route, a curving street with a switchback on the confusing mess of a hill, where adjoining streets can be inaccessible to each other, necessitating long journeys like the one she was on now, wasting precious time, zigzagging up the *butte*, not dissimilar to the plateau of Luxembourg surrounded by deep gorges, another place where Kate used to chase people, and get chased.

In fact, these very same people.

Kate comes to another stop, this time on a steep street next to a tall retaining wall that prevents a lush garden from spilling onto the sidewalk. The houses here look almost suburban: driveways, yards, fences with gate latches. Hard to believe this is the same city.

She looks at her watch, that present from Dexter. Kate thought she knew what he'd been apologizing for with the exorbitant gift, but now she's less sure.

The gunfire was more than two hours ago, a long time with a gunshot wound. More than time enough to go into shock, to bleed out, to die. Also more than time enough to find a doctor, to treat the wound, to bandage up, to escape.

Kate may get only one chance here. If she barges into the wrong doctor's office, the police will be called, and a unit might be anywhere, just around the corner, one minute from responding, on-edge from the day's events, ready to fire first and ask questions later.

If she barges into the right office? She might get shot that way too.

And if she does neither? Then she will have no leverage, nothing to bargain for Dexter's freedom.

Nothing except twenty-five million euros.

Kate reminds herself, yet again, that it's not her money. It's not even her government's money. It's no one's money, and it's sitting untouched in that numbered account, accruing minuscule interest, which is exactly how it will remain for eternity, unless someone transfers it out, reintroduces it to the economy, to the pockets of chambermaids and grocers and restaurateurs and the devious woman who tricked Dexter into stealing it. Would the world be any worse off?

The street is paved in cobblestone, bordered by an exceptionally narrow sidewalk even by Paris standards, barely wide enough for one person to walk. Kate peers down at the pavement directly in front of the build-ing, examining every discoloration, chewing gum, dog poop—

There.

She kneels, and dabs her finger into the ovoid splat. Nearly dry, but not quite. Blood.

The front door is recessed in a shallow alcove. The doctor's buzzer is at the very top, number 1, it must be the ground floor, front of the building.

Kate steps backward, into the street, trying to get an angle to see through the windows. But the shades are all drawn, she can't even tell if lights are on.

She checks her phone: still no message from Inez. No flight plan. No further information.

Kate senses movement, it's the door opening, someone is exiting, and she returns to the alcove just in time to catch the door before it closes—

The lobby is very small. The door to the doctor's office just steps from the front.

Kate has known a good number of policemen. American cops, Mexi-can, Colombian, Italian, German. All of them somehow able to subsume the completely rational fear of dying, to subjugate that fear to the will of their professional responsibilities, enabling themselves to do this su-premely terrifying thing: go through the door.

It has never really been Kate's job to burst through doors, but she has nevertheless done it a handful of times. And even in this very finite sam-ple size, she has managed to confront, more than once, the thing that no one wants to confront, ever: an enemy with a gun.

She draws her own. Puts her other hand on the doorknob, and exerts just the tiniest pressure, testing to see if the door is unlocked, if the knob turns—

It does.

70

"Your phone, please."

"What? Why?"

"You ask that question way too fucking much." The police officer extends his hand, the one that's not holding an automatic weapon. "Just give me your goddamn phone."

Hunter complies.

"Yours too," the guy says to Colette. He no longer seems to have a French accent. How long has that been going on?

"Please," Hunter pleads. He's not sure exactly what he's pleading for, but he doesn't like the look of this junkyard. "What are you going to do to us?" He knows he sounds like he's about to cry, it's definitely not an attractive sound, but he's finished trying to be attractive. Now his focus is staying alive.

"The State Department will deny any involvement," the man continues. It's now clear that he's neither French nor a cop. "The CIA too will decline to comment one way or the other. No one will answer any questions posed by anyone, including you. So it would be better if you didn't bother asking."

"Why?"

"There you go again, with that fucking question. Can't you just accept anything?"

Hunter obviously doesn't want to argue with this guy, who's pointedly holding a gun.

"You'll look like a self-important, delusional, conspiracy-theory lunatic. And you see how easy we got to you today? We can do it again tomorrow. Keep your fucking mouth shut."

"Understood."

"So what are you waiting for? Go."

"What? Where?"

"There's a Métro station five minutes in that direction."

"And?"

"And? And you'll probably want to get on it."

"I mean: and that's the end of it?"

"Of what?"

"Of . . ." Of what? That's a damn good question.

"You should just be grateful that you're alive. There were other possible outcomes, you know?"

Hunter nods.

"In fact"—the guy raises the gun—"there still are."

71

The whole transfer could not have been easier—apartment to speedboat to airport to private jet, gangplank raised and wheels up, all in less than a half-hour. It's amazing, the conveniences that can be bought with immense amounts of money. The appeal of this whole operation. One of the appeals.

Susanna can't decide what she's looking forward to most: the riches or the revenge.

Kate Moore had taken their liberty. Kate Moore had taken their identities, their families, friends, homes. Kate Moore had taken their twenty-five million euros.

In the end, Kate in her ostentatious largesse had allowed them to avoid arrest, had let them loose to flee Paris, a sinuous trip of local trains that lurched from one station to the next, snack-bar fast food, increasingly disgusting bathrooms, saggy beds in the sorts of hotels that don't maintain records, and finally a third-class ferry across the Mediterranean on their way to erasing their trail in the undocumented anarchy of North Africa, a grueling twenty-hour crossing in rough weather.

That's where it happened: on the ferry. In an iron-walled windowless bathroom off the main lounge, three toilet stalls, only one of whose doors had a fully functioning lock.

She was barely showing. Almost no one knew. There were few people to tell; she didn't have many friends, not that much of a life, her career had come to an abrupt end. All she had was this new husband and this new human growing in her, and the promise of a large fortune on the immediate horizon.

When that fortune was yanked away at the last minute, she fell into a tailspin of anxiety and furor, exacerbated by frantic uncomfortable travel, and finally that rolling, groaning ferry.

She banged into that middle stall clutching her spasming stomach, bent over double, one hand bracing herself against the door while she fumbled with the lock.

That middle stall. That was where she lost her baby.

Just a few minutes after the plane levels off, Richie mutters, "Jesus."

She looks up. Richie is sitting across from her in a quartet of big soft leather seats that are the exact same color and visual texture of tiramisu. He's staring at the computer in his lap. "It happened."

"*Che?*" asks Gianna, who clearly serves double-duty as girl Friday and concubine. She also adores Matteo. It seems to be universal, the way Italian women love babies. That might be useful later. Soon.

Richie doesn't answer Gianna. He leans forward, extends the laptop to Susanna.

Even though she knew this was coming, still she recoils when it happens. The sequence ends, and she can't help herself, she hits REPLAY.

What does she see? The footage is blurry, grainy. A man is standing in a vast courtyard, all alone. He shifts his weight. She imagines that his feet are aching, his lower back too. Maybe he's thirsty. He needs to pee, or he already has, relieving himself inside the rubber liner he's wearing for this exact purpose. He has been standing in this position for nine hours. You can see the fatigue in his posture.

With no warning there's a sharp crack, and a spray explodes from the side of his head, and he slumps to the ground.

The camera angle changes slightly, and the image blurs while the lens refocuses on the body—the corpse—in this new prone position.

A sizable portion of his head is, simply, gone. Blood is gushing from the crater. The image is horrifying, the undeniable reality of a life ended violently.

The vest: intact, undetonated.

The silver briefcase: just sitting there.

And everyone in Paris wondering: what happens next?

❧

This was built into the plan, it was preordained, to be followed inevitably by outrage, protests, unrest, reprisals. Markets will continue to stagnate and suffer for days, for weeks, stocks will be falling everywhere, short positions will be immensely lucrative.

"What if they never decide to shoot him? What if they take him into custody?"

"He'll resist. Then he'll be shot."

"Why will he resist?"

"Because that's what we're paying him to do."

"You're actually paying a guy to get killed? That's sorta fucked-up."

"Is it?"

"Isn't it?" Richie seemed amazed that she was willing to be so brazenly inhumane. This was at their follow-up meeting, she was providing some of the details that she'd withheld at first. Now she had Richie's money.

"Not necessarily. Listen, Richie, this is the same principle as a high-value assassination. All it takes is one person willing to sacrifice his life, and you can kill any other person in the world. That has always been the case, and probably always will be."

"The trick is still the same: finding the one person willing to die."

"Exactly. But everybody dies. In ten years, or twenty, sixty. It's hard to find a willing participant if he thinks he has sixty great years ahead. But what if he knows for certain that he doesn't?"

Richie nodded, then moved on. "So what's the big secret in that scary briefcase?"

"It will appear to be a dirty bomb. Probably nuclear."

"*What?* Are you out of your fuckin' mind? You're gonna detonate a nuke? In Paris?"

"Please. I'm not even going to procure one. But that's what it'll look like."

"What, just because it's a metal briefcase? Won't the police or army—whoever—won't they have a, whatchamacallit, one of those things that measures radiation?"

"The police will call military experts, scientists. They will procure a device that can measure ionization-induced fluorescence—"

"The what?"

"—and they will indeed detect alpha-particle radiation—"

"The fuck is an alpha particle?"

"—but the device will not be a *bomb,* Richie. Just a piece of hard lug-gage with some radioactive material packed in, surrounded by explo-sives. But the triggering mechanism will not work. Literally impossible to detonate."

"And where in the name of Christ Almighty will you get radioactive waste?"

"Asia." As if that explained it all. It ended up being a strange trans-action, a surprisingly modest sum of cash.

"You understand that this can't be used for a weapon, yes?" the man asked. He didn't want her coming back, demanding a refund.

"I do."

He glanced down at her pregnant stomach. "It's just really *bad* for you."

"Yup." She had done her research, as always. "Got it."

"The nuclear bomb is a hoax, Richie. With the very specific goal of preventing the military or police from acting too aggressively, too early. They wouldn't risk an escalation to a nuclear detonation, or a conven-tional explosion that releases lethal agents."

"Lethal agents, huh?"

"Although the case's contents won't be known for certain, the possi-bilities are too terrifying, especially at the Louvre."

"You're fuckin' crazy, you know that?"

"Richie," she said, "I'm going to take that as a compliment."

Ten minutes later, Susanna and Chris were back out on the *calle,* walking away from the hotel with a bagful of cash.

"How can you trust that guy?" her husband asked. "He's complete slime. He's not only a career criminal, but also a snitch. He's not even an honorable crook."

"You're completely right. I don't trust him, and I don't like him. Those are two of the main reasons why I want to use him."

"I don't understand."

"Don't you? For the same reason we're using that sociopath to drive the van in Paris."

Chris continued to not understand.

For a long time, she'd hoped that one day her husband would eventually prove himself to be smarter than all previous experience had suggested. But he kept disappointing her, again and again. Luckily, he had other useful qualities.

"We're going to need to destroy the evidence, every last shred. Every link to us."

That's when he finally figured it out; she could see the recognition cross his face. "Who?" he asked. "*Me?*"

"No, you'll be taking care of that piece of shit in Paris. Me, I'll handle Benedetti. I've been waiting a long time for it."

Susanna looks down at the Alps, bathed in the last of the rosy late-afternoon light. She can see the Matterhorn, its shape easily distinguishable even from up here. Some things are unmistakable, no way to be wrong no matter how you look at them.

They must be flying above Switzerland.

Huh.

It hadn't occurred to her until this moment that the pilot would need to file an international flight plan, but of course he did. All rules may not apply when flying private, but some do.

This is a nice plane, less opulent than she expected from Richie, but then again he bought it used from a distressed seller, so he didn't get to make any choices about the décor. The pilot is polite, the hostess obsequious. There was no waiting to take off, there will be no long taxi at the other end; the travel time is minimal.

There are many undeniable benefits to flying private, but for this flight the most operative one to her is this: no one cares if you bring a gun.

72

The door bangs open, Kate pushed it too hard, not calmly, not in control, expecting that on the far side will be a gun pointed at her—

There isn't.

What's in the waiting room is a doctor wearing a white coat, her sleeves dabbed with blood and a large stain on the front. Beside her is an old man, naked from the waist up, next to a messy pile of clothes exuding the stench of vodka.

"You are here for an American with a gunshot wound?" the doctor asks, in English. She seems completely unsurprised by the appearance of a woman with a gun. "He left. Two minutes ago? Perhaps three. He too has a gun. I should tell you that I have already called the police."

Kate glances at the old man, who looks furious, his mouth working up to something, eyes burning into her.

"That man," he finally sputters. "He stole my clothes!"

Kate can feel the Vespa's tires on the verge of slipping as she tears around the corner, onto a broader street with at least ten pedestrians in her sight-line, but none is a man wearing a tweed jacket or a pink shirt.

She continues to accelerate, then has to slow to turn another corner onto an even busier street, a commercial thoroughfare, there are dozens of people visible, near and far, and her eye is drawn down the hill, where a gaggle is gathered under the glass *édicule* of a Métro entrance, a large group emerging from the subway, trying to get their bearings—which way is the Moulin Rouge, Picasso's studio, Sacré-Cœur—and dispersing just in time for Kate to see a grayish jacket, and just the sliver of pink collar, disappear down the stairs.

She lunges for the elevator doors—

Too late.

Stairs, then. This platform is the deepest in Paris, more than a hundred feet underground, signs tell you how many more steps before the top, encouraging you, pep talks. The two hundred stairs are divided into sets of ten, to make the climb up seem more manageable.

But Kate is going down, down, racing around the circular stairwell, the murals whizzing by.

She bounds onto the platform. A train is already in the station, and all the disembarked passengers are moving away, others are now boarding, she doesn't see the gray jacket anywhere, and she's sprinting toward the train, sprinting, the doors are beginning to close, she has just a few more steps but she can see that she's not going to make it, but she keeps trying anyway, another step, another—

Fuck.

She doesn't make it. The doors are closed.

"Mademoiselle?"

She is grateful for two things. One is that a man is holding open the next set of doors for her. Two is that he's a good-looking young man who just mistook her for a *mademoiselle.*

She can't waste time. If he's even on this train, he might exit at the next station, he might change directions, he might depart the system.

She pushes her way through the crowd. It's rush hour now, the subway is packed. Luckily there are no doors between the cars, no barriers of any sort, so she can see a long distance.

He's relatively tall, the man she's looking for. She suspects that his face won't be recognizable, not from afar. Maybe he's wearing facial hair, or eyeglasses, or he has an unusual hairstyle, or he's cue-ball bald. She knows what he looked like a couple of years ago; she spent no small amount of time examining his face.

She can still remember his frank open stare, his unabashed invitation to adultery, propositioning her right there on the Grand Rue. She wishes her memory is that she never even considered it, but that's not what happened.

He wouldn't look the same now, not here, doing what he's doing. He'd be disguised. As she is, but more so. Much more.

The train is already slowing for the next station and she's only halfway through, and hasn't seen him yet.

Kate's phone dings an incoming text: *Destination Le Bourget.* Paris's general-aviation airport. That woman is on a private plane en route to Paris.

Of course.

There's a pair of very tall, very skinny African men standing in her path, and Kate can't see much beyond them. "*Excusez-moi,*" she says, and when they part she can see all the way to the rear of the train, she can see everything clearly.

73

The Métro is nearly empty when they board. They take seats in a corner, ride in uneasy silence. The train sits for long stretches, delays that are explained by PA announcements that neither listens to. Colette and Hunter are not concerned with service delays, not after what they have been through.

They disembark in a big station where three lines meet. Colette will transfer here to get home, and Monsieur Forsyth can find his own way to wherever he wants to go—home, office, embassy, police, the bar at the Meurice, she does not care anymore.

"À demain," she says. Now that home is within grasp, she is growing extra-impatient to get back to her husband and daughter, away from her boss, his problems.

"Colette, wait."

She stops, but does not immediately turn back.

"We should discuss this," he says. "What we will tell people."

With her slight pause, she hopes to make her boss understand that she has had enough of today, does not want to discuss this, cannot. Tomorrow, that will be another day, she is planning to go to the office, they can talk then. Not now. Tomorrow.

That would be the smart thing to do, the rational and sensible thing: go to work tomorrow. She will be able to tell the story to her colleagues, the whole ordeal, the guns, the fight, the flight, the life-or-death confrontations. People will stand around with their mouths hanging open, gasping, *Mon Dieu*, clutching her arm.

Her narrative will help everyone understand, later, when she resigns. It was too traumatizing, she will say. She could not get over her fears, her flashbacks, she could not sleep, she was having panic attacks, yes she had seen a therapist, she was taking anti-anxiety medication, but the drugs left her feeling stupid, dull, tired, unable to enjoy eating, drinking, fucking.

She has no choice, she will say. It is for her own health, and also for her role as wife, as mother. She simply cannot function this way.

"Are you okay?"

He takes both her hands in both of his, and she forces herself not to recoil.

"*Oui Monsieur.*"

Colette has faced many indignities in her life, an attractive woman in the business world, working in tech, every office populated almost exclusively by men. Come-ons of every type, double-entendres, sexual innuendo, lewd jokes, overt propositions. She has been massaged, she has been caressed, cornered, kissed, squeezed, groped, all manner of sexual assault short of the traditional legal definitions of rape.

But perhaps the greatest indignity has been the ignominy of pretending to enjoy the company of this man, this sexist elitist anti-intellectual lout. His eyes always on her, his lust oozing off him, enveloping her in its suffocating stench.

On second thought, maybe she will not go to the office tomorrow. That too will make sense to everyone. After all, it was just minutes ago when she was climbing out of that car, thinking she was about to be shot, stuffed into a rusted-out automobile, and set afire.

Everyone will understand if she needs to take a day or two.

She had not known exactly what would happen, or when, but she had definitely not imagined that she would end up dragged into today's events. That was M. Forsyth's fault—he was the one who insisted she accompany him. If he had not, she would have been left behind with Didier the bodyguard. She would have gone to the office. She would have stood around with everyone else, speculating, wringing their hands, making reports, taking ineffective action.

"At least let me get a car to take you home," he says.

"*Merci bien, Monsieur.*" She shakes her head. "But the train will be faster."

Colette had also not expected that anyone would be in any physical danger. Certainly not herself. She had been well assured of the contrary. And she had continued to believe that this was the truth, right until the moment when it was not.

But it had all turned out okay, just as the handsome bearded American had promised. No one had been hurt, at least not seriously. The two Americans had gotten the worst of it, wounds inflicted on each other, by each other.

"All I want is to be home with my family."

It was just a few small pieces of information that she provided. Details about M. Forsyth's morning routine, his bodyguards and police escort, the security code to his building, the location of the telecommunications boxes, the model and operating system of his mobile.

The entire meeting had taken an hour, at a working-class *bar-tabac* out in La Villette, someplace where Hunter Forsyth would never deign to visit. Colette left that café with a thick envelope bound in a rubber band.

"Je suis épuisée, Monsieur."

Then this morning she had been slipped another large sum, this time tucked inside the oversize sunglasses case that is right now sitting in the zippered compartment of the leather bag hanging from her shoulder. Twenty thousand euros cash, nontaxable.

"I will see you tomorrow," she says.

She will tell her husband that this money was part of 4Syte's settlement, alongside the actual settlement they end up paying. It will not be insignificant. She has been through a lot.

"Okay," M. Forsyth says, with a smile. "Good night, Colette."

Then she smiles back at him, it is for once a genuine smile that she gives Hunter Forsyth, because she just decided that she will not see him tomorrow, nor ever again.

74

He eases back into consciousness, a fade-in, the lights coming on slowly, images resolving themselves, awareness resuming . . .

He's on the Métro. He's been riding for—how long?—who knows. He has changed trains, trudged through those tunnels, rush-hour crowds, delays, more crowds.

And now he remembers: he has been shot.

He fingers the lapel of the sport jacket that he commandeered from the old man in the doctor's office, and peeks inside. The bandage has leaked, and there's a fist-size blot of blood near the shoulder of the old man's pink shirt.

The pain medication is fading.

The subway crowd has dwindled, and the few remaining passengers are giving him a wide berth. He thinks he may stink—yes, he rolled through a pool of urine in a dark alleyway, right after he was shot. His pants are filthy, his shirt and jacket don't fit, he's wearing facial hair that could be mistaken for a homeless man's beard, and a large fake scar on his cheek, and crazy-person hair. He has been fading in and out of consciousness.

He'd stay the fuck away from him too.

He wonders what his wife decided to do. She could have stuck with Plan A, and is already in Croatia, settling into the top-floor flat with a view of the sea, feeding the baby, unpacking the bag, waiting for her husband.

Thankfully the police have left him alone. The cops have priorities far more urgent than sweeping bums off the subway.

He is almost positive he's not going to make it to Croatia by morning. He's not going to make it to Croatia ever. He's not going to make it at all.

He feels this definitively in the pain in his shoulder, in the coldness that has enveloped his body, in his inconstant consciousness, in the echoes of the doctor's warning, "It is necessary for you to have surgery."

He nodded, trying to climb into the old man's clothes, failing. She helped him.

"This wound will not repair itself. You will bleed, and bleed, until you die."

"How long?"

"Impossible to say."

"How about a guess?"

She said *Pfft.*

"Please."

"At very most, twenty-four hours." She shrugged at the unlikelihood of this. "Probably much less."

Maybe his wife didn't go to Croatia. Maybe—hopefully—she opted for Plan B, or some secret Plan C. But he doubts he'll ever know.

75

K ate is growing impatient, riding this Métro, watching this man, wondering if this is futile. But he's her only leverage. And he must be on his way somewhere relevant.

He suddenly stands, exits the train, staggers down the platform.

Kate lags behind to take off her jacket, to change her first-glance appearance, even though this is probably an unnecessary precaution. The man she's following isn't aware of other people, he's not using any countersurveillance tactics, not making any evasive maneuvers. This man's situational awareness isn't heightened; it's nonexistent. He must be in intense pain, or on intense pain relievers, or both. He has been easy to monitor—moving slowly, falling asleep on a Métro seat. She thought, briefly, that he'd died.

She follows him into the *correspondance* tunnel, continues round a bend, up some stairs. Then she confronts a fork in the tunnel. Which direction would he take? She has no inputs to help her choose, it's a coin toss. She walks left.

This transfer tunnel deposits her onto the middle of the platform, rather than at the end. From just inside the tunnel, she can't see any of the other people waiting on the platform she's about to enter. But she can see across the tracks, to the far side of the station, to the platform for trains heading the other way.

That's where he's sitting, eyes staring straight in front of him. Straight at her.

⚜

No. He cannot recognize her, there's no way. It has been years, and she's disguised. She's wearing a wig and glasses that cover half her face, she's fifty yards away, the light is not great, there's no way he's prepared for Kate Moore to possibly appear on the opposite Métro platform.

She glances at the arrivals board. The train on her side is due to arrive in one minute. The other one in two.

Yes, that will work.

She turns to face the direction from which the train will arrive, presenting her profile to the man she once knew as Bill MacLean. Profiles are much harder to recognize.

Kate waits.

She can see the train arriving, it should be here in seconds. At that point she'll be shielded from his view, and she'll spin on her heels and dash through the station to his platform, and he'll think that this woman had simply boarded the—

But what's this? The train for her platform has stopped, just short of entering the station.

Across the way, she can see that the other train is due to arrive in one minute, while the train on Kate's side is now just sitting there, waiting for something, for the love of God what? She can hear the opposite one getting near.

Damn.

She can't continue to wait. She retreats into the tunnel.

Behind her, she can feel the rumble of the other train arriving, and she turns a curve into the corridor, and now breaks into a full sprint, up a flight of stairs, another turn, a dead sprint on a straightaway—

Kate can hear it down there, the doors are open, people are exiting.

Down the stairs three at a time, each jump a chance to miss, to twist her ankle, to lose balance and go tumbling down facefirst, breaking her nose, her jaw, splitting her forehead open on the sharp edge of a riser—

She lands at the bottom, and it's just another few steps around the corner.

This is one of those Métro stations whose platform entrances and exits don't use the same corridors. People who are arriving don't need to face off against people trying to depart, no trench warfare of shoving, shuffling, bags bumping, elbows flying . . .

So no one impedes Kate as she bursts onto the platform, and through the train's open doors, and into the very same car where he is already sitting, watching her board.

She doesn't make eye contact. She turns and walks away, grabbing seat backs for balance, passing empty rows. Anyone observing her closely would realize that she's putting distance between herself and someone else, who must be that disheveled wild-eyed man.

Does he himself realize? Did he notice that she's the same woman who was on the opposite platform? And on his previous train? Not to mention the same woman who deprived him of twenty-five million euros? The same woman whose husband he has come to Paris to frame for kidnapping, conspiracy, insider trading, maybe even murder?

Kate takes a seat, one that faces his side, so she can watch him unobserved but he'd have to turn to see her, it would be obvious.

Her adrenaline is spiked. She takes deep breaths, focusing on the PA, the recorded woman's voice announcing the next station, they always say each station name twice, the first as a matter of fact—perhaps a gentle suggestion, maybe a bit tentative—but the second with a completely different inflection, as if this woman has had enough of your shit, she's putting an end to the whole debate, severe stress on the final syllable—Chate*let*—and now shut the fuck up. This is a woman who has ample experience disciplining small children, firmly, the way French mothers do. Kate has respect for this woman.

The train is pulling into the station when Kate's phone rings.

She knows, from just the single syllable: "Kate." According to her screen it's no one, no area code, no country, no way to ID, to locate.

Kate doesn't respond.

"It's been a long time."

It's been two years.

This subway is relatively empty, there are no conversations going on. When mobile signals were introduced to the system, Kate worried that the Métro would become unbearable, like commuting in a customer-service call center. But surprisingly few people choose to have conversations here. If Kate starts speaking in English, it will be noticeable. She remains silent.

"Do you have any idea how much evidence there is, Kate? The police are going to solve this so quickly."

Kate stands, and walks farther away from him.

"The first thing that's going to happen is that a Métro worker finds a duffel bag that contains a wardrobe change. Clothes that are the exact same outfit that your husband wears basically every day. Displaying the same lack of imagination today that was apparent even two decades ago, back in college. People don't change, do they, Kate?"

Not much.

"This bag also has lots of visible residue from a tennis-court surface, which will be easily ID'd as from the Luxembourg Gardens. This bag, it's obvious, is your husband's tennis bag."

That's all explainable, Kate thinks. All could have been fabricated. But she knows there's more to come, and it will be worse. She knows how this woman tells stories, little to big.

"But what makes this bag *really* suspicious—what provokes an emergency call to the police—is that it also contains disposable phones. Burners that were purchased on the boulevard St-Germain, just a few minutes from your apartment. The American who made this memorable purchase—he's six feet even, tortoiseshell eyeglasses—was also wearing a unique article of clothing. You know what that was, Kate?"

Kate's mind hops around for a second before she alights on the answer. But still she says nothing.

"A white hat with a ludicrous logo. How many American men in Paris could possibly own such a cap?"

One.

"The police are right now examining surveillance footage of the landmarks that were targeted today. They will notice that one person appears again and again, standing around in the place Vendôme, at the Gare de Lyon, Notre-Dame. Often wearing this navy jacket and white shirt and blue jeans and brown shoes. Sometimes wearing that ridiculous cap. And always—*always*—looking around, taking notes. As if what, Kate?"

This is far worse than Kate had imagined.

"As if casing the joint."

She'd thought it was going to be a few clusters of circumstantial evidence, digital footprints that could be explained away, or obliterated.

"But wait, Kate, there's more. Your husband also received calls on a regular basis, for weeks, from a phone that will be discovered on a dead body. Do you know what body?"

Of course she knows: the suicide bomber at the Louvre. Those were Dexter's daily robo-calls. Not from an insurance salesman.

"So then, to summarize: *means,* yes; *opportunity,* yes; and what about *motive*?" She chuckles. "In addition to your husband's compulsive research into 4Syte Inc., his browser history also features an obsession with the personal life of Hunter Forsyth that, frankly, looks a lot like stalking."

How much of this browsing history will still be retrievable, now that Kate has thrown Dexter's hard drives into the Seine? That depends on how careful he had been.

"A disturbing pattern. But an easy narrative to understand, isn't it? An ex-friend, ex-employee, afflicted with debilitating jealousy of Forsyth's gigantic success. The tech boom passed Dexter by, didn't it? While everyone around him got filthy rich, especially this guy he hates *so much.* It's almost impossible to *not* believe that Dexter would plot revenge. He is, after all, a master plotter of extremely complicated crimes."

This is mind-bogglingly thorough. Psychopathic, is what this is.

"But don't worry, Kate. Because although there's plenty of evidence that implicates Dexter—though, no, it's more than *implicates,* isn't it? There's ample slam-dunk evidence. But there's also evidence that exonerates him."

Yes, Kate knows: there must be, because he's innocent. But she can't think of a single shred of it.

"There are a few witnesses who saw him at strategic times this morning. People who can prove that there was no way for Dexter to be kidnapping Forsyth, or dropping off any bombs, because he was somewhere else at the time."

Now she understands the old man at the intersection, the attractive woman at the Luxembourg Gardens: setups, planted in Dexter's path, for this purpose.

"And the incriminating electronic trail, that too can be disguised. Dexter already installed the sequence to do that, unwittingly, when he opened an e-mail from the so-called inside source, forwarded to him via his tennis pal. You know what source I'm talking about, right? The one who supposedly leaked the negative intel about this merger?"

What forethought, planning, legwork. Investment of money too. The payoff must be commensurate.

"The malware is just waiting for my—"

"Enough," Kate says, firmly but perhaps too quietly.

"Excuse me?"

"That's *enough*." A few decibels louder. "What do you want?"

"Are you kidding? You know exactly what I want."

She does. "And what do I get in exchange?"

"Certain tips will not be called into the police. Instead, evidence will be destroyed. And other evidence provided, constructing a different, equally credible narrative. Pointing to a different suspect."

Kate is not in any position to bargain; this isn't a negotiation. She has been outplayed. The patrolmen have already interacted with Dexter, and unless the cops start searching somewhere else, they're going to track him down and look at him ever more closely. It won't take long.

She has to capitulate, or flee. At this moment, Kate still has the choice. "How do I know you'll keep your end?"

"The normal way."

"How's that?"

"Half now."

Half?

"The other half after the second suspect is ID'd, exonerating Dexter."

Half doesn't make sense. What this woman wants from Kate—what Kate can provide—is a bank account number to go with the password that the woman already possesses. This account number is stored on Kate's phone, in her notes app, on a page that seems to be filled with details about the kids' teachers, and a few school administrators, and the kids' American social security numbers and passport IDs, and Ben's doctors' names and specialties and addresses. This page is a one-stop resource for all this parental data, the items that Kate used to have to hunt for every single time the need arose, which was always in situations that were unpleasant to begin with.

It had taken Kate a few years to realize that there was a simple solution to this recurring problem, if she'd only recognize that it wasn't a one-time problem that just happened to repeat itself, unexpectedly, again and again. It was an expected, ongoing state of affairs. And the only person who could mitigate it was herself.

The long string of digits is labeled SCHOOL ID. No one who glanced at this page could have any idea what that could mean. There's no such thing as a school ID number.

The code is a simple one. If you knew you were looking at a code, and you knew anything about cracking codes, you could do it in minutes. But even if you succeeded in decoding the number, you'd still have only half of the puzzle, with no way to obtain the other half. Not unless you were the sole person in the world who already knew it.

If Kate provides this number, the woman she once knew as Julia MacLean will have access to a bank account containing twenty-five million euros. You either have access to the account, and everything in it, or you don't. There's no possible half about it.

"Half? What are you talking about?" But even as she's asking it, Kate realizes with a sinking heart what the only possible explanation is.

"Are you fucking kidding me? You know exactly what I'm talking about."

"We don't have—"

"I'm assuming you spent—how much? That's a nice apartment of yours, fancy vacations, et cetera. But you're not profligate, I know that about you. Maybe you've spent two million? Three?"

It has been only one. Not even spent; just set aside.

"So, tell you what, Kate: for that second payment, I'll take just twenty."

"Are you out of your mind? We don't have *any* of that money anymore."

"Then find it. Twenty-five million right now, twenty by the end of tomorrow. Forty-five million euros, or Dexter goes to jail."

"I don't . . . I can't . . ."

"I guess you have to ask yourself, Kate: what's your husband worth?"

76

Hunter is hailed as a hero by the staff who still remain, the vice-presidents and lawyers who have spent the afternoon fighting the fire of his disappearance, plus the handful of assistant-levels who understood that they should not leave the office until their bosses do, all these people gathered in the conference room, everyone except the young guy with the spotty beard and eyebrow ring and tattoos—the full complement of millennial self-adornments—whom Hunter sent to the apartment to pick up a clean suit and shirt and tie.

"I'll explain everything later," he says to the assembled. "But our first priority is to reverse the stock slide." The stock did not slide so much as fell off a fucking cliff, but Hunter is in spin mode now.

"Let's do everything we can, as quickly as we can, to reassure share-holders, investors, the international financial community, our business partners, our employees. Let's get a teaser out that I'll be making an announcement"—he checks his watch—"at eight-thirty local."

"That's too late for legacy press."

"Of course. So we'll need to do this live on 4syte.com, and feed the video to all digital and social. Georges and, um, Ninon, you two collaborate on the asset. Élodie, put together distribution lists for text-messages."

"*Oui Mons—*"

"Something like this: due to terrorist attacks and personal safety concerns and inconvenient luck, CEO was forced to take precautionary measures that unfortunately rendered him unreachable for some hours, a situation that was one hundred percent unrelated to 4Syte business or its major announcement, which has been rescheduled to, um"—he pauses, recalculates—"let's make it eight P.M. Central European. Not eight-thirty."

"That's too long for Twitter."

"Fix it, split it, do what you need to do. Get me language within five minutes. Then start working on a revise of the release, a new top graph with apologies." He looks around the room. "Everyone help everyone, we'll get through this, and you can all go home at a reasonable hour."

The stock slide will halt within minutes. Maybe even begin to climb again, baby steps first, then a giant leap after the announcement.

"Someone order some food," he says. Leave it to them to figure it out.

Hunter reminds himself that he has not yet lost any actual wealth today. He still has time to turn this day completely around, and fall asleep an enormously rich man.

"Let's go," he urges, and for good measure claps his hands, the quarterback breaking up the huddle, and winces from the pain in his swollen knuckles. "Time is—literally—money."

What's that noise? Dexter holds his breath, listening, seized by fear. He approaches the door, puts his ear to the wood—

It's people. Women, talking. The plunk as a cork is pulled, the glurp of wine pouring.

He walks down the hall. Three young women are sitting around the table, a baguette, a pile of pink ham, a wedge of pale-yellow cheese, an open bottle of red. Dexter is hungry.

"Evening," says one of the young women. She has a laptop open in front of her.

"Is there any news?" Dexter doesn't know what's happening out there, and he can't go see for himself. "My phone is out of juice."

"Not really, no."

The window faces the Seine, the cathedral of Notre-Dame. A tourist barge floats by. Things must be getting back to some level of normal. "Mind if I take a look?"

"Be my guest."

He leans over the laptop, types in a search, looking for—

Shit.

"Sorry, could I use this for a few minutes? I really need to take care of something."

"Sure," she says.

Dexter logs onto his account, fingers flying, desperate to get to the transaction window, to confirm, to unload his position before it's too late. The share price has been inching up, but it hasn't gotten very far. Not yet.

He executes the first trade, doesn't waste any time figuring out his profit, he has no time for that now, he logs onto the other account, he can see the share price has already ticked up again, but—what?—*Access denied.*

Fuck. He clears all the fields, and starts afresh, typing slower, precisely. Whew.

He looks up. The young women are all pretending they weren't staring at him.

"Thanks." He closes the window, quits the browser. "That was really helpful."

Now he allows himself to calculate, quickly. Then a second time, carefully. Both times, the result is the same.

"You want a glass of wine? You seem like you need a drink."

He smiles at this small kindness, at these young people just starting out, embarking on this adventure, they haven't yet made any major mistakes, even if they think they've faced disasters—that year wasted on the wrong major, or the wrong boyfriend—they don't realize how eminently overcome-able it all is, even while in the middle of overcoming it.

"Thanks," he says. Dexter's mistakes have been much bigger, much harder to overcome. But with a couple of clicks, he just did.

Harder, but not impossible.

78

Paris is on the same latitude as Vancouver; north of basically everywhere in the United States that's not Alaska. Seasonal daylight swings are extreme. In spring, in early summer, dusk seems to last forever, the sun just hanging there, reluctant to dip below the horizon, the last drunk guest to leave a raucous party. Then after sunset, the sky continues to clutch onto last light, and it doesn't get fully dark till ten at night, after all the blue has slowly drained away.

But in autumn and winter, the opposite: nightfall jumps out of nowhere, a predatory mugger lurking in a doorway, attacking with quick furtive movements before anyone has time to react. That's what happened while Kate was on the Métro: night fell.

"Okay," she said as the train sped under the city. Kate had weighed her options, and realized she had none. The only thing she could do was surrender—or pretend to—and buy herself time. "But I don't have the number with me."

"You have thirty minutes."

Then the line went dead.

Kate's eyes were fixed fifty yards down the train, at the man slumped in the seat. Was it possible that Julia just offered to throw him under the bus? Her own husband? Is he the other suspect? Or is there no other suspect? Is she bluffing?

But of course there must be another suspect, because Dexter is not guilty, and someone obviously is. That guilty someone must be Julia's husband. So who else could she offer . . . ?

There *must* be another man whom Julia set up to look guilty, a man with Dexter's build who wore Dexter's clothes, his cap, and bought a bunch of mobiles on the boulevard, and loitered around landmarks, and delivered bombs. That's the man who will look guilty. That's the man who already does, if only people will search for—

Kate's mouth fell open; she actually muttered "Oh" to herself. She realized that she doesn't need to find this alternative suspect. He's not going anywhere. He's already dead, killed in that gunfight in the *onzième*. His opponent is right here, wounded.

For much of her life, Kate had been reluctant to ask for help, she'd seen it as a sign of weakness, a fatal flaw for a woman in her career, working for her organization, all the men would say, *That's exactly what we thought, women can't hack it, always need help.*

It took her a long time before she was able to stop worrying about what all the men thought. That's when she realized that asking for help wasn't a weakness.

She sent Inez another message: *One more favor?*

He staggers into the park. Kate follows at a safe distance.

She realizes that her children are not far from here, this is Hailie's neighborhood off the Champ-de-Mars, the rue St-Dominique is Hailie's hashtag high street, with her daily bakeries and *boucheries,* the same expat-housewife life as Kate's. Almost.

Kate checks her watch. There has been more than enough time to arrive at Le Bourget and then drive into the center of Paris. That woman could be right here, now. She could be waiting up ahead, or following from behind—

But no, she isn't going to preemptively kill Kate. She can't get what she wants from a dead Kate. After she gets her money, though? That'll be different.

Kate feels the weight of the two guns, one in each pocket.

She still thinks of the woman's name as Julia MacLean, though for years now Kate has known that Julia is not her real name. That real name is Susan Pognowski, an ex-FBI agent who has recently been living in Italy as Susanna Petrocelli with identity documents procured in Sicily. Her husband is now called Cristoforo. Their newborn son is Matteo.

Julia MacLean had been nothing more than a character, a role this woman played in Luxembourg. Julia MacLean had been Kate's friend, her best friend, briefly. Her BFB, her frenemy, then her arch enemy. A relationship that was always on its way somewhere, though Kate never knew exactly where, until now. Here.

It ends tonight.

Kate sends another ping of her location. It won't be hard to triangulate the path she's on.

The queues to ascend the Eiffel Tower are staggeringly long; there's no way that's his destination. Kate had briefly imagined this was where he was heading, tricked by a lifetime of movie-watching experience to expect that real life might look that way.

He passes the tower, and exits the park. Across the street, the small carousel is packed, the concessions mobbed, everyone wants ice cream. Kate pauses, watches him turn, make the descent to the riverbank. She looks left, looks right, and here it comes, the lime-green Vespa, puttering near the curb, pulling to a stop.

"He went down to the quay," Kate says.

"*Oui.*"

"Are you sure you want to do this?"

Inez gives a *what-are-you-kidding* smirk. Kate recognizes the attitude: obviously I'm willing to do this, more than willing, this is what I do. Kate too.

"*Merci,*" Kate says. She reaches into her pocket, where she retrieves Inez's gun, wrapped in a silk scarf. "I got my own."

Down on the riverside, there are more long queues for the *bateaux-mouches,* hundreds of people waiting to board the barges for nighttime cruises under the bridges, past the islands, the grand monuments, the splendid museums, the elegant apartment buildings, the busy boulevards, everything lit up in full glory. It was Baron Georges-Eugène Haussmann who ordered more than fifty thousand gaslights installed as part of his ambitious plan to transform a dirty diseased agglomeration of villages into the world's metropolis—mapping a new street plan, erecting train stations, parks, boulevards, row upon row of apartment buildings, a central market, everything. This one man Haussmann created this City of Light.

Kate unlocks another bicycle, and pedals along the street, high above the riverside quay. Beyond the barge docks, the crowds dwindle quickly, just a few couples strolling hand-in-hand, sitting along the embankment, drinking, kissing, until finally it's just the one lone man, walking slowly.

There's limited egress down there, ramps or steps every few hundred meters. He has nowhere to go but straight along the riverside. To where? Why is he down there?

He walks past a houseboat, seemingly unoccupied. And another. Is he going to a houseboat?

A bridge is looming. A lot of bridges cross the Seine, and their undersides tend to be well lit, well maintained, for obvious safety reasons. But the lights under this particular bridge seem to be out, it's dark under there, though not completely, Kate can still see vague forms, the line of the embankment, a supporting pillar, and—

Damn.

⚜

She pedals furiously to the bridge, abandons the bike at the top of the stairs, and scampers down, spins around a landing, down again to the bottom.

This is a wide, low bridge, with a big dark space underneath. Plenty of room to shelter from the elements, to hide from people, to wait unobtrusively. To rendezvous in a prearranged fallback position. To tie up a motorboat, like the one right there.

Kate can see someone standing in the bow, a man holding a gun.

Shapes resolve themselves, backlit by the indirect ambient light of a big city. A person is bent double at the waist, reaching down to the paving stones. It's her—Julia, Susanna, Susan. She's trying to pull up someone, it must be her husband, he has apparently collapsed.

They are just steps from the boat, mere seconds from escape.

Kate raises her weapon, and creeps forward in the darkness that clings to the embankment. She can barely hear Julia's voice. "Come on, you can do it," she implores. "Get up."

Julia can't hoist him all by herself, not the dead weight of a full-grown man.

"I . . . can't."

"Richie?"

"Yeah?"

"Help me."

The man in the bow tucks his gun into his waistband, and gingerly steps up onto the gunwale, careful to keep his balance, this guy doesn't want to stumble, to tumble into the Seine, he's preoccupied at this moment, and so is Julia—

Now is Kate's chance.

She charges forward, gun sighted in front of her. "Stop!" she yells. "Don't move!"

Everyone freezes. A long second passes before Julia asks, "What is it you think you're going to do here?" She lets go of Bill's arm, stands.

The three people in front of Kate form a dimly backlit tableau vivant. On the street above, the traffic light changes, and now there's the noise of engines, the thrumming of wheels.

"Lie down on the ground," Kate orders, continuing to advance.

Julia doesn't obey. "This doesn't change anything, Kate. I still own Dexter's freedom. And your livelihood."

The traffic noise grows more insistent, the buzzing of an engine.

"Unless you're going to kill us all? In cold blood?" Julia doesn't seem to be worried about that possibility, not at all. "Is that what you're going to do, Kate?"

This engine buzz is different, on a different aural plane. Kate realizes what it is.

"*Murder* us all?"

"You!" Kate yells at the guy called Richie, who has moved a few steps away from the boat. "Very, *very* carefully, toss your gun into the water."

She can see him pretending to consider his options. Maybe he's the type of guy who's never willing to admit defeat, not without making a show of something.

"Understand that I will not hesitate to shoot," Kate says. "And there is absolutely no chance I'll miss."

He begins to comply, reaches into his waistband, then Kate senses movement on the boat, she cuts her eyes over there but keeps the gun trained on the man, and—damn, yes—it's definitely another person—

"*No!*"

—and Kate hears Julia's scream but doesn't know who her scream is directed at, or why, and she rotates her arms in a rapid arc toward the boat, to find this new target, to neutralize—

Shit.

It's a young woman. She's holding a baby to her chest. Another unexpected young woman. Another unexpected baby.

Shots begin to explode.

brahim Abid exited the *préfecture* headquarters through the public doors on the place Louis Lépine, around the corner from where the media was camped, waiting for formal comment, which would be edited down into a seven-second sound bite and spliced into a ninety-second package, leading the hour before moving on to whatever is the latest crisis in the Middle East, and the worst of today's sub-equatorial natural disasters, and the inevitable Johnny Hallyday retrospective.

What they would have loved, these reporters, was to talk to him. The shooter.

They would never imagine it, this dark-skinned man wearing baggy jeans and a hoodie. The media were more likely to imagine that such a man was a relative of the bomber, or a friend from madrassa, just now being released after an hour of questioning, cell phone confiscated, ordered not to leave town.

Ibrahim's debrief had taken an hour. There will be more tomorrow, plus psychological evaluations, and trauma specialists, and solicitous meetings with upper echelons, pats on the back, firm handshakes. Sooner or later, someone will present him with a medal, a private ceremony. But no press release. No public acknowledgment.

He bypassed the Métro entrance. Without making a purposeful decision not to take the subway, he started to walk in the direction of home. Through the flower market, where on Sundays street vendors sell birds, which makes the place seem more like Africa, or Asia. He took the pont Notre-Dame, walked past the Hôtel de Ville, from whose roof someone was at that moment looking down on him, another sniper up there, wondering who was that man, what did he want. Ibrahim did not look up. Past

Beaubourg, all that self-referential intellectual-architecture exoskeleton; he does not go to museums, not since primary-school class trips.

Ibrahim took a zigzag through the Marais, the sidewalk cafés full of men, tight jeans and tight tees and tightly cropped facial hair. Then the Jewish street, which had become a shopping street plus falafel, hundreds of people standing in queues for sandwiches, dozens more simply standing, taking pictures of their overstuffed pitas, shopping bags at their feet.

Up through Oberkampf, young people spilling out of loud bars, tattoos, cigarettes. Graffiti here and there, dilettante stuff, token resistance. Like the tattoos.

One Paris after another, none his own.

Little by little, the grandeur gave way to concrete apartment blocks with laundry hanging from twine lines, radar dishes, pinned-up bedsheets as curtains. Jackhammering, a torn-up street, a crumbling building behind rusted-out fences, covered with graffiti that was more political, more convincing.

As Ibrahim climbed the hill, store signs began to appear in Eastern alphabets. The languages he heard were no longer English and German and Japanese; what was not French was Arabic, Chinese, Farsi. There were Turc kebabs, Moyen-Orient grocers, the *traiteur chinois,* the smell of five-spice everywhere.

He was exhausted. He had awoken before dawn, was at the museum by eight, worked a full and horrible day, and now had walked for an hour into the night.

After taxes, his net salary today was 120 euros. Some days, his job is an easy way to earn that money, enough for a new pair of shoes, or a few days' meals for the family; his household responsibility is the midweek *supermarché* run, bags of rice and dried beans and the dark-meat parts of chickens, the sinewy segments of lamb, the less expensive everything.

Today was definitely not one of the easy days.

Some people earned a lot of money today, sitting around, pushing buttons on a keyboard. Not Ibrahim. He worked hard, for not much.

His feet are sore, his body aches from the tension of the day, his brain is tired, he is not thinking clearly. So when he sees the police lights flashing, it does not occur to him that he should turn the other way.

✤

It is dark here, the nearest streetlight is not functioning, but even in the darkness and from a distance of hundred meters, Ibrahim can see that it is Samir who is being hassled, frisked. A handful of people are watching with passive interest, but no one is surprised, Samir is a small-time neighborhood operator, no stranger to the police. But Ibrahim has known Samir since crèche; this guy is no terrorist.

The two patrolmen do not look familiar to Ibrahim. But it is dark. Maybe when he gets closer, he will recognize them.

Samir says something that must be really inadvisable, because one of the *flics* kicks Samir's legs out from under him, and Ibrahim's childhood friend face-plants into the concrete, starts screaming in pain.

It all happens so fast.

Samir spins on the ground and lashes out, kicking upward in anger, catching the arm of one of the *flics,* who responds with his nightstick, one quick shot to the ribs, one to the face. It is a disproportionate reaction, brutal.

"Hey!" Ibrahim yells. He takes a couple of quick steps, then yells "Hey!" again, this time louder, and breaks into a jog. "You are hurting him!"

The *flic* who is not beating on Samir spins, his gun already drawn.

Fifty meters away.

It is so obvious, to Ibrahim, that he himself is one of the good guys.

"I am police!" he yells, continuing to jog toward the confrontation. Today of all days, it does not occur to him that he could look like anything else. But it is dark, he is wearing civilian clothes, a beard, it is a tense scene, he understands that misunderstandings are possible, of course he does, so he knows he needs to clear things up, which is why he reaches his right hand into his sweatshirt's pocket, for his badge.

Crack.

He hears the sound, but he does not understand where it came from, who is shooting at whom, another overreaction, he certainly hopes no one is taking potshots at cops, the whole neighborhood could end up in flames.

Then he feels it, and understands.

He stops running.

Most people see it coming from a distance, from the clear vantage of hours or days, from months or even years or decades, they can see the rapid organ failure or the slow general decline, the inexorable march, the inevitable end.

But other people do not, especially young people, people who are on the cusp of the prime of their lives, people who have never given any real thought to it, nothing more than a few fleeting seconds, now and then, in a completely abstract way, nothing like this:

Ibrahim Abid staggers, and stumbles, and falls to one knee, then the other, and is kneeling there in the middle of the street, holding his badge in his palm, never even realizing that he is already dead.

80

K ate drops to the ground, her ears ringing from the booming reports bouncing off all the surfaces under this bridge, the stone, the iron, the water.

She might have been shot, but she can't feel it yet, she doesn't seem able to feel anything, she's rolling to free her right arm, her shooting hand, bringing the weapon up, sweeping left, and right—

Where the hell is Julia?

It's all very dark, then suddenly it's not: the moped's headlight ignites, and now she can see Bill lying there, unmoving, and the man who threw a shot at her, he's kneeling near the wall, and Kate is about to squeeze the trigger when another shot explodes in bright fiery light, and the man crumples. Hit by Inez.

But where the hell is Julia?

This has been Kate's main question for years, her primary mission, the target of her professional resources. Kate recruited policemen, she recruited hospital administrators, shopkeepers, she eventually had dozens on her payroll, in Sicily and then in Venice, to track this woman who never went anywhere recently except a couple of nights alone at a hotel in the Lido, but otherwise stayed put in Santa Croce with her baby, it must be the same baby who's in the boat right now, but Kate can't see—

No.

That's not possible. Is it? No. It's impossible that she shot a baby.

No, no, NO, she did *not* shoot the woman holding the baby, she did not shoot *anyone.*

Did she?

How long has it been? One second? Five? Fifty? She can't tell. Shouldn't the baby be crying? Why would a baby not be crying from all this noise, this yelling, this gunfire? *Why?*

Kate feels like she's falling, down, down through the paving stones, the packed-earth of the embankment, the bedrock beneath, down through the earth's crust to its core, to the molten burning pit of a hell that until this moment she didn't believe in.

⚜

What is the very worst thing you can do? What if you do it? How do you live with yourself?

She just did it.

Kate lies in the dark, frozen with fear, with horror, with self-loathing. She just killed a baby.

Kate should show herself, that's what she should do. She should stand up, present herself in the harsh light of judgment. She should leave her gun lying on the ground, she should leave her hands at her sides, she should wait for her penance, her punishment.

Yes. That's what she deserves. She shifts her weight, pulls in her arm, starts to—

Another startling burst of light, this one in the distance, it's the Eiffel Tower's light show commencing, and—*there!*—there's a backlit Julia, who in turn sees Kate in this sudden illumination, and raises her arm—

⚜

So this is it, Kate thinks. This is how I die.

Time stands still.

I did all right, I guess. The children I made are wonderful, they will go out into the world and be good people, lead fantastic lives. What else does any of us leave behind? Kate Moore is not Baron Haussmann, she is not fashioning a world capital out of her imagination, not creating lasting art, curing disease, leading nations, peace among men. Whatever second act Kate may have conjured would have been smaller, not larger, than her modest first. She has led one insignificant life, and it will have continued to shrink until she became nothing but an unremarkable ex-spook, hoping her children phone on Sunday night.

What had she wanted? It's hard to remember, exactly. She'd tried to do no harm, but she did plenty of it, didn't she? That's disappointing. And it's a failure if you can't tell your husband, your children, what it is you've done with your life, if you have to be ashamed. That's obvious.

What should she have done instead? Should she have had more fun? More sex with her husband? With someone else? Torrid affairs, scuba diving, hang gliding, Antarctica? Should she have played more, kissed more, tried more? Done more?

You don't get any medal, at the end. There's no ceremony, congratulations, you've been a paragon of goodness, we are pleased to present you with this fine gold watch. And she already has the gold watch anyway. Her husband gave it to her.

She watches Julia, flickering in the tower's light show, turning toward Kate, toward Kate's end, both arms up, swinging in her direction.

This is it.

With all this light, all this sound, all these bullets and adrenaline and fear, Kate has not realized that when Inez fired her gun just a few feet from Kate's right side, the loud close explosion deafened Kate's right ear, the same ear that's facing the river, facing the boat, and this deafness is what's preventing Kate from hearing the loud noise that's emanating from the boat: the sound of a terrified baby crying at the top of his lungs.

Nothing happens.

Then: still, nothing happens.

Then Kate begins to hear something, a high-pitched sound, yes, it's the baby, and Kate opens her eyes, and what she sees is that Julia's arm is raised, and what she's holding is not her gun, it's her baby.

Bill is dead.

The other man too, whoever he is.

The woman who'd been holding the baby has run into the night, sobbing.

Inez has also fled, and advised Kate to do the same. The police will be here very soon, and there will be a lot of them.

Julia, unarmed, is holding her baby, staring at Kate, who is holding her gun.

In that final instant before death, this is what Kate realized was the thing she'd done wrong with her life: she should have been better. She should have been nicer, more frequently, to more people.

That's what she regretted. That's what had led her to tonight's mortal crisis: she'd chosen to be mean.

That's what she will do differently. Beginning right now.

"Here," she says, and thrusts something into the other woman's hand.

Julia looks down, confused. It's Kate's business card—phone number, e-mail address, affiliation with an ersatz consulting enterprise. Kate turns over the card to where she has just written a long string of digits.

Julia turns her eyes back up to Kate. "Why?"

Kate doesn't have the time to explain everything, all the people she has wronged, and killed, all the lives she has ruined, all the times she has deceived her husband, screamed at her children, all the things she has done that she absolutely knew were wrong.

She can see police lights flashing, the cars are coming over another bridge, they'll be here in a minute.

"Because I'm sorry. And I want this to end." Kate pulls off her wig, tosses her gun into the Seine. "But if you ever come near me or my family again?"

Julia nods, she understands.

"Please try," Kate says, "to do something good."

Then she turns away. Her bag is still slung over her shoulder, but a few items spilled out when she dropped to the ground. The case for her reading glasses, that unofficial credential of middle age, like a badge you have to carry everywhere, all the time, if you hope to be able to do anything. The old hardcover from the bookshop, Graham Greene's *The End of the Affair*. And the box of Lego, a bit crushed, trampled upon, but all the contents are still inside. Not perfect, but it'll do.

A moment will come when the boys are finished with Lego, it will happen without warning and sooner than expected, and it will be months later before anyone notices that the Lego has gone untouched, the kids don't play with it anymore, they've moved on to video games, to board games, to sports, to girls, to alcohol, and from that future vantage Lego will look so innocent, Kate will long for the past, for that period in life when she did this tedious thing every single day, this top-line job description: she bends over to pick up Lego.

Then she sprints up the stairs. At the landing she can see that Julia is pulling the boat away from the riverbank, throttle in one hand and baby in the other, speeding away from the police.

Kate never did pull her trigger tonight. It wasn't Kate who shot anyone on the quay. And she never will again.

Her bicycle is lying on the sidewalk. She looks over her shoulder, sees the police closing in. She pedals away with all the energy that her exhausted middle-aged body can muster, which as it happens is not inconsiderable; she can still be mistaken for a *mademoiselle,* after all. She bikes at breakneck speed back toward the park, back toward the twinkling tower, back toward her kids. Back to her life.

After weeks of rain and gray and increasingly hostile chill, today was an autumnal jewel, a reprieve that everyone knows will be brief, and the warm weather has drawn out not only throngs of tourists but also flocks of locals, it looks like everyone in Paris has arrived in a good mood at a surprise party, Kate cycles by young and old and everyone between, the cafés are all full, people packed onto the terraces, making conversation with strangers and neighbors, making out in corners, holding hands across tables filled with glasses of wine and bottles of beer, bowls of peanuts and ashtrays overflowing and half-eaten slices of tarte tatin, it's still early enough that children are everywhere, playing on sidewalks and in the park, running and jumping and joyous noise, chasing balls and dogs and that final bit of fun before the unseen clock expires, and suddenly you're called to come here, to go home, to go to bed, kids know this better than anyone, that you have to do it all right now, everything, because this can always happen without any warning whatsoever: you're out of time.

ACKNOWLEDGMENTS

"This book would not exist without" is a phrase that has a very loud ring of inauthenticity. For this book, it's demonstrably true:

The Paris Diversion is my fourth published novel, but I've also written bits and parts and entireties of others that are lying around, as if in long-term care, awaiting a new drug or a revolutionary surgery that will breathe fresh life into them. As we're reminded every day, life is short. I haven't yet gotten around to removing some metal ornaments that we found screwed to our garage when we bought an old house, back when the kids were infants; they're now in high school. I won't have the time to pursue every single book idea.

I've spent all of my forties—a decade when we're supposed to know important things about ourselves—writing novels, but I still don't have a solid answer to this fundamental question: how do I choose which books to write, which not?

A few years ago, I was happily writing a completely different fourth novel. Midsummer arrived, and my wife took the kids to remote Ontario for an annual week-long vacation that as a rule I choose to skip. This Canada trip coincides roughly with my birthday, and Madeline's gift was sending me by myself to Paris, where as soon as I arrived an entirely new book idea intruded on my consciousness, urgently, merging an old idea—an apparent terrorist attack that turns out to be something else—with my long-simmering desire to write a sequel to *The Expats,* and a new impulse to set a novel in Paris.

I started immediately, with a laptop in a café in St-Germain-des-Prés every morning, then setting out for the afternoon. I didn't have any responsibilities. I didn't need to worry about anything, not the kids, the dog, the house, bills, taxes, inexplicable sinkholes in the driveway. I could free my mind completely, and immerse myself in these characters, in this story, trudging mile after mile, stopping on street corners to scribble notes. Over the course of a few days, the entirety of *The Paris Diversion* resolved itself—every plot twist, all the characters, the most important scenes and reveals and red herrings. It all became clearer and clearer to me, more and more exciting. Each night after dinner, I'd open the computer and write some more.

This was my most productive week of work ever, and it was a gift to me from my wife, who has always allowed me ample space to pursue this second career that I'd chosen to hurl myself into in midlife, when I could no longer countenance the idea of going to an office every day. This was an irresponsible, indulgent, irrational choice that I'd made, but she supported me without hesitation or criticism or the barest hint of doubt.

Thank you, Madeline McIntosh.

In the middle of that Paris week, I went to have a drink with Sylvia Whitman at Shakespeare & Co., and I ended up staying for five hours, talking to regulars who came and went, and Sylvie's husband and son and dog, seeing this whole expat life laid out, in this remarkable bookshop that hosted events in the *place* facing Notre-Dame, and the stream of visiting authors, and the tumbleweed kids reshelving books, the whole terrific operation guided by this wonderful principle: be open to new people, be welcoming to strangers. It seems so obvious as a decent, deliberate way to go about life. But it's not usually a business plan.

I was struck with a newfound sense of the enormous importance of deliberateness, about everything. I spent the rest of the week focused on how *The Paris Diversion* should relate to *The Expats,* and what the themes of the new book would be, and whether it should really be the next thing I wrote, and why the book should exist in the world.

Productivity isn't just moving forward; it's also figuring out which direction to move in.

Thank you, Sylvia Whitman.

After I'd turned that week's frantic scribbling into a hundred pages of readable manuscript, I sent it to my literary agent, David Gernert, who was already in possession of a hundred pages of that other novel I'd been working on.

The business of book publishing revolves around the judgment of individual people; almost everything is subjective, matters of taste. I think one of the hardest choices for everyone is figuring out whom to trust, about what, and this is especially true for authors: whom we trust can make all the difference.

I first met David more than a quarter-century ago, when he was editor in chief of Doubleday and I was a junior copy editor. He was the supreme authority, the person in charge. I'm now (alarmingly) a lot older than David was back then, but for me he's still the authority, and there's no one I trust more about editorial matters or publishing ones, and possibly everything else too.

So I asked David: which of the two different 100 pages do you prefer? His answer was the book I was calling *Diversion* (he didn't think the title was quite right), and that's why you're holding this one.

Thank you, David Gernert.

And now, the more traditional acknowledgments:

These people provided invaluable feedback on early drafts: Ned Baldwin, Layla Demay, Jack Gernert, Kathryn Lundstrum, Libby Marshall, Libby McGuire, Alex McIntosh, Hannah Marie Seidl, and my editors Lindsay Sagnette at Crown in New York and Angus Cargill at Faber & Faber in London. Sincere thanks to all of them, and also to everyone who helped turn the manuscript into a book: Chris Brand, Caspian Dennis, Rose Fox, Rebecca Gardner, Elina Nudelman, Mary Anne Stewart, and Heather Williamson.

My novels have all been published simultaneously by Crown and Faber, and I'm immensely grateful for the years of support—expertise, enthusiasm, and energy—from everyone at both houses, and especially the essential handful who've been working with me since the very beginning: Sarah Breivogel, Terry Deal, David Drake, Maya Mavjee, Steven Page, and Molly Stern.

Finally, a note about facts:

There is no International School of St-Germain; the Louvre's real-life security measures do not exactly match those depicted herein; I'm unaware of any bookstore that features an escape hatch built during the Occupation; it's not so easy to short-sell stocks anonymously; et cetera. These are purposeful deviations for legal, ethical, and dramatic reasons. I didn't try to write a guidebook to Paris, nor a manual for perpetrating a terror attack or manipulating securities. This is just a novel.

ABOUT THE AUTHOR

CHRIS PAVONE is the *New York Times* bestselling author of *The Travelers,* *The Accident,* and *The Expats,* winner of the Edgar and Anthony awards for best first novel. He was a book editor for nearly two decades and lives in New York City with his family.

To continue reading about Kate Moore, please go to
www.PRH.com/TheExpats.